THE SILENT SERVICE

GRAYBACK CLASS

H. JAY RIKER

AVON BOOKS NEW YORK

AVON BOOKS, INC.
An Imprint of HarperCollins*Publishers*
10 East 53rd Street
New York, New York 10022-5299

Copyright © 2000 by Bill Fawcett & Associates
Excerpt from *Seals, the Warrior Breed: For Extraordinary Heroism* copyright © 2000 by Bill Fawcett & Associates
Published by arrangement with Bill Fawcett & Associates
Library of Congress Catalog Card Number: 99-95331
ISBN: 0-380-80466-2
www.harpercollins.com

First Avon Books Printing: February 2000

AVON TRADEMARK REG. U.S. PAT. OFF. AND IN OTHER COUNTRIES, MARCA REGISTRADA, HECHO EN U.S.A.

Printed in the U.S.A.

WCD   10   9   8   7   6   5   4   3   2   1

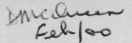

INTO THE BREACH

They call it the Cold War—but there are those who burn in its heat. The year is 1985, and two great superpowers—the U.S. and the U.S.S.R.—are locked in a lethal, escalating race of arms and technology.

No war has been officially declared. But for those forced to fight in secret, it is do . . . or die.

Reports have been received of a devastating new Soviet weapon. It is called *Akula*—a prototype attack submarine more advanced than anything in the U.S. undersea arsenal. Unchallenged, it will give America's enemies dominion over the Earth's waters—and an advantage that could prove nothing less than catastrophic to the Free World.

Now America's greatest hope travels within the hull of a nearly obsolete *Grayback Class* submarine. A platoon of SEALs—the nation's most skilled fighting men—is heading into the jaws of the bear on a mission to penetrate *Akula*'s home port, the heavily defended Severodvinsk shipyard on the White Sea. But it is the *Grayback*'s crew—along with the Navy men manning the accompanying Los Angeles class attack sub—who will be put through the most strenuous trials. For when the mission gets hot, it is the warriors of "The Silent Service" who will be called upon to fight their way out of impossible straits.

Also by H. Jay Riker

SEALS, THE WARRIOR BREED

SILVER STAR
PURPLE HEART
BRONZE STAR
NAVY CROSS
MEDAL OF HONOR
MARKS OF VALOR
IN HARM'S WAY

Coming Soon

FOR EXTRAORDINARY HEROISM

To the memory of Dorothy D. Keith, Navy wife,
who always kept the home fires burning

AUTHOR'S NOTE

This is a work of fiction. Although the USS *Pittsburgh* is an actual Los Angeles class submarine which has served in the Atlantic Fleet since the mid-eighties, there is no evidence that she was ever involved in a covert operation in the White Sea or had a combat encounter of any sort with the Soviet Red Banner Northern Fleet in the last decade of the Cold War. All of the characters are fictional, as is the submarine USS *Bluefin* (though it is modeled on a real sub, the *Grayback*, which did indeed serve as the first dedicated submersible transport for covert operations, as described).

The *Bars* is an actual submarine, the first of a class of Soviet high-technology submarines which NATO knows as the *Akula*. It was, indeed, launched in the summer of 1985, and would have undergone testing while based at the Soviet naval shipyards at Severodvinsk. It incorporated new design elements which made it fully the equal of the early Los Angeles class. The circumstances described in this book, however, are entirely derived from the author's imagination.

There *is* a persistent story in submariner circles of an American skipper taking advantage of a lucky break and making several close passes, cameras running, around a brand new Soviet sub which was surfaced and apparently not keeping a good watch. Like all navy scuttlebutt it has undoubtedly grown in the telling, and there has never been a shred of evidence to confirm the story or even narrow down the class of the sub in question or other details. It suited the purposes of this story to have the *Pittsburgh* and the *Bars* be the boats in question. But like the rest of the story, the encounter is the author's vision of what *might* have happened.

In truth, though there were many minor incidents during the Cold War, it is a tribute to the professionalism of the captains and crews of our submarine fleet—and their counterparts in the Soviet Union—that encounters of the sort portrayed in this book were few and far between, and such clashes which did occur never escalated out of control despite the tense atmosphere and pressure-cooker environment of life in a nuclear attack boat.

The real *heroes* of "The Silent Service" must always remain the men who did their duty as "bubbleheads" and helped *to keep the peace.*

H. Jay Riker
April 1999

PROLOGUE

Friday, 19 July 1985

Soviet Shipyard Facility Number 402
Severodvinsk, USSR
1342 hours GMT

Captain Second Rank Viktor Nikoleivich Kalinin tried to mask his surprise as he recognized the man who stepped forward to meet him, but it was plain that he failed. The leathery face of Rear Admiral Arkov creased in a smile.

"Well, Viktor Nikoleivich, it has been a long time since the Academy, true?" At the age of seventy, the admiral had a shock of white hair and careworn features, but his ice-blue eyes still glittered with the intensity Kalinin remembered from the days when Arkov had been an instructor in submarine tactics at the Leninsky Komsomal Higher Naval School in Leningrad who had made young Lieutenant Kalinin's academic life miserable. That had been nearly fifteen years ago, but the look in those eyes made it seem as if no time at all had gone by since the last time the grizzled old veteran had handed out a tough assignment for the younger man to complete.

1

"Yes, Admiral," Kalinin responded carefully. "A very long time."

"I have followed your career since then, Captain. You were a student who showed considerable promise, and you have more than lived up to that promise since then."

"Thank you, Admiral . . . but I am not sure what I have done to earn your praise, sir." He smiled. "It is not as if I have been out there racking up kills for the glory of the *Rodina*."

"No, you have been doing something much more difficult." The admiral smiled thinly. "You have been doing your duty, quietly, competently, neither a hotheaded Cossack nor a frightened timeserver, but an officer who gets the job done. Your part in the *Riga Komsomolets* incident did not pass unnoticed."

Kalinin gave a dismissive shrug. "I did not feel that any of us came out of that cluster-fuck looking good," he said, deliberately coarse. He had been the Exec aboard the *Riga Komsomolets*, a nuclear guided missile submarine which had gone down in the Bering Sea two years back. Kalinin had been one of the lucky few who had managed to escape the stricken vessel, and the Court of Inquiry convened on the disaster had found that his efforts had probably been responsible for saving the lives of those who had managed to make it off the boat. That same court had found the captain of the sub guilty of negligence, but as he had died with his command, their assessment hadn't meant very much in the long run.

Viktor Kalinin had received his promotion to captain second rank for his efforts, but he had long since found out that the higher rank didn't do much to combat the nightmares that still haunted him from time to time.

"Whatever you may think, Viktor Nikoleivich, the fact is that you are well thought of. And you have been picked for a very important role." The admiral motioned with one arm. "Come, walk with me."

Kalinin followed his old mentor past the huge building that had once been intended for the construction of

two battleships at a time, back in the days of the Great
Patriotic War when Stalin had been determined to build
up the *Rodina*'s surface fleets to match the power of
Germany, Britain, Japan, and the United States. Those
days were long gone, and the Severodvinsk shipyards
now concentrated entirely upon submarines, the modern
naval wonder weapons that had replaced battleships as
the status symbols of the Cold War era.

At the end of the long walkway they reached a railing
that overlooked the cold, choppy waters of the White
Sea. Below them was a complex of docks and piers, with
perhaps twenty submarines of various types and designs
testifying to the volume of work that went on there. Kalinin saw one sub cradled in a dry dock, with a swarm
of workers performing repairs to a damaged hull. Another, an immense *Tyfun* SSBN, was just getting under
way. For a moment he allowed himself the luxury of
pride. In many ways, the Soviet Union lagged far behind
their Western rivals, but in the design, construction, and
deployment of submarines the *Rodina* was clearly superior.

The admiral pointed. "You see that one, Viktor Nikoleivich?"

Kalinin followed the gesture and studied the long,
sleek black shape Arkov was pointing to. It was a design
unlike any sub Kalinin had seen before, with the sail
twice as long as anything he was familiar with, but
lower, and a pod rising from a strut above the stern. The
boat had the menacing look of a predatory cat . . . or a
shark.

"An attack sub?" he asked.

Arkov nodded slowly. "Project 971," he said proudly.
"But he has been named *Bars*." The name meant *Snow
Leopard*. Arkov turned to face Kalinin. "He is our newest attack sub design, Victor Nikoleivich. Based on a
whole new way of thinking in the areas of stealth and
surprise. A titanium hull, and quieter systems throughout. We believe that past intelligence reports may have

badly underestimated American tracking capabilities, but there is every reason to be confident that *Bars* can evade even the most sophisticated Western boats."

Kalinin let out an impressed whistle. "This could change . . . everything." Soviet doctrine envisioned the need for effective attack subs to be able to take out Western carrier battle groups and convoys should war ever break out in Europe, but so far they had been unable to prove themselves able to carry out such a mission. It always seemed that American detection and tracking was just far enough ahead of the Russians to keep them at arm's length when they tried to infiltrate Western fleets in peacetime "observation" efforts. If the *Rodina* could put large numbers of boats into play that *could* defeat American detection systems, it might mean a huge shift in the balance of power. Ronald Reagan's vaunted "six-hundred-ship navy" would become virtually useless if it couldn't prevent boats like this new *Bars* from stalking and killing prey at will.

"The boat was launched late last year, but has only now been completed. He has taken on a full crew and is ready for sea trials. All he lacked was a captain . . . until you arrived."

"Me, sir?" Kalinin was stunned. Even after Arkov's earlier praise, he hadn't expected this kind of honor. Sea trials of a newly commissioned sub, based on a new and untested design, were put in the hands of the very best of the navy's submariners. Kalinin had only held one sub command since his promotion. . . .

"You, Viktor Nikoleivich." Arkov smiled. "It was not easy to convince the High Command that you were ready for this task, but I wanted you for it. We need a younger man for these tests, a man who is not afraid of new ideas or new tactics. So I am expecting great things of you . . . and if you fail me, I fear both of us will face an uncertain future."

"I will not fail you, Comrade Kontr-Admiral," Kalinin said stiffly.

The admiral clapped his onetime student on the shoulder and squeezed it with a surprisingly strong grip. "That is why I fought to give you this job. Now, go aboard and meet your officers and crew. We will begin a series of briefings later in the week, and begin the actual tests before the end of the month."

They turned away from the railing together.

Monday, 22 July 1985

**Control Room, USS *Pittsburgh*
The GIUK Gap, Off Keflavik, Iceland
1245 hours GMT**

"Conn, Sonar. Designating contact Sierra One. Bearing, zero-three-four degrees. Range . . . two-one nautical miles, closing."

Commander Mike Chase leaned over the plotting table, studying the chart displayed there. He considered his options for only a moment before he looked up. "Stop engine," he ordered crisply. Inside he felt a little thrill. He was still new enough in command of a Los Angeles class attack boat to be excited at the thought of action. USS *Pittsburgh*, SSN 720, had only been on patrol for seven weeks, without contacting anything more exciting than a pod of whales off the coast of Greenland. Maybe this would be something more interesting, something to test their mettle. *Pittsburgh* was one of the newest attack subs in service, and Chase knew there were plenty of fellow skippers who envied his luck in getting her.

"Aye aye, Captain." Lieutenant John Quimby, USS *Pittsburgh*'s Dive Officer and the Officer of the Deck for the afternoon watch, gave a quick nod. He turned to look down from the watch officer's station on the raised periscope platform toward the two sailors manning the helm station at the forward end of the control room. "Make it 'Stop Engine,' helm. Rudder amidships, maintain depth."

"All stop, aye aye, sir," the helmsman replied. After a long moment, he went on. "Answering 'stop engine,' Lieutenant."

Chase nodded as Quimby turned toward him to repeat the announcement, smiling faintly. "Let's wait here until we find out what we've got, Lieutenant," he said casually. "Always a nice idea to know what the neighbors are up to, wouldn't you say?"

"Yes, sir," Quimby replied. He sounded a little nervous. This was his first tour of duty as a full lieutenant and a department head, and he took his duties seriously . . . especially when he had to take responsibility for the duty watch under the critical eye of his commanding officer. Chase knew he had a wry, devilish sense of humor, but he let it show only infrequently.

Chase picked up the intercom microphone and thumbed the key. "Sonar, Conn. Can you give us anything more on the contact?"

"Wait one." Chief Bob Franco replied, a testy edge to his voice. There was a pause before he went on. "Conn, Sierra One is a submarine. Haven't got it IDed yet, but it's definitely an underwater contact. Depth two-zero-zero feet. Speed fifteen knots. We'll have the course figured in a minute."

Chase looked across the width of the control room at Quimby. "Any other friendly subs working our side of the street, Lieutenant?"

The OOD looked flustered, then collected his wits. "Not that I remember seeing, sir."

"Same here. Last summary I read put the nearest friendly sub as the *Dallas*, and she was assigned to patrol off the east coast of Iceland." He kept his tone casual, like he was making conversation about a baseball game or some other ordinary occurrence. Chase liked to promote a relaxed atmosphere on his boat . . . relaxed, but always ready for action.

Silence followed, long seconds in which the only sounds in the *Pittsburgh*'s control room were the faint noises made by the ship's systems. Finally, the intercom speaker came to life once more. "Conn, Sonar. Sierra One on course two-five-five degrees."

Chase consulted his chart again, marking the course of the unknown sub and studying it for a moment. It was headed west, away from the Icelandic coast. More and more, he was becoming convinced that boat was no friend.

"Mr. Quimby, sound General Quarters, if you please." Even if it turned out to be friendly, tracking that stranger out there would be good practice for the crew. And if it wasn't . . . well, one of the main missions of Los Angeles class fast-attack subs was to keep an eye on their counterparts from the other side of the Iron Curtain.

Quimby picked up a microphone. "All hands, now, General Quarters. General Quarters. Hands to stations. General Quarters." A siren hooted briefly, then fell silent.

Chase turned his attention back to the chart. The other sub wouldn't be passing very close to the *Pittsburgh*, which meant they would have to do some maneuvering if they were going to follow her. And that would mean risking the possibility of detection themselves. Drifting as she was, the *Pittsburgh* was almost impossible to detect, but once her screws began to turn a good sonar operator on the other boat might pick up the sounds and realize they were not alone.

Additional men entered the control room, foremost among them the dapper Executive Officer, Lieutenant Commander Frederick Yates Latham. The newcomers quickly settled into their accustomed positions while Quimby, looking happy to be out of the hot seat, moved

forward to join the helmsman and the planesman at their
dual control station. Latham joined Chase at the plotting
table.

"Unknown submarine," Chase told him, tapping the
chart. "Headed just south of west, submerged at two
hundred feet, making fifteen knots."

"You're figuring it for a hostile." Latham's voice was
flat, more statement than question.

"Safe bet. We're not supposed to have anything else
in these parts, and that bearing and heading tells me he's
trying to slip through the gap and go play in the pond."

Latham nodded. "Follow him?"

"I'd like to. At least long enough to see how long he
maintains this course. Maybe if he gets too complacent
we'll have to . . . take other steps."

The Exec met his eyes with a level gaze. "Don't tell
me you're turning into a hot dog, Skipper. You wouldn't
be wanting to start an incident, would you?"

Chase smiled at him. "Farthest thing from my mind,
Rick. But you have to admit that nothing can ruin your
day like an unexpected ping."

Chuckling, the Exec nodded and straightened up. No
submariner liked to hear the warbling ping of an active
sonar painting his boat. It meant that an opponent had
the drop on him, had him precisely targeted . . . and that
meant the possibility of torpedoes slashing through the
depths to savage the sub. Subs that stayed out of contact
for long periods of time might not hear word of an outbreak of hostilities, and that targeting sonar ping might
be the only warning they had of a shooting war.

Or it could just be a bad joke. That was the way the
game was played.

A sailor crossed the control room to hand Latham a
clipboard. He scanned it, then looked back at Chase.
"All stations manned and ready, sir," he said.

Chase glanced at the clock mounted on the bulkhead
and gave an approving nod. "Fast work. I do believe

you're getting this bunch of yahoos in some kind of shape."

"Yes, sir. We're getting there."

"Very good. You have the conn, Rick. I want to see what else we can find out about our friends."

"Aye aye, sir." Latham's expression and voice remained perfectly controlled as he took over the command position from Quimby. Chase admired that in his XO. He never seemed to be thrown by anything, not even a captain who walked off the bridge during a tense maneuver.

Not that Chase was going far. He walked forward through the control room, through the hatch that stood next to the helm position, and turned to enter the sonar shack. The lighting there was dim, and four techs huddled over their displays with a single-minded devotion to their work while CPO Franco watched over them like a border collie guarding his flock. He stiffened as Chase entered, then relaxed at the casual gesture the captain gave him.

"Who made the contact, Chief?" Chase asked quietly.

"Who do you think, sir? Rodriguez."

"Why am I not surprised?" Chase said, hiding a grin.

Sonarman Third Class Enrique Rodriguez had only finished his specialty training a few weeks before being assigned to the newly commissioned *Pittsburgh*, but he had already earned a reputation as a young man to watch. He was one of those rare birds whose affinity for his equipment and his work was little short of magical. Nobody, least of all Rodriguez himself, knew how he was able to do it, but he could get more information out of his sonar station, and faster, than anyone else in his department.

"Anything further?"

"No, not yet, sir . . ." Franco broke off as Rodriguez looked up.

"Nailed him! That's a Victor III, or I'm an Anglo!" The swarthy young sonar operator flushed as he realized for the first time that his commanding officer was in the compartment. "Ah . . . sorry, sir."

Chase and Franco stepped forward, one looking over either of Rodriguez's shoulders and studied the display for the submarine's BQQ-5 sonar system. Rodriguez, at a sign from Franco, unplugged his headset from its jack and allowed the audio signal to fill the compartment. Cocking his head, Chase listened to the slightly irregular throbbing sound, but to his ear it was just noise.

Franco moved to another console and began entering commands into the sub's powerful BC-10 computer, frowning. "You sure about that, Rodriguez?" he demanded. "Brainiac over here hasn't narrowed it down yet . . . wait a minute." The printer came to life, chattering for a moment as a sheet of paper unrolled into Franco's hands. He tore it off. "Victor III, all right," he announced. "Looks like old Number Three . . . I remember playing tag with that one off Cuba aboard the *Phoenix* a couple of years back."

Rodriguez nodded. "Had to be. You can tell a Victor III by the sound the twin screws make. This one sounds like there's a little bit of an imbalance between the props, though."

Chase held up his hand. "Thank you both. Very impressive performance. Stay on top of this guy. I figure between you two and that box of printed circuits over there, you ought to be able to tell me if the captain gets indigestion after he eats his borscht. Right?"

Franco grinned. "We'll do our best, Skipper," he said.

"I'm counting on it. Pass the word to the control room, Chief." He turned and headed aft before either man could respond, striding briskly back into the control room just as the speaker came on with Franco's announcement.

"Conn, Sonar. Positive ID on contact Sierra One. It's a Victor III . . . looks like good old Number Three. Still holding course and speed. I don't think she's noticed us."

Chase motioned to Latham to join him back at the plotting table, his eyes meeting the level gaze of the Executive Officer. He gave a small nod. "Let's follow him, Rick," he said quietly. "See how long we can keep on Ivan's tail without being noticed."

"Aye aye, sir," Latham replied. He straightened up and moved into the center of the control room, raising his voice slightly as he began to snap out orders. "Bring us about, helm. Course zero-one-five degrees. Speed zero-five knots. Maintain depth."

"Course zero-one-five, aye," the sailor at the helm responded. "Speed zero-five."

"Maintaining depth at one-five-zero," his companion, who manned the diving controls, chimed in a moment later.

"Nice and easy, gentlemen," Latham added. "Until we can get into his baffles I don't want to attract any attention, so keep it quiet and don't go scaring our little friend."

Lieutenant Quimby stepped between the two men at the helm, watching over their shoulders as they worked the controls. "Be vewy, vewy quiet," he said softly in a passable imitation of Elmer Fudd. "We're hunting wabbits."

"Mr. Quimby," Latham said. His voice was flat and neutral, but conveyed volumes. The Dive Officer glanced back, looking sheepish, and shrugged.

Glancing around, Chase saw a few of the men grinning at the exchange. *Pittsburgh* was a new boat, and she had only been out on patrol for seven weeks. The crew was just starting to settle in, and it was good to see their morale was high.

Chase braced himself as the submarine began a slow, stately turn, maneuvering to follow the Russian attack sub that had passed them by just a few minutes before without seeming to detect their presence. It was all part of a game that was played out over and over in every ocean of the world, every day. Soviet and American submarines played cat and mouse with one another, stalking their opposite numbers and trying to avoid being stalked in turn. In the peacetime conditions of the Cold War it really was just an elaborate game, but for forty years now everyone who had played that game had been forced to live with the realization that it could suddenly change without notice into a life-or-death situation, should someone in Moscow or Washington lose his mind long enough to let slip the dogs of war.

"Mr. Jackson, I want a firing solution ASAP," Chase ordered. "Get a torp in the spout and be ready to use it. Just in case."

"Aye aye, sir," Lieutenant Jackson, the Combat Systems Officer, said in his slow Virginia drawl. The son of a Civil War buff and stubbornly pro-Confederate history teacher from the Shenandoah Valley, Jackson's given name was Stonewall, but he preferred to be called Stone.

"Course is zero-one-five, sir," the helmsman reported.

"Steady as she goes, Abrams," Latham ordered curtly. "We're on him, Skipper."

Chase returned his attention to the chart table, where the onboard computer was displaying constant updates of the sub's position and course. Creeping along at five knots, the *Pittsburgh* wasn't exactly living up to her role as a fast-attack sub, but she was making very little noise for the Soviets to detect. Unless they used active sonar, they were unlikely to notice the American boat. And as the Russians passed, *Pittsburgh* would be perfectly placed to slip into her baffles, the dead zone in the sub's wake where sonar detection was virtually impossible as long as the Victor III was under way.

It wasn't like anything else in the catalog of modern warfare. This sort of stealthy submarine operation was more like a stately dance, a precisely choreographed ballet that unfolded with maddening slowness. And one missed step could spell the difference between life and death for 133 officers and men aboard *Pittsburgh*. Even in peacetime there was always the risk of a miscalculation.

At length the intercom sounded again. "Conn, Sonar." Chief Franco's voice was gruff. "Contact is maintaining course and speed. Bearing three-two-five degrees. Range is one-point-one miles, opening."

"He's passing us," Latham commented, joining Chase again at the chart table. "Still want to tail him, Skipper?"

"Is a bear Polish?" Chase misquoted with a smile. "Yeah, bring us around and close the range."

"Aye aye, sir," the Exec said, turning. "Helm, course three-zero-zero. Increase speed to fifteen knots."

Chase picked up the intercom mike. "Sonar, Conn. Tell Rodriguez to keep that Russkie in sight any way he has to. Say an incantation, spin a prayer wheel, rub Franco's belly for luck . . . whatever it is he does, do it now. I don't want to lose that boat while we're maneuvering."

Franco's chuckle echoed on the speaker. "He ain't rubbing *my* belly, sir, but I'll make sure he stays on top of the Russkie."

This was always the worst part of the war of nerves that was the essence of stalking an opponent's submarine. The faster you moved, the more noise you generated, and hence the more likely you were to give your own position away to the other guy. At the same time, increased speed cut down the efficiency of your own detection systems, so it became harder to keep track of the target you were pursuing. But you needed that extra speed to catch up with the quarry.

Usually a sub on the hunt alternated short sprints with periods of drifting, fixing the opponent's position and course, then maneuvering to a position near where the enemy *ought* to be. Crossed fingers, rabbits' feet, and the occasional prayer were just a few of the tools sub skippers used to increase their chances of success at times like these.

Chase, for the moment, preferred relying on his sonar

wizard, and the *Pittsburgh*'s top-of-the-line technology. Crossed fingers would come later, when he really needed some extra luck.

Minute followed minute as the sub slowly settled in to her new course behind the Russian sub. Latham ordered their speed up to eighteen knots to begin to close the range, and through it all the sonar operators never lost their fix on the Russians. Finally, when Franco reported that the range had been reduced to a thousand yards, Chase breathed out a sigh of relief. "Reduce to fifteen knots, Rick, and stay on his tail," he said quietly.

"Fifteen knots, aye aye, sir," the Exec repeated. He turned toward the helm station to begin issuing orders, while Chase again spoke into the intercom mike.

"Sonar, Conn. Keep an eye out for aspect changes on the target."

"Aye aye, sir," Franco replied. When another boat turned, sonar readings could measure the change in its relative position. It was essential to watch for this if *Pittsburgh* was going to be able to continue to follow the Victor III . . . or to avoid the favored Russian maneuver, known as "Crazy Ivan," where a sub would periodically execute a complete 360-degree turn to check for American pursuers.

Chase rubbed the bridge of his nose. So far, the whole operation had been flawless. He wasn't sure, though, how long he should maintain his position behind the Soviet sub, or what else he should do. It was good practice for his crew to track the Russians, but he wasn't about to follow them all the way out of *Pittsburgh*'s designated patrol area. And there was always the risk of some unfortunate incident in a situation like this. The Soviet skipper might discover the American boat and overreact, even to the point of firing torpedoes. Or one of them might maneuver the wrong way at close range, leading to a collision. It happened more often than people realized, when Cold Warriors met far out at sea.

"Conn, Communications." The intercom crackled

with the slightly quavering voice of Lieutenant David Erskine, *Pittsburgh*'s Communications Officer. A nervous little man who looked more like a bank clerk than a submariner, Erskine was damned good at his job, but somehow didn't seem like he'd ever learn how to be an officer of the U.S. Navy.

Picking up the intercom mike, Chase tried to keep any trace of irritation out of his voice. Sometimes it was hard to live up to the phlegmatic, unruffled image required of a sub commander, especially in a tense situation like this one. "This is Conn. Go."

"Skipper, we just registered the beginning of an ELF transmission. Recorders are running now."

By their very nature, submarines were hard-pressed to stay in touch with the outside world. Subs working deep underwater didn't mix well with the properties of ordinary radio waves, which simply couldn't reach to normal operating depths. Antennae and buoys could be used to connect the sub with the surface world and transmit or receive information, but these tended to make the submarine easier to locate, the cardinal sin to be avoided at all costs.

One method that did work, after a fashion, was the use of Extremely Low Frequency radio transmissions. Giant antenna complexes in the central United States broadcast radio waves which pierced the depths, and subs trailed long antenna wires through the water behind them that could pick these up without compromising the sub's stealth. The problem with ELF transmissions was the low information content they could convey, on the order of a single character in thirty seconds. That made it a trifle inefficient for casual conversations with home, especially since the sub couldn't transmit on the same band because of the size required for an ELF transmitter's antenna.

So ELF was used to broadcast coded messages to subs at sea. Simple three-letter code groups broadcast over the ELF channel were transcribed by the radioman on duty, and the Communications Officer consulted a code book to translate the letters into specific words and phrases. It could take half an hour or more to receive one of these ELF messages, but at least they could alert a submarine to specific situations—like a declaration of war, for instance—and pass instructions for the captain to make contact with higher authority through more conventional means.

When the ELF started transmitting, sub captains listened.

"Very well, Mr. Erskine," Chase said. "Keep—"

"Conn, Sonar!" the intercom interrupted him. Franco's voice was taut. "Aspect change on target!" There was a pause. "Crazy Ivan! Port side!"

"Communications, monitor signal and keep me informed," Chase snapped. He looked up at Latham. "XO, stop engine. Maintain course and depth. Silent running."

"Aye aye, sir," Latham replied laconically. He turned to repeat the orders, while Chase swallowed and looked down at the chart.

The Victor III was making a Crazy Ivan turn, circling around to make sure no one was following. There wasn't much a pursuing submarine's captain could do when his quarry pulled that kind of maneuver. The one response that gave any hope of remaining undetected was to shut down engines, maintain complete silence, and simply drift while the other sub made its circle. With luck the enemy boat would go all the way around her and never realize there was anything there, for a submarine on silent running could be very, very hard to notice with passive sonar, even at close ranges.

Of course, it was the close range that was the problem with that tactic. If the pursuing sub happened to be in the wrong place at the wrong time, the boat performing the Crazy Ivan might plow right into her because she had managed to be just a little too stealthy.

Or if the Russians *did* detect the American boat, so close behind and with no time to prepare, they might decide they were about to be attacked and open fire. And *Pittsburgh* would be a sitting duck, powered down, unable to dodge torps launched at point-blank range. They'd barely have time to hear torpedoes leaving the tubes.

And those were just the normal risks that a sub captain dealt with at a time like this. Right now Chase had to deal with another fear that gnawed away at his gut while he tried to maintain an outward appearance of calm.

What was in that ELF message Erskine was receiving? Every time a signal came in, a sub captain couldn't help but wonder if it might not be the message no one wanted to hear, but every man in the Navy had to be prepared for. War. The two superpowers had been playing a high-stakes game of poker for over thirty-five years now, meeting each other's raises time and again, bluffing when necessary. Someday one side or the other might decide to call instead of raise, and on that day the Cold War could turn hot in a matter of moments.

Maybe the signal was announcing the outbreak of hostilities somewhere. And maybe the Russians on that Victor III already knew about it. They might even have been aware of *Pittsburgh* all along, and were turning not for a routine check of their baffles, but to launch the opening rounds of a surprise attack designed to knock out an American fast-attack submarine. Both sides knew well that a major key to winning the next war, if and when it came, was to take down as much of the opposition's submarine fleet as possible before they had a chance to vanish into the ocean depths.

If that was what the captain of the Victor III was doing now, Chase told himself, then it was his own order to pursue the Russian that would lead *Pittsburgh* and her crew to a watery grave in the cold, dark depths off the Icelandic coast. . . .

A submarine skipper's lot was not a happy one. Ulcers were an occupational hazard, and a nervous breakdown the all-too-common outcome when a captain failed to learn how to cope with the stress. And always there was the need for the command mystique, the myth of nerves of steel, a mind like a computer, and perfect judgment under any and all circumstances. None of those things was real, Chase thought wryly, at least not for him, and very likely not for any captain who had ever sailed. The best a man could do was to make the tough calls, try to look confident while he made them . . . and pray that his best would be enough to get the ship and crew out of trouble.

Minutes passed, a long, slow interval when the control-room crew hardly dared draw breath. They could hear the noise of the other boat's screws as she passed; Chase even fancied he could hear the slight irregularity Rodriguez had commented on before, an imperfect balance between the two propellers. If this had been a movie, Chase told himself in a fit of gallows humor, it was just about time for a crewman to drop a wrench or accidentally activate a noisy alarm. . . .

But *Pittsburgh*'s crew was well trained. The boat was silent as a tomb as each man listened, and waited, and a few, including Mike Chase, prayed in silence.

After an eternity, Latham crossed over to the starboard side of the bridge and bent over the sonar repeater console. Less detailed than the monitors in the sonar shack, the display there was still useful for summarizing the data processed by Franco and his technicians. Latham studied it a moment, then approached Chase.

"She's passed astern of us," he said softly. "Now moving up our starboard side. Looks like they haven't noticed us."

"Keep an eye on them," Chase told him, equally quiet. "We need to know when he's out ahead of us so we can drop back into his baffles again."

Latham nodded rather than replying aloud, returning to the sonar repeater. Chase breathed a little easier. It looked as if the Soviet boat really had been performing a routine Crazy Ivan turn, and not stalking *Pittsburgh* after all. And it had passed astern of the American sub, which meant the danger of a collision was receding. A few more minutes, and all would be well again.

Until the next time.

After another interval, Latham was back. "He's resumed his original course, Skipper," the Exec said, still low-voiced.

"Very well, Rick. Secure from silent running and get us under way. Back in his baffles, match course and speed."

"Aye aye, sir," Latham replied. Any other man would have been smiling, or at least looking relieved, but not Frederick Yates Latham. He simply looked briskly efficient as he strode forward, rattling off orders to Lieutenant Quimby.

Chase hoped his own face betrayed as little as Latham's. He *was* relieved, now that the other boat had resumed course without noticing *Pittsburgh*'s presence.

"Captain?"

He turned to meet the owlish gaze of Lieutenant Erskine. Clutching a sheet of teletype paper, Erskine stood near the forward hatch. He had a hangdog expression that was infectious. Slowly, the little Communications Officer crossed to join Chase.

"Mr. Erskine," Chase replied, neutral.

"Just finished transcribing and decoding the message off the ELF, sir," Erskine told him. He passed the paper to Chase, who studied the message as Erskine headed back for his lair in the communications shack, just across the passageway from Franco's sonar shack forward of the control room.

AFW	VHR	NDP
FROM COMSUBSPECLANT TO USS PITTSBURGH		CANCEL
LJB	WMQ	FCO

CURRENT PATROL ORDERS COMMUNICATE SSIX FOR REDEPLOYMENT

He read it through twice, absently rubbing the bridge of his nose while he pondered the significance of the message. First off, it originated not with his regular superior, Commander Submarine Force Atlantic, but with another office entirely—the Navy's Special Submarine Warfare Command. That was unusual enough; COM-SUBSPECLANT controlled the operations of the various submarines used for mounting covert commando operations in the Atlantic Theater of Operations, and shouldn't have had anything to do with a 688-boat like *Pittsburgh*. But the order was clear enough. They were to break off their regular patrol routine, go to periscope depth, and contact the geosynchronous orbiting Submarine Satellite Information Exchange, a comsat dedicated entirely to sub operations. Presumably SSIX would relay new orders.

Chase shook his head. It had been five years since he had last worked for the people at Special Submarine Warfare, and he had been happy to put those days behind him. Commanding a Los Angeles class boat was the work he had been pointed toward for years now, and he had finally achieved it. Now this new order felt like a step backwards.

He motioned for Latham to join him and showed him the paper. The Exec never quite lost his usual bland expression, but Chase could tell that he was as surprised as his captain. "I guess Ivan gets off easy today," was his only comment.

"Looks that way," Chase said, nodding. "Tell you what, though. Before we break off and head for periscope depth, why don't you let Mr. Jackson give him a good old-fashioned targeting ping, just to let him know he's been tagged."

The corners of Latham's mouth twitched, as close to a smile as he was likely to come on duty. "It would be a shame to waste all this effort," he agreed.

As the XO turned to carry out his orders, Chase was frowning at the message once again.

A submariner was a creature of routine. Chase didn't like it when that routine was disrupted . . . especially when the disruption came from his own side.

U.S. Navy Amphibious Base
Norfolk, Virginia
1610 hours GMT

Lieutenant Junior Grade Bernard Gunn turned a page in his book and reached for his half-finished sandwich without looking up from his reading. B.H. Liddel Hart's *Strategy* wasn't the kind of book most people Gunn knew would describe as light reading, but then Gunn himself didn't have a lot in common with most of those people. He had always been a solitary, studious young man, not at all what people thought of when they pictured an officer of the U.S. Navy SEALs.

The popular image of the SEALs came from some kind of cross between John Wayne and that silly Rambo movie he'd seen a few weeks back—the strong, silent, lone-wolf killing machine, short on brains and big on body counts. That was a long way from the truth, of course. The Navy's SEa-Air-Land teams were physically tough and trained in all manner of ways to dispatch their foes, but they were also men who understood the importance of planning, thinking, and working together as a unit. There was no room for the lone Rambo in the ranks of the SEALs.

At the same time, Gunn thought with a tiny, self-deprecating smile, there wasn't a whole lot of room for the Bernard Gunns of the world in those ranks, either. In his Basic Underwater Demolition/SEAL class, he had barely squeaked through the course; he was the very bottom of his class to still get the prized "Budweiser" device that proclaimed him a member of the Teams. And while he worked well with his fellow SEALs, he was out of step with them in many ways, preferring to read books on history when the others were perusing the latest issue of *Playboy*, and spending quiet evenings in his quarters when the others were partying in the bars and dives around Norfolk.

He slipped a bookmark into the book, deciding that Hannibal and Scipio Africanus could wait for a while, and finished the sandwich and his last swig of coffee. Leaning back in his chair, Gunn turned his head to study his reflection in the mirror that hung near the door to the little cubicle he called home. He still didn't look much like a SEAL, either, he decided. He wasn't quite as chubby and moonfaced as he'd been when he went into BUD/S training—nobody could stay chubby through the waking nightmare known as Hell Week—but he wasn't exactly the lean fighting commando of popular legend, either. There were times when Gunn wondered why he had followed this particular career path, when there had been plenty of other options open to him. With his academic background and test scores, he could have had his pick of specialty schools. But he had chosen BUD/S, and stuck with it even though it had been even harder than he'd imagined it could have been.

His father had been a SEAL, back in the days of the Vietnam War, and Arthur Gunn hadn't come back from his fourth tour of duty there in 1971. Bernard had been only eleven when the telegram came, and he could still remember his mother's tears and that shattered, hopeless look that had taken months to fade away. Part of him had wanted to step in to fill his father's shoes ever since . . . and another part had recoiled from the thought that he might someday cause someone that same kind of wrenching grief.

But the first part had won out, and Gunn was a SEAL now, however unlikely. He'd been through his baptism of fire in Grenada and come out of it all in one piece. But it didn't stop him from wondering, sometimes, if he had made the right choices. . . .

A knock on his door jerked him from his reverie. "Come in," he called, straightening up in his chair.

Machinist's Mate Third Class Johnny Silverwolf entered the room, looking like he'd stepped off the set of some old-time Hollywood Western. Silverwolf was a full-blooded Lakota Sioux who had only joined Gunn's SEAL platoon a month earlier. Unlike Gunn, he was the very model of a proper SEAL despite his unlikely heritage and Amerind features. On duty he was tight-lipped, efficient, and totally dedicated to the job at hand. Off duty and away from the base, he was quite a different person. Gunn had already bailed him out of jail twice after some of the most spectacular brawls anyone in the platoon could remember . . . and SEAL brawls were always pretty spectacular. The last time out, the thin, wiry Silverwolf had taken on three Marines, none of them less than twice his size, after they had baited him with bad Hollywood Indian accents and ill-judged comments about firewater—ill judged because Silverwolf's older brother, an alcoholic, had died in a drunk-driving accident. The SEAL had won the ensuing fight and hardly broke a sweat doing it.

"Sir, Lieutenant Anderson wants you in his office. Right away."

Gunn stood up, wiping a few crumbs from the front of his uniform and grabbing his cap. "Any idea what it's about?"

Silverwolf's face broke out in a grin. "I think it's orders, Lieutenant," he said. "Some kind of op. At least that's the scuttlebutt."

"Orders . . ." Gunn smiled and shrugged. "Well, we can only hope so. But with our luck it'll probably be orders to clean the latrines before some veep from D.C. shows up for an inspection."

Gunn hurried out of his room, through the barracks that housed Third Platoon, SEAL Team Four, and out the door into the blinding afternoon sunlight that beat down on the "grinder," the open space nestled between the buildings within the corner of the Amphibious Base that housed the SEALs. A platoon from Team Two was doing sit-ups in the Tidewater heat under the watchful eye of a grizzled old chief petty officer; Gunn had heard there had been some training screwup the day before that had resulted in one of the most unpopular forms of punishment known to SEALkind—extra calisthenics.

He skirted the perimeter of the grinder and headed for the Admin Building, where the CO of Third Platoon had said he'd be buried in paperwork all day. Gunn smiled to himself at the thought. When the SEALs had first gotten started in his father's day, more than twenty years back, they had been noted for the free-wheeling approach they took to such mundane matters as requisitions, safety regs, and procurement procedures. Now that the Teams had finally come of age, they had acquired more respectability . . . and mountains of red tape and tedious paperwork, just like any other branch of the service.

Rambo didn't have to deal with any of that in the movies, either.

He found Lieutenant Ted Anderson going over his papers with another officer from a different platoon, evidently assigned to take over for him. Gunn waited outside the office until Anderson came out.

"Bernie . . . good." Anderson smiled broadly. "Sorry for the delay. Had to get Mancuso up to speed so we could get to work."

"Silverwolf said we had an op," Gunn said quietly as they started down a hallway. "Any idea what it is yet?"

"Nothing definite," Anderson told him. "But it's overseas . . . we're traveling by sub. We're supposed to report aboard tomorrow morning . . . which means we've got to get our gear picked out and packed up today. Commander Warren sent over a list of what we're supposed to need. From the looks of it, I don't think they're sending us to teach beach surveying to the Swiss."

Gunn chuckled. That was Anderson's favorite way of

describing the typical SEAL training deployment to one
of the NATO allies, and it was apt. Back in his father's
day, Special Warfare had been a new idea, and SEAL
training units had done plenty to spread the gospel of
commando tactics to other countries. These days,
though, everybody had their own elite forces, with their
own ideas of how to get the job done. Training missions
rarely seemed to have much impact anymore, but the
Pentagon still loved to order them.

But from what Anderson was saying this sounded like
a serious op. And every SEAL waited eagerly for The
Real Thing, instead of one more training deployment or
practice mission.

Every SEAL . . . including Bernard Gunn.

The Old Harbor Inn
Norfolk, Virginia
2335 hours GMT

"You look like you're a thousand miles away, Frank.
Still playing the sub skipper?"

Commander Frank Gordon shook his head vaguely,
only half-hearing his wife's words. Then he looked
straight at her and forced himself back to the here-and-
now. "Sorry, dear," he said. "I'm afraid I'm not doing
too good a job at this whole anniversary thing."

"Well, you haven't exactly had a lot of practice, have
you?" she said, but smiling enough to take the sting out
of the words. "Last year it was . . . what? A training exercise in Norway? Or was that two years ago?"

"Norway last year," he said. "Turkey the year before.
And in '82 it was that staff assignment at Pearl . . ."

"Well, this is number fifteen, Frank. And you're home
for a change . . . so *try* to look like you're enjoying yourself, okay? For me?"

He grinned at her. "I'll try, Becca. You know I've

always chosen you over the Navy, even if it doesn't always look that way."

Gordon leaned back in his chair and let his eyes rest on his wife. At thirty-eight, and after bearing two daughters, she still looked as lovely as when he had eloped with her, against her father's wishes and at great risk to his own Navy career. Rebecca Gordon's father had been a senior admiral—still was, in fact—and his displeasure with a certain young officer had definitely placed Gordon on the slow track.

Fifteen years later, his career still lagged in comparison to his contemporaries', even though he had earned a second chance for his part in a difficult covert operation during the Iranian hostage crisis. He would have thrown his career away again and again, though, for the sake of the woman who sat across from him in the venerable old seafront restaurant.

"Really, though, Frank . . . what is it that's got you so preoccupied? Is anything wrong?"

"No . . . not really, I guess," he said reluctantly. "It's just . . . well, the word came down today. *Bluefin*'s being decommissioned come the end of this tour. She'll probably be scrapped."

"You knew it was coming. You told me her days were numbered when you took command."

"Yeah. It's just different to have it in black-and-white, with all the Navy officialese." He shook his head. "I've gotten kind of attached to the old girl, is all. She's kind of like me. Solid service for all these years, but outstripped by the newer models."

He didn't mention the other reason for his preoccupation. It wasn't the kind of thing he wanted to burden Rebecca with tonight of all nights. Gordon had hoped that command of USS *Bluefin* might be a springboard to other postings, maybe even to one of the Los Angeles class attack boats so coveted by the captains in the Silent Service these days. But his request for a new command had been turned down. He would command *Bluefin* right

up until she ended her days as a Navy boat . . . and then
he would probably be shuffled off to another dead-end
staff job, just like the ones he had held so many times
before.

It seemed his past was never going to let him go, not
completely. For a few short years he had been back on
track, but he hadn't managed to add to his laurels
enough to erase the blemishes that had dogged him for
so long.

As if she could sense what he was thinking, Rebecca
took his hand and looked straight into his eyes. "And
you, Frank? Where are you going to be posted next?"

"I don't know, yet," he said, truthfully enough. "I'm
sure the boys at the five-sided squirrel cage will have
some ideas, though."

"You don't think my father would do anything to hurt
you? Not now?"

He shrugged. "You know how he's always been about
us, Becca. Even if he's finally started to unbend a little
with you, he still hates my guts. But the fact is he
doesn't need to do anything for my career to stall again.
My own record will do that just fine. I was an Exec
when most of my Academy class had boats of their
own." His voice got bitter. "Including Mike Chase. Now
I'm commanding a beat-up old diesel transport sub destined for the scrap heap, and he's got himself a brand-
new shiny LA-class to play with."

"It was Mike's recommendation that got you a command, Frank," she said seriously. Rebecca Gordon had
known Mike Chase long before she'd met her husband.
In fact, he had introduced her to Frank at a party in
Washington fifteen years ago. Though her husband's
onetime friendship with Chase had turned to a long and
bitter feud, she had never allowed herself to be drawn
directly into their dispute.

He let out a sigh, trying to force himself into a less
confrontational frame of mind. "I know," he said. "And
I know he can't help it he's still your father's fair-haired

boy, with all the advantages that go with it. But you know how I feel. I love you, Becca . . . but I also love the Navy. And I hate being shut out of it."

She was about to reply when his beeper went off. Frowning, he switched it off before it could draw every eye in the room to their table, and rose reluctantly. "I'd better check the service," he said. "Be right back."

He hastened to a phone in the back of the restaurant, cursing under his breath. This was turning out to be one hell of a poor excuse for a romantic night out with his wife. First he had managed to bring his personal thunderclouds along to plunge the evening into gloom, and now this interruption.

Sometimes Gordon thought he should just resign his commission and forget about the Navy, since it was plain that the Navy didn't want him. Any life would be paradise with Becca beside him. But no matter how badly his career had gone awry over the years, he still loved the Navy. The sea. The Silent Service.

As he had feared, the page had been from his Executive Officer, Lieutenant Commander Edward Hogan. As he dialed and waited to be put through to *Bluefin*, Gordon found himself wondering what could have been important enough to make Hogan call him. The XO knew Gordon would be celebrating his anniversary tonight, and that cheerful extrovert would have faced down the entire Soviet Navy and a couple of dyspeptic admirals rather than interfering with his captain's night out.

When a chain of subordinates eventually passed him up to Hogan, Gordon was brief and to the point. "What's the problem, Commander? Nuclear war? Martian invasion? Sea monsters in the Potomac?"

"Worse than that, Captain," Hogan answered with a chuckle. "Orders. Just came in by courier. Straight from Goldman's office . . ."

"Goldman?" Admiral Benjamin Goldman . . . Rebecca's father, and COMSUBSPECLANT. *Bluefin* was part of the Navy's Atlantic Special Submarine Warfare Command, but it was rare for orders to come straight from Goldman's office, rather than down the torturous chain of command. Frank Gordon was generally pleased that this was so, and imagined his father-in-law felt the same. "Any idea what's up?"

"There's an envelope for you that's sealed, Captain," Hogan told him. "But I was instructed to prepare the boat for sea. We're taking on passengers and gear in the morning. And I don't think it's a sightseeing tour."

Gordon glanced at his watch. If he left now, dropped Becca off at the house . . .

"Captain, far as I can tell there's no need for you to get back here right away," Hogan said, as if picking up his thoughts. "Finish your evening with your lady. But I thought you'd want to know about this. Better than a rude surprise later tonight."

Gordon smiled. "Very thoughtful, Mr. Hogan," he said.

"Part of my duty as your Exec, Captain."

"All right, get the preparations in train. Do you see any problems?"

"Just the usual hassles of getting the dockyard to cooperate with topping off our stores. Nothing we can't handle."

"Good. I'll be in . . . later. Let me know if anything comes up that you can't handle in the meantime."

"Aye aye, sir," the Exec replied.

Gordon hung up the phone and returned to his wife, his mind in a whirl. He certainly hadn't expected to be facing a mission tonight.

It might be *Bluefin*'s last.

Tuesday, 23 July 1985

U.S. Naval Base
Norfolk, Virginia
1311 hours GMT

The truck's brakes squealed as it lurched to a stop, and Lieutenant Junior Grade Bernard Gunn had to grasp a hanging strap firmly to keep from being thrown against Master Chief Callahan. The grizzled petty officer glanced his way with raised eyebrows, and Gunn nodded quickly.

"All right, you squirrels," Callahan growled. "Grab your gear and move out! Move it! Move it! Move it!"

The other eleven enlisted men were grinning at the Master Chief's imitation of a boot camp DI as they got to their feet and slung their seabags over their shoulders. Ever since the orders had come down assigning SEAL Team Two's Second Platoon to this special operation that would throw them into close contact with the "black shoe Navy," there had been endless jokes about discipline, organization, and clean noses. SEALs were a breed unto themselves, and paid as little attention as possible to the niceties of the more formal military structure of the regular service.

31

Gunn watched the men clamber down from the back of the truck, with Callahan following them. He finally stood, pulled his own bag out from under his bench, and brought up the rear.

The morning sun was beating down on the quay at the Norfolk Naval Base, and Gunn wiped sweat from his brow. He squinted against the glare from the water, and wondered how soon they would be missing the heat and humidity of summer in Virginia. Their orders had been sketchy, but the equipment they'd been issued suggested a considerably cooler climate. A couple of the younger guys had speculated that they might be headed for a training mission with NATO forces in Norway, but Gunn doubted that. A routine training mission didn't come wrapped in mysterious orders and require the services of a Special Ops submarine.

Gunn suddenly smiled. *A couple of the younger guys*, he repeated inwardly. Martinez and Silverwolf were both twenty years old, and not long out of BUD/S. At twenty-seven, Gunn was the third youngest in the outfit, and had been a SEAL himself for less than two years, but he was coming to look on his unit as "his boys." He wondered how Callahan, who had seen action with the SEALs in Vietnam and was approaching retirement age, would react to that idea.

He swung his seabag over his shoulder and took the lead, walking briskly toward the gangplank with the other SEALs trailing. As they reached the smooth, featureless deck of the USS *Bluefin*, each man saluted twice—to the colors hanging limp in the humid, still air, and to the OOD who watched them with an unreadable expression. The officer returned the salutes crisply.

"Good afternoon, Lieutenant," Gunn said with a brief smile. "My name is Gunn, and my men and I will be your cargo for this cruise."

"Lieutenant Shelby," the OOD replied seriously, not reacting at all to Gunn's humor or his smile. "Dive Officer. Welcome aboard the *Bluefin*." His gaze wandered

over the SEALs and back to Gunn, before he consulted
a clipboard under his arm. "You're one man short, Mr.
Gunn," he said.

"My CO, Lieutenant Anderson, had some briefing material to collect. He'll be along in a while."

"Right." Shelby waved a hand toward the deck hatch,
where a short, broad, tough-looking fireplug of a sailor
dressed in oil-stained dungarees was standing, looking
bored. "If you gentlemen will go with Chief Matchett,
he'll get you installed in your quarters."

"Thank you, Lieutenant," Gunn replied. "Is the rest
of our gear aboard?"

"This morning," Shelby told him. "All stowed and
ready for sea. Except for the SDVs, that is. They're
scheduled to be loaded later."

The SEALs followed him to the deck hatch, where
the CPO whom Shelby had called Matchett was waiting.
Even uglier up close than he'd seemed when viewed
from the gangplank, Matchett wore an Engineering
badge and nearly as many hash marks on his sleeve as
Master Chief Callahan. "If you'll follow me, sir?" he
said gruffly. The words were formal and respectful
enough, but the chief had the air of a tough noncom
who didn't care much for officers or members of fancy
elite units—and didn't give a damn who knew his feelings.

He led the way down the hatch, and the SEALs soon
found themselves within a warren of narrow corridors
and tiny compartments. *Bluefin* was an old-style diesel
boat, not much more advanced than the subs that had
fought Germany and Japan, though as a former nuclear
missile sub converted into a transport she was less
cramped than most of the Navy's submersible arsenal.
Still, that didn't qualify her as roomy, by any means.
Gunn was reminded of the childhood trip to Chicago
with his mother, when he'd toured a German U-boat at
the Field Museum of Natural History. *Bluefin* wasn't

quite as claustrophobic as that boat had been, but on the other hand Gunn wasn't a child anymore.

Chief Matchett stopped for a moment in the cubicle designated *Ship's Office* and emerged with a clipboard before going on. Twice the SEALs were forced to flatten themselves against one side of the corridor as someone shouted, "Make a hole!" and pushed past, and once they were forced to wait several minutes while a pair of sailors maneuvered a large crate through a narrow hatch into a storeroom.

Finally, Matchett held up a beefy hand. "Okay, listen up!" he growled. "Here are your berthing assignments. Silverwolf! Woods! Davis!" He jabbed a blunt thumb toward a curtained stack of bunks, each one about the size of a coffin. "Callahan! Jenkins! Martinez!" This time he indicated an adjacent set of bunks. He went down the line, pointing out more bunks for the other six men in the unit. "You men will share this area with the SDV platoon, which has not yet come aboard. We have plenty of accommodations for all of you, so I don't expect to be hearing any complaints about berthing. Am I understood?"

Callahan gave him a lazy smile. "I think we can handle things, Chief," he said. "Beats the hell out of some billets we've had, eh, boys?"

"You can say that again, Cal," Electrician's Mate First Class George Jenkins, fondly known among the SEALs as "Jinx," chimed in. "Remember that time in Panama? No tents, rain all the time, and mosquitoes big enough to carry off a small cow!"

The submariner turned to Gunn. "There are separate accommodations aft for SEAL and SDV officers, sir," he said. "If you'd come with me . . . ?"

Gunn followed him aft, to a tiny cubbyhole that might charitably have been called a cabin, but only by someone with poor eyesight or a very large sense of humor. Still, for this mission there would only be four SEAL officers aboard—Anderson, Gunn, and the two officers who would command the SDV platoon Matchett had mentioned—which meant each of them could have a private cabin, instead of being forced to double up.

As he unpacked his seabag into the cramped storage areas available under the lower bunk, Gunn found himself hoping this mission wouldn't take too long. Claustrophobia was something SEALs couldn't afford to suffer from, and he was very much afraid that too much time in this so-called cabin would leave him with a major case.

Enlisted Mess Hall, USS *Pittsburgh*
North Atlantic Ocean
1445 hours GMT

"So, Archie, whaddya think? Any idea what's behind it all?"

Boatswain's Mate Second Class Archibald Douglas took a cautious sip of "bug juice" and shook his head. "Not a clue," he said with a grin. "Yonder's the man you should be asking." He nodded his head toward Radioman First Class Eugene Markowitz, who was maneuvering between the crowded tables of the mess hall with a loaded tray precariously balanced in his hands.

"Hey, Genie! Over here!" Petty Officer Third Class Tom Edwards, the sub's youngest and greenest enlisted man, chimed in. "Got a seat open here if you want it."

Markowitz smiled and nodded, steering for the table. *Pittsburgh*'s mess hall was the single largest compartment on the boat, but with six tables—each capable of holding eight men on attached benches if they were reasonably friendly—it was still fairly crowded. Especially when nearly fifty people, close to half the crew, were packed in at once eating lunch. The radioman had to be nimble to weave his way over without managing to dump his tray on any of his shipmates. But he made it without incident, and settled in at the end of the table next to Quartermaster First Class Bob Reinhold.

"Here's the man who knows it all," Reinhold said. "What about it, Genie? Give us the inside dope on these new orders, will ya?"

Markowitz, known as "Genie" because of his magic touch with electronics gear of all kinds, didn't answer right away. He first took a large bite from his burger, plainly savoring the taste. That was one of the few compensations a submariner enjoyed for an otherwise difficult existence—the food, whether it was hamburgers or Lobster Newburg, was always first-rate. At least in the early stages of the cruise.

Setting down the burger, Markowitz took a drink of his orange-flavored bug juice, causing some of the others around the table to grimace in disgust. Most of the crew found the red juice tolerable, but thought the orange was awful . . . and took glee in pointing out that it was generally used as scouring powder for cleaning decks aboard. But Markowitz, perversely, claimed to like the foul stuff.

"Come on, Genie, give!" Edwards urged, unable to contain himself in the face of the radioman's elaborate silence.

"Not much to tell, guys," Markowitz told them. "You already know about as much as I do. The orders were to break off the patrol and head for Holy Loch. Best possible speed." He shrugged. "What else can I say?"

"I wonder what it's all about?" That was Hospitalman First Class Harry Norris, the sub's independent duty corpsman, from his place next to Douglas. Like almost all corpsmen in the Navy, he'd been hung with the rather plebeian handle "Doc." "Why pull us in for no good reason, huh? Seems pretty damned stupid if you ask me."

"Well, I didn't ask you," Reinhold told him, but grinning. "Look, don't knock it. This your first time in a sub, Doc?"

"Yeah. What about it?"

"Be grateful for the break. Trust me on this one. I've been in subs for close to ten years now, and I know what I'm talking about. Six months out on patrol is a damned long time. This way, I figure we'll at least have a shot at some liberty. We get a little fresh air, a chance to hit the bars in town, and best of all we get to get out this underwater coffin."

"Anyway," Douglas put in, "I've always wanted to see Glasgow. My family came from that part of Scotland, you know. Might be kind of cool to see where my people came from . . . and I might not get another chance."

"Ha! Listen to Kunta Kinte here. Gonna look for your *Roots,* Archie?" That was Engineman Second Class John Bowen, one of the few African Americans aboard *Pittsburgh.* He was loud and opinionated, especially about racial issues, but he was popular with his shipmates because he never let his personal beliefs get in the way of his performance of duty. During a mishap in *Pittsburgh*'s first sea trials Bowen had pulled four other men out of a compartment before it flooded . . . one of them Torpedoman Third Class Jerry Connors, with whom Bowen had been arguing just a few hours earlier after Connors proclaimed himself to be proud of his father's membership in the KKK. Connors was sitting next to him today. They still weren't exactly buddies, but they had learned to bury their differences and get along. You did that aboard a sub, if you wanted to stay sane.

"Gonna get a kilt, Archie?" Norris added, laughing. "Bet you've got great legs, huh?"

"Next thing you know, he'll want to transfer to Engineering so he can start telling the Skipper, 'I canna do it, Captain. She just canna take any more!' " Reinhold's imitation of *Star Trek*'s Scotty was good enough to set them all to laughing.

"Geez," Douglas said. "Don't any of you guys have

any interest in your heritage? Or is Glasgow all about
bars and strip clubs to you?"

Reinhold and Bowen exchanged glances. "Bars and
strip clubs!" They said it in unison.

Jerry Connors spoke up. "I know what you mean, Archie," he said in his soft, Mississippi-accented voice. "I
had a chance to visit the battlefield at Murfreesboro one
time. My great-granddad fought there. Walking around,
lookin' at where the fighting happened, it was like he
was there beside me, talkin' to me."

"Hearing voices. That's when you know you're losing
it." Norris spun his forefinger beside his head. He'd
never been fond of Connors, and frequently needled
him.

"Lay off, Doc," Douglas said. "Connors's got it right,
for a change. Y'know, history's something more than
just something to put kids to sleep in school. And just
because Alex Haley made the big splash with *Roots*
doesn't mean you blacks have the market cornered on
wanting to know where you came from, Bowen. One of
my ancestors was shipped over to Virginia as a slave,
too. Because he fought with Bonnie Prince Charlie
against the Brits." He jabbed a finger at Bowen. "Come
on, tell me something. When some black guy dresses up
in one of those dashiki things, everybody talks about
how great it is he's getting in touch with his ethnic heritage. But everybody laughs and makes rude jokes about
a Scotsman and his kilt. What's the difference?"

"The Scotsman's got better legs?" Reinhold suggested. That produced some more laughs, though Bowen
was nodding thoughtfully.

"This is getting way too deep for me," Norris commented. "Hey, Rodriguez, you gonna finish those fries,
or just stare at them all afternoon?"

"Here, Doc. Take 'em." Enrique Rodriguez pushed his
tray across the table. The corpsman started cleaning up
the food left on the plate. Along with the common nick-

name, Norris also shared the general reputation of Navy hospital corpsmen as a chowhound.

Douglas glanced at Rodriguez and frowned. The sonar operator had barely picked at his food, and he was frowning darkly now, paying little attention to the banter at the table. "Hey, Roddy, you okay, man?"

Rodriguez looked up at him, suddenly seeming very young and vulnerable. "You really think we'll get some time ashore, Archie?" he asked.

"Well, there's never any percentage in trying to outplay the house or outguess the brass," Douglas said slowly. "But I'd figure there's a pretty good shot. What's the matter, man?"

"It's my wife," the Hispanic sailor said softly. "She's . . . we're going to have a baby." He swallowed. "It's due in a couple of weeks . . . damn, I wish I could be home for it. To be with her."

"Your first?"

He nodded. "Yeah . . . I married Carlotta right out of high school. Had everything all planned out, until my uncle's store closed, and I had to find something I could do to make a living. We didn't figure to start a family, but . . . well, you know what it's like when you get your first big leave after boot camp."

Douglas couldn't help but grin. "That I do, Roddy, that I do."

"Thing is, I haven't heard *anything* about the pregnancy. Not one damned word in two months! Eight of those goddamned familygrams and nothing about the baby at all!"

"Hey, don't work yourself into a state, Roddy," Douglas said.

"Yeah, you know what they say, man, no news is good news," Reinhold interjected.

Inwardly, though, Douglas wasn't sure if they were right to try to allay the younger man's fears. Because of the difficulties of maintaining communications with a submarine on patrol, contact between crew members and their families was limited to a single message a week, a forty-word missive known in Navy parlance as a familygram. Not only were they short and limited in the amount of information *or* emotion they could readily convey, they were also heavily censored before being transmitted via satellite to the subs at sea. It was the Navy's notion that the crews of subs out on patrol were better kept insulated from the problems, crises, and general difficulties that might be going on back home, as these might distract the men from the efficient performance of their duties.

Of course, in cases like Rodriguez's, *not* knowing could be just as distracting and inefficient. But the Navy rarely considered such things when framing policy.

"Don't sweat it, kid," Reinhold went on. "We get any time ashore at all, you can find yourself a telephone and put in a call. Hell, we'll even pitch in to make sure you can afford it. Right, guys?"

"You bet," Edwards said eagerly. Markowitz nodded, as did Bowen.

"Guess these fries oughta be worth a little something," Norris said with a grin.

"Sure thing," Connors added. "I got a couple dollars stashed that could go to a good cause."

"Save something to give to the dancers at the strip clubs," Douglas advised. "But that's a good idea. We'll get a whole fund going . . . I bet everybody in the crew would chip in, Roddy, so you can talk to your wife and see how the kid's doing."

"Hey, thanks, guys," Rodriguez said. "Maybe you Anglos aren't as bad as my folks were always telling me."

"Watch who you call an Anglo," Bowen said, glowering.

"So what do you guys think of our captain now, huh?" Norris asked hastily. "I mean, now that you've had a chance to see him work."

It was a recurring topic of conversation in the mess hall. *Pittsburgh* was a brand-new boat, and her captain had been something of an unknown quantity from the beginning. He had come out of Special Warfare, rather than following the more customary career path for an attack-sub commander. The typical submarine officer followed a carefully planned course, alternating active duty aboard a boat with time in one of the sub schools in Groton, Connecticut. Extensive training in engineering and reactor technology and a short stint in the Submarine Officer's Basic Course was followed by a tour as a junior watch officer on a boat. Then shore duty and more schooling in the Submarine Officer's Advanced Course, followed by an assignment as a department head on a boat at sea. The successful officer would then continue to alternate training with shore-duty and sea-duty assignments as he rose to be an Executive Officer, and then a CO with command of his own boat.

But Captain Chase had taken a step sideways sometime in his career and ended up serving in diesel-electric subs attached to the Special Warfare command. He'd risen to command there before slipping back into the "regular" submarine fleet. That made him a little older than some of his fellow attack-sub skippers. It also meant that he hadn't had much recent experience with nuclear boats, and in the Silent Service captains were expected to be expert in dealing with reactors safely and efficiently. So there had been considerable speculation about Chase's qualifications for the job. It was fairly widely known that he had a powerful patron at the Pentagon, and while everyone knew the Old Boy Network was still an important part of Navy life, there were those who resented the way it worked and worried about the quality of the officers it brought to the fore. That had been especially true in the last few years, when President Reagan's efforts to rebuild the fleet after the cutbacks of the post-Vietnam era had required a rapid expansion of the Navy's officer corps.

"He's a cool one," Reinhold admitted grudgingly. "When we were tracking that Victor III, he looked so

relaxed I thought he was getting ready to take a nap."
Reinhold had been acting as helmsman that day, the only
one of the group at the mess table who had been in the
control room during their encounter with the Soviet sub.

"You bet he's cool," Douglas said. He had served under Chase once before, when the captain had command
of USS *Bluefin* back in 1980. During the Iranian hostage
crisis, *Bluefin* had carried a SEAL unit into the dangerous waters of the Persian Gulf to pull a group of CIA
operatives out of harm's way. The mission had gone
down at the same time as the failed effort to get the
American embassy hostages out of Tehran, and it was a
testament to the skill of the Navy Special Warfare elements involved in the operation that *Bluefin*'s mission
had been a spectacular success . . . yet it had never been
in the public eye the way the failed Operation Eagle's
Claw had been.

Douglas had been as green then as Rodriguez was
now—greener, in fact—but he'd come to recognize his
captain's qualities during that difficult and dangerous
mission. "I don't care if he *is* some admiral's fair-haired
boy. He's a damned good skipper, and we're lucky to
have him."

"I'd feel better if—" Bowen began.

"Hey, guys, look at the time," Rodriguez interrupted,
pointing to the clock on the wall. "I gotta report to Chief
Franco! Got an inspection this afternoon . . ." He got up
hastily, retrieved his tray from Norris, and carried it
across the mess hall to the counter by the galley. The
others at the table started getting up as well. The mess
period was almost over, and they all had work to get
back to in preparation for the VIP visit the next day.

Douglas was the last one to rise. He stood for a moment, studying the retreating back that belonged to John
Bowen, and wondered what the engineman would have
felt better about, with regards to *Pittsburgh*'s captain.

U.S. Naval Base
Norfolk, Virginia
1620 hours GMT

Frank Gordon pulled the car up close to the dock and cut the motor. "Well, end of the line," he said, trying to inject a note of hearty cheerfulness into the proceedings. He glanced across at Rebecca, who met his look with eyes barely holding back tears.

It was always like this, when he was leaving on another mission. Unlike the attack subs or the boomers in the Navy's submarine arsenal, *Bluefin* wasn't out at sea for patrols that lasted six months at a stretch. Instead she was in and out of port frequently, sometimes on training missions, sometimes on genuine ops, but never gone for more than a few weeks at a time. In some ways that was harder on the families than a clean break for an entire duty cruise would have been. Rebecca, in particular, hated the good-byes, and Frank Gordon hated putting her through it each time.

He opened his door and climbed out, and Rebecca did the same on her side. She stopped to fold the passenger seat forward to allow the other two occupants of the battered old Skylark to join her. Ellen Gordon, aged fourteen, and her ten-year-old sister Margaret didn't betray any sadness over their father's coming departure, only excitement at the chance to see the sights.

"Daddy's boat still looks funny," Margaret opined, pointing. "It's not like any of the other ones . . ."

"That's because there isn't any other boat like *Bluefin*," her older sister replied patiently. "Right, Dad?"

"That's right," he said, smiling faintly. The same exchange seemed to follow every time he brought his daughters to see *Bluefin*. It was true enough that the sub's looks were unusual. Originally designed to carry the Navy's Regulus missile during the late fifties, *Bluefin* and her sister ship, *Grayback* (the boat that had given the class its name), had been rendered obsolete by the development of the Polaris missile and the nuclear boats that carried it. So they had been converted for use as submersible transports, retaining many of the distinguishing characteristics of their earlier incarnation.

First and foremost, she was big. Displacing 2935 tons submerged, *Bluefin* measured 334 feet from bow to stern, had a 30-foot beam, and a draft of 17 feet. Now that *Grayback* had been decommissioned, she was the largest diesel-electric submarine in the world, though of course there were nuclear boats that were larger still. With a crew of eighty-seven and the capacity to transport sixty-seven commandos and their gear, *Bluefin* had been part of the first real step toward giving the Navy's Special Warfare branch the range and striking power it needed to function in the modern world. Subs and SEALs had gone together from the very beginning, in places like Cuba and Vietnam, where SEALs had been deployed from ordinary attack subs on covert recon missions and the like. But *Grayback* and *Bluefin* had taken the concept to a new level by introducing the idea of a *dedicated* covert-ops sub, capable of transporting larger SEAL units into trouble spots. Newer boats, like the *Sam Houston* and the *John Marshall*, were only refining and carrying forward the ideas embodied in the reliable old *Bluefin*.

Gordon's gaze wandered along the length of her hull, from the stern to the towering fairwater and on up to the bow, *Bluefin*'s most distinctive feature. Built to house four missiles in enormous forward bays, the bow section of the *Bluefin* bulged up and out, seventy feet long and eleven feet higher than the rest of the sub's hull, giving the sub an incongruously chubby look in front. The missile compartments had been replaced by bays that could hold four of the Swimmer Delivery Vehicles, or SDVs, developed to extend the underwater strike range of the SEALs carried aboard the transport into action. Collectively the bays were referred to as "the batcave."

One of those bays was open now, in fact, and Gordon could see a cluster of *Bluefin*'s sailors working under the supervision of the sub's crusty Chief of the Boat guiding a crane operator who was swinging an SDV over the gaping mouth of the portside compartment. There were some other sailors there as well, no doubt the SEAL specialists who were in charge of the stubby cylindrical minisubs, who seemed to be engaged in a heated argument over how to proceed.

Gordon smiled inwardly. Master Chief Preston wouldn't be intimidated by anybody, not even a flock of bad-ass SEALs. As *Bluefin*'s senior enlisted man, and Gordon's direct link with his crew, Preston had seen it all. And the rumor aboard the boat was that he ate SEALs for breakfast.

"Daddy, will you be back in time for my concert next week?" Margaret asked him. She had been taking Suzuki violin lessons, and was anxious to show off her budding musical skills.

He dropped to one knee so he could be at eye level. "Sweetie, I don't think so," he said softly. "There's a good chance I'll miss it, I'm afraid." He touched her chin with his finger and made her meet his look. "But when I do get back, if I'm too late for the concert, you can put on a special performance just for me. Okay? And your mom will take a tape recorder, too. I'll be thinking about you, even if I can't be there in the audience. Okay?"

She nodded. "Okay. But I hope you make it back in time."

"I do too, sweetie. I do too."

He stood up again. "Ellen, you know the drill by now," he said to his older daughter. "Help your mother out every way you can, all right? If everybody pulls their own weight—"

" 'Nothing will weigh too much,' " Ellen chimed in. "Yeah, Dad, I think I know the speech by now."

"Knowing it is one thing. Doing it is what counts. Right?"

"Sure, Dad." Ellen was going through a blasé phase, refusing to take anything that had to do with family life very seriously, but she was a good kid underneath, and Gordon was reasonably sure she'd pitch in when it counted.

He turned to Rebecca. "Damn stupid anniversary present, Becca," he said. "Next year I'll try for a necklace or something."

"Just bring me back what's really important, Frank. You."

He took her in his arms. "Count on it, honey," he said softly in her ear. "It's just another milk run, anyway, I'm sure of it."

"Don't play games with me, Frank. I know better. Milk runs don't start with last-minute sailing instructions. And they don't come with sealed orders, either." Her voice was soft so as not to reach the two girls, but urgent. "I know you want to make a mark, Frank. For you, and for your boat's last mission. But don't do anything stupid. Just come back safe."

He let her go, took a step back, and met her eyes. "I'll come back," he said firmly.

Then he kissed her, and his two daughters, before turning away to make the walk to the gangplank.

That walk had never seemed quite so long before.

SEAL Officers' Quarters, USS *Bluefin*
Norfolk, Virginia
1930 hours GMT

A knock on the partition that passed as the door to Gunn's cabin made him put down his book and sit up in his bunk, narrowly avoiding hitting his head on the empty bunk above him in the process. It was definitely going to take some time to readjust to life aboard a sub, he thought with a grimace.

He opened the partition and found himself looking up at his platoon leader, Lieutenant Anderson. "Settled in nicely, I see," the lieutenant commented.

"Figured I was best out from underfoot," Gunn told him with a grin. "All those busy worker bees out there look like they'd just as soon run over a guy as ask him to make a hole."

"Yeah, I know what you mean. I swear some of those guys don't shout the warning until *after* they've stepped on your feet."

"You find out anything more about what this is all about, Ted?"

Anderson shook his head. "I must've called in every marker I had, and I still came up dry," he said. "Nobody's talking. I think this is a bigger deal than we've seen in a long time. The kind of op you only hear about after six or seven beers . . . and then get sworn to secrecy over the next morning by a couple of suits with attitudes."

"Yeah. SEAL platoon. SDV platoon. Transport sub. This is more than a sneak-and-peek to keep an eye on some pissant terrorist cell somewhere."

"Well, that's what we signed on for," Anderson said with a faint smile. "Look, I'm going to report in to the CO. Want to tag along?"

"Think you can find him? I want a trusty native guide and three days' rations before I try to find my way around this tub. It's not that it's too big, you know . . . it's just too damned confusing."

"Buck up, SEAL," Anderson told him. "You've survived Hell Week . . . surely you won't get lost on a submarine? Anyway, I've already got the native guide lined up. Come on."

Gunn followed Anderson out into the corridor and forward into the area where the SEAL enlisted men were housed. The same CPO who had guided Gunn and the others before was waiting for them, looking impatient. But he said nothing. He simply nodded and led them out of the compartment at a brisk pace.

Gunn had trained aboard submarines before, like all SEALs, but his previous exposure to subs had been aboard the newly recommissioned *Sam Houston*, a converted Ethan Allen class nuclear boat, and he had understood the layout better than he did *Bluefin*'s. He was happy the two SEALs could allow Chief Matchett to be their guide while he tried to get his bearings.

They finally stopped at a plain door that had several notices stuck on with Scotch tape. The only ones Gunn could see plainly said KNOCK AND ENTER and THEY ALSO SERVE WHO ONLY SNEAK AND WAIT. Matchett knocked briskly and held the door open for Anderson and Gunn. "The SEAL officers to see you, Skipper," he said, and for the first time Gunn heard a note of respect in his gravelly voice.

"Come in, gentlemen, come in." The captain of the *Bluefin* rose from his small bunk and stepped forward to meet them. "I'm Frank Gordon. Mr. Anderson, isn't it? And Mr. Gunn?"

"Yes sir," Gunn replied crisply. Beside him, Anderson nodded curtly.

"Have a seat, please. We're pretty informal around here. Maybe not quite as wild as some of you SEAL types, but we're not nearly as stuffy as the surface boys." He waited for Anderson to perch on the office chair at the tiny desk on one side of the cabin. Gunn leaned against the cabin door behind him, while Gordon sat back down on the bunk. "Got your people aboard, then?"

"Yes sir," Gunn said again. "And I understand our gear is stowed as well."

"Yeah. All we have to do now is finish taking on the SDV platoon and the two Mark Eights, and we'll be ready. They're still working with my people to get their gear stowed. A Lieutenant . . . uh, Harriman, I believe, is in charge. Do either of you know him?"

Anderson shook his head. "Only the name. Haven't worked with him before."

Gunn nodded slowly. "I do, sir." Lieutenant Vincent Harriman had gone through the same BUD/S class as Gunn, and he'd consistently outperformed him at just about everything thrown at the SEAL trainees. But Harriman had been a little too much of a wild man, and a few of the stunts he had pulled had come back to haunt him later when his attention—and his performance—had wavered during important exercises. As a result his final evaluation hadn't been quite as good as Gunn's, and he hadn't quite made the cut to go on to a SEAL Team after BUD/S. Instead he had been routed into an SDV unit, rising to command a platoon that maintained and crewed the Swimmer Delivery Vehicles that were more and more becoming a major component of SEAL covert operations. Although every effort was made by Navy officialdom to deny that the SDV units were inferior to the SEALs, that was a common perception . . . and Gunn knew that Harriman had resented his posting. Maybe the fact that some of the instructors at Coronado had started comparing Gunn and Harriman with the Aesop characters of the Tortoise and the Hare had been part of the man's irritation. "Hare" Harriman had become something of a legend in Gunn's graduating class. "He had an . . . impressive record in training," Gunn finished blandly.

"Good, good," Gordon said. "This mission is going to take good men, gentlemen."

"You have details, sir? So far my men and I are still pretty much in the dark." Anderson was frowning. The NSA men who had briefed them the day before hadn't been very forthcoming on details, only general parameters for a covert op in Russian waters. They were supposed to find out more at another briefing at the sub base at Holy Loch, Scotland. The whole thing had the air of a military "hurry-up-and-wait" sort of situation, with the mission all too plainly being thrown together in a hurry. The SEALs were less than pleased at that aspect of things.

"Nothing firm," the sub skipper told him. "We're to get a briefing and detailed orders at Holy Loch . . . from Admiral Goldman." For a moment his features hardened, as if the mention of the admiral's name had sparked some unpleasant association. "If Goldman's personally involved, you can guarantee this isn't going to be a cakewalk, Mr. Anderson."

"I see, sir. I hope nobody's expecting my men to go in on an op cold. We'll need time to rehearse, train . . . the works." Anderson was still frowning.

"I'm sure you'll get all the time you need, Lieutenant," Gordon said. He paused a moment. "Have either of you seen action before?"

Gunn nodded. "Grenada," he said shortly. "First thing out of BUD/S."

"Missed that one," Gordon said. "Pulled a desk job at New London."

"Be glad you did, sir," Gunn told him. "A right royal screwup. I hope to God the brass keeps their noses out of this op, whatever it is, because I'm damned if I ever want to see any more long-range micromanagement."

Gordon gave him a thin-lipped smile. "Believe me, Lieutenant, the brass doesn't have much chance to meddle with the likes of *us*. A sub's the last of a dying breed, gentlemen. Like the old-time frigates. We cruise for weeks or months at a time with only the briefest contacts with home, and when a sub captain has to make a decision there's no time to call up the Pentagon and take a poll of the admirals who are parked behind their desks that day. We'll be having to make all the tough decisions on our own. By the time this cruise is over you might be wishing you had somebody to fall back on."

"Maybe so, sir," Anderson said, but he knew his voice didn't carry much conviction.

The cabin was quiet for a moment. Then Gordon stood up suddenly. "Listen, Lieutenant. This mission is going to be the last cruise for the old *Bluefin*. She's the last of her kind, you know. LPSS-570. After they decommissioned *Grayback* last year, she's the only one of the old conventional Amphibious Transport Submarines left in service, and now that *Sam Houston* and *John Marshall* are being converted the penny-pinchers have decided to retire the old girl."

Neither of the SEALs spoke. They let the sub's skipper carry on, his features animated as he spoke. If the cabin had been larger, the man probably would have been pacing. "I intend for *Bluefin*'s last op to be a success. The kind of last entry her logbook deserves. So I want you and your people to know you can count on me to back you up. Whatever you need, if I can help you with it, I will. You follow me?"

"Yes sir," Anderson said. He leaned forward in the chair with an intent look on his craggy features. "And believe me, sir, nobody wants you to be able to write up a good mission report when this is all over more than I do . . . since it's my SEALs who are going to be out there doing the dirty work, whatever the hell it turns out to be."

Gordon grinned suddenly. "Good, Lieutenant. I think we're all going to get along just fine." He paused. "We'll be getting under way tonight, after sunset. Keeps us from being noticed by prying eyes—either on shore or in orbit. So our sailing doesn't crop up in any reports at the Kremlin, *or* on CNN, and by the time anybody knows we're not in port anymore we'll be submerged and well on our way. That puts us at Holy Loch by the end of the weekend. After that . . . I guess it'll be up to the Admiral. But *Bluefin* will be ready. That much I guarantee!"

Wednesday, 24 July 1985

Bridge, USS *Bluefin*
Norfolk Harbor, Virginia
0425 hours GMT

"All stations report 'Ready to get under way,' sir."

Frank Gordon rested both hands against the rail that ran along the front of the tiny bridge perched at the front of *Bluefin*'s fairwater and took a long, slow breath. The light evening breeze was off the sea, tangy with the smell of salt. Hard as it was to leave his family behind yet again, Gordon loved that smell and everything it represented.

He allowed himself a quirky smile. Once she was clear of the harbor *Bluefin* would run submerged, and "fresh sea air" would be replaced by the bottled variety. Nonetheless, there was something about leaving the land behind that always drew him. It was what had made him cling to his career against all the odds for so many years, when the easy answer would have been to take his engineering degree and his skill as a sailor to a high-paying job in the private sector where no one knew about any scandal involving an admiral and his daughter. It wouldn't have been the same, Gordon told himself.

Straightening up again, he turned to Lieutenant Commander Hogan. "Let's do it, XO," he said quietly.

"Aye aye, sir," Hogan responded. Then, raising his voice, he added, "Prepare to get under way!"

Beside them, BM/3 Jake Cohen spoke into his microphone headset. "Prepare to get under way," he repeated, his intercom hookup passing the orders to the control room below the sail.

Hogan leaned forward to survey the deck. "Single up all lines!" he called.

The line handlers fore and aft hastened to obey, moving carefully on the narrow, rounded decks as they readied their lines. Despite the darkness that shrouded the harbor, the dock was well lit and made it easy to follow the action.

"Forward lines singled up, sir!"

"Aft lines singled up, sir!" The two shouted reports were within moments of one another, and Gordon smiled again. *Bluefin*'s crew might not be managing a flashy LA-class attack boat, but he'd match them for efficiency against any submarine crew in the Navy.

"Start engine," Hogan said.

"Engine room, start engine," Cohen repeated.

From the stern of the boat the engine grumbled to life, and Gordon could feel a faint vibration through the deck plates under his feet. It was part of what made *Bluefin* seem almost alive when she left the shore.

"Engine room confirms engine started, sir," Cohen added a moment later.

Hogan raised his voice. "Cast off forward!"

"Cast off, aye aye!" The line handler skillfully released the forward line from a cleat on the dock and began to coil it up. Another in the party used a boathook to fend off from the pier.

The Exec waited a moment before calling out again. "Cast off aft!"

"Cast off, aye aye!"

"Engine ahead dead slow. Hard right rudder!"

Cohen duly repeated the instructions, and the submarine slowly began to move free of the dock. As she entered the main channel Hogan studied the water for signs of current and wind. "Make it ahead one-third. Helm, heading zero-one-zero."

"Very nicely done, Mr. Hogan," Gordon told him.

"Head of my class in Driver's Ed, sir," Hogan replied with an easy smile. He was, Gordon thought, the perfect subordinate, cheerful and laid-back, but competent. Gordon could still remember his stint as XO of the *Bluefin*, under Mike Chase during a covert operation back in 1980, and how hard it had been to fit himself in with a commanding officer he resented and a crew trained up to another man's standards. These days there were no such problems, though. Captain, Exec, and crew functioned together smoothly, a well-trained and well-practiced team.

The sub made her way slowly through the harbor, past Navy ships and then civilian traffic toward open water, guided by Hogan's confident shiphandling. Gordon let himself play the passenger, watching the other shipping, the water glittering with the myriad lights reflected from the waterfront. He was thinking of the historical significance of this place. Hampton Roads had seen the first clash of metal-hulled warships, *Monitor* against *Virginia*. And farther out, at the mouth of Chesapeake Bay, the French had turned back the British in the Battle of the Virginia Capes and thus made the Colonial victory at Yorktown possible. One of the first great amphibious attacks, a daring prelude to MacArthur's Inchon strike, had been mounted down this coast when General McClellan had launched his Peninsula campaign . . . even though he had bungled it later, it still ranked as an impressive use of Union naval superiority.

It was all a part of the long Navy tradition . . . and Frank Gordon liked to think that he was helping to add a new chapter to the saga, however little-remarked the doings of a single submarine carrying out covert operations under the cloak of the Cold War might be to the world at large.

Eventually, they were clear of the crowded harbor. Hogan glanced at Gordon with slightly raised eyebrows. "Shall we go below, sir?"

Gordon nodded. "Might as well," he said, with a wistful look around the sub. He decided he had been born two centuries too late. What he would have given to have served as captain of a frigate in the days of wooden ships and iron men. . . .

But the world of steel coffins and silent warriors would have to do for him.

Cohen undogged the small hatch at the rear of the crowded little bridge and started down the ladder into the submarine's sail. Hogan followed the enlisted man, and Gordon brought up the rear, pausing long enough to dog the hatch shut after him. He followed Cohen and Hogan down the ladder, through the sail, a distance close to three stories in all before they reached the end of their journey. They were in a corridor just forward of the sub's control room, and just aft of the sonar shack.

All three headed for the control room, while a sailor waited patiently for them to clear the foot of the ladder so that he could go up to begin double-checking the hatch seals well before the sub prepared to dive.

Inside the control room, all was purposeful activity and quiet attention to duty. Brightly lit, the compartment hardly looked like the hub from which a Navy warship was managed. It might have been almost any sort of civilian control center, in a TV studio or a factory somewhere. Only the men in their dungaree uniforms really set the place apart.

"Status, Mr. Shelby?" Hogan asked as they walked past the helm station near the front of the control room.

Lieutenant Shelby was standing behind and between the twin chairs manned by *Bluefin*'s helmsman and planesman, each man in a bucket seat with safety belts buckled, operating steering yokes that looked more like the controls of a jumbo jet than a Navy vessel. Close by a third seat was occupied by Master Chief Preston, who had charge over the myriad valves and gauges that monitored the sub's buoyancy during dives or ascents.

"Maintaining course and speed, sir," Shelby replied.

"Very good, Lieutenant."

"Conn, Comm Shack," the intercom announced with the voice of Lieutenant Ronald King, *Bluefin*'s Communications Officer. "Message from Admiral Westfalen. 'Good luck and Godspeed.' "

Gordon took the intercom mike from Hogan. "Comm Shack, Conn," he said laconically. "Acknowledge." He put the microphone down and met Hogan's eye. "Shall we take her down, Mr. Hogan?" he asked with a smile.

"It's where she belongs, sir," the XO responded.

"Do it."

Hogan picked up an intercom mike beside the periscope platform. "All hands, all hands, diving stations! Diving stations!" A siren hooted warning.

There was little outward change in the control room, but Gordon could picture the activity elsewhere in the boat as the crew prepared to take *Bluefin* beneath the waves. The deck crews would have finished checking that all gear was secured and the hatches were sealed tight, while extra care would be taken forward in the SDV bays to make sure those four vital pieces of equipment were snug in their cradles with bay doors tightly closed. The engine-room crew would be getting ready for new orders, while damage-control parties got ready in case the dive might cause unexpected leaks that would have to be met by sealing off compartments before the entire submarine was endangered.

The increased tension was a palpable thing. It didn't matter that it was *Bluefin*'s natural element; it didn't matter that the crew had been through this scores of times in the past two years. There was always a moment of uncertainty when a submarine crew prepared to trust their very existence to a thin metal hull in an environment men had never been intended to visit.

BM/3 Cohen cocked his head to one side as reports began coming through his headset. "Engine room reports ready at dive stations," he relayed. "Torpedo room reports ready at dive stations . . ." The chant went on, almost a mantra. After a time Cohen said, "SDV bay reports ready at dive stations, all secure and ready to dive. All stations ready, sir . . ."

Hogan picked up the intercom mike again. "Prepare to dive! Prepare to dive! Close all hatches. Prepare to dive!"

Shelby looked back at his superiors from the helm station. Hogan met his quizzical look with a smile. "Maintain present course, ahead one-third, Mr. Shelby. Set ten degrees down-angle on the diving planes. Prepare to dive."

"Aye aye, sir," Shelby responded. "Engine at one-third, maintaining zero-one-zero. Bubble at ten degrees down. Ready to dive." The helmsman and planesman each repeated the orders that applied to him. Redundant it might be, but it was the routine which kept the crew from mistakes in a realm where any mistake could prove fatal to the boat and crew.

"All tanks and vents show green," Master Chief Preston reported, studying the ballast tank board intently. "Ready to dive." Shelby passed the report on to Hogan.

"Now, dive! Dive! Dive!" Hogan chanted into the mike. A Klaxon sounded.

"Flood all ballast tanks!" Shelby ordered. "Take her down!"

Preston ran his fingers over a series of switches that opened the vents into each of the sub's ballast tanks, admitting enough water to change the sub's buoyancy. Combined with the angle of the diving planes and the *Bluefin*'s forward motion, this was enough to cause the old sub to begin to edge downward, into the depths.

"Bring her to periscope depth, Mr. Shelby, and level her off there," Hogan ordered.

"Periscope depth, aye aye!"

The descent was gradual, barely enough to disturb anyone's equilibrium, but Gordon could feel every shift in the boat's angle as she began her downward course. It took only a few minutes before she began to level off again, running at a depth of sixty feet below the surface.

"Mr. Shelby," Hogan ordered, "let's put her through her paces. Adjust the trim, and then let's check the angles and the dangles." Gordon smiled gently at that. The next few minutes would tell him a lot about how good a job the crew had done stowing their supplies and equipment. The "angles and dangles" were a series of steep maneuvers, up and down, to check the sub's overall performance under way . . . but sudden sharp dives also had a way of revealing when things hadn't been secured properly, a useful bonus as far as an efficiency-conscious Exec was concerned.

"Aye aye, sir," Shelby said. "Adjust the trim, Chief."

That was Preston's signal to begin experimenting with the controls on the ballast board, altering the amount of water in the various tanks in search of a perfect balance, negative buoyancy, which would keep the sub from either rising or descending except as dictated by the angle of the diving planes and the power put out through the engines. It was more of an art than a science, and Master Chief Preston was an artist of rare talent.

As the sub began to enter the "angles and dangles" phase, a steward appeared through the forward hatch of the control room balancing a tray against the steep angle of the sub's farther descent. He approached Gordon with an almost cocky stride. "Coffee, Captain?" he asked with a grin.

Gordon reached out and took his mug, prominently bearing the word CAPTAIN. "Thank you, Madison," he said, taking a sip of the steaming brew. It was something of a tradition aboard *Bluefin* now, ever since the first time they had left port and the newcomer Madison had tried to impress his captain by serving coffee as they made their way out to sea, knowing nothing about "angles and dangles" or any of the other routines of a sub making a first dive. That performance had ended dismally, but now at every opportunity Madison trotted out his coffee and made a show of delivering it without spilling a drop, whatever evolutions the boat might be going through at the time.

Hogan also took a mug, grinning at the steward. "Better every time," he said. "You can hardly tell it's Navy coffee."

"Thank you, sir," Madison said with an answering smile before scurrying back toward the forward hatch.

"Level her off back at periscope depth, Mr. Hogan," Gordon said as he finished another sip of the scalding brew. "Then get together with our esteemed Navigation Officer and work us out the best course to Holy Loch. I have a feeling that our lords and masters will want us to make time."

"Aye aye, sir," Hogan responded. "Mr. Shelby! Make it periscope depth again. Cohen, I want all departments to check for any signs of gear adrift or loss of hull integrity. Check her over from stem to stern, boys. I don't want our SEAL guests having to start their swimming before they're supposed to!"

Gordon drank more deeply from his mug, satisfied.

No matter how powerful the attractions of home and family, it was good to be at sea again, back in his own element once more.

Wardroom, USS *Bluefin*
Mid-Atlantic Ocean
2235 hours GMT

"Read 'em and weep, gents. Full house, kings over threes."

Bernard Gunn dropped his cards onto the pile at the

center of the table, shaking his head in disgust. "You must have the cards marked, Doc. That's all I can figure."

Lieutenant Doug Waite grinned. "Clean living, son. Nothin' but clean living." Waite was something of an anomaly in the submarine service, a full-fledged Navy doctor serving aboard a submarine. Most subs made do with independent duty hospital corpsmen, but the Amphibious Transport Subs—*Bluefin* and her now-decommissioned sister ship *Grayback*, and the new nuke boats *Sam Houston* and *John Marshall*—called for a doctor to head up the medical department. The requirement was based on the number of men in the unconventional warfare detachment the sub was supposed to carry, but *Bluefin* hardly ever carried the full sixty-seven man complement aboard. Dr. Waite's duties were usually light . . . unless a mission went badly. Then his presence might be critical.

"Yeah, right. That and the fact that our sawbones here has nothing to do most of the time except practice cleaning out his shipmates." That was Lieutenant j.g. Carl Vanderberg, the Damage Control Officer, a slender, wiry little man who seemed perfectly suited for life aboard a submarine.

"What can I say, guys?" Waite said. "Poker is a game of skill."

Poker was also looking likely to become a way of life for the SEAL officers traveling aboard *Bluefin*. There was a more-or-less permanent game going on among the off-duty officers in the sub's small wardroom, and the SEALs had been invited to join in as soon as the submariners had realized there was fresh blood aboard. Lieutenant Anderson hated card games and had found other ways to keep occupied, but Gunn had accepted the invitation. It was more out of curiosity than from any love of the game, a way to get to know the sub officers better.

Unfortunately, it also threw him into the company of

Vincent Harriman. Harriman was an enthusiastic poker player, and he could turn a friendly game into a war to the knife faster than anyone Gunn had ever seen. Harriman was a poor winner . . . and a worse loser.

"Fuck!" he said predictably, slamming his cards down on the table to reveal the three tens he'd been betting heavily on. He was a short, powerful man with dark hair, bushy eyebrows, and a bristly mustache, all combining to give him a fierce, threatening aura that Gunn well knew was warranted by his temperament. "You damned truck drivers have some kind of signals set up, or what? I've been getting nothing but shit for hands all morning!"

Next to Gunn, Harriman's junior officer in the SDV platoon, Lieutenant j.g. Mitch DuQuense, muttered, "It goes with shit-for-brains." Gunn was sure he was the only one who overheard the comment. The others were too busy with their own angry retorts over the "truck-driver" comment.

The younger SDV officer was tall, gangly, and fresh-faced, very much out of place in the cramped confines of a submarine. He made a good first impression, but Gunn had already discovered that he also had an underlying sarcasm that belied his innocent looks. Gunn was torn between laughing at DuQuense's assessment of Harriman and warning him to watch what he said where others might hear him. He settled for doing neither; he pushed back his chair and stood up, instead. "Deal me out of the next one, guys," he said.

"What's the matter, Gunn?" Harriman demanded. "Game getting too rough for you?"

"Just getting some coffee, Lieutenant. And stretching my legs. I'm not used to sitting in one position for hours at a time. It's just not a SEAL thing, you know?"

Harriman flushed red with anger. The comment would have sounded innocuous enough to most people, but Harriman had recognized the dig for what Gunn had meant it for, a reminder of the man's role as an SDV

driver who never left the cockpit of his minisub ...
while the SEALs did the real work ashore. "Watch it,
asswipe! SDV platoons are as much a part of the SEALs
as your lot. Don't you forget it!"

"Aye aye, sir," Gunn said with a smile. That only
made Harriman more angry. He started to stand, but
Vanderberg held up a hand.

"Hey, knock it off," he said. "I'd tell you two to take
it outside, but that would be a little too wet. Are we
going to sit around taking swipes at each other or get
back to playing cards?"

Flashing a last angry look at Gunn, Harriman sat
down again and grabbed the cards, shuffling with a savage flourish. Gunn shook his head again and stepped
over to the counter where a coffee machine was bub-
bling away. He found a mug and poured himself a cup.

So far, it had been a quiet crossing. There wasn't
much to do except eat, sleep, read, or play cards, though
Anderson had insisted on the platoon spending part of
their first day at sea checking and rechecking their gear
and familiarizing themselves with those parts of *Bluefin*
that concerned them—mostly the SDV bay and the escape trunks. He had requested time to conduct some
practice lock-outs and lock-ins, but Gordon had deferred
that until they reached Holy Loch. *Bluefin*'s orders
called for them to reach Scotland in the shortest possible
time, and Gordon wasn't going to take time out for drills
and training runs along the way.

The time spent essentially inactive weighed heavily
on the SEALs. It was all well and good for the submariners; they were used to these cramped conditions. But
the essence of SEAL life was activity, calisthenics,
drills, practice runs, rotation to different schools and
training grounds ... for all their complaints about the
amount of work they were expected to do, a busy SEAL
was a happy SEAL. A bored SEAL, Gunn told himself
with a smile, was dangerous. He could still remember
the stories that circulated through the Teams about the

SEAL rotated to a boring desk job that involved studying the vulnerability of VIPs to terrorist attack who had ended up mounting an elaborate stalking effort against a well-known Hollywood actress and anti–Vietnam War activist.

Luckily, they wouldn't be at sea all that long, and once they had all the details of a mission to focus on there would be plenty to keep the SEALs occupied.

Until then, there was always poker.

Sipping his coffee, Gunn studied the men at the table as the hand played out. He was interested in the similarities—and the differences—between the submarine officers and the SEALs. Both groups tended to regard themselves as standing somewhat apart from the regular Navy. SEALs and submariners alike were considerably less formal in their relationships between officers and enlisted men.

For the SEALs, the vital bond was Hell Week, that period of their BUD/S training where everyone, regardless of rank, was pushed to the edge and beyond. Anyone who survived that was a SEAL, and anyone who hadn't been through it wasn't worth knowing. Differences in rank, social class, even race and religion faded in the face of Hell Week.

He didn't know enough about the submarine service to be able to say what the exact nature of the bond was that held the "Dungaree Navy" together, but he could see it was there. There was more formality than in the SEALs, but much less than was common aboard surface ships or ashore. Probably it had to do with the enforced isolation these men shared. Crowded cheek to jowl in a tin can that stayed underwater for weeks or months at a time, with few contacts with home and family, the men who shared this life would have to become an extended family themselves if they were going to stay sane. Like any family, they had their disagreements, their quarrels, even their occasional blowups, but mostly they seemed to get along together pretty well.

Gunn knew that the Amphibious Transport Subs had it fairly easy compared to the attack boats or the boomers. An extended patrol with hardly any chance to communicate with the people left behind would be a killer, Gunn reflected. Having lost his father to the war in Vietnam at a fairly young age, Gunn thought a lot about families left behind. Perhaps, he thought, that was why he still hadn't been able to pop the question to Pamela. They had been seeing each other for nearly three years now . . . but the thought of turning their relationship into one where she would always be the one he left behind made him pull back from taking things further.

How much worse would it be for the wife of a submariner? A sub by its very nature couldn't communicate freely with its home port. There were no letters or phone calls to allow sailors to keep in touch, not unless they were lucky enough to call at a port somewhere during their cruise. Maybe, in some ways, it took a tougher breed of men to fill the ranks of the Silent Service.

"Yeah, me and Burn-Out go back a ways," Harriman was saying. Gunn snapped out of his reverie at the sound of the nickname he had hated at BUD/S. "He was this chubby little butterball who could barely keep up with the rest of the class when we were training at Coronado." He brayed a laugh and drew two cards.

"Well, I have to admit, he doesn't *look* much like a SEAL," Vanderberg said.

"What's a SEAL supposed to look like, Lieutenant?" Gunn spoke up mildly. "We aren't all stone-cold killers with dead eyes, you know. Some of us hardly even drag our knuckles on the deck when we walk."

Dr. Waite spluttered a laugh. "Wait a minute, that's the Marines you're talking about."

"No, the Marines are still pretty much at the knuckle-dragging stage, I'd say, Doc," DuQuense put in. "You've gotta look at the family tree. It starts in pond scum, goes up through Marine DIs, then to regular Marines, and finally ends in SEALs."

"With the rest of the Navy farther up," Vanderberg added. "And submariners at the top. Right?"

"I don't know about that," DuQuense said judiciously. "Aren't fish and amphibians pretty far down the food chain?"

"Come on, come on, whose bet is it?" Harriman demanded. He didn't sound interested in the mockery making the rounds of the table. "Are we gonna talk, or play?"

Gunn smiled behind his coffee mug. Human nature, it seemed, was the same for both branches of the service.

SEAL Enlisted Berths, USS *Bluefin*
Mid-Atlantic Ocean
2351 hours GMT

"You guys ever see *Ice Station Zebra*?" Johnny Silverwolf asked, looking around the small open area near the SEAL bunks that served as a very inadequate rec room. Most of the SEALs were sitting around the various small tables, along with a few of their counterparts from the SDV platoons. There was a card game in progress at one, while at another a couple of the men were writing letters. The few who weren't in view were still within earshot, in their bunks, benefiting from the closest thing to privacy they were likely to find on board *Bluefin*. "Maybe it's something like that. Up in the Arctic somewhere. We're packing enough cold-weather gear to go hunting polar bears."

"Nah, that shit only happens in the movies, Wolf." That was Radioman Second Class Danny Woods. He was one of the card players. "No, I figure Norway's the best bet. Probably some NATO war game to see who can sneak in and out of the fjords the best."

"I don't know," Silverwolf said. "I thought that, too, at first, but if it was a training mission I think the L-T would've told us. This whole thing seems pretty hush-hush to be some routine war game."

"Don't be too sure," George Jenkins put in. "I've been reading some stuff in the *Proceedings*." That was one of the Navy's more prestigious magazines, dedicated to exploring various aspects of modern Navy policies and programs. It was usually considered to be the sort of thing only officers and armchair strategists read, but Jenkins had never made a secret of his hopes to one day get a commission.

"I tried that once," Woods said. "But then I found out the closest thing to a centerfold was a cutaway view of the *Nimitz*, and I lost interest."

"Like I was *saying*," Jenkins went on. "The Russkies have their own commando force, you know. *Spetznaz*, they're called. Supposed to be really hot shit, too. There's been stories floating around that these guys are trained to take out military installations ahead of an invasion, infiltrating, blowing up stuff, assassinating VIPs, all sorts of stunts like that. They already did it when they invaded Afghanistan."

"Yeah? So?" That was BM/1 Mark Davis, who looked up from the August issue of *Playboy* he'd been perusing at a nearby table to join in the conversation.

"So I think NATO's worried the Russkies might try something like that in Norway, and they're trying to find out how vulnerable they'd be if it happened. They'll have us play the part of the *Spetznaz* and see if we can penetrate any important bases. The secrecy's just part of the game, see?"

"In case you squirrels didn't notice it," Master Chief Callahan spoke up, "we're carrying live ammo. Real guns, not just those MILES laser toys they use for practice these days. Last time I heard, NATO was on our side, and we hardly ever do live-fire exercises against our own side." He paused. "Well, not intentionally, anyway."

There were a few chuckles from around the compartment.

"What do you think we're being sent to do, Chief?" Silverwolf ventured.

"Sonny, I stopped asking questions like that a lot of years ago. I'm a SEAL. I go where they tell me to go, I shoot who they tell me to shoot, I blow up whatever they don't want left standing, and in between I try to grab some extra sack time."

"You tell 'em, Chief." That was the platoon's corpsman, HM/2 Randy Carstairs, part of the platoon's first squad. "Sounds like you've got the SEAL life down."

"It's served me well enough, over the years, youngster," Callahan said. "Learned it in 'Nam."

"You really served in Vietnam, Master Chief?" someone else asked from the anonymity of one of the bunks. Silverwolf thought it must be one of the men from the SDV platoon. The man sounded awestruck.

Well he might be. Most of the SEALs barely remembered those days. Silverwolf himself had been born in 1967. For him Vietnam, like Watergate and Armstrong's moon landing, was something his parents had talked about sometimes. Too recent to be "history," too far gone to have any real meaning to him personally.

"Two tours," Callahan said, letting a little pride creep into his gruff voice. "First time out I was about Wolf's age, and so green I didn't need camie paint. Next time I went over we were winding things down, before the big pullout, and I didn't see much action, but that first tour was something else."

"Guess you were one of the lucky bastards, huh, Master Chief?" Hull Technician Second Class Chuck Moultrie commented as he discarded his cards. "Damn, I wish I'd been around for a real fight, like 'Nam."

"No you don't, Chuckles," Callahan contradicted him. "Believe me, nobody in his right mind would wish for that."

"What are you talking about, Callahan?" Electronics

Technician First Class David Briggs, one of Harriman's SDV men, demanded. "C'mon, you're a SEAL! Quit talking like some kind of wimpy liberal whiner!"

Callahan shook his head slowly. "You people just don't get it, do you? You're still thinking war's like some goddamned John Wayne movie. Well, I'm here to tell you, boys, it ain't. Vietnam was mud, blood, stupid officers, and stupider politicians, but not one little bit of glory."

"If that's the way you feel, what the fuck are you still doing in?" someone asked. "You could've got out after ten, instead of reupping."

"I'm in because I'm good at what I do," Callahan growled. "And because somebody's got to do it. But that doesn't mean I'm in any hurry to see another war. The way I got it figured, the brass hats are finally starting to figure out that it's better to use folks like us to keep from fighting a real war, and I'm all for that."

"I don't get it, Master Chief," Sonarman Third Class Alberto Martinez piped up. "What do you mean?"

"I mean that it was stupid to use SEALs and Green Berets and such like regular troops in 'Nam. We're trained for covert ops. Surgical strikes. The kind of missions we draw in peacetime. And every time we pull off one of those, it might just mean we won't end up having to send in the jarheads or start up a full-scale war somewhere. So I figure I'm doing my part by staying in and helping you guys out with these little surprise parties, so that maybe, just maybe, you won't have to spend your time the way I did, squatting in some rice paddy surrounded by a bunch of enemy soldiers who intend to do you some major bodily harm."

"Still seems to me you must have some idea where we're going, Master Chief," Silverwolf insisted. "You've been at this a hell of a lot longer than the rest of us."

"Speak for yourself, kid," Senior Chief Quartermaster Sam Burns said acidly. "Maybe I didn't get a shot at

'Nam, but I sure as hell put in my time, okay?"

"Don't worry about it, Junior," Callahan told him with a grin. "Just 'cause you're wet behind the ears—"

"At least I ain't old and decrepit!" Burns shot back. "And I'll tell you what I think, Wolf. I think we're going to play tag with the Russkies. Maybe somewhere up north—Murmansk or Archangel or some place like that."

"Russia!" Martinez said sharply. "You serious, Chief?"

"It makes sense," Burns told him. "Like the old man here said, we're carrying live ammo, and it looks to me like we're going on a serious op, not some training mission. We're fitted with enough cold weather gear to keep the Alaska National Guard happy for a year or two. And we're staging out of Scotland, which also points north . . . and what kind of hostiles do we have that far north? Just the Russkies."

"Is that what you think, Master Chief?" somebody pressed.

"The man makes sense," Callahan admitted. "Even if he is still young and innocent. But, like I said, I don't think about it much. Our lords and masters'll tell us what they want, soon enough."

"You think those two officers of yours are up to it?" Briggs asked.

"What's that supposed to mean?" Woods shot back hotly. "You got something against Mr. Anderson?"

"Oh, not him, he's okay," Briggs replied. "But what about the other one—Gunn? I hear he's a real pantywaist. Shouldn't even have passed BUD/S."

"But he did," Jenkins said reasonably. "Fuck it, man, if he went through Hell Week, he's okay by me."

"I hear he has some pull with the brass," another of the SDV men, BM/1 Bill Joor, chimed in. "His dad was a SEAL . . . and the family's friendly with Tangretti."

"You mean Steve Tangretti?" Martinez said, his voice tinged with a little awe. Every SEAL knew that name.

Tangretti was the First SEAL, the onetime enlisted UDT man who had become a mustang officer and the founder of the SEALs in the early sixties. He was a legend more than a decade after his long-delayed retirement from the Navy.

"You know as well as I do that friends in high places don't count for shit in Hell Week," Callahan said. "Where've you guys been getting this crap?"

"Well . . . Lieutenant Harriman knows the guy," Briggs said slowly. "Was in the same BUD/S class as he was. Don't you think he'd know?"

"Maybe. Maybe not." Callahan shrugged. "The day I start taking the word of taxi drivers about the qualifications of a SEAL is the day I'll eat my Budweiser, no salt." For emphasis he touched the trident insignia, commonly known as a Budweiser, that labeled him a SEAL.

"Okay, okay, man, don't get all huffy about it," Briggs said. "I was just wondering, that's all. If you old-timers are right and we're heading for a brush with the Russkies, I just figured you'd be worried about what kind of guys were going to be giving you your orders, that's all. I'd sure as hell want to be sure I can trust the guys who're telling me to go out and get my ass shot off."

"Yours is big enough it probably wouldn't matter," Burns commented brightly. "Thanks for the kindly thoughts, Briggs, but next time keep 'em to yourselves, okay? You guys know as well as we do that one of the things that makes SEALs special is knowing that everybody's got what it takes. We all go through the same training. They don't pull punches because you're an officer or the admiral's nephew or whatever. What's the matter with you guys? You forget what it was like at BUD/S after you went off to play with your bathtub toys?"

"Maybe we'd remember it a little better if *you* did," Joor said loudly. "We go through the same training, but all we get are put-downs. 'Taxi driver,' 'playing with bathtub toys.' Got a little bit of a double standard going for you, don't you, Chief?"

"I call 'em like I see 'em," Burns told him. "You guys start acting like you've been through Hell Week, I'll be glad to give you all the respect you deserve. You sit there and take potshots at us, and you can be damned sure I'll return fire. *Capisce*?"

"Hey, guys, let's take it down a notch or two, okay?" Silverwolf said. He wasn't happy with the turn the conversation had taken. "We're supposed to be on the same side, here. Right?"

No one answered his sally. But at least nobody went back to the war of words between SEALs and SDV men.

Saturday, 27 July 1985

U.S. Submarine Base
Holy Loch, Scotland
1640 hours GMT

Rain lashed from an angry sky, giving rise to a steady
hiss from the waters of the harbor that softened the
harsher sound of raindrops beating against the metal hull
of the boat. A typical day on the western coast of Scotland, Chase thought as he squinted into the falling rain
for a moment before settling his raincoat more comfortably across his shoulders, picking up the briefcase that
sat beside the open deck hatch, and starting toward the
gangplank.

It seemed ironic, somehow, that almost the only time
he had to deal with getting wet was when he was called
ashore.

Chase paused at the gangplank, saluted the drooping
flag and the equally rain-soaked sentry, then made his
way down to the pier. Ignoring the rain, he turned back
to study the sleek lines of the boat—*his* boat—and felt
the same thrill of pride he'd enjoyed the day he'd first
taken command.

What she was doing in Holy Loch was a question that

had been nagging him since the sub's arrival in the Clyde estuary the evening before. The orders they'd received after breaking off contact with the Soviet Victor III off Iceland had been short and succinct. *Proceed at best possible speed to U.S. Submarine Base, Holy Loch, Scotland. Report in and await orders.* They left a lot of room for doubts and speculations.

Then, this morning, he'd been given equally terse and mystifying orders to present himself to the COMSPEC-SUBLANT. There had been no further elaboration or explanation, and Chase was feeling very much out of the loop.

Almost reluctantly he turned away from the boat and started toward the car waiting a few yards from the gangplank, its motor running and its windshield wipers sounding somehow insistent. His stride was purposeful as he crossed to the car and climbed into the back seat, settling his briefcase beside him. The admiral had been kind enough to save him a walk across the base in this weather, and it was never good to return an admiral's kindness by being late.

The driver was a female yeoman who looked over her shoulder as he closed the door. "I hope you're Captain Chase, sir," she said. "Otherwise, I'll have to throw you back into the rain."

"I'm Chase," he said, chuckling. "So don't even think about it. Let's go."

He leaned back in his seat, falling silent as the driver started the engine and guided the car over the rain-slick roads that wound through the base. Chase spent the trip as he had spent the last several hours since receiving the admiral's summons, trying to decide what business the skipper of an attack sub had with the Commander, Special Submarine Warfare Office, Atlantic. It was true that Admiral Goldman was an old family friend, but that wasn't any reason for the man to leave his Pentagon office to fly to Holy Loch in Scotland . . . or to have the

Pittsburgh pulled from her normal patrol so that Chase could be summoned to a meeting.

Chase had been in the Navy long enough to know when there was trouble in the wind. It was there now, and he was going to be a part of it.

It didn't take long to reach the brooding building that housed the base administrative offices. A painfully young ensign met the vehicle as it pulled up, opening the car door for Chase and stiffening to attention with a crisp salute. Chase returned it in a more relaxed fashion.

"This way, sir," the ensign said, leading the way in.

The activity inside was low-key but steady, a sort of controlled chaos he remembered with a certain fondness. Chase had served in Holy Loch once before, as a young lieutenant posted to the base commander's staff, but a lot had changed since his tour. There had been some remodeling, and there were now computer terminals and high-tech equipment taking the place of the typewriters and old-fashioned office machinery he'd grown used to there.

Well, submarines had changed in much the same way since he'd taken his training in the sixties. The whole Navy was becoming more high-tech every day. The differences between the old *Bluefin*, which he still remembered fondly, and his new love, *Pittsburgh*, were staggering.

Chase was glad to have the ensign for a guide, especially once they had left the lobby and plunged into the labyrinth of offices and cubicles that were the heart and soul of the building. At length they reached a fourth-floor office, where Chase was handed off to a lieutenant who relieved him of his wet raincoat and conducted him to the inner sanctum. The aide announced him and ushered him inside.

"Mike! Come on in, son, and have a seat!" A wiry man with iron gray hair and weathered features rose from behind the imposing desk on the far side of the office and advanced to meet Chase, extending a hand.

Chase took it warmly, surprised as he always was by the strength of the man's grip. Admiral Benjamin Goldman's small stature and advancing years were deceptive, and could even fool someone like Chase, who had known him for most of his life.

"It's good to see you again, Admiral," Chase said. He waited for Goldman to return to his own seat before he settled into a chair and set his briefcase on the ground beside him. "How's the family, sir?"

"Good, good," Goldman said. "Miriam's getting settled into the new quarters in Arlington. I hope this is the last move for a while. When you get to be our age, son, moving is a lot more complicated than just throwing some gear into a seabag and finding yourself a MATS flight."

"I've already been finding that out, sir."

Goldman grinned. "Finding it a little hard to justify all the moving around to Ellen, are you?"

Chase shook his head. "Not really, no . . . but it was hard on Scott, growing up. I don't think the poor kid was ever in the same school two years running."

"Yeah, they kept you bouncing around pretty good the last few years, didn't they?" Goldman's grin took on a wicked cast that suggested he knew more about it than he was willing to admit. "Well, I'm afraid when you're the best, son, you get more than your fair share of calls on your time."

"Thanks, Admiral . . . I think."

The older man barked a short laugh. "You sound like your father, Mike."

Chase didn't respond. His father had served alongside Goldman aboard the USS *Hammerhead* during World War II, but Alexander Chase hadn't made it home. Goldman had kept an eye on his friend's family over the years, but for all his help and all his genuine affection he had never quite filled the void left by the man Mike Chase had never had a chance to know.

There was a long moment of silence before the conversation resumed, and for a moment the shadow of the long-dead man seemed to fill the room. Then the admiral cleared his throat and spoke again, changing the subject. "What do you think of your boat, son? Settling in aboard her all right?"

A smile sprang unbidden to Chase's lips. "Yes *sir*," he said, leaning forward in his chair. "She's quite a change from the old *Bluefin*. One hell of a good boat, Admiral."

"Glad to hear it." Goldman pursed his lips thoughtfully. "Any problems? Anything you feel should be taken care of?"

"Sir?" Chase studied the older man, looking for some hidden meaning behind the careless-sounding questions. "We've only been out of New London for eight weeks, Admiral. And she was fresh from her trials when I took command."

Goldman nodded. "I know. But you know as well as I do that a new boat sometimes shows a few . . . quirks on her first tour. Things that never show up during the shakedown process. I want to know if you think there's anything that might make *Pittsburgh* less than . . . combat-ready."

"Combat-ready." Chase repeated the words flatly. "Somehow that doesn't sound like something you'd be saying if I was taking her back out on patrol, sir."

"You're not, Mike," Goldman told him. "You've drawn a special mission. I asked for you and *Pittsburgh* in particular for this, because of your experience in the Gulf back in '80."

The Gulf. Those two simple words brought back a flood of memories for Chase. While the hostage-rescue mission of Operation Eagle's Claw had been falling apart at a remote airfield called Desert One, Chase and the *Bluefin* had been engaged in a covert operation delivering a team of U.S. Navy SEALs to the small Iranian port of Bandar-e Shapur near the head of the Persian Gulf to rescue a group of CIA and NSA operatives on the run from Iranian government troops. It had been a difficult and dangerous mission, involving the insertion of the SEALs in the very heart of enemy waters, complicated by the treacherous shallows of the Gulf and a delicate political situation. But the operation had fared far better than Eagle's Claw, perhaps because it had been an all-Navy show from first to last, not marred by the interservice rivalries and incompatibilities that had derailed the hostage-rescue mission.

"Admiral, I'm not sure I understand," Chase said slowly. "What could my experience at Bandar-e Shapur have to do with a mission for *Pittsburgh*? A Los Angeles class isn't exactly intended to insert SEALs anywhere . . ." He trailed off. There was no reason an attack boat like the *Pittsburgh couldn't* put a stick of SEALs ashore on some remote coast, but there were better resources available for those types of ops. Resources like the *Bluefin*, for instance.

"No, and that won't be your job." Goldman smiled, but the expression was devoid of warmth or humor. "But you'll be going in as escort to a sub that's equipped to do just that . . . *Bluefin*, in fact. And in another spot where you're not going to have a whole lot of water under your keel. Hence my idea of calling on you. You know *Bluefin*'s capabilities, and you're used to swimming in the shallow end of the pool."

"Escort," Chase said quietly. "We didn't get an escort in the Gulf."

"You weren't going up against the entire goddamned Soviet Northern Fleet, either," Goldman told him. "This time *Bluefin*'s going knocking at the Bear's front door, Mike, and I want an attack boat backing her up that can cover her backside if there's trouble. *And* a skipper I know I can count on."

"You're sending a commando op into the White Sea? To Archangel?" Chase was stunned. The White Sea was an almost landlocked body of water along the northern coast of the Soviet Union, with a single relatively narrow

entrance easily guarded by naval and aerial patrols. It
was also a shallow, treacherous sea, full of shoals and
uncharted obstacles . . . uncharted because the Soviets
claimed it all as their own, and didn't allow foreign ships
to map the area. Moreover, Archangel was a major port
for the Soviet Red Banner Northern Fleet, the most powerful striking arm of the Soviet Union's navy, and both
the White Sea and the approaches to it could be expected
to be full of hostile warships at any given time.

Chase knew that a few American submarines had penetrated those dangerous waters from time to time. Some
had even carried out covert ops there. But it wasn't the
sort of mission the Pentagon would order casually . . . or
the kind of op a sub commander could contemplate with
anything but a knot of apprehension in the pit of his
stomach. Sub ops in the open ocean could be dangerous
enough. Chase's Gulf experiences had taught him how
much worse they could be in constricted, shallow waters.
And, as Goldman had said, that time he hadn't been
facing the Soviet navy . . .

"Damn it, Admiral," he went on after a moment.
"That's about as close as those guys can get to suicide
without pulling the triggers themselves. Not to mention
the risk if the Soviets catch us with subs and commandos
operating in those waters. They regard that as their own
private preserve . . . it'd be like us finding Soviet subs
cruising the Gulf of Mexico off New Orleans! What
could possibly be worth us putting everything on the line
like that?"

Goldman leaned back in his chair, looking deceptively
relaxed. Chase knew from long experience, though, that
when the admiral looked that detached, that distant, it
could only mean he was lost in concentration on a problem that required all of his mental and physical energies
to deal with. "Some of our humint resources inside
Archangel have reported that the Russkies are beginning
to test a newly constructed submarine," he said quietly.
"We don't have many details as yet. Security is damned

tight—even tighter than when they were working on the first *Typhoon* a few years back. What we know so far is that this new baby's probably an attack sub . . . and the Soviets are supposed to be damned proud of her."

"A new class of attack sub." Chase rubbed the bridge of his nose thoughtfully. "I'm still not sure I see that warranting a sneak-and-peek right into the White Sea. They're always experimenting with new sub designs, Admiral."

Goldman fixed him with a steely eye. "This one could be different," he said. "What I'm about to tell you doesn't leave this room. As a matter of fact, I probably ought to shoot you as soon as I tell you, but I suppose that would sort of defeat the whole purpose of the meeting." He mustered another smile, but it wasn't very convincing. "Ever since the FBI busted the Walkers, we've been starting to trace some of the information they passed to the KGB. And there's one area where it's pretty damned clear that the Walkers have been busy. Submarine and ASW ops."

Chase frowned. It had been barely two months since the arrest of members of the Walker family, who had been spying for the Soviets since the sixties, had shaken the Navy. One of them had been taken right off the carrier *Enterprise*, where he had been serving, unsuspected, just one more ordinary American sailor . . . with full access to all of the Navy's most sophisticated communications technology, codes, and security protocols. His father and others had been in even more trusted positions. The firestorm generated by the case was still sweeping through the service, from the lowest ranks to the very highest. Chase had heard it estimated that it might take a decade or more to undo all the damage this one spy ring had caused.

"Our big advantage over the Russkies in submarine warfare has always been the fact that we've stayed leaps and bounds ahead of them in technology," Goldman went on. "They don't seem to have realized just how *good* our detection systems are . . . or just how damned noisy their boats are. You've played enough war games out there to know that if the balloon goes up, we're set to knock out every Soviet boat we can find. And we can find just about all of them, given the technology gap between them and us. Their attack boats, that is. Some of their boomers are pretty damned sneaky, especially the new *Typhoons*."

"You're saying this new sub might incorporate more advanced technology? Some of our stuff the Walkers could have passed on?"

The admiral nodded slowly. "That's what we're afraid of. Our sources inside the Soviet Navy have reported that there has been a sudden surge of interest in underwater stealth. New hull materials . . . quieter propulsion systems. On the other side of the coin, there's been work on improved sonar and such, and some of what we're hearing about could be coming straight out of our own R&D. It seems pretty certain that the Walkers have been feeding the Russkies all the information they need to close the gap and start deploying subs we might *not* be able to find and sink if a war breaks out." He paused, his eyes assessing Chase.

Ever since the start of the Cold War, the balance had always been the same. The Soviets had the numbers— more men, more aircraft, more ships, and especially more subs. Their leadership had embraced the military potential of submarines in a way that only a handful of Americans, men like Rickover and Goldman, had ever considered. But the United States and her allies relied on their technological edge to maintain parity, outnumbered, but with high-tech systems and better-educated, better-trained men to operate them. It was that technological advantage as much as the number of nuclear missiles trained on the Soviet heartland which had kept the Russian Bear at bay all these years.

If the Soviet Union could steal a march on the West and modernize their navy to a point where it could close that technological gap, the whole balance of power would shift dramatically. In ten or fifteen years, given the Soviets' dedication to submarines and their willingness to experiment with inventive new designs—something the United States had lost in the battle to trim the budget—the Soviet navy could be strong enough and skilled enough to sweep the seas clean of American boats like *Pittsburgh*.

"The question is," Goldman continued after a moment, "how good are these new systems? Are they on a par with the LAs?"

"And this mission is to find that out?"

"Exactly. The Pentagon wants details on this new attack sub before it goes into full production. If it's what we think it is, it will incorporate all their new tricks. If we know just what those tricks are, we'll be able to concentrate on coming up with ways to overcome them, to stay ahead in the technology battle. The specs on that boat may also tell us what *their* detection systems are able to do . . . which could be critical if we want to keep *them* from hunting down *our* boats."

"So we send in SEALs to try to penetrate the submarine base at Archangel? Admiral, nobody admires those guys more than I do, after what they did in the Gulf, but that's one hell of a tall order."

"That it is," Goldman agreed. "But short of turning some insider in the Soviet hierarchy at their sub base in Archangel—something I don't think either the CIA or the NSA has any great hope of pulling off anytime soon—this is our best chance of getting the intel we need. And it won't be Archangel itself, but the shipyard at Severodvinsk. About thirty miles west of Archangel . . . by the mouth of the Dvina River."

"Just about the same thing," Chase said. "Security will be tight."

"Damn right it will. But this is the kind of thing the SEALs are good at. Just a quick in-and-out operation. Photographs, measurements, that sort of thing. If they

can manage it, maybe they get a look at the files inside
one of the admin buildings—copy some schematics or
purchase orders for hull materials." Goldman leaned forward. "If this new sub is actually into sea trials as we
suspect, you and *Bluefin* will both be placed to watch
and listen. Get some sonar readings on the beast."

Chase nodded reluctantly. "I see the possibilities, Admiral. But I also see a hell of a lot of risks."

"Risks we have to take," Goldman told him. "Look,
this is the kind of thing subs are perfect for. You know,
Mike, I've watched a lot of things change since I was
in subs back in World War II. The technological changes
have been incredible . . . frightening, sometimes. We've
got satellites and computers and high-tech gizmos that
can listen in on conversations a mile or more away . . .
but there's no substitute, even yet, for good old-
fashioned human intelligence. A guy with a notebook
and an eye for detail, on the ground, studying whatever
it is that needs to be studied and taking a report back to
his bosses. Did you know I was aboard one of the first
subs used for this kind of covert recon work? The old
Burrfish, back in the PTO in '44. We had some UDT
swimmers, and some OSS guys, mixed up together in
this crazy little recon unit to find out if we could take
the Japs by surprise in the Palau Islands. One night, three
of them didn't make it back."

The admiral sat up, a sudden intensity in his eyes. "I
remember a lot of talk in the wardroom about whether
it was worth it, sending guys in to scout out enemy
beaches when any damned little screwup would mean
they wouldn't make it out again. But I said then, and I
still think today, that sometimes you've got to put a few
good people at risk if you're going to save hundreds,
thousands . . . hell, today it could be millions more. So
I'll risk a platoon of SEALs ashore in Archangel if that's
what it takes. Otherwise, we run the risk of the Russkies
pulling up even with us, and maybe when the balloon
goes up they slip their subs past our guards to take out

a convoy of troopships heading to reinforce NATO. And I'll risk *Bluefin* . . . and *Pittsburgh*, too, if need be. Because whether we're in a cold war or a hot one, it's still a war, and you have to risk people sometimes if you're going to win that war."

"Yes, sir," Chase said slowly. "But . . . aren't you also risking the chance that we'll end up *starting* a war? A real one?"

"If somebody miscalculates, maybe," Goldman said flatly. "Frankly, I doubt it. We have these little 'incidents' all the time. They violate our waters, we violate theirs . . . they 'accidentally' ram one of our destroyers, we 'unintentionally' play chicken with one of their cruisers. Odds are that the worst that would happen if things went bad would be a more elaborate version of the U-2 incident, or something like the *Pueblo*. Lots of rhetoric, lots of posturing, but all for the benefit of swaying world opinion. The Russkies know they're too far behind us in most military technology to be able to guarantee victory in a good old-fashioned conventional war, and they're not quite crazy enough to go nuclear as long as it might leave Holy Mother Russia looking like one big cinder." He gave Chase a lopsided smile. "Just keep in mind, Mike, that just because they might not start a war over finding Americans in the White Sea doesn't mean they'll give you a slap on the wrists and a warning never to do it again. The game is played for keeps . . . on both sides. And you can get just as dead in an 'incident' as you can fighting World War III."

"Yes, sir," Chase said wryly. "I'll try to keep that in mind."

Goldman's eyes remained on him for a few long seconds before the admiral spoke again. "There's one other thing you should know, Mike."

"Admiral?"

"*Bluefin*'s skipper . . . it's Frank Gordon." There was a tightness to Goldman's voice as he said the name.

Even after fifteen years, he wasn't one to forgive and forget.

Chase and Gordon had been roommates together at Annapolis, and had gone through Sub School together as well. Gordon had even been best man at Chase's wedding to Ellen Chandler, the young Navy nurse he'd met in Manila after a shipboard accident on his first cruise aboard USS *Perch*, a Special Operations submarine operating off the coast of Vietnam in 1967. But three years later, their friendship had come to a sudden, bitter end . . . and all because of another woman. Benjamin Goldman's daughter, Rebecca.

Chase had grown up regarding Rebecca Goldman almost as a sister; there had been a time when they had shared a brief romance, but they had gone their separate ways without losing the friendship that had existed long before any other feelings had surfaced. Rebecca had met and dated a senator's son in college, and the two were planning to marry with the blessings of her parents and the good wishes of the Chase family. But at a party in Washington mere weeks before the wedding day, Chase had introduced his friend Frank Gordon to the bride-to-be . . . and Gordon, who already had quite a reputation as a lady's man, had swept the admiral's daughter off her feet. After a whirlwind romance that lasted precisely three days, Gordon and Rebecca had eloped.

The fallout from that fiasco had nearly wrecked Gordon's career. The admiral had refused to speak to his daughter again for years afterward, and Gordon had found himself on dead-end assignments and the bottom of the promotion list ever since. Chase, as the admiral's godson, had tried to soften the old man's ire, as much for Rebecca's sake as for Frank's, but he'd soon realized that there was no hope of changing Goldman's mind. Frank Gordon had blamed him for not trying hard enough, even accused him of using the older man's influence to get ahead in the service at the expense of his friend.

Circumstance had thrown the two men together again during the mission in the Gulf, when Gordon had been assigned as Exec on the *Bluefin* under Chase's command. Professional officers both, they had managed to work around their personal differences despite considerable friction. In the end, Gordon's quick thinking had saved the mission from disaster, and Chase had been careful to acknowledge his role in his report, which had contributed to Gordon's finally getting a long-delayed chance at a command of his own.

Now, apparently, they were destined to serve together again, this time both of them commanding submarines. Gordon would have the more dangerous part to play, since *Bluefin* would be the boat that had to deliver the SEALs right to the Soviet doorstep. But he would have to trust Chase as his backup. Would he be prepared to extend that kind of trust to a man he had long claimed had betrayed him once before?

Chase met the admiral's flat, expressionless gaze. "Sir, I know what you think of Frank Gordon. I also know that he's a damned fine officer, whatever else he may be. If anybody can take *Bluefin* into the White Sea and bring her out again without tipping off the Russians, it's Frank."

"Hrrmph." Goldman cleared his throat noisily. "Maybe so. Becca claims she made the right choice." Father and daughter had finally resumed contact a few years back, but it was still a difficult dance for the two of them. "And Miriam says I'm a fool to keep on being so stubborn. But, damn it, he knew she was engaged . . ."

"Yes sir," Chase said stiffly. "But after fifteen years and two granddaughters, maybe it's time you took a look at him for what he is, instead of what he did."

"Now I know you sound like your father, Mike," Goldman said thoughtfully. "He gave me almost that exact same speech once, when he thought I was being too hard on an ensign aboard the *Hammerhead*. And he was right, too. I was." He shrugged. "Well, it doesn't much matter what I think of Frank Gordon. I'm not the one who has to work with him. You are."

"Yes sir," Chase said. "Is he here at Holy Loch?"

"Not yet. *Bluefin* sailed from Norfolk at the beginning of the week. That gives you a few days in port before she gets here. Make sure your boat and your crew are both in top shape, Mike. And ready to sail as soon as Gordon and the SEALs are ready." Goldman paused. "This mission stays strictly classified until you're notified differently. Don't discuss it with anybody, not even your Exec. We've got a cover story to explain why you were pulled off your patrol, and why you'll be here at Holy Loch over the weekend. Everything you need to know will be with your briefing materials. You understand?"

"Aye aye, sir," Chase responded formally.

"Good. I'm counting on you, Mike. This mission is damned important, and I rely on you to make sure we get the info back, one way or another. If need be, you consider everything else expendable . . . but bring back that information."

"Everything, sir? You don't mean . . . ?"

"The SEALs. *Bluefin*. Hell, your own boat if you can think of a way to get that data to us. Am I clear?"

"Aye aye, sir," he repeated. It was hard to hold back the dismay he felt at the admiral's cold, calculating orders.

The interview was over, and Chase left the office with his mind already grappling with doubts and uncertainties. This was not going to be any ordinary, straightforward mission for *Pittsburgh* and her crew.

Wardroom, USS *Pittsburgh*
Holy Loch, Scotland
2245 hours GMT

"Okay, Rick, what have you got for me this evening?" Mike Chase leaned back in his chair and picked up a coffee mug that bore the submarine's logo. Taking a sip of the strong, acid brew, he studied his Executive Officer with what he hoped was a properly nonchalant eye. Every morning and every evening, without fail, he made it a point to meet with his XO in *Pittsburgh*'s small but well-appointed wardroom for a few minutes over coffee to discuss ship's business and go over any problems which might have arisen. Tonight, with his mind still grappling with everything he had learned from Admiral Goldman, it was harder than usual to concentrate on the mundane details of managing the day-to-day routine of submarine life.

Lieutenant Commander Frederick Yates Latham managed to look elegant and unruffled, as he always did, but Chase had known him long enough to know that under his recruiting-poster features and unflappable air he was just as harassed and perpetually worried as any other Exec in the fleet. Latham was merely better at hiding his feelings than most.

Latham had first caught Chase's eye as the Navigation and Operations Officer aboard *Bluefin* during the Bandar-e Shapur operation, and Chase had pulled a few strings to get him assigned as his Exec on the *Pittsburgh*. He came from an Ivy League background, with an uncle in Congress and a brother-in-law one of the rising stars of the foreign service, but he was the first of his venerable and distinguished family to join the Navy. Chase had him pegged as likely to be on the fast track to command and, ultimately, flag rank. Meanwhile, he was a damned good second-in-command.

"I've taken the opportunity to have Mr. Vanyek put in requisitions for fresh stores," Latham said. As always when he mentioned Lieutenant j.g. Walter Vanyek, the Exec pursed his lips disapprovingly. The young Supply Officer of the *Pittsburgh* was competent enough, but his easygoing style and disorderly record-keeping brought him into frequent conflict with Latham. As a result, the sub's XO tended to keep him on a tight leash. "As long as we have the extra time in port, I figured we could fill up on perishables."

"Good." Chase nodded and sipped his coffee again. "The men will be happy to get some extra fruits and vegetables while they can. Maybe Chef Andre can hold off making any three-bean salads for a couple of weeks longer."

Latham smiled thinly. Fresh fruit and vegetables were a submariner's passion, since they normally spent months at a time out of touch with land and quickly went through the stocks of perishable items laid in at the start of the voyage. *Pittsburgh*'s cook, a second-class petty officer named Andy Lee, but most often referred to as Chef Andre by the crew, was a wizard in the cramped galley that served the 133 officers and enlisted men aboard the submarine, but even his best efforts would ultimately end up petering out into the ubiquitous three-bean salads that were a staple aboard boats finishing up a lengthy cruise. "I'm sure that will go a long way to improving morale, Skipper."

"That reminds me. I want everyone to have a chance at liberty while we're in port. Start it up right after the big do tomorrow. Twenty-four hours each, rotate by watches. Any problems with that?"

"No sir," Latham said, but he frowned just slightly nonetheless. "Might slow down the loading a bit ... nothing we can't take care of, I suppose." He met Chase's eyes with a level stare. "So we're going to be in port at least four days?"

Chase grinned. That was the closest Latham had come to asking about the sub's new orders since he had returned from his meeting with the admiral on Friday.

"Sorry to keep you in the dark, Rick," he said quietly. "It would be a damned sight easier to plan things if you knew what was going on. But Admiral Goldman didn't leave me any options. Security. I promise you'll know everything as soon as I'm able to fill you in."

"Of course, Skipper," Latham said. "Four days?"

His grin broadened. *Pittsburgh*'s XO was not just known for his dapper good looks and calm demeanor. He also had a stubborn streak wider than any three bulldogs put together.

"At least, Rick," Chase agreed.

"Good. That means we can concentrate on getting ready for the show-and-tell tomorrow and still have time to deal with the resupply later." Latham made a quick note on the clipboard on the table in front of him, then looked up at Chase again. "Still bugs me that they'd haul us in off patrol for this thing, though. There are plenty of subs in and out of Holy Loch all the time."

Chase shrugged elaborately, hoping it was convincing. "Beats the hell out of me, Rick," he said. "The admiral made it sound like he was doing us a big favor. Maybe he figured I'd like meeting royalty."

Actually, he knew exactly why *Pittsburgh* was getting a visit from His Royal Highness, Prince Andrew, and various other Royal Navy VIPs and media types. Goldman had set the whole affair up to provide a cover story to explain why *Pittsburgh* had made an unscheduled stop at Holy Loch. The prince, an officer in the Royal Navy and a veteran of the Falklands War, had expressed an interest in touring a 688-class attack boat, so Goldman had decided to oblige. Chase was a little uncomfortable with the whole thing. Not only would he have to play host to royalty, but there would be inquisitive reporters poking around his submarine with cameras . . . and he was sitting on a dangerous secret mission into Soviet waters. It wasn't exactly his ideal of how to prepare for a covert op, but Goldman had assured him it would be the perfect cover to keep *Pittsburgh* in port until *Bluefin* arrived and the final briefings could be arranged.

Latham studied him for a long moment in silence. "Right. Requests for VIP tours always go through Navy Special Warfare." He smiled thinly. "Looking forward to hearing the real story, Skipper. Really looking forward to it."

"Not half as much as I am to being able to tell you, Rick," he said. Inwardly, though, Chase had to admit that the security measures were vital. After all the revelations about the Walkers, it was plain that even the most seemingly trustworthy crewmen might turn out to be security risks. And the fewer people who knew about the White Sea operation, the better. When secrets fell into enemy hands, men died. It was as simple as that.

Chase couldn't help but think back to the Ivy Bells operation. For more than a decade, the Navy had operated a secret tap on an undersea phone cable in the Sea of Okhotsk, listening in on Soviet naval communications. The Russians hadn't suspected a thing, hadn't even bothered to encrypt their communications, so the listening device attached to the cable had been one of the finest intelligence assets the Navy had employed. Subs had been required to visit the site of the tap every so often, carrying SEALs to go out, remove a tape, and place a new one. Every mission had gone smoothly . . . until another American traitor had revealed the operation to the Russians in 1981 and brought large numbers of Russian ships converging on the area to locate and remove the tap. The American sub on the way to make the standard exchange of tapes had sailed right into the middle of it. The official story was that the sub had avoided contact and escaped without incident, but Chase had heard plenty of rumors about what had really happened out there.

He didn't have any desire to act out such a scenario with *Pittsburgh* and *Bluefin* in the treacherous waters of the White Sea.

"We going to be ready for this royal shindig, Rick?" he asked to change the subject. "Wouldn't want to offend anybody by not being up to the mark, now, would we?"

"Inspections all day today, sir," Latham said. "If there's anything wrong with any part of this boat, I'll find it and have the man in charge of it keelhauled personally."

"If I'm not mistaken, Rick, I think somebody had keelhauling taken off the list of approved punishments," he said with a smile.

"No, really?" Though not usually given to flights of wit, Latham had a flair for a kind of heavy-handed sarcasm that he could use to great effect on occasion. "Next thing you know they'll want to get rid of flogging. But not on my boat . . . Around here we still do things the old-fashioned way."

"Before you get us both cast in another remake of *Mutiny on the Bounty*, why don't you just settle for making sure things look good for the visitors tomorrow, okay, Rick?" He finished his coffee. "Wish I knew how to act around royalty, though. Closest I've ever been was when I took Ellen to an Elvis concert, and I don't think this is the same thing."

"I had a dog named Prince once," Latham countered. "Does that count?"

"Somehow I doubt it." Chase leaned back in his seat. "Anything else I should know about, Rick? Now's your best chance to unload. When those VIPs come aboard tomorrow I'll have plenty of worries of my own, so I won't be nearly as eager to share in yours." He gave his Exec a weary smile.

Latham didn't speak right away, but his frown was eloquent.

"Come on, man, out with it," Chase said. "What have you got? Moonshine still in the engine room? Nothing but orange bug juice in the dispensers? Doc selling drugs on the side? What?"

"As far as I know, Doc wouldn't prescribe an aspirin without orders countersigned by the CNO, much less sell them," Latham said heavily, his own brand of wry humor. Chase laughed appreciatively. Everyone knew by now that Norris, the independent duty corpsman, was opposed to using medications of any kind unless absolutely necessary. "As for the bug juice, rumor has it that we have plenty to last us. And the still, the last time I heard, was in the torpedo room, not Engineering. Petty Officer Douglas will, however, be disassembling it shortly." He gave Chase a thin smile, and the CO decided not to try to find out if his Exec was joking or not. Archie Douglas, whom he remembered fondly as a brand-new submariner from the *Bluefin*, had developed into something of a character in the time since Chase had last seen him, and was perfectly capable of running a still, or a floating crap game, or perhaps the world's first submersible brothel, if he took it into his head that it might be amusing and/or profitable to do it.

After another short pause Latham continued. "No, sir, there is one minor matter I thought you should hear about, but I'm not sure what to do about it."

"Speak up, Rick."

"It's about Rodriguez. Scuttlebutt has it that his wife's expecting, and he hasn't had any news in any of his familygrams. Word is he's going to make a call home. There's even a collection going around so he can make the call and have plenty of time to talk." Latham frowned again. "If there is something wrong, and it's been censored out of the man's familygrams, it could be bad for morale for him to talk to his family."

"Hmmm." Chase pursed his lips. He had never been a big believer in censoring the news from home, but that was official Navy policy, and it wasn't up to him to dictate it. "Might be equally bad for morale if he didn't get the chance, don't you think, Rick?"

"It's just . . . look, I know you can't tell me what's going on, Skipper, but I know enough to know we've been tapped for something more than a Royal junket. And Rodriguez is our best man in the sonar shack. The whole idea behind censoring the familygrams is to keep our people from getting distracted by a bunch of problems they can't deal with. If there's something wrong back home, can we afford to have it messing up Rodriguez's head? You'd know better than I would . . . since you know what's going on."

Chase nodded. "I know where you're coming from, Rick. But I'm not going to keep Rodriguez under lock and key. It wouldn't work anyway. One of those other nutcases would just make the call for him. Look, if he seems preoccupied after he comes back off liberty, we'll make a point to talk it over with him. Get him compassionate leave, if need be."

"But—"

"And don't start talking about him being our best sonar man. It's true, he is, but he's not irreplaceable. It's more important, as far as I'm concerned, to put the men first. They're what makes the sub more than just a metal hull. What Rodriguez does when he's ashore is his business, not ours. Got me?"

"Yessir," Latham said softly.

Chase studied his subordinate for a long moment. "You don't agree with me on this one, do you, Rick?"

"That's not my place, sir," the XO said stiffly.

"Never mind the perfect little second-in-command routine, Rick. Nobody here but us chickens. Want to talk about it?"

"Sir . . . Captain, I don't like the idea of going into a mission with less than our total assets. Rodriguez is an asset. Putting one individual ahead of the mission . . ."

"Is the only way we're ever going to do things as long as I'm the captain of this boat," Chase told him firmly. He was thinking of Admiral Goldman's words, that the SEALs, *Bluefin*, even *Pittsburgh* herself were deemed expendable, provided the mission was carried out.

If necessary, Chase would make those sacrifices. They

were the natural outgrowths of the oath he had sworn as a naval officer. But Mike Chase didn't believe in making sacrifices if there was any way around it, and that applied as much to a single sailor in his crew as it did to the sub under his command.

"The way I see it, Rick," he continued, "we never have the right to reduce our people to just so many assets to be used or expended as we need them. Rodriguez is the best damned sonar operator I've ever seen, but I'm damned if I'm going to let that enter into my thinking if he's got a problem. Okay? Or do you have a problem with that?"

Latham shook his head slowly. "Not . . . a problem, exactly, sir," he said slowly. "It sounds good . . . but I just hope you don't live to regret those words, when we need a sonar wizard and you've let him go home on leave . . ."

"We'll cope if we have to, Rick," Chase told him. "But this is one position I don't budge from."

Inwardly, though, he found himself agreeing with Latham's hope.

Sunday, 28 July 1985

Enlisted Mess, USS *Bluefin*
Firth of Clyde
0845 hours GMT

"Secure from Divine Services! Let's clean it up, people!"

Gordon smiled as Hogan bellowed orders in a most unworshipful fashion. Of all the many difficulties and inconveniences to be dealt with aboard a U.S. Navy submarine, providing spiritual comfort for the crew was among the most vexing, at least as far as he was concerned. Subs were just too small and cramped to allow for the luxury of a chaplain; *Bluefin* was one of the few that could actually rate a full-fledged doctor, and medical services were needed considerably more often than religious guidance. On the other hand, the demands of living in such a tightly enclosed community often gave rise to the kinds of problems that needed spiritual rather than material assistance, and even in a day and age when religion as a whole often seemed more honored in the breach than in any regular observance, the Navy did like to provide its people with the regularity of a weekly service if that was at all possible.

As a result, it generally fell to the captain of a sub to organize and run whatever religious services were held, and Gordon took that duty as seriously as he did any other. When *Bluefin* was operating in and around Norfolk, as she usually was, he saw to it that the crew could visit one of the chapels ashore for whatever services they wanted to attend. But at sea, on Sunday morning, he led a short nondenominational service in the enlisted mess hall. He and his Exec also tried to field individual problems among the men as best they could, though neither officer pretended to be trained as either a priest or a psychiatrist.

There was also Petty Officer Second Class Pete Jones, from Engineering, who held regular prayer meetings with a handful of born-again Pentecostals, open to anyone who wanted to drop in and didn't mind the "joyful noise unto the Lord" that passed as hymn-singing there. Lieutenant Commander Hogan had been heard to remark that if the Russians ever heard one of "Brother Jones's" prayer meetings on sonar, they were liable to sail for home complaining of either technical malfunctions or mass insanity. Needless to say, Jones and his fellow worshipers had to curtail their activities during actual missions.

Now, with another Sunday service past, Gordon could put away his Bible and his hymn book once again and revert to being the captain of the *Bluefin*, a change he greeted with considerable relief.

Hogan joined him at the temporary podium at the end of the mess hall. "Message came in from Holy Loch during the service, sir," he said. "We're to lie off the mouth of the Clyde and not enter until after eighteen hundred hours."

"Hurry up and wait," Gordon said, frowning. "Guess we shouldn't have bothered making such good time this trip."

"What's it all about, do you think, sir?"

Gordon shrugged. "There's probably some good reason. Maybe Admiral Goldman doesn't want *Bluefin* to be too visible when she comes in. By eighteen hundred on a Sunday evening things are liable to be slowing down a bit. Or, maybe he just likes to think of me sitting off the Scottish coast cruising in circles and going slowly insane. Who knows?"

The XO chuckled dutifully, but didn't look very amused. "Well, whatever the reason, I sure as hell am looking forward to getting this boat into port. The sooner we get this mysterious mission started, the sooner I can get home to the wife, the kids, and the dog."

"Especially the dog, right?"

Hogan smiled sheepishly. Everyone knew he and his dachshund, Schultz, were virtually inseparable when he was ashore. He was happily married, loved all three of his kids ... but everyone on *Bluefin* claimed it was Schultz the Wiener-Dog that really called him home from the sea.

Gordon picked up his books and headed for the hatch. It was time to get back to being a captain.

SDV Bay, USS *Bluefin*
Firth of Clyde
1442 hours GMT

"Okay, that checks out! What's next, Briggs? Oh, right. Radio check ... testing, one, two three ..."

"Five by five. Sounding good."

Lieutenant Vincent Harriman listened to the exchange between the two technicians as they checked over Swimmer Delivery Vehicle Number Three with only part of his attention on their progress. His technical people were good, and really didn't need his supervision, but Harriman was a by-the-book man when it came to the platoon's day-to-day operations. He kept an eye on everything his people did, and he let them see him doing

it, so they always knew the Old Man was on the spot
and ready to step in if the need arose.

It was rarely necessary. Briggs and Scanlon, the platoon's two electrical technicians, knew their jobs and
knew their way around a Mark VIII SDV. All four of
the cylindrical vessels had been thoroughly checked
back at Norfolk, and Harriman had ordered daily spot-
checks while *Bluefin* made her way across the Atlantic,
more to keep his men busy than out of any real concern
for the readiness of the minisubs. The checkups were as
much an extra chance for the nontechnicians in the platoon—the unit consisted of four pilots, four navigators,
the two electronics experts, and two mechanics, plus
Harriman and DuQuense—to brush up on their own
maintenance skills under the supervision of the technical
gurus. Everything was going like clockwork, which was
exactly what Vince Harriman expected.

That left him with the opportunity to allow a part of
his mind to dwell on other matters, far removed from
the communications subsystems of SDV 3.

Matters such as anger . . . and ambition.

Sometimes Harriman was bitter at the chance that had
catapulted him into the SDV platoons rather than the
regular SEAL Teams. He'd breezed through most of
BUD/S training, taken everything the instructors could
throw at him during Hell Week in stride, and then one
stupid mistake had dropped his qualifying scores just far
enough to get him siphoned off into the SDV program.

There were some who argued that the SDV service
was actually more demanding, in some ways, than the
standard SEAL program. The technical skills needed to
maintain and operate the cranky little minisubs required
hours of specialized training and a completely different
mind-set than was common to the rough-and-tumble life
of an ordinary Navy commando. But so far that was the
kind of argument most often advanced by jealous SDV
men looking for a way to put down their more glamorous counterparts, and it hadn't won wide acceptance.

Maybe someday, if the SDV program proved its worth often enough. At the moment it was still new enough that it drew from the bottom, not the top, of the SEAL barrel.

Harriman didn't subscribe to the theory about SDV men being superior. He didn't like his job, and he wanted nothing more than a chance to join the Teams as a full-fledged member of the Navy's elite, not as a kind of freakish afterthought. But the SEAL establishment was already overloaded since the decision to disband the old UDTs and merge them into the SEALs, which meant that competition for slots in the Teams was fierce, and there were plenty of men with more seniority and standing than Vince Harriman ready to snatch up any openings that did show up. So he had to be content with his role, for the moment.

Or at least as content as he could be.

"Lieutenant? Do you have a minute?"

Harriman turned to find Lieutenant Anderson at his elbow. The SEAL platoon CO seemed competent enough, though Harriman hadn't really seen enough of him to form much of an opinion. Two years older than Harriman's thirty years, and senior to him in both time in service and in time served since BUD/S, he wasn't the sort to flaunt any of that when he dealt with other officers. Anderson was soft-spoken, genial, but stayed fairly aloof most of the time. Certainly he hadn't joined in the ongoing poker game in the wardroom, and most of Harriman's contact with him had come when their respective duties had brought them together.

He laid his clipboard down. "What can I do for you?"

Anderson didn't answer right away. When he finally spoke, his voice was quiet, hard to hear over the noise of the technicians continuing their equipment checks behind the two officers. "Look, Harriman, we need to talk about whatever it is that's between you and Gunn. Want to tell me about it?"

The name Gunn brought a black frown to Harriman's

brow. "Did he send you here? What did he say? That I was picking on him?"

"He didn't say anything," Anderson said, shaking his head. "But you'd have to be a blind deaf-mute not to pick up the vibes you two give off every time you come within ten feet of each other. And I hear things. Like about how some of your guys have been running Gunn down in front of my platoon . . . and how the two of you strike sparks even over a friendly little poker game. Now what's the story?"

Harriman shrugged. "Nothing much. I happen to think young Mr. Gunn isn't qualified to be a SEAL. He scraped through BUD/S near the bottom of the class. Too soft by half, if you ask me."

"I see. And the fact that he made it into the SEALs and you didn't . . ."

Flushing, Harriman clenched a fist, then forced himself to relax. He wasn't going to be drawn into doing anything stupid. "Was blind, dumb luck, Lieutenant," he said stiffly. "I had one bad day and did poorly on an exercise. Gunn was lucky and happened to breeze through it. But it counted for a big chunk of our scores . . . even though Gunn consistently screwed up on plenty of other tests." He shrugged elaborately. "Can you blame me for being ticked off? That little moon-faced nerd will never make a proper SEAL . . ."

"That little moon-faced nerd, as you call him, led the stick of SEALs that captured the transmitter for Radio Free Grenada during Urgent Fury," Anderson told him coldly. "According to his file, Mr. Gunn was wounded twice and still managed not only to capture the station and take it off the air, but also withdrew his unit successfully in the face of heavy opposition after destroying the facilities. He *is* a SEAL, Lieutenant, no matter what you happen to think of him."

"Ah, Grenada was a cluster-fuck from first to last," Harriman growled. "Didn't I hear that the radio was supposed to be knocked out before it could ever get on the air in the first place?"

"That's right, but the Army messed up the timetable and our people went in late—*and* against heavy opposition. Look, Harriman, you don't have to like Gunn. But you damn sure have to work with him, and while you do I'll see you extend the same courtesy to him that any SEAL officer deserves, or I'll kick your ass so hard you'll stand at attention with your butt over your head for a month. That goes for your men, as well. I don't want to hear anymore about how they're questioning his abilities in front of the people he's going to have to command. You understand me? I won't have this op put in jeopardy by some stupid rivalry between two of my officers."

"Hey, lighten up, Lieutenant," Harriman said, raising a hand. "So I called the kid a few names. Big fucking deal."

"I asked if you understood me, Lieutenant," Anderson said, his voice even softer but more menacing than before. "Do you?"

Harriman met the other's angry glare, unwilling to simply back down. But Anderson looked and sounded dead serious . . . and Harriman, for all his pride, knew better than to push him too far. This wasn't the time to test Anderson's resolve, or his loyalty to his subordinate. Not over something this stupid. A bad report from Anderson could destroy whatever was left of Harriman's prospects for breaking out of the SDV platoons and into the regular SEALs where he belonged.

"All right, all right," he said. Then he drew himself up as if standing at attention and sounded off in his best military manner. "Aye aye, sir! I understand and will obey, sir!"

"That's enough, Harriman," Anderson told him. "Look, all I'm asking for is some professionalism. From *both* of you. Don't think I won't be having this same little talk with Lieutenant Gunn. As far as I'm concerned, neither one of you has been behaving the way I expect my officers to act." He smiled faintly. "Now, on to more pleasant matters. How do the SDVs look? Any problems?"

Harriman breathed out slowly and fought back his dislike of being put down. He picked the clipboard back up and thumbed through the pages. "Nothing my boys can't handle," he said smoothly. "One of the valves on the UBA system in Number One was sticking, but that's a minor fix. I'd be glad of a chance to take these puppies out for a walk around the block, though."

The other officer nodded gravely. "Me too," he admitted. "I was kind of hoping that the little delay this afternoon would give us a chance to do some work in the water. But Captain Gordon has other ideas. Looks like we'll have to wait until we get to Holy Loch before we get a chance to start any real drills."

"We'll be ready for it when we do get the chance," Harriman told him. "We've been over these beauties every day since we left Norfolk, but I always find that you don't really get to know how ready they are until you try them out on a cruise."

"That's what I generally say about my platoon," Anderson said. "Glad to hear you've got the same attitude on your end, Lieutenant." He paused. "And listen . . . thanks."

Harriman nodded, but didn't reply.

He'd do what he had to, in order to do his job. But he was never going to believe Bernard Gunn belonged in the SEALs . . . or that Vince Harriman didn't.

Forward Deck, USS *Pittsburgh*
Holy Loch, Scotland
1645 hours GMT

"A most impressive tour, Captain Chase. I'd like to thank you, both for myself and on behalf of Her Majesty's government, for an interesting afternoon."

"Thank you, Your Highness," Chase replied, schooling his features sternly for the cameras trained toward
the little knot of officers near *Pittsburgh*'s gangplank.
Prince Andrew, Duke of York, resplendent in his Royal
Navy dress whites, was a fresh-faced younger edition of
his famous brother Charles, his face a little too long, his
nose a trifle too sharp to be considered handsome, but
certainly striking in appearance and aristocratic in bearing. The Duke of York's ears weren't quite so prominent
as his brother's, which helped somewhat. It wasn't hard
to imagine Andrew treading the wooden decks of some
sailing ship out of the Napoleonic Wars, as his ancestors
had done, though Chase had more trouble picturing him
flying a Harrier jump jet off the deck of one of Great
Britain's aircraft carriers. It seemed somehow incongruous, this blending of monarchical tradition and modern
naval technology.

At least the tour was almost over, save for a few more
platitudes for the benefit of the press and the promotion
of better relations between old allies. Chase hoped
they'd get it over with before the rain that had been
threatening since morning finally decided to break loose
on them all.

Beside Chase, a lieutenant commander from the Public Information Office named Miller coughed discreetly.
When Chase glanced his way the man used his eyes to
point toward Petty Officer Douglas, standing a few yards
away, and the plaque he held under one arm. Forcing
himself not to frown at the officious little bureaucrat
disguised as a naval officer, Chase gave a curt nod instead. He hadn't forgotten the plaque; he'd just wanted
to make sure the other formalities were over with first.

"Your Highness, I've been asked by my crew to present you with a little something they made in honor of
your visit." And he nodded toward Archie Douglas, who
stepped forward smartly.

"From the crew of the *Pittsburgh*, Your Highness,"

the petty officer said, stammering a little. Chase hid a smile. That wasn't like the brash, almost cocky Douglas he knew. Maybe it took a brush with royalty to put the man off his stride.

Douglas held out the plaque, which the duke examined with every appearance of interest. It was a simple mahogany slab decorated with the logo of the *Pittsburgh*, showing the silhouette of an attack sub against a stylized skyline of the Golden Triangle, and bearing the sub's name and number. Some of the crew had gotten together to make it soon after the announcement of the Royal visit, and Douglas had won the drawing to present it.

"Excellent," the prince said in his clipped accent. He gestured to an aide, who took the plaque from Douglas. "What's your name, sailor?"

"Douglas, sir . . . Your Highness. Petty Officer Second Class Archibald Douglas."

The prince smiled at him. "Ah, Archibald Douglas, is it? You should be at home on this visit, then. Plenty of Archibald Douglases have been making history in Scotland down through the years, you know."

Chase was startled to see Douglas blush a little. "Yes, sir . . . Your Highness. I was hoping to get to see some of the old home country while I was on liberty this week . . ."

"Excellent!" Andrew repeated. He looked over at another aide. "Moffet . . . see to it that Petty Officer Douglas receives a tourist booklet for Douglasdale."

"Aye aye, sir."

"Th-thank you . . . Your Highness," Douglas said, saluting crisply. The prince nodded and returned the gesture, then turned back to Chase. "Captain, once again, my thanks to you and your crew. I don't believe I would want to leave aviation, but if I did, I believe a submarine like yours would be an excellent billet."

Chase responded dutifully, though inwardly he was betting that was the phrase the prince used at every such occasion, whatever it was he was currently inspecting or visiting.

The final minutes of the visit were purely ceremonial on all sides, and at length Commander Miller escorted the British VIPs back to the dock and into the waiting line of staff cars. A few more photographs and additional video footage exhausted the Fourth Estate's interest as well, and *Pittsburgh* reverted to being once more American attack sub with nothing to distinguish her from any of her sister ships.

As the word was passed that the inspection was over, more crewmen erupted onto the deck. Archie Douglas had become a center of attention, now. Many had seen him talking with Prince Andrew, but only Chase and the officers with him had heard the exchange. Now the questions and comments were flying freely.

"Guess you're gonna be too big now to talk with your bunkmates, huh, Archie?"

"Hey, Arch, did you get Koo Stark's phone number?"

"Phone number? How about a picture of her, huh?"

"How's it feel to talk to a Royal?"

Chase was smiling gently as he decided to help his old shipmate out. He strode toward the knot of sailors briskly. "All right, let's break it up, gentlemen," he said loudly. "I'm afraid Archie here didn't get a knighthood *or* an invitation to Buckingham Palace, so he's not going to be able to introduce any of you guys to high society. For which fact Great Britain should be extremely thankful. Now . . . I happen to know that liberty will be starting for some of you in a few hours, but before that time let's make sure things are shipshape, all right? Back to your duties . . . and if you don't have any duties, just give me a moment and I'm sure Mr. Latham and I can find a few to pass out!"

Before he was done, most of the sailors were already hastening to be somewhere else.

Chase turned back toward Latham and the other senior officers, and the smile was already fading. Now that the visit was over and done with, they would need to start preparing for *Pittsburgh*'s real mission.

Bridge, USS *Bluefin*
The River Clyde, Scotland
1822 hours GMT

From the top of her sail, *Bluefin* looked like some ungainly aquatic beast that had strayed from its natural habitat. Even Gordon, who loved the old boat, couldn't help but acknowledge the fact as the sub made her way slowly up the wide mouth of the Clyde estuary. Her high bow rose from the water like the domed head of some sea monster come to ravage the Scottish shore.

Gordon smiled. He wondered what folks would make of *Bluefin* if he was to take her through the Caledonian Canal and into the waters of Loch Ness. . . .

Probably, he told himself, they'd decide the old girl wasn't nearly as glamorous as Nessie.

Gordon allowed himself a moment to play the sightseer as the sub steered north-northeast between the jutting promontories that defined the mouth of the river. From the looks of sea and sky, it had been raining not long ago, but the clouds to the west had started to break up by then. The afternoon sun reflecting off high-banked clouds gave the sky a startling golden hue, and there was a hint of a rainbow to the south that struck Gordon as a good omen of sorts . . . for those who believed in omens. He didn't . . . but he could certainly appreciate the glorious beauty of this distant coast. It was his first time to visit Holy Loch despite years in the submarine service, but he had heard plenty of stories about the natural splendor of the Inner Hebrides.

The land rising in ever-higher ridges on either side of them was impressive, too, in a different way. Clad in thick green forest, there was something unspoiled about this coast that was enhanced rather than marred by the buildings clustered between mountain and shore, quaint old structures that looked as if they had been there for centuries, watching ships of all kinds come and go. They probably had, too, Gordon thought. He considered the sense of history he always experienced off Norfolk, and shook his head slowly. Over here, that history was just the blink of an eye.

Beside him, Lieutenant Commander Hogan remained intent on studying the water ahead through his binoculars, barking occasional orders. Unlike Gordon, he had been to Holy Loch before, and from some of his grumbled comments Gordon was fairly sure the XO disliked having to bring a boat up the Clyde to the American submarine base.

He could understand why. The Clyde was navigable all the way up to Glasgow, a distance of nearly thirty miles by a dogleg route that ran north, then sharply southeast. In the outer part of the estuary the current was sluggish, but there were tricky eddies all the way up, and as one approached the Rhu Narrows, where the river turned inland toward Glasgow itself, the current became much more difficult to deal with. Fortunately *Bluefin* didn't have to negotiate that treacherous route to reach Holy Loch, which was a long inlet on the western side of the estuary that opened up before the incoming boat had to turn east into the Rhu Narrows. According to stories Gordon had heard, British submariners based at Faslane Submarine Base, which was on Gareloch, on the other side of the Narrows from Holy Loch, frequently cursed whatever Royal Navy bureaucrat had decreed the location of their base without ever realizing what it actually meant to steer a submarine in or out of port there. The fact that a yacht club overlooked the Rhu Narrows didn't help, either. Skippers were all too conscious of the fact that every mistake, every accident that befell them would be seen and laughed at by part-time, civilian sailors lounging around the club tossing back an afternoon pint and comparing notes on the shiphandling deficiencies of the Navy's sailing men.

At least Hogan didn't have all that to worry about. But getting *Bluefin* safely into Holy Loch was still a chore, and Gordon was glad to let the XO's prior experience give him an excuse to play the tourist.

Eventually the mouth of the sea loch appeared to port, and under Hogan's stern guidance *Bluefin* edged over out of the main channel on course for the narrow confines of the American base. Once again Gordon was struck by the way the buildings seemed to fit in so well with the surrounding landscape, without the urban sprawl that marred places like Norfolk and even Groton, the home base for the Atlantic submarine fleet in Connecticut. A stately old church caught his eye, small and square, built of gray stone, with a tall spire that seemed to stand guard over the place.

Then they were into the loch, and ahead Gordon could see the base itself. There was a long quay, with the sleekly menacing shape of a Los Angeles class sub tied up alongside, presumably Chase's *Pittsburgh*. Gordon preferred not to dwell on the fast-attack boat, since it rubbed salt in the angry wound of his fading career to realize that his onetime Annapolis roommate was standing at the very pinnacle of his career, while Gordon himself languished in obscurity aboard a boat that would soon be just another footnote in maritime history. . . .

To one side he saw the USS *Holland*, a sub tender, nestled alongside the oversize shape of an Ohio class ballistic-missile submarine. It was the "boomers" that had always taken first place at Holy Loch, a facility designed from the very beginning to give America's Polaris and Trident missile platforms an advanced base through the long years of the Cold War. Presumably if the not-quite-hostilities between East and West ever came to an end—say through the implementation of the Strategic Defense Initiative that was in the news so much lately—then Holy Loch and other such overseas bases would be abandoned as too costly and no longer necessary for the maintenance of the fragile peace based on the doctrine of Mutual Assured Destruction. But Gordon didn't see it as likely. The Cold War, he thought, was one of those institutions that would go on under its own power for decades longer. It was just the way the world worked.

There isn't much activity over there today, Gordon thought, *except for the harbor tug creeping out into the middle of the loch to meet us.*

He exchanged looks with Hogan, who shrugged and made a face, but then passed orders through the telephone talker to assemble line-handling parties fore and aft and break out the towing cables. No Navy ship-handler ever liked to admit the need for tugs and tows, but in fact they were often essential for maneuvering submarines in the cramped confines of a harbor. Sub design had long since settled on single-screw propulsion as the norm, because one propeller was less likely to make unwanted noise than two ... particularly when twin screws could become unbalanced and give rise to unfortunate vibrations that a good sonar man could latch on to with appalling ease. Yet a single-screwed vessel, particularly one as long and narrow in its proportions as the typical sub, was a bear to handle in close quarters, places where twin engines could literally be used to "walk" the boat sideways.

So it was normal to take a sub in tow when it entered a harbor. But that didn't mean that a man like Hogan—or Gordon—had to like it. There was something inherently wrong about surrendering control of one's vessel to the tender mercies of some tugboat skipper.

The dungaree-clad deck parties came boiling out of the hatches fore and aft, transforming the previously placid scene into one of controlled chaos. Hogan gradually slowed *Bluefin* to something close to a standstill and allowed the tug to maneuver alongside. Then, as lines were passed across and fenders rigged to protect both hulls, Gordon let out a little sigh. They were in the hands of others, now, and there wasn't much reason to continue on the bridge. In fact he much preferred to be out of sight for the next hour or so, since he knew all too well that his boat would be under scrutiny from two men whose watchful regard he preferred not to think about—Mike Chase and Admiral Goldman.

Suddenly Gordon had a great deal more sympathy for those British skippers passing under the eyes of the yacht club. He understood how they must have felt.

Leaving Hogan to finish supervising, he left the bridge and descended into the bowels of the submarine, where prying eyes couldn't reach him.

The Pussycat Club
Dumbarton, Scotland
2240 hours GMT

"What do you think, Rodriguez? Hot enough for you?"

Enrique Rodriguez shook his head, starting to frown before the expression was converted midway into a wince as a pair of speakers on either side of the club's runway stage blared the opening bars of some rock song, heavy on the bass and loud enough to be picked up without sonar half an ocean away.

Hastily he set down his drink and excused himself from the little table, not even tempted to remain when the pert, bare-breasted redhead began her gyrations. Rodriguez pushed past a party of British sailors just coming into the club and ducked through the door out into the cool night air.

He leaned back against the stone wall of the club, now only distantly aware of the throbbing music within.

Rodriguez reminded himself not to go out on the town with Norris, Markowitz, and Reinhold again. He knew

their offer of treating him to a night on the town was
meant as a kindness, but all three of them were barbar-
ians, in his eyes, for their complete lack of musical taste.
There weren't too many people in the Navy, in fact, who
showed much discrimination as far as music went, he
told himself glumly. Of course, Rodriguez was constantly aware of sounds; they were his profession, almost
his life. While others abused their ears with rock and
roll or some mournful wailing country song, Rodriguez
preferred gentler fare, Bach or Mozart. No one believed
him when he said that concentrating on the individual
threads of a Bach Brandenburg Concerto had taught him
how to read the sounds he picked up in his sonar headphones better, but it was true.

Even if he could have tolerated the so-called music,
Rodriguez wasn't in the mood for hanging out at a strip
club anyway. He'd been out with his buddies to places
like this one back in the States a time or two, and enjoyed a "boys' night out" as much as the next guy, but
tonight he had other things on his mind.

Like Carlotta.

Before they had left Holy Loch Rodriguez had found
a telephone on the base. Feeling flush from all the
money his shipmates had raised for him, he had invested
in a call home. It had been about noon, Stateside, when
he had called, and Carlotta had been just about to leave
for a prenatal visit at the base hospital in Groton.

After the initial shock of hearing from him so unexpectedly, Carlotta hadn't taken long to let slip the truth.
His fears had been well-founded—there were complications with the pregnancy. Getting the word second-
hand, and through a worried and not always coherent
wife, Rodriguez still wasn't sure what the problem was.
All he knew for sure was that the doctors had Carlotta
on a strict program of frequent visits, a carefully controlled diet, and extra counseling. Still, the verdict
seemed to be that mother and child could both come out

of things just fine as long as Carlotta paid close attention to doctors' orders.

Rodriguez had immediately thought of trying to get emergency leave so he could hop a MATS transport and fly home, but Carlotta herself had refused to hear of it. She had been concerned when her first two familygrams had been returned by the Navy with suggestions for changes—leaving out all reference to the problem, basically—but now she thought she had everything as much under control as it was likely to get. Having Enrique home and fussing over her, she had claimed, would only make things worse. His mother and her sister were looking after her, and the quality of care given by the Navy doctors at the base hospital was all that she could hope for . . . far better, in fact, than a poor Hispanic wife could expect from civilian health care. So he had agreed to say nothing of the matter to his captain or his shipmates. The next few familygrams would tell him everything, either by announcing the arrival of a baby girl . . . or by saying nothing. Or, perhaps, coming in that special code that only Captain Chase could penetrate, with an announcement of tragedy at home that he would have to decide to reveal or withhold according to the needs of the boat and her crew.

The noise from inside grew louder for a moment, and Rodriguez looked up to see Norris approaching with a worried expression on his blunt features. "You okay, Roddy?" he asked.

"Yeah. Sure." Rodriguez touched one finger to his ear. "Just didn't appreciate that noise in there. Bad for my ears, you know?"

Norris laughed. "Well, Reinhold and Markowitz are in there going deaf as we speak, but I doubt they'll even notice, the way they're drooling over those babes. There's a blonde in there with boobs that defy gravity, I'm tellin' ya."

"Don't let me keep you, Doc." He mustered a half smile. "I know how much science means to you."

Harry Norris shook his head. "I don't like to just abandon you out here, Roddy. You okay, man?" None of the sailors had asked directly about Carlotta yet, but Rodriguez knew she was on all their minds. The knowledge that he had friends who were concerned for him, and the wife they'd never met but heard endless details about in bull sessions aboard *Pittsburgh*, gave him a warm glow of *belonging*. That was one of the things the Navy had given him that he might never have found on his own.

"I'm good, Doc," he said.

"Carlotta?"

"She's . . . had some problems. Something medical, I guess, to do with the baby . . . but the doctors say they'll both be all right." He shrugged. "Who am I to say different?"

Norris clapped him on the shoulder. "If they're saying that, you don't have anything to worry about, Roddy," he said gravely. "I know. I was an OR tech before I drew independent duty. I've watched those guys work close up."

"Thanks, man. *Mira* . . . look. You go watch your blonde with the big mariachis. I'll be fine out here. It's a nice night, and I think I just want to look at the stars for a while, okay?"

"Sure, Roddy, whatever you say," Norris said. "Just watch out for those Scotsmen. I never trust a man in a dress."

Rodriguez watched his friend amble back to the front door of the club. He was a barbarian who didn't understand the first thing about music, but Norris was all right. All of his buddies from *Pittsburgh* were all right, in his book.

He looked up at the night sky and conjured up the sounds of the "Ode to Joy" in his mind. Enrique Rodriguez hoped it was a fitting selection.

Monday, 29 July 1985

Administrative Building, U.S. Navy Submarine Base
Holy Loch, Scotland
0954 hours GMT

Mike Chase was the last to arrive at the conference room where Goldman had scheduled the mission briefing. He took a certain secret pride in having managed the delay, since it meant that he hadn't been forced to be a part of whatever discomfort had surrounded the meeting between the admiral and Frank Gordon. The last time he'd been caught in the middle between those two strong-willed individuals, he had lost a six-year friendship. Now he wanted to avoid reopening old wounds, at least long enough to carry out the White Sea operation successfully.

He still anticipated sparks, and when he opened the door and entered the conference room it was with the same knots in his stomach as he always had the first time he dived a new boat or waited for a positive ID on a sonar trace.

The oval table was already occupied by eight men. Gordon sat in lonely defiance at the far end, an open briefcase at his elbow, delving through a stack of papers that probably had nothing to do with the briefing. They gave him a good excuse to ignore everyone else, though. But his eyes did flick to Chase as he entered, and the man gave him a sort of distant nod. Not friendly, but courteous.

It looked as if they were going to revert to their respective roles from the Persian Gulf mission.

In the center of the table, four young officers faced each other in groups of two. All of them had a lean, rawhide look to them, even the slightly chubby, round-faced junior grade lieutenant. They didn't exactly look like brothers, but they were obviously all stamped from the same mold . . . and Chase didn't need to see the trident devices of their Budweisers to know that mold had been the U.S. Navy SEALs. These were the men on whom the mission really depended. *Bluefin* and *Pittsburgh* were responsible for getting them into the White Sea. After that, these SEALs would be taking the real risks. He didn't envy them.

Finally, at the head of the long table, Goldman sat flanked by an aide Chase had met briefly on his first visit there, Captain Walter Steadman, and a nondescript man in an equally dull suit whose very blandness shouted "Spook," though whether he was CIA, NSA, or something even more covert wasn't clear.

"Ah, Mike, there you are," Goldman said. The look in his eyes told Chase that the old man knew exactly what his protégé was doing in coming late. "Take a seat so we can get down to work."

"Aye aye, sir," Chase replied formally. He was feeling the pressure already, and trying to counter it as best he could. Goldman's genial, first-name manner was no doubt intended to remind Gordon of his place in the scheme of things . . . so Chase took refuge in distancing himself. It was the kind of deadly little social dance that made him very glad of the time he spent dealing with the "loneliness of command" that romantically inclined historical novelists talked about when describing ship captains. Just then Chase was wishing he had stayed out on patrol, where he belonged, accepting that loneliness in place of having to deal with these particular people.

He found a chair, inevitably near Gordon. He felt uncomfortable, and no doubt his onetime friend did as well. But the moment of tension was relieved as Goldman began introducing the SEAL officers.

"And this," he finished up, gesturing to the suit, "is John Dreyfuss. National Security Administration. He flew out from Washington last night with the latest updates on the planned operation."

Dreyfuss seemed to take that as a cue to take over the briefing, though Chase had his doubts that Goldman had intended it that way. Clearing his throat, the man in the suit leaned forward in his chair. "Gentlemen, Washington regards the mission you are being given as a top-priority item. It is vitally important to our national security interests that we discover the progress being made by the Soviets in their latest attack-sub design project. To that end, you and your men are to do whatever it takes to penetrate the Soviet submarine yards at Severodvinsk on the White Sea, gather as much information on the project we have code-named *Akula,* and ensure that it is returned safely."

Chase noted, but didn't comment on, the fact that it was the information that Dreyfuss wanted returned safely. Evidently two boats and close to three hundred men were still being considered far less important in the grand scheme of things.

Goldman took over again when Dreyfuss paused for dramatic effect, going over the same basic ground he had already covered with Chase in their earlier meeting, for the benefit of Gordon and the SEAL officers. They took it in with little comment. Chase had the impression that the SEALs had worked out at least some of the details among themselves already, while Gordon merely nodded and looked wise.

Then the admiral nodded toward Captain Steadman,

who touched a series of buttons on a small box in front of him which dimmed the lights and switched on a rear-screen projector behind Goldman's spot at the head of the table. Dreyfuss took over again, gesturing toward a map of the Murmansk/Archangel area of the Soviet Union that had appeared on the screen.

"Severodvinsk is a city which happens to be the location of one of the major Soviet shipbuilding facilities," he said dryly. "This is officially designated Shipyard Number 402 in Soviet naval parlance. Originally it was known as the Molotovsk yard, after V.M. Molotov, who served as foreign minister under Stalin. After Molotov fell from grace the name was changed. No doubt the Russians are happier to use the numeric designation to avoid the necessity of changing names every time a new regime takes power and discredits everything done by its predecessors." He smiled thinly.

"The shipyard is located farther north than any other shipbuilding facility in the world, and it is believed to be the world's largest submarine construction yard as well. It was built in the 1930s as part of Stalin's attempt to make the Soviet Union a serious naval power in the years leading up to World War II. Having a major yard on the White Sea enabled the Russians to build up their Northern Fleet without having to rely on their established facilities around Leningrad on the Baltic, which of course were vulnerable to interdiction by the Nazis. From the beginning the yard was intended to be one of the largest in the world, capable of battleship construction. However, work was only done on two battleships shortly before the war, and these were never completed due to the German invasion of Russia and the diversion of war materials to more pressing military needs. Destroyers and a few S class submarines were produced at the yard in the forties, and destroyers and cruisers were built there in the early fifties. More significantly, it was the site where the first of the Soviet Zulu class diesel attack boats was constructed in 1953, followed by production runs of the Golf and Hotel class ballistic-missile subs and the November SSN. Some commercial work was done there as well, but this ended in the mid-fifties.

"Since that time, production at Severodvinsk has shifted exclusively to submarines. Virtually every class of sub in the Soviet arsenal has been built there, and the majority of new designs and prototypes have been created at the yard and tested in the waters of the White Sea."

"Why is that, sir?" Lieutenant j.g. Gunn spoke up for the first time. "I mean, you'd think that the White Sea would be a poor testing ground. It's shallow, it's icy for a good part of the year, and it's at the far end of the Soviet transportation net for everything from raw materials to parts to food supplies."

The NSA man gave him a look that suggested he wasn't used to being interrupted by questions that sounded more like idle curiosity than an attempt to understand the tactical situation. Chase found himself liking the young SEAL officer instantly. Anyone who could throw one of the NSA's suits off his stride was all right as far as he was concerned.

It was Goldman who answered the question, and he didn't sound at all perturbed. "It isn't as if the Soviets have a lot of choice in the matter, Lieutenant," he said. "Both the Baltic and the Black Seas are handicapped by being locked behind narrow straits easily denied to their navy in wartime, and currently held by powers that aren't under Soviet domination. Their ports in the Far East have the same handicaps as the White Sea, and a far longer supply line. And the White Sea offers a couple of major security advantages. First, as you say, it is shallow and difficult to operate in . . . but that applies much more to us than it does to them. After all, it's their own backyard, and they can and do patrol the area heavily. There is also the fact that it is almost landlocked. Access is restricted by a relatively narrow strait between the Kola and Kanin Peninsulas, but this time the Soviets control the strait, so they can dictate who gets in or out."

"Guess we'll just have to show them that their security isn't as tight as they think," Gordon said.

Chase gave him a sharp look. He hadn't expected Gordon to have much to say, especially when it was the admiral who had the floor.

The admiral's reply was cool, but controlled. "That's our job, Commander," he said stiffly.

Dreyfuss took charge again, nodding to Captain Steadman to change the view on the screen. This time it was a satellite image, a fairly wide view of the White Sea from orbit. "Severodvinsk lies on the Dvina Gulf, approximately forty-eight kilometers west of the major city of Arkhangelsk. The Dvina River enters the gulf between the two cities, spreading out in a low-lying delta which is marshy in summer and largely frozen over in winter. It is the feeling in Washington that the Dvina offers us unique possibilities for the employment of SEALs and SDVs, extending the available landing zones for a commando operation. We will discuss the possibilities in more detail later."

The satellite view changed again, this time focusing on the shipyard facilities proper. "This is the yard, gentlemen. Admiral Rickover once said that this one facility had several times the shipbuilding capacity of all U.S. submarine-building and repair yards combined. He was exaggerating, but it is certainly true that Shipyard 402 is large." He began using a pointer to indicate specific buildings. "This is the original battleship construction hall, built in the 1930s. To give you an idea of scale, it is three hundred thirty-five meters long and one hundred thirty-seven meters wide. Think of three football fields sitting side by side. It has since been supplemented by two other construction halls, here, and here. This one is even larger than the original, and was used in the construction of the first Typhoon class ballistic-missile submarine a few years back. All three of these construction halls are covered and heated to permit year-round work on submarine construction."

He tapped another area down at the water's edge. "There are a series of docks located here, including dry-dock facilities for repair or refurbishing not deemed important enough to require the use of one of the major construction halls. The number of subs deployed at the facility varies from week to week, but averages between ten and twenty boats." The image changed again to a close-up of the dock area, and the pointer indicated a long, dark shape in the water. "This is the new sub. She's been in the water since the early spring. Major work stopped on her about a month ago, and since that time she appears to have been taking on various stores and supplies. We believe that her sea trials have either just begun, or are about to begin. So far we haven't spotted her away from the dock, but it is possible she has been out on limited maneuvers while our satellites weren't overhead watching."

Anderson and Gunn studied the docks with particular intensity. Chase was examining the picture as a whole, noting the overall layout of the docks and the distribution of all the subs there, not just the target. It looked to him as if two of the boats in port were not likely to be going anywhere for a while. One, which he suspected was a Victor II, was in dry dock, with what looked to be a hump-backed Delta I SSBN close by, as if awaiting a turn. There also appeared to be a freshly launched Alfa near one of the construction halls that might not be ready for sea yet, but that wasn't something Chase could tell on the basis of a few satellite photos.

It left plenty of subs on hand at Severodvinsk to deal with any unwanted intruders, aside from the patrols and fleet units that would be operating out of Archangel and other ports in the area. His initial doubts about the mission were only crystallizing now as he studied the intelligence information. Slipping two subs into the White Sea required taking an incredible risk to begin with.

Keeping them there while a SEAL platoon reconnoitered ashore was only compounding the danger.

But what real choice did they have? In theory they could launch the SEALs in their SDVs a long way from Severodvinsk, marginally reducing the risk to the two subs but making the SEAL op that much harder to carry out. Swimmer Delivery Vehicles didn't have the most sophisticated navigation systems in the world, nor were they very fast. Extending the distance they would travel would only make them that much more open to discovery.

The view on the screen reverted to the previous image of the entire shipyard complex. "From what we've been able to determine," Dreyfuss continued, "the administrative buildings for the facility are located here." Again his pointer gestured. "We believe that there are extensive records of all the projects undertaken at the yard in this building here. It is likely that the files will be found in a room on the first floor of this structure, Room 115, though we do not have an accurate layout of the building to work with."

"How do we know the room?" DuQuense asked.

Dreyfuss seemed reluctant to answer him, but finally responded. "We have a useful humint resource within the Kremlin, Lieutenant. He does not have direct access to the shipyard, but he is acquainted with some elements of the administration there. He also informs us that the Russians refer to the new attack sub as 'Project 971,' so presumably if you can locate the right set of files you can track down the records that will tell us what we need to know about the sub. I presume you have men in your platoon who can read Cyrillic and speak Russian, Lieutenant."

Anderson nodded. Gunn looked up and said, "I do, for one. Enough to find my way around, at least."

"Good. Then assuming your SEALs can penetrate the facility and reach the proper files, you should be able to get us the kind of information we'll need. Blueprints and reports on the construction of the new sub would be best, of course, but even parts requisitions or inventory lists would be useful in showing us what's going into the construction of this new boat. And that will enable our experts to decide just how much the Soviets have moved forward in underwater stealth and detection technology."

"How much do we know about what the Walkers might have handed over?" Chase asked. "From our end, I mean . . . interrogations and that kind of thing. Surely we must have gotten something out of Walker and his associates."

"I'm not at liberty to disclose details of an ongoing investigation," Dreyfuss said stiffly. Chase took that to mean that he didn't know. Cracking the spy ring had been an FBI job, for the most part, possibly with help from the CIA and Naval Intelligence. When that many agencies were involved, the flow of information tended to slow to a trickle. No doubt everyone involved was jealously guarding whatever tidbits their operatives had turned up. It might be years before the full story of the Walker case was known . . . far too late to be of any use to this operation.

It looked like they'd have to collect the information the old-fashioned way.

"While the SEALs attempt to gain access to the Severodvinsk records," Admiral Goldman said, "we'll want to pursue other possible avenues of information gathering as well. First, if your platoon can manage it along with the main op, Lieutenant, I hope that you can send swimmers into the harbor area itself. If they could get accurate measurements, photographs, possibly even a sample of the hull material of the new sub, it would make a very useful supplement to whatever your people come up with inside the compound. It's even possible that alone would be enough if the mission ashore proves impractical."

Anderson nodded. "I'm sure we can manage it. Fourteen SEALs can cover a lot of ground, Admiral." His smile was faint, but genuine.

"Why don't we take in some mines and smash the damned boat while we've got the chance?" Harriman, the SDV platoon commander, asked gruffly. "Seems a pity to be sending people in just to take pictures."

"That would be counterproductive," Dreyfuss said sternly. "Our purpose is to learn what advances the Soviets are incorporating in this new production line of attack boats. If we were to destroy the prototype, or if they realize that we have obtained detailed information on it, they might well make extensive modifications which would leave us right back where we started. That is why it is absolutely imperative that the mission be carried out in complete secrecy. You must get in, obtain as much information as possible without betraying your presence, and then get out."

Harriman shrugged and settled back in his seat.

Chase caught the admiral's eye. "I assume you'll also want us to try to monitor the boat if they take her out while we're in the area, sir?"

"If you can do it without being caught," Goldman replied with a terse nod. "But your primary job in *Pittsburgh* is to provide backup for *Bluefin*. Specifically, to obtain copies of all the information that the SEALs bring out, to double our chances of getting it back safely. Also to protect *Bluefin* from Soviet patrols . . . always provided you can do so without compromising the mission as a whole."

"I'm more concerned about getting in and out in one piece," Gordon said, leaning forward. "I know what the SEALs are capable of once we deliver them to the target, but this is one target that's damned tough to get at."

Dreyfuss nodded. "True enough, Captain," he said. "And you should know about it. I was quite impressed with your file. *Sea Devil*'s record was very impressive."

Sea Devil . . . Chase had forgotten about Gordon's tour aboard the USS *Sea Devil* back in 1976. No wonder the admiral had gone along with using him for this mission, despite their history. There were probably only a handful of officers on active duty in the Navy who could match Gordon's experience.

Gordon had been a senior lieutenant assigned as Navigation Officer aboard Captain Daniel Brady's *Sea Devil*, a Sturgeon class nuclear attack sub. In one eight-month tour of duty, *Sea Devil* had penetrated the waters of the White Sea three different times to mount a series of covert operations against the Soviets. The details were still largely classified, but Chase had heard that a stick of SEALs deployed on the sub had pulled a party of Russian dissidents out from under the very noses of the KGB, among other achievements.

The older sub's exploits were proof that the White Sea's defenses could be pierced . . . but that had been nine years ago. A lot of things had changed in nine years, and not all of those changes would be good for the Americans.

"*Sea Devil* was able to get in and out of the White Sea because Captain Brady was a patient man," Gordon said. Chase noted the respect that still crept into his voice after all these years. Brady had been one officer who had never turned against Frank Gordon, and had plainly earned his loyalty. "We waited for a week off the Kanin Peninsula until we spotted a noisy freighter headed in toward Archangel. Then we slipped into her baffles and followed her right past every patrol ship the Russkies had deployed. Got out pretty much the same way, too." He frowned. "We can do that again, I guess . . . but it'll take time. You can never tell when you're going to catch a break like that. And getting two subs in, instead of one . . . ?"

Goldman shook his head. "We don't have that kind of luxury, time-wise, gentlemen," he said, answering Gordon but carefully addressing all of them. "For one thing, we can't be certain how far along their trials are. If they're close to finishing, that new sub could redeploy almost anytime. And whether they send her to Vladivostok or just to the base at Polyarny, she'd be out of reach. Might be years before we got another crack at her."

Chase found himself nodding in silent agreement. Once the new Russian sub was fully operational, she'd be put to work. It would be a matter of pure, dumb luck to run across her in the open ocean, and the first time someone did they'd have no way of knowing what she was or where she came from. She'd just be an "Unknown Contact." There'd be no hope of gathering much information on her under those circumstances. And he didn't even want to *think* about what it would take to send a covert op in against one of the big Soviet submarine bases, like the one at Polyarny near Murmansk. That place was almost legendary, with its underground sub pens reached by long tunnels and protected by every kind of defense the Russians could assemble. Even the SEALs would be hard-pressed to penetrate something like that. Severodvinsk was going to be a tough enough nut to crack.

"In any event," the admiral was continuing, "we have a very brief window of opportunity that could help you reach the target area, carry out your mission, and exfiltrate again with a much lower risk factor than you would normally expect . . . but only if you can carry out the mission within the next three weeks. That's the main reason we've pushed this operation forward so quickly."

"I was kind of wondering about that, Admiral," Lieutenant Anderson said. "I would have expected some time Stateside running some rehearsal missions. Mockups of the target area, different scenarios . . ."

"If we could have worked it in, we would have, Lieutenant," Dreyfuss said. "But as Admiral Goldman said, our window of opportunity isn't very large. We've received information that the Red Banner Northern Fleet is going to be conducting a major series of exercises off Novaya Zemlya during the first half of August. In essence, that means their patrols in the White Sea area will be drastically reduced. Still formidible, but not nearly as dangerous to your submarines as having the entire fleet in port would be."

Chase leaned forward. "That could make it doable," he said. "A major fleet exercise would probably mean they'd only have a few capital ships in the target area. Maybe some subs . . . but probably older ones."

"Patrol boats," Gordon added. "And aerial recon. But nothing we can't outfox." He was looking positively wolfish now, anticipating the possibilities.

"So you understand why this has to move ahead right away," Goldman said. "The main question is, do you think you can get in close enough to Severodvinsk to deliver the SEALs ashore by SDV?" For the first time he was looking and talking directly at Gordon.

Bluefin's captain nodded without waiting for Chase to weigh in. "I know those waters, Admiral," he said, and for once there was only enthusiasm, with no trace of resentment or caution, in his tone. "The White Sea is damned shallow, tricky maneuvering for a sub especially if you're not sure of the bottom terrain. We only mapped a small portion of it aboard *Sea Devil* . . . but I remember that part of what we did map was a very nice little underwater highway that can take us in very close to Severodvinsk. Or Archangel, for that matter."

"We have *Sea Devil*'s charts on hand," Dreyfuss put in.

"Good. We'll need copies . . . and I'll want to see them when we get down to brass tacks planning the op."

"You'll have them," the admiral said, making a gesture to Captain Steadman to make a note. "Tell us more about this, uh, 'highway' of yours."

"It's a fairly wide channel of relatively deep water," Gordon said. "Formed by the currents from the Dvina where it enters the White Sea. Water's pretty sluggish there now, but I'd say that once upon a time, before the delta was formed, those currents were pretty strong.

Captain Brady found that we could slip right up that channel until we were just off the mouth of the river, if we had to. Some tricky navigating in those days, but with the newer sonar terrain-imaging systems it ought to be a piece of cake."

"I wouldn't advise taking the subs in too close to shore, channel or none," Dreyfuss said. "But it sounds like an ideal route for the SDVs to follow to deliver the SEALs to target. I take it the channel decreased the chance of detection for *Sea Devil*, Captain?"

"Some," Gordon said. "For one thing, there are some sharp temperature gradients in those waters, especially off the river mouth. Changes in salinity, too. You get thermoclines in some pretty odd places, and if you're lucky you can keep just underneath one when you're running up that channel. Also, the irregularities in the bottom terrain around it make it harder for passive sonar to pick up a boat against all the clutter. Not just natural stuff, either. In close to the mouth of the Dvina you've got shipwrecks, garbage dumps, all sorts of stuff. Our SEALs even came across a pile of rusty old cars near the entrance to the harbor at Archangel."

"Excellent. It sounds as if the SEALs will be in little danger of being detected, provided we keep the subs far enough out . . ." Dreyfuss wore a thin-lipped smile. Chase thought it was probably as close to happy as the dry little man would ever look.

"Keep the subs too far out, and you're running a different set of risks," Harriman growled. "Don't forget, my SDVs aren't all that fast, and our oxygen supply ain't exactly unlimited. You've got to let us out close enough to the target so that we can get to shore, let the SEALs carry out their mission, and then make it back out to the subs before the air tanks run dry."

The NSA man frowned. "Well, those are details to be worked out between you and Captain Gordon, I should think . . ."

"Let's stay focused on *getting there* before we start

worrying about what happens on the op itself," Goldman
cut in. "You've been quiet, Captain Chase. What do you
think?"

"Frank's the expert on navigating in the White Sea,"
Chase said slowly. "And I'll definitely want to go over
those old *Sea Devil* charts with him . . . *and* with my
Exec and my Navigator. As far as the rest of it goes . . .
I can see some possible problems in coordination. Communications, for instance. We have no way of knowing
which, if any, of our codes are secure right now, so
transmissions between the boats could be chancy." *Another legacy of the Walker betrayal*, he thought bitterly.
Both the father and the son had been involved with communications technology and protocols, and they had
both had access not only to current Navy codes but to
others that hadn't even been put in place yet. There was
a frantic effort under way throughout the Navy to rewrite
the codebooks and come up with a new measure of operational security, but that would take months to complete. Meanwhile there was no way to tell when a private
conversation was really private.

"Agreed," Goldman said. "But you'll have to do what
you can. I'd suggest limiting radio contact between your
boats to routine matters, and trying alternative methods
of communicating. Rendezvous and set up personal
meetings before you get to the White Sea, if you need
to go over plans for any reason. Possibly send divers
back and forth when the need for stealth is stronger. Be
inventive."

Gordon nodded. "We can come up with ways to deal
with the problem," he said. "But I would suggest we set
up a regular schedule for running at periscope depth so
that we can transmit a rendezvous request and contact
SSIX for changes in orders or information updates."

"Good idea, Frank," Chase said. "If we keep transmissions to a minimum, we won't be giving anyone
much information, but we'll still be able to maintain
enough contact to stay coordinated."

"And we can use the SDVs if we need to send a message to you once we've entered patrolled waters," Gordon went on. It was starting to feel like the old, pre-quarrel days, with ideas bouncing back and forth easily. Chase wondered how long it could last, and dared to hope it might be a real step forward between them.

"Not sure I like the idea of treating my pups like a goddamned taxi service," Harriman said, surly.

Chase saw Gunn stir as if he was going to respond, but a look from Lieutenant Anderson silenced him.

From the head of the table, Dreyfuss cleared his throat. "If we can get down to specifics, gentlemen?" he began. "Now, the thinking in Washington is that the SEAL platoon should be deployed in this manner . . ."

Chase settled back in his seat. They still had a lot of planning to do.

Outside the Tourist Information Center
Douglas, Lanarkshire, Scotland
1703 hours GMT

Archie Douglas saw the woman pause at the door as she left the small building and realized she was fumbling with a set of keys. He glanced at his watch and uttered a muffled curse. The place was closing . . . and he'd come too late.

He hastened up the sidewalk. "Excuse me, ma'am?" he called.

The woman turned and looked his way. Slight and slender, she had dark hair and a pretty smile. She looked to be in her mid-twenties, about Archie's own age, but she carried herself with an assurance he hadn't often encountered in the women he normally met.

"Actually, it's 'miss,' " she told him. Her accent was charming, something of the clipped upper-class British combined with a hint of a delicate lilt. "Can I help you?"

"Er . . . I was hoping to get a chance to see the Tourist Center," he said. "Ask a few questions."

She shook her head. "I'm terribly sorry, but we're closed for the day." Her startling gray eyes assessed him thoughtfully. "An American sailor, I take it? We don't get many of your lot this far from Glasgow."

He smiled. "I can believe that," he said. "My name's Douglas . . . Archie Douglas. I had a little free time, and I wanted to come see the place my ancestors were supposed to come from . . ."

"You'll find Douglases all over Scotland, Archie Douglas," she told him. "Not just here in Douglasdale. The family owned wide lands, once."

He shrugged. "Maybe so," he said. "But I was steered here when I asked about the family background."

Actually he knew very little about his family heritage, only the tradition that one of the family had been shipped over as little better than a slave for his part in Bonnie Prince Charlie's fight against the British sometime before the American Revolution, and some of his grandmother's references to members of the family being "true Black Douglases" in their looks. There was also a story about one of the family having lived in Glasgow, and Archie's original plan had been to try to learn more about him while he had the chance. But after Prince Andrew's visit to *Pittsburgh*, a small packet of maps and a thin guidebook had arrived addressed to Douglas from the Prince's office, describing this area known as Douglasdale as the ancestral home of his family. It lay within fifty miles of Glasgow—he was still trying to get used to the fact that Scotland, indeed all of England, was so *small* compared to what he was used to back home—so Douglas had changed his plans, rented an inexpensive car, and driven through some of the most beautiful country he had ever seen to reach the town of Douglas. Since arriving he had been trying to get his bearings . . . but he'd been too slow, apparently, to get the information he'd hoped to find once he had finally tracked down the tourist office.

He considered trying a little name-dropping and telling the woman he'd been directed here by no less a personage than the Duke of York himself, but decided that wasn't the way to go. That kind of line might have worked on some bimbo from one of the waterfront dives in Groton, but he had a feeling this young lady was less likely to be impressed.

She was still studying him curiously. "I could swear I've seen you somewhere recently," she said, frowning. He stifled a smile; now *there* was a pickup line if he had ever heard one! "Wait, I know. You were on telly last night, weren't you?"

"Telly?" Douglas was baffled.

"The box . . ." She shrugged. "Sorry. I thought you Colonials spoke English." Her smile softened the comment. "The television. You were in a clip on the news last night, weren't you? Aboard an American submarine, wasn't it? You made some kind of presentation to the Duke of York when he visited your ship."

"Boat, miss," Archie said with a smile. "If I have to learn to call the TV set a 'telly,' then you have to know that we call submarines 'boats' in the Navy."

She laughed. "Two peoples divided by a common language," she said. "Who said that? Churchill?"

"I wouldn't know, miss," he said, shrugging. "I'm just a poor sailor from western Pennsylvania."

"Hold on for just a moment, won't you?" she asked. Turning, she finished locking the door behind her before turning back to face him, holding out her hand. "I'm a Douglas too, as it happens. Kate Douglas. I work here."

He took the hand, surprised at the firm grip from her soft, cool fingers. "Hi, Kate," he said with a grin. "Does that make you a cousin, or something?"

"I doubt that," she told him, releasing his hand. "Look, if you can come back tomorrow morning I'm sure I can help you out. Answer your questions, maybe point you to some sites you might enjoy . . ."

He shook his head. "Afraid I can't," he said. "My liberty's up tomorrow morning. I'll have to be back at Holy Loch early. And I doubt we'll be in port long after that."

"Oh, that *is* too bad." She hesitated a moment. He could tell that she was sizing him up . . . and he had the feeling that his little television appearance—and more importantly the way he had steered clear of boasting about it—had produced a favorable effect. "Tell you what, though. If you'd care to stop off at a little pub I know, perhaps I can answer a few of your questions over a pint of something cold and wet?"

"*You're* asking *me* to come have a drink at the pub?" Archie shook his head. "No, no, wait a minute, you've got it all wrong, Miss Douglas. It's the big, crude American sailor who is supposed to go around asking all the local girls out. You see?"

"Well, sailor, if you're going to start inviting other ladies to join us, then I'll just leave you to it . . ." She smiled at him. "You seem fairly decent, for a Colonial *and* a sailor."

"Maybe I'll stick with you, then . . . at least for the moment." Archie was beginning to enjoy fencing with her this way. The British reputation for understatement and reserve certainly seemed borne out in this young lady, at once friendly and aloof. He had to admit it was more than just a hope of learning about Scotland that made him want to have that drink at the pub with her. "Do you want me to follow your car?"

"Car?" She raised one eyebrow. "Oh, of course, you'll have driven down from Glasgow. No, I walk to work. It's only half a mile from home."

"Well, let me drive you to the pub, then," he said. "If you won't think I'm too soft or anything. You don't do a lot of walking every day when you're serving aboard a submarine, you know."

"No, I don't suppose you would, at that. I suppose

being driven about won't cause any lasting damage."

The pub was a quaint old stone building near the edge of town, quite a contrast to the modern tourist office where Kate worked. The sign in front showed a long-haired man with a mustache, pointed beard, and a large plumed hat, and bore the words "The Montrose Arms, established 1665." Archie stopped and stared at it for a moment, hard-pressed to believe it.

"The story is that it was founded by a soldier who served with the Marquis of Montrose at Philiphaugh," Kate told him. "After the Restoration the fellow decided to show his gratitude for having escaped the massacre after the battle, so he invested everything he had in this little inn and spent the rest of his life living on stories of his days with the great Montrose."

"I'm sorry to say I don't know anything about Montrose, or Philiphaugh," Archie told her. "Forgive an ignorant Yank, won't you?"

She smiled. "As long as you don't mind if I don't know very much about your American heroes," she said.

They entered the pub together. An aging man, white-haired with a weather-beaten face, greeted the woman with a wave and a grin. "Katie, lass. Och, 'tis good tae see you." Unlike her, his accent was thick. Archie was put in mind of Bob Reinhold's impression of *Star Trek*'s Scotty.

"Donald! How are the grandkids?" Kate led him to a pair of seats near the end of the bar. It wasn't crowded, but the people who were there all studied Archie keenly. "I'll have a pint of the usual. What about you, Archie Douglas?"

"Er . . . the same as she's having," he said.

"Archie Douglas, is it?" the barman said as he filled their glasses. "Do you hae American relatives you didna tell us about, Katie?"

"No, nothing like that," she replied. "Just another American come to trace his roots."

"Weil, noo, laddie," the barman said with a twinkle

in his eye, as he deposited a mug in front of Archie.
"The first thing you'll be wantin' tae ken is that *Scots*
are the people, and *Scotch* is the drink!"

Archie smiled and took a sip of the beer. "Thank
you," he said formally, suppressing a smile. "I think that
was one of the few things I knew already ... being a
Navy man, I know plenty about Scotch, but not nearly
as much about Scots."

"Good for you," Kate said. "You'd be surprised how
many American tourists pass through these parts every
year who can't even get that much right."

The atmosphere became more relaxed after that. Evidently, wary as these folk were of outsiders, they took
their cue from Kate and Donald. Since Archie had
passed muster with them, he was tolerated by the others
as well. The conversation turned to his quest for information.

"And what was it that you were wanting to ask at the
office?" Kate asked him.

"Oh, I don't really know ... just wondering if there
was anything special to see that tied in to the Douglases." Archie shrugged. "I read something about a
Douglas Castle. Is that around here? I'd love to see it,
if I ever get back."

"You're forty years too late for that, I'm afraid," she
told him. "Douglas Castle used to be a great tourist at-
traction, but in the forties a coal seam opened up under
it and the place was ruined. There's nothing much left
there now. It was a terrible loss. All that history. Douglas
Castle was where the Black Douglas first made his
name, you know."

"The Black Douglas?" Archie looked at her. "My
grandmother used to talk about some of us taking after
the Black Douglases, but I never really knew what she
was talking about."

She smiled. "Well, the first Black Douglas was one
of the great heroes of our Scottish War of Independence.
Almost seven hundred years ago. His real name was Sir

James Douglas, and he helped Robert the Bruce drive out the English. He was supposed to be a dark, grim-faced man, and his descendants often had that same look. They came to be called the Black Douglases, to distinguish them from another line of the family known as the Reds. Actually, though, it wasn't so much their looks that gave them those names. It had more to do with family connections and such. The original Black Douglas line all but disappeared a long time ago, so don't get the idea that just because you're connected to the family you're actually the long-lost heir to the Earls of Douglas!"

Donald chuckled. "That's another thing our American visitors tend tae do, lad," he said. "I dinna ken hoo many braw lads I've seen who were aye sure they had only tae claim their inheritances in order tae tak their rightful places as earls or dukes or such."

"No worries there," Archie said. "Like I said before, I don't know that much about the family, either back home or around here. But I've always been interested in finding out more."

"Och, better keep this one, lass," the barman told Kate. "You'll nae find another American like this lad, I'm thinking."

The young woman laughed. Archie Douglas decided he liked that laugh.

Somehow a drink at the pub turned into dinner, with Kate giving every appearance of being glad to keep on talking as they shared a plain but plentiful meal. Archie couldn't help but compare the food with what they would have found at almost any affordable restaurant back in the States. He had a simple plate of meat and potatoes, nothing like the kind of slick, preprocessed fare he would have expected at home, and in portions that rivaled *Pittsburgh*'s galley for quantity as well as taste.

Meanwhile, they talked. Archie learned more about the Good Sir James, the great Douglas ancestor, who had such a reputation as a fighter that English mothers used to use him as a sort of bogeyman to quiet their children at night.

"So the story goes," Kate was saying as she pushed her plate away and drained the last of her cup of tea, "that one night this young mother was sitting out on the ramparts of an English castle, trying to rock her baby to sleep. And she starts crooning some lullaby that says 'hush, little baby, and the Black Douglas won't come near you,' that sort of thing, when what should happen but a lot of grappling hooks come up over the walls, and the first attacking Scotsman to climb up and confront the woman is . . ."

"The Black Douglas, of course," Archie said with a grin.

"Of course. But being a good knight, he naturally treated the woman courteously, and let her know that all the stories about his eating babies for breakfast were just a wee bit exaggerated."

Archie laughed. "You know, that's the first time tonight you've said something that really sounded Scottish."

"Och, aye, are ye implyin' that I dinna sound like a bonnie lassie frae Scotland, then?" Kate said, her accent suddenly as broad as Donald the barman's. Then she went on in her accustomed tones. "I'm afraid I'm doomed to sound like a Sassenach all my days," she said. "Four years at Cambridge will do that to a girl . . . especially when speaking with too much Scots in your voice gets you branded as some kind of half-civilized barbarian."

"You're not serious," he said.

She smiled. "Don't tell me America is free of regional bias. Surely the wrong accent or the wrong birthplace will earn you some ridicule there, too."

He nodded, a little sheepish, thinking of the way people were treated if they sounded like "hicks" or "hillbillies." "You're right, of course. I just thought folks here were a little more civilized than that."

"That's the problem with feeding you Yanks nothing but the high-class cultured shows from BBC-1," she said. "You think all of us are these upper-crust aristocratic types with nothing but good breeding and stiff upper lips."

"While I imagine you think all Americans are rough-and-ready cowboys who are rude, crude, and ignorant."

"Not all Americans," she said with a little smile. "Only the tourists from Texas . . . and perhaps the sailors."

After dinner she took him for a long walk. In Scotland, in summer, it was never truly dark, but when they reached a hillside that shielded them from the lights of the town they could see the stars overhead. They sat there, saying little, and Archie found himself appreciating the calm and quiet more than he would ever have expected to.

It was late when he finally tore himself away to start the drive back to Glasgow and Holy Loch, and even so he was reluctant to leave.

More startling still, as far as Archie was concerned, was the way Kate urged him to return. It had been an evening unlike any date he had ever had before . . . and he could only hope that someday he would have the chance to repeat it.

Wednesday, 31 July 1985

Enlisted Mess, USS *Pittsburgh*
Holy Loch, Scotland
1321 hours GMT

"Hey, Archie!"

Douglas looked up from his lunch tray as Bob Reinhold hailed him from the other end of the mess hall.

"Special delivery, Arch," Reinhold went on, dodging his way through the dense traffic. He held up a small box. "Somebody handed this in at the main gate. They actually got their asses in gear enough to get it to us."

Douglas accepted the box from his friend and studied it curiously. It was long and flat, wrapped up in plain brown paper like any parcel, but it hadn't been mailed. A label on the front, neatly typed, proclaimed it was to be delivered to *Archie Douglas, USS Pittsburgh, U.S. Naval Base, Holy Loch.*

It wasn't as fancy as the packet he'd received from Prince Andrew's staff, and he frowned at it for a moment. There was one person he could think of that he would have been happy to hear from, but he didn't think she would be sending him anything. For one thing, he had never actually told her the name of his boat . . .

which had been causing him to berate himself unendingly ever since he had left Douglasdale.

"Well, come on, man, open it," Reinhold said with all the impatience of a nosy friend just dying to know Archie's secrets.

Without answering, Archie tore open the paper to reveal a flat cardboard box. Inside was an envelope and a short length of cloth, neatly folded. It was a plaid pattern in black, dark green, and blue, with a prominent white stripe.

"Ha! So you did get a kilt, huh, Archie?" Reinhold said with a grin.

Douglas held up the cloth. It was more like a scarf than a kilt. "I don't think I'd be decent if I tried to wear this as a kilt," he commented wryly. Then he picked up the letter. This time the address wasn't typed, but written in a neat script that had a decidedly feminine look to it. His heart jumped, just a little, as he opened the envelope and extracted a single page from within.

Archie,

I thought you might like to have a sample of the Douglas tartan to remember your evening in Douglasdale.

Please visit again when you can. Until you can come back in person, write if you will.

I'll be thinking of you.

Kate

He read through those simple lines several times, shaking his head slowly. Kate must have remembered the name of Archie's submarine from the television coverage, which said volumes all by itself. And her note—along with the gift—told him even more. That she had enjoyed their time together as much as he had. And she was hoping for something more.

Archie Douglas had pursued women with the same
careless energy as any other sailor these past six years,
but Kate was different from anyone he had ever set his
sights on before. Although the Navy strongly encouraged submariners to marry and raise families, as a way
of providing stability at home to counterbalance the
strains of their long isolation on patrol, Douglas had
never really considered settling down.

Until now.

He wondered what Kate would think of the idea. . . .

Wardroom, USS *Bluefin*
Holy Loch, Scotland
1545 hours GMT

"All right, gentlemen, I think that covers everything,"
Chase said quietly. They were meeting to finalize
plans for the White Sea mission, which had received the
typically dramatic Pentagon code name of Operation
Arctic Fox. *Bluefin* had been chosen as the meeting
place mostly for logistical reasons—more of the officers
involved were already aboard the transport sub, after
all—but also because the diesel boat held some fond
memories for Chase, and he was glad of the chance to
walk her decks again, even for just a few hours. "Unless
you have anything further, Captain?"

Frank Gordon shook his head. "No. No, between all
the briefings with Dreyfuss and the admiral, and this
session, I think we've gone over things enough." He
mustered a tired smile. "Maybe too much."

" 'Too much planning,' " Chase said, quoting Captain
Ralph Bricker, one of their instructors from their days
together at the Submarine Officer's Basic Course at
Groton, nearly twenty years ago now. " 'Too much planning can sometimes be more of a problem than not
enough . . .' "

" 'And sometimes your best choice is just to start shooting,' " Gordon completed. Both men laughed, drawing some strange looks from the other officers in the wardroom, especially Frederick Yates Latham. No doubt he remembered the strained relations between the two men aboard this very boat during the Gulf operation all too vividly.

Latham and Hogan, the sub XOs, had been included in this last planning session, though no one had actually asked the NSA man, Dreyfuss, if they could relax security that much while they were still in port. Goldman had given his permission, and that was what counted. If there was one thing Chase insisted on, it was having his Exec fully up to speed on any mission, and Gordon apparently felt much the same now that he was in the hot seat as a captain.

The SEAL officers and their SDV counterparts had also attended the meeting to go over the final points that had to be coordinated before the subs left port. They would continue to refine their own plans right up to the moment they left *Bluefin* to carry out their end of the operation, but that planning would be strictly tactical. Most of the efforts at this meeting had been focused on getting the subs and their human cargo to the White Sea, and extracting them afterward without bringing down the entire Soviet Northern Fleet on the boats in the process.

As senior officer, Chase had chaired the meeting, but it was Gordon's boat. He gave *Bluefin*'s captain a brief nod, and Gordon picked up on it immediately. "Well, we sail tonight. Unless someone comes up with a bright idea that requires all of us to approve it before then, I'd say we ought to adjourn."

"Aye aye, sir," Anderson said, standing. Gunn was on his feet at once as well, followed by the two SDV men. It was clear enough they didn't care to be closeted with mere chauffeurs any longer than they absolutely had to be. At any rate, Anderson was hoping to get a few hours of diving practice in before the boats left port. Promises of some additional practice time both for divers and SDVs while en route to Severodvinsk hadn't deterred him from his desire.

After the commandos had left the wardroom, Gordon turned to his Exec. "Perhaps Mr. Latham would like a chance to look around the old girl before he returns to *Pittsburgh*. Make sure he gets a good look at things, Mr. Hogan." He looked at Latham. "The orders have come through to scrap her this fall, so this may be your last chance to reminisce."

"I'm sorry to hear that, sir," Latham said. "She was a damned fine boat in her day."

"Still is, Commander. And don't you forget it." There was passion in Gordon's voice. Chase recognized it, and hid a small smile. Once he, too, had spoken of the old *Bluefin* that same way.

The departure of the two XOs left Gordon and Chase alone in the wardroom for the first time since *Bluefin*'s arrival at Holy Loch. In fact, the two of them had not been together this way, alone, face-to-face, since the Persian Gulf mission, when feelings between them had been running tense and high. The air was noticeably more calm today.

Gordon stood up and crossed to the coffee urn. "Want a cup?" he asked casually.

"You bet," Chase told him. "I feel like I've been running on the stuff for close to a week now."

Bluefin's captain poured two cups and passed one to Chase. "Don't push yourself so hard you have a breakdown, Mike," he said quietly. "I like Rick Latham well enough, but I don't think he's the man I want backing me up in the White Sea."

"And I am?" Chase asked mildly. "I wouldn't have figured on that."

"Neither would I," Gordon admitted with a shrug. "Funny how things go, isn't it? Fifteen years, and we only work together a few weeks one time . . . yet when we sit down here, it's like we were a couple of junior grades again."

Chase took a sip of the coffee. It wasn't much different from the way he had the mess crew prepare his, back on *Pittsburgh*. They'd shared a taste in strong Navy coffee from their days as roommates at Annapolis. "I'm not sure the admiral was right pulling me in for this op, Frank. I feel like he picked me because he figures I'll keep a closer eye on you, or something. You know none of this was my choice."

"Yeah, I know," Gordon said, nodding curtly. "I also know that there are some damned good reasons why you *should* be the one riding shotgun with me. You know *Bluefin* and what she can do. You know how to handle a boat with precious little water under her keel. And, though I hate to admit it, you know me pretty damned well. It's a good combination."

"Glad to hear you say it, Frank," Chase told him. "We can't afford to butt heads on this one. Too many things stacked against us as it is." He didn't say anything about Goldman's priorities, about the possibility of having to sacrifice *Bluefin* if it would help finish the mission. He didn't have to. He could tell that Gordon had already sized up the situation and come up with the same answer. "So they're really going to scrap the old girl, huh?" he added instead, looking around the small but well-appointed wardroom. It hadn't changed much from when he'd been captain.

"That's the word from on high," Gordon said. He sounded a little bitter.

"No chance of lobbying for something different? A museum, maybe?"

Gordon shook his head. "If they wouldn't do it for *Grayback*, I don't see what chance this old girl has." Chase understood what he meant. *Grayback*, *Bluefin*'s sister ship, had not only been the first Amphibious Transport Submarine, but had also been flagship of the U.S. Seventh Submarine Fleet out of Subic Bay in the early seventies. Yet she'd been scrapped a year ago without the tiniest hesitation. *Too old*, the Pentagon judgment ran. *The day of the diesel boat is over.* Now was the time for the new covert-ops subs, the *John Marshall* and the *Sam Houston*, and the converted Sturgeon class boats that were just starting to come into their own.

"Well, the old warhorse deserves a rest, I guess," Chase said. "She's done her job with distinction, even if the job wasn't one that ever earned her any public recognition." He was thinking about the VIP tour with Prince Andrew, while *Bluefin* lurked outside the Clyde Estuary, unwanted, unheralded.

"Just so long as she does her last job just as well," Gordon said. "I don't want anyone to say that she didn't measure up the last time out."

"She'll measure up, Frank," Chase said quietly. "And so will you."

"Me? I've about run my course, too, Mike. They turned me down for a new command to follow this old lady. I'll probably end up at some sub pen in the Aleutians, trying to decide if I should be pouring antifreeze into the harbor, or just drinking it." He shrugged. "Guess I just fought the system too damned long, and wore out my welcome."

"Don't say it yet, Frank," Chase said. "Remember all the 'attaboys' and slaps on the back I got when we got back from Iran? Well, my next post after *Bluefin* was teaching at SOBC in Groton for three years. I had to pull every string I could find to get on the list for an attack boat of my own."

"You had them to pull."

"Not as many as you'd think. I was in covert ops too long. And Admiral Goldman might be fond of playing my patron, but he's not in the loop with the regular submarine service anymore either." Chase paused. "Look, I know you've been pushed to the bottom of the list too many times to have much faith in the Navy any longer. But don't give up now. I think the admiral's finally figured out that you and Becca aren't going to break up just because he frowns . . . and while I doubt he'll ever hug you and call you 'son,' I don't think he's really your enemy anymore. And without him leading the charge, you don't really have that bad a reputation. Oh, everybody in the goddamned Navy knows you're a stubborn, pigheaded mule who steals admirals' daughters away and picks fights with fellow officers for no good reason, but who's going to hold that against you? Our beloved Admiral Rickover was a hell of a lot worse than that in some ways, you know, and now he's a gen-u-wine all-American hero."

Gordon chuckled. "Yeah, maybe you're right, Mike." He paused. "Look, man, I have to be honest with you. I doubt you and I are ever going to do the best-buddies thing again. Too many things were said . . . on both sides. You know it."

"I know it," Chase echoed.

"But, for what it's worth . . . I really do think you're the best man to have watching my back out there."

Chase met Gordon's level gaze. That had been a hard admission for the man to make. One of the strongest of those words that lay between them from their original quarrel had been "traitor." Frank Gordon had expected his best friend to support his cause, and Chase had let him down. To put his trust in Chase now, after all these years, Gordon must have done a lot of hard thinking.

His reply was reserved, but he knew Gordon could read him well enough despite that. "Thanks, Frank. *Pittsburgh* will be there when you need her . . . and so will I." And if the time came when he was faced with the admiral's orders to sacrifice *Bluefin* if it would complete the mission . . . Chase mentally crossed his fingers and hoped fervently that it would never come to that.

SEAL Quarters, USS *Bluefin*
Holy Loch, Scotland
1852 hours GMT

"Good job out there today, Gunn."

Bernard Gunn studied Lieutenant Anderson's bland features thoughtfully. The SEALs had spent several hours outside the sub today, practicing with SCUBA gear and rehearsing the easier part of the planned operation in the White Sea—the recon swim to take measurements and photographs of the new Soviet attack sub. Anderson had seemed happy to finally be getting a chance to do something, anything, but as usual his face gave away nothing of his thoughts.

It was too bad the lieutenant didn't like card games, Gunn thought. He would have been one hell of a good poker player.

They were sitting in what they laughingly referred to as the SEAL wardroom, a tiny cubbyhole adjacent to the SEAL officer berths with just enough room for a cramped table equipped with two benchlike seats. A coffee urn took up most of the tabletop, and their two cups accounted for the space that was left. The faint sounds of banter drifted back from the enlisted SEAL billets, where the rest of the platoon was unwinding.

"I just wish we could get a rehearsal for the Severodvinsk ground op," Gunn said. "Like maybe two solid weeks in a full-scale mock-up?"

"It would be nice," Anderson admitted, taking a swig of coffee. "But you know it isn't going to happen, so we might as well not shed any tears over what we can't have."

"Yeah," Gunn grunted. "Just seems like too much of a rush job, is all."

"It is. Has to be. Nobody knows how far along the sea trials for this new sub are right now, or how much more time they'll need. I think the Pentagon brass is afraid that the bird will have flown by the time we get there, and they're smart enough to know that the best chance of collecting information is the recon swim, not this raid on the files."

"You don't like that part of the op, do you?"

"Believe it," Anderson said sourly. "The suits at NSA may like the James Bond bit, but I think it's a fool's game. We have to make sure we can get as much info from studying the boat firsthand as we can. That way we can abort the other op if things look dicey, and we'll still come out with what we need." He leaned back. "I figure that's Admiral Goldman's thinking, too. He wants the photos and that sort of thing . . . and maybe some sonar readings to find out how noisy this *Akula* thing is underwater. It's the NSA morons who think we can bring back more."

"But we're going to try, aren't we?" Gunn didn't like to think of the SEALs deliberately skimping on a mission.

"Oh, yeah, we'll try. We might even come up with something. Who knows? This is the job we've been training for, and we'll give it everything we've got. But I want you to keep something important in mind, Gunn. If things get ugly ashore, keep in mind that the most important aspect of the mission is secrecy. It's like the man said when Harriman started talking about sabotaging the target when we had a chance. If the Russkies figure out that we've learned what they've done building their new boat, they'll go back to the drawing board and come up with a new and better design that might have bells and whistles we don't know anything about. So we want as much info as we can, but we want to make sure they never know we've been there. If you end up having to call any of the shots, you remember that. Don't charge ahead with the mission if you're going to end up compromising information we've already collected."

"You sound like you think I'm going to be running things, L-T," Gunn said. "What's the matter, planning on catching a dose of the flu or something?"

Anderson shook his head. "Not if I can help it. But you're my second-in-command, Gunn. You have to be ready to take charge if something happens to me. And you'll have to jump in with both feet if you do. Know where you're coming from and what you have to do. You should know by now that the bad guys don't generally give you time to mull things over in the middle of a firefight."

"If there's a firefight," Gunn pointed out, "we've already screwed up the secrecy angle."

"Not necessarily," Anderson said. "You might keep in mind that people see what they expect to see. Even if we're spotted . . . hell, even if we get into a shooting match . . . the important thing is to convince them that they've mopped the floor with us. That we didn't accomplish anything worthwhile before being driven off, or better yet that we're all dead and nobody has to worry about us. This op isn't like Grenada, Gunn. There it was take the objective no matter what. This time around you have to learn a little something about priorities and how to juggle them. *Capisce*?"

Gunn nodded slowly. "Yeah, I guess I do."

"Good. Because no matter how easy things look on paper, they're a lot harder when you're in the middle of chaos trying to sort things out without taking a bullet in the process. Right?"

Gunn rubbed his arm just above the elbow, one of the places he'd been hit during the fighting on Grenada. Anderson was right. He could still remember how quickly all their prepared plans had flown out the window that day . . . and how hard it had been for Gunn to rise above it all and hold his command together. This time around they didn't expect to walk into that kind of opposition. But it always paid to expect the unexpected.

"Yes, sir, L-T," Gunn told him. "So, do you want to go over the satellite maps of the shipyard again? Or shall we just wing it?"

Control Room, USS *Pittsburgh*
Holy Loch, Scotland
2311 hours GMT

"How are we doing, Rick?" Chase asked quietly.

The atmosphere in the control room was thick with tension as the submariners waited at their stations for the orders to get under way. It was always like this, Chase thought, when the time to leave port loomed near. No one aboard save Chase and Latham knew that they were heading into hostile waters on a risky covert mission rather than returning to their routine patrol station in the GIUK Gap, but that didn't matter. Whether it was a short shakedown cruise, or the beginning of a nine-month patrol, or a dangerous special mission that lay ahead, there was always this period of somber reflection that gripped almost every man aboard, from the captain to the veteran Chief of the Boat and right down to the newest enlisted man or the greenest young officer.

In the Silent Service, leaving port meant turning your back on everything familiar and safe, consigning yourself to life in a tiny, fragile shell surrounded by water at pressures that could crush a man in seconds. A minor flaw, a single foolish mistake, could snuff out the boat and the 133 lives that sailed with her.

Submarines demanded a special kind of man to serve aboard, someone who was trained to an exceptional level of excellence. And who was steady, levelheaded, and able to come to terms with psychological pressures as potentially devastating as the crushing physical pressure that constantly beat against the hull of the boat. Locked up in the overcrowded confines of the submarine for months at a time, with hardly a sight of open sky or green land to relieve the monotony of metal bulkheads; living in coffin-sized bunks with nothing more than a curtain to give the illusion of privacy, often sharing the berth with another man who worked a different shift because "hot-bunking" was the only way to fit the entire crew into the available space; cut off from friends and family with none of the usual Navy amenities of mail or phone service . . . it was a harsh and demanding life, and those who chose to live it had to be not only competent sailors, but stable and dedicated professionals who could do their jobs even knowing the risks and the strains that went with it.

"Just sent Johanssen outside for his hull inspection," Frederick Yates Latham reported. He didn't appear particularly affected by the mood Chase sensed so strongly, except for a certain thoughtful look in his eyes.

"Good." Chase nodded. PO/2 Pete Johanssen was one of *Pittsburgh*'s handful of divers. It wasn't widely known that all subs carried trained SCUBA divers aboard. Their principal purpose was to be available in case emergency repair work needed to be done outside the boat, but they were also tasked with an important security function. It was Navy doctrine that no boat leave a foreign port without first sending a diver out to inspect the hull and the surrounding waters. No one had yet thought to attach a mine to a sub's hull as part of some terrorist statement, but it was a prospect that frightened a lot of senior Pentagon staffers. Especially with the recent car-bomb attack on the Marine barracks in Beirut that had claimed so many lives and brought home the dangers of terrorism to an American public that had been largely ignorant of the dangers that lurked in the modern world.

Not that anyone particularly expected trouble in a place like Holy Loch. Great Britain and the United States were the closest of allies, and there was no strong anti-American sentiment to contend with there. The Scottish home-rule movement was anything but radically militant.

On the other hand, the Irish coast wasn't that far away from that corner of Scotland, and the "Troubles" there had been known to spill over before. Bombing an American submarine in port didn't sound much like a typical

IRA ploy, but you could never be sure what some fanatic might decide to do these days. Precautions were always in order, even if all Johanssen turned up on his inspection tour was a litter of soft drink cans on the bottom of the loch.

Chase noticed Chief Franco talking quietly with the crewman manning the sonar repeater station. It brought another matter to mind.

"Did you have a chance to check on Rodriguez, Rick?" he asked.

The Exec nodded. "He made his call as soon as he got off the boat," Latham said. "A couple of his buddies thought he was pretty quiet the next couple of days, and Norris told me there was some kind of complication with his wife's pregnancy that had Rodriguez worried. But when I spoke to him myself, he denied there was anything wrong and ignored some fairly strong hints I dropped about the possibility of emergency family leave. I didn't see any way I could go any farther at the time, so I let it drop."

"Best you could do, probably," Chase said. "If he wants to be the macho tough guy, that's his prerogative."

"As long as he doesn't screw up," Latham said darkly. It was the most emotion Chase had seen from the XO in a long time.

"I don't think he will, Rick. But you should probably have a chat with Franco, and maybe with Torricelli as well." Master Chief Eddie Torricelli was *Pittsburgh*'s Chief of the Boat, a slender, graying, fatherly man whose kindly voice could bellow like a foghorn at a moment's notice. As the sub's senior NCO, he had the special responsibility of forming a bridge between the captain and the enlisted ranks. "Tell them to keep an eye on him, discreetly, of course. We want to offer him whatever support he needs . . . but I don't think he'd appreciate being smothered with care and concern."

"I already mentioned it to Franco, sir. I'll see Torricelli about it tomorrow morning."

"Good man. Why don't I just stay at Holy Loch and let you run the boat?"

Latham shook his head. "Not in my job description, sir," he said with a ghost of a smile. "I'm supposed to do my job efficiently, secure in the knowledge that I have a captain to do all the real worrying."

"Well, good to know you aren't ready to replace me just yet," Chase said with a smile. It didn't last long. More somber, he went on. "Now that you know the score, Rick, what do you think? About the mission?"

"On the whole, I'd rather be in Philadelphia," Latham said quietly. "It isn't my idea of the best thing to do if I want to live long enough so I can tell the story over and over again to annoy my grandchildren someday." He shrugged elaborately. "But I hate kids anyway, so maybe it's better this way."

"Careful, Rick. Too much of that kind of cheerful optimism and we'll have a mutiny on our hands."

"You want the truth, Skipper? I'm not too worried about our prospects. *Pittsburgh*'s quiet enough to slip past just about anything the Russians can put on patrol up there. If any boat in the fleet can go sniffing around the White Sea, I'd say it would be a Los Angeles class. But I'm a little more concerned about . . . Commander Gordon." That last came out as if with the greatest reluctance. Latham was enough of a straight-arrow type to take very seriously the traditions of never criticizing a superior officer.

"Speak freely, Rick," Chase told him. "I respect your opinions . . . and you're one of the few people I've got on hand who knows Frank."

Latham still looked uncomfortable. "No disrespect meant to the commander, sir . . . but I think he's taking the mission a little bit too personally. Some of his comments in the briefing session today . . ."

Chase nodded. "I know. He's pushing hard to make this thing work."

"Exactly, sir. I don't know if it's because of *Bluefin*

being scheduled for decommission, or if it's because of his history with Admiral Goldman, or what, but I'm not sure his judgment is what it used to be."

"I think it's a little bit of both those things, Rick," Chase told him. "And the notion that this might be his last chance to make good. But he's still a damn fine officer."

"I didn't say otherwise, sir," Latham said stiffly. "To be honest, sir, I believe he's the reason we came out of the Gulf in one piece. A lot of other Execs wouldn't have stood the pressure, but he did. All I'm saying is that *Bluefin* could be our weak link, this time out. I think we need to keep an eye on things, like you're doing with Rodriguez. Just in case there's a problem."

"And if there is?"

Latham managed to look even more unhappy. "I don't know, Skipper. A hell of a lot is riding on that old boat . . . and on the way Commander Gordon handles her."

"They're both up to it, Rick. I'm sure of it."

Chase turned away and walked forward toward the communications shack. He didn't want to keep on that line of conversation if he could help it. Not when he had his own worries about Frank Gordon's state of mind that he didn't want to communicate to anyone else.

He hoped that Gordon could handle the special pressures that were building up within him.

Control Room, USS *Bluefin*
Holy Loch, Scotland
2335 hours GMT

"All stations report 'ready to get under way,' Captain."

Frank Gordon nodded at Lieutenant Commander Hogan's formally worded announcement. "Stand by stations," he said crisply. Turning, he caught sight of the

Communications Officer, Ron King, near the forward hatch. He beckoned the lieutenant closer.

"Messages just came in, sir," King announced. "From *Pittsburgh* . . . Ready and waiting. Proceed at your discretion."

Gordon nodded, and the short, prematurely balding young officer went on. "And one from Admiral Goldman, sir. He says, er . . ." King glanced down at the hard copy of the message in his hand. "Good luck to you all, and come home safely."

"Are you sure that one was tagged for us, Mr. King?" Gordon asked. It didn't sound like any message he had ever expected to get from Admiral Goldman in this lifetime.

"Yes, sir. It was sent to both subs."

"All right. Acknowledge both messages." Gordon turned back to Hogan. "Commander, are you sure you want to take her out without help from a tug? This isn't exactly Norfolk, you know."

"No problem, Skipper," Hogan said with a confident smile. There had been some concern over how to go about leaving port. Dreyfuss and Admiral Goldman had both been worried over the amount of attention it might stir up if the Holy Loch base was treated to the sight of two submarines getting towed clear of the docks and leaving together, especially when one of them was *Bluefin*, her oddly shaped bow "kenspeckle" in the local Scots lexicon. If Soviet agents were operating in the neighborhood and learned that a Los Angeles class attack boat had accompanied a covert-ops transport sub out of the base, there was every likelihood that Russian ships from Scotland to Archangel would be warned to keep an eye out for the American boats. So it had been suggested that the two subs could slip away without fanfare . . . if they were willing to forgo the services of the tugs. Someone might still report that they had both sailed, but a lower-key departure for both might make the whole situation a little less noteworthy.

Hogan had claimed it wouldn't be a problem, and Chase had decided *Pittsburgh* could manage it as well. Gordon hadn't argued. His Exec was the expert on these waters, and probably a better ship-handler, overall, than he was.

"Very well, XO," he said. "The boat is yours. Take her out when you're ready."

"Aye aye, sir." Hogan motioned to the enlisted rating who was doing duty as telephone talker, and the two of them headed forward to take charge from *Bluefin*'s bridge, high atop her fairwater.

Gordon watched them go, his whole body taut with expectation. After the long voyage from Norfolk and the seemingly endless time here at Holy Loch, they were finally about to be on their way.

The operation they'd been handed was a nasty one, far worse than the Persian Gulf mess back in 1980. Gordon didn't fancy working so deep in the Soviet Northern Fleet's private bailiwick, and he wasn't at all sure that even U.S. Navy SEALs could carry out the mission they were being asked to perform. But none of that mattered to Gordon just then.

He was being given a chance to show, one last time, what *Bluefin* could do. And, just incidentally, what her captain and crew could do as well. He wasn't sure if he was ready to believe Mike Chase's reassuring comments about his prospects for the future, but he was damn well sure that he'd show the Pentagon bureaucrats how a job like this should be done.

He glanced at his wristwatch. Like the clocks aboard the boat, it was set for Greenwich Mean Time, the standard for all American subs at sea anywhere. Gordon had to do a quick mental calculation to come up with the time back home. It was Wednesday evening in Norfolk, about dinnertime . . . no, wait. Tonight was the night of little Margaret's violin concert. The whole family was probably on the way to the Arts Center. Wistfully, he found himself wishing he was there with them to cheer her on, but in his heart he knew he wouldn't have chosen a different path for himself even if he'd had a choice. He loved Rebecca and the kids with all his heart . . . but his soul was still in thrall to *Bluefin* and the Silent Service.

Frank Gordon needed to make this mission work. When it was over, when he had proven himself, his boat, and his crew, maybe then he could face the prospect of letting his career wind down while he devoted himself to his family. But not yet.

Not just yet.

Bridge, USS *Pittsburgh*
Holy Loch, Scotland
2346 hours GMT

"There she goes, sir."

Chase followed Latham's gesture, swinging his night-vision binoculars over to the pier where *Bluefin* had been tied up since her arrival in Holy Loch. The submarine was now angling out of her berth, slowly but steadily leaving the land behind as her high-thrust bow pointed out to sea like a compass needle swinging to find north. Hull black against the loom of the land on the far side of the loch, she was hard to spot despite the cluster of running lights at the top of her sail.

He watched as she eased into the channel and headed southeast, toward the Clyde estuary. The old sub's stately departure went apparently unnoticed; no ripple of excitement ran through the base, no official sendoff heralded her leaving.

That was the way submariners liked things, Chase thought. Theirs was a world where stealth was all-important, where victory went not to the biggest guns or the largest hull, but to whoever was quieter, more cunning . . . to the sub whose commander had the best sonar ears and the most patience. They weren't known as the Silent Service for nothing.

"They're clear now, Rick," he said, forcing aside his musing to focus on the job at hand. "Let's get this little lady moving, shall we?"

"Aye aye, sir." Latham's teeth gleamed in the darkness in a quick flash of a smile. He turned, raising his voice. "Deck parties! Single up all lines! Make all preparations for getting under way!"

It was time for *Pittsburgh* and her crew to head back out to sea. To carry out their mission . . . or to die trying.

Friday, 2 August 1985

Captain's Quarters, USS *Pittsburgh*
The North Sea
0037 hours GMT

A harsh buzzing penetrated Mike Chase's dream, and he awoke from a vivid image of a World War II era sub's control room in the midst of a depth charge attack to the more prosaic surroundings of his tiny cabin. The buzz went on and on.

He rolled over in his narrow bunk and slapped the intercom switch. "Chase," he said, managing to sound a great deal more awake than he actually was.

"Captain, Officer of the Watch," the intercom replied in Lieutenant Jackson's gentle Virginia drawl. "Sorry to disturb you, sir, but I think we might have a problem. Sonar's getting intermittent traces of something behind us . . . about ten degrees off the port quarter. Nothing definite, but . . . well, it's Rodriguez who made the call, sir, and . . ."

"I'm on my way, Lieutenant. Sound General Quarters."

"Aye aye, sir." After a moment the public-address system came on, and Jackson's voice sounded from every intercom speaker on the sub. "Now, General Quarters, General Quarters. All hands, General Quarters."

Chase rolled out of his bunk and opened his locker, reaching for a pair of uniform trousers. So much for turning in early, he thought morosely. First his dreams had been restless and disturbing, a cross between the stories Admiral Goldman had told of the long patrol of USS *Hammerhead* and the imagery of some old war movie Chase had watched years ago. And now . . .

A sonar contact astern. That was always a submarine's weak spot. Unless she remained virtually dead in the water, a sub was mostly blind back there. The whole goddamned Soviet Northern Fleet might be holding war games out there, and *Pittsburgh* might not know it unless she cut her engines or turned in the water in one of those Crazy Ivan maneuvers. *Bluefin* was apt to be even worse off, since her sonar gear was considerably older and less effective.

Once again it was Rodriguez who'd gotten lucky—if it *was* luck that gave him such an edge with his equipment—and spotted the contact. With anybody else Chase would have checked the contact, but in the full expectation that it was just a glitch, or fatigue, or some other fault giving a false reading. But with Rodriguez making the original report, he was ready to believe they had picked up a tail.

He finished dressing automatically and left his cabin moving at a brisk walk, fast enough to convey urgency, but slow enough to preserve the dignity of the boat's captain. By the time he reached the bridge all the stations were manned and ready, and there was an air of subdued urgency hanging over the officers and enlisted men as they waited.

Latham had arrived first, and looked immaculate as ever. He even seemed to have shaved more recently than Chase, and there was no indication that he'd been off watch and probably asleep just a few minutes earlier. He joined Chase at the plotting table, where Jackson was waiting with a look of relief at being able to pass the burden of decision making to his superiors.

Jackson tapped the chart with a slender finger. "Last reported contact, sir," he said. "Six minutes ago. All we have is the bearing. No idea of range or any ID yet."

"And we're not likely to get it, at this point," Chase said. "Not as long as we keep to this course and speed."

"If we maneuver, he'll know we're on to him," Latham pointed out.

"True enough. But we might get a good enough look at him before he does." Chase turned, raising his voice. "Helm, on my mark you will cut the engine."

"Cut the engine on your mark," Quimby repeated back. "Aye aye, sir."

"We'll want to deploy the towed array as we reduce speed, Rick," Chase added to his Exec.

"Aye aye, sir." *Pittsburgh*'s ordinary sonar reception, despite the sub's high-tech equipment, wasn't all that reliable by itself, but the range and accuracy of her sensors could be vastly improved by using her towed sonar array. Essentially a very long string of hydrophones trailed behind the sub, the towed array was a wonderful way of avoiding the shipboard noises that hampered the sub's regular receivers. Unfortunately, a towed array could only be deployed at comparatively low speeds. It wouldn't hold up under higher power, and the speed *Pittsburgh* and *Bluefin* had been maintaining since leaving Scottish waters would have snapped off a deployed array.

Chase walked to the nearest intercom station and picked up the mike. "Sonar, Conn," he said. "We're going to be cutting speed and reeling out the array. I want your people to be ready. Report *anything* you see out there, people. Understood?"

"Conn, Sonar, aye aye." That was CPO Franco, sounding terse. He would probably have been off watch when the GQ warning went out, too.

"Helm, prepare to change course. Come to new heading of . . . three-four-four degrees."

"Prepare for course change to three-four-four degrees," Quimby repeated.

"Bring her about, Mr. Quimby," he ordered.

"Come to three-four-four degrees!" the Dive Officer barked. "Planesman, keep her level."

"Cut the engine," Chase said.

"Cutting engine, aye aye."

The distinctive throb of the engine, felt more than heard, died away. Carried by momentum alone, the sub continued the ninety-degree turn Chase had ordered, slowing as she did so but with plenty of inertia to work with.

"Towed array is deploying," Latham announced.

"Course three-four-four degrees," Quimby added. "Meet her, Helm." After a moment the Dive Officer's voice changed to an angry rasp. "Watch her trim, damn it! You don't have the planes to do the work!"

The enlisted man at the ballast controls muttered something that might have been an apology and obeyed.

"Conn, Sonar!" Franco called. "One contact. Underwater . . . bearing two-zero-seven degrees . . . range is six nautical miles . . . course . . . zero-seven-zero degrees, speed is thirty knots."

"Not a biological, then," Latham said blandly.

"Not unless it's a whale with a jet ski," Chase replied.

"I think we've got him IDed," Franco went on. "She's an Alfa . . . Number Two in the database, I think."

"Yeah, that's him," they heard Rodriguez confirm in the background.

"Don't think I like the sound of that," Latham said, though the words were as flat and cold as ever.

Chase nodded. The Alfa was one of the newest Soviet attack subs in service, produced in the late seventies and incorporating a number of important innovations. Though still behind the American fast-attack boats in stealth and detection capabilities, the Alfas used a titanium hull that combined light weight with high endurance. They were reported to be fast—possibly faster than *Pittsburgh* and her kin—and capable of diving far deeper than American subs.

An Alfa dogging their steps could be a real danger to the mission. They couldn't outrun her, and they might not be able simply to shake her, not without more luck than Mike Chase wanted to rely on. Nor could they turn and attack her. That wasn't the way the game was played, not even when the stakes were as high as they were for the White Sea mission.

"Aspect change!" Franco announced. "She's reducing speed . . . bearing is changing . . . We're getting the sounds of tanks filling, Captain . . ."

"Spotted our course change," Latham said.

"Not fast enough," Chase said.

"Conn, Sonar. We've lost him again, sir. Probably dropped under an inversion layer."

That was one of the many tricks of the trade a good sub skipper learned to use. There were layers of seawater with different average temperatures stacked one on top of the other in the ocean, and the rather sharp dividing line between two such layers had properties that could scatter a sound wave in unpredictable ways. These inversion layers or thermoclines were as important to submarine warriors as the rise and fall of a ridgeline could be to an infantry officer. Knowing how to use the underwater terrain to hide a sub from searching sonar was one of the most important skills a captain learned.

"What now?" Latham asked. "Do we dive after him? Or do you want to go active?"

Chase shook his head. Active sonar would light up everything in the neighborhood even through the thermocline . . . but it was definitely an aggressive move to make, and Chase didn't want to go that route as long as he had *Bluefin*'s safety to think about as well as *Pittsburgh*'s. As for playing cat and mouse with the other sub, diving below the scattering effects of the inversion layer to spot him again, then waiting for the inevitable countermove, all that would just prolong the chase without doing anything to end it. He had another idea in mind.

"Negative," he said. "To both."

"Then what do we do, sir?"

"Resume the turn at one-third speed. Take us in a complete circle, then resume our original heading. As far as our friend out there is concerned, we didn't see a thing."

"You'll let him follow us?"

"For a while. How soon to the next radio check with *Bluefin*?"

Jackson checked his watch. "One hour, fifteen, sir."

"Good. We'll let our shadow have that long, at least. Then we'll take him for a little ride." Chase gave his officers a wolfish smile. "Hope Ivan's up to it."

Communications Shack, USS *Bluefin*
The North Sea
0212 hours GMT

"Sorry to wake you, sir, but this message from *Pittsburgh* . . . it's damned strange."

Frank Gordon looked from Lieutenant Daniel Harper, *Bluefin*'s Combat Systems Officer and the current OOW, down to the radioman sitting behind the assortment of arcane electronics that constituted the sub's communications center. "Strange? How? Are they having a party over there?"

He wasn't feeling his most tactful and diplomatic, not routed out of his bunk at this hour of the morning. According to the procedures they had agreed on back at Holy Loch, the two subs rose to periscope depth every four hours and deployed a radio antenna. This allowed them to pick up any recent updates broadcast from Holy

Loch or the States through the Submarine Satellite Information Exchange, and also permitted the two captains to exchange messages if need be. So far actual radio contact hadn't been necessary . . . but now, apparently, *Pittsburgh* had transmitted a message addressed personally from Chase to Gordon.

"Er . . . best you should hear it for yourself, sir," Harper said. "Saunders?"

The RM/1 tapped a key and a tape recorder started playing back through one of the speakers. After a short crackle of static, Chase's voice came through clearly. *"Chase calling Gordon. Like you were telling me the other day, Commander Richardson had the right idea. Looks like the first part of the alphabet, all alone. Personally, I prefer Thor to Odin, but you can take a day or two to decide for yourself. Take a good look around, and keep in mind you could be closer to home than people think. As for me, sauce for the gander. See you later, buddy."*

Saunders cut off the tape. "That's all there was, sir."

Gordon looked at Harper. "What've we got on *Pittsburgh*'s movements?"

"That was another odd thing, sir. They transmitted the message and then did an immediate dive. Didn't wait for an acknowledgment."

"That's because Chase doesn't want one. At least not by radio." Gordon rubbed his chin thoughtfully. "Saunders, I want a transcript of that message ASAP. I want to make sure I don't overlook anything."

"Aye aye, sir," the radioman said. He still looked mystified, as if afraid whatever madness had robbed the *Pittsburgh* CO of his wits might now have infected his own captain.

Gordon didn't elaborate. He didn't intend to stand and explain things now, not until he was sure he knew everything Chase had tried to pass on to him.

The first clue that he seized on was the reference to Commander Richardson, the crusty, veteran sub officer who had taught at the Submarine Officer's Basic School in Groton when the two officers had first entered the Silent Service together nearly twenty years ago. Richardson had been fond of pointing out the perils a submariner faced. The phrase he had been best remembered for was "You never know who might be out there stalking you while you're stalking some other guy."

Chase had been trying to tell Gordon that *Pittsburgh* had spotted someone trailing them. As they had discussed back at Holy Loch, there was no telling how secure their current codes were. The Walkers had not only compromised current Navy codes, but had also had access to new ones under development, and until completely secure new codes could be developed there was no telling what the Soviets might be able to decode. So Chase had couched his message in references that had little meaning to anyone but Gordon, then broadcast in clear.

It was a gutsy move, Gordon thought. Something like using the Navajo code talkers back in World War II to baffle the Japanese. *Pittsburgh*'s captain was taking one hell of a chance, though, in counting on Gordon to understand the entire message. After all, they'd barely been on speaking terms for close to fifteen years, except for that brief tour in the Gulf together. Yet Chase figured that Gordon would pick up on the hidden meanings in the message.

"The first part of the alphabet, all alone" . . . that made Gordon frown. What was Chase driving at with that? There were different ways to read that . . . but suddenly Gordon saw how different interpretations could all lead to the same answer. Chase was pinpointing the nature of the tailing vessel. The Navy used designations for Soviet subs based on letters from the phonetic signal code in common use in the West. *Alfa* was one of the newest sub classes, and whether you took it as sounding like the first letter in the code, or the first part of the word *alphabet*, it came out the same way. "All alone" meant they had only spotted the one enemy sub.

What else could he figure from Chase's message?

Well, the reference to Thor and Odin was easy enough. Odin was the code word they had selected for a rendezvous off Bergen, while Thor represented Trondheim, another Norwegian town farther north. Chase had said he preferred Thor, so that was where he wanted *Bluefin* to go. But Gordon would start by heading toward Bergen, until he was sure he had lost any pursuit. By saying "a day or two" Chase was probably giving Gordon a time frame for the meeting. If *Pittsburgh* didn't arrive off Trondheim within forty-eight hours, there was definitely something wrong.

Time enough to worry about what to do in that event later.

But what about the rest of the transmission from *Pittsburgh*? "Sauce for the gander . . ." All Gordon could think of in that connection was the old cliché, *what's sauce for the goose is sauce for the gander.* Goose . . . as in wild goose? And "as for me" reinforced it. Chase— wild-goose chase. That confirmed the idea that Chase wanted the subs to split up and rendezvous later. *Pittsburgh* would do her best to lead the pursuers, whoever they were, on a wild-goose chase while *Bluefin* proceeded to the rendezvous point.

That left one line, the vaguest of them all. Gordon turned back to Saunders. "Can you play the message back again?"

Saunders had one hand pressed to his ear, holding a headphone in place while he wrote something down. Now he looked up. "Better than that, sir. Here's the transcript. If you wait I can type it up . . ."

"Never mind that." Gordon took the paper and studied that curious sentence. "Take a good look around, and keep in mind you could be closer to home than people think." What the devil was that supposed to mean?

Of course he'd take a good look around. Once *Pittsburgh* broke off and started trying to lead the Alfa away, he planned to bring *Bluefin* to a dead stop and lie low for a while, listening to passive sonar until he was sure there was nothing else in the neighborhood. But what was the rest of it all about?

He stared at the paper until the words began to blur, and then, at last, he had an idea. Something Chase had told him once, shortly after the Gulf mission. "*Bluefin*'s one of the last of a dying breed, Frank," he had said. "The future's with the nuke boats, and before too long the old dinosaurs like this old lady will be gone. Diesel boats will be for the third-rate navies that can't build the nukes but still need subs for coastal patrols."

Bluefin was one of the last diesel-electric boats in the American sub fleet. That made her distinctive, especially given her size. But by her nature she had kept a low profile over the years. There was a good chance that the Soviets didn't even have her acoustic signature on file, the way they would boats they encountered all the time on patrol operations. Out here in the North Sea, finding an old diesel sub would suggest to most captains an encounter with a boat that belonged here. Britain, Denmark, Norway, and other NATO powers all had old-style conventional subs, many of them operating regularly in these waters.

Chase was suggesting that *Bluefin* might pass as one of those boats, most likely a Norwegian Ula or Kobben class boat. Such a false ID wouldn't stand up to prolonged scrutiny, of course, since *Bluefin* was considerably larger than those sub types and wouldn't have a very similar acoustic signature. But it was a truism that people saw what they expected to see, and given outdated Soviet detection gear—and, hopefully, no sonar operators as good as the one Chase had been boasting about—*Bluefin* might not attract much notice if she stayed in close to the Norwegian coast.

It also meant that Chase's decoy plan ought to work. No doubt the captain of the Alfa would be a hell of a lot more interested in a Los Angeles class attack boat than he would be in some aging diesel boat that was probably just out patrolling the coasts of Norway for a few days.

Gordon studied the handwritten transcript for a few moments longer, but he was fairly sure he'd wrung all the information it contained from those few enigmatic lines. Finally, he looked up at Lieutenant Harper.

"Mr. Harper, we'll be changing course in a few minutes. I want you to lay in a course for Bergen. Also, get together a profile on the inversion layers around us. We may need to do some quick dodging later."

"Sir?" Harper looked confused.

"Just do it," Gordon said sharply. He still didn't feel like trying to explain his reasoning. He was sure of what the message meant, and that was all that mattered.

It was strange, he thought, that he and Chase should have been so much attuned to each other for that short transmission to convey so much. After fifteen years of going their separate ways, it seemed their old friendship still meant something after all.

Control Room, USS *Pittsburgh*
The North Sea
0237 hours GMT

"Conn, Sonar. Aspect change on *Bluefin*. She's turning to starboard."

Mike Chase allowed himself a smile. So Gordon had deciphered at least part of the message . . . that was good. Now all they had to do was make sure their friends in the Alfa followed the right boat. . . .

"Reel in the towed array, Rick," Chase said. "Time to do some sprints."

"Are you sure he'll follow us, Skipper?" Latham asked quietly. "And how will we be able to tell, if we're running at high speed and don't have the towed array out?"

"Put yourself in our Russian friend's place." Chase gestured toward the chart. "You have two targets. One's a diesel sub heading toward the Norwegian coast, which a lot of diesel subs call home. The other is a big, bad American Los Angeles class, new enough that you probably don't even have acoustic records on her yet. Suddenly the LA increases speed and changes course, like she's got some kind of business somewhere else. Who do you follow? The plodding, old-fashioned diesel boat, or the attack sub with some kind of mission?"

"That's assuming they really think *Bluefin*'s a Norwegian patrol sub," Latham said. "If they know she's a covert-ops boat . . . well, then we could be in trouble. Or *they* will be, without an escort."

"Now that Frank knows they're out there, he'll play it cagey," Chase told him. "He knows every trick in the book, and one or two that never made it into print. And I'm figuring the Soviets don't have any reason to suspect *Bluefin*'s in these waters. Soviet captains on patrol out here wouldn't have a clue that there was anything special going on back at Archangel, so they wouldn't be on the lookout for any special American covert ops. Admiral Goldman kept security tight from word one, too. So I don't think they'll be paying that much attention to Frank. No, we're the ones he wants in his crosshairs . . . figuratively speaking, of course." He smiled. "Anyway, we'll find out one way or another soon enough."

Latham nodded, but his expression was still sober. He picked up the intercom mike. "Sonar, Conn. Bring in the towed array." Then, setting the mike aside, he turned toward the helm station and raised his voice. "Mr. Quimby, prepare to alter course. Let's look alive, people."

Chase, meanwhile, gestured for Lieutenant Jackson to join him. "Lieutenant, I want two torps ready in the tubes. Also a couple of noisemakers ready to deploy.

Just in case our Soviet buddy out there turns out to be the trigger-happy sort."

"Aye aye, sir," Jackson responded. He looked nervous, but headed back to his station with a determined set to his jaw.

Routine reclaimed the control room as the crewmen went about their jobs, the only breaks in the silence the occasional job-related comments, reports, or orders that passed between officers and men. Eventually, though, the intercom came alive once more. "Conn, Sonar. Array has been retrieved and secured." Franco didn't sound happy to be reporting that. The men who worked with *Pittsburgh*'s sonar "ears" didn't like to operate without the array streaming behind the sub. Not when they knew something was out there, hunting them.

"Change heading, Mr. Latham," Chase said formally. "Bring her to the designated course. Take us to one hundred feet, engine ahead full."

"Helm, course zero-zero-zero," Latham said loudly. "Engine ahead full. Make your depth one-zero-zero feet. Five degrees up-angle on the planes."

"Aye aye, sir," Lieutenant Quimby chimed in, repeating the orders for the benefit of the helmsman and the planesman in front of him.

Chase could feel the power vibrating through the deck plates as *Pittsburgh* gathered way. Running at full speed was hardly common for the vessels of the Silent Service, which relied far more on stealth than on raw power. But the Los Angeles class boats were capable of either, as the need required. They could stalk the ocean bottoms, all but undetectable . . . or run free like a sea-going greyhound at speeds in excess of thirty knots. Of course, running flat out that way not only hampered their own ability to detect others, but also made enough noise for anyone listening to track them easily. That was exactly what Chase was counting on at the moment. What Soviet captain could resist the lure of finding out what the crazy Yankee cowboys were up to?

Control Room, USS _Bluefin_
The North Sea
0250 hours GMT

"Conn, Sonar. _Pittsburgh_'s just increased speed. By God, he's going like a bat out of hell!"

There were a couple of chuckles around the control room at that report, and even Frank Gordon smiled. _Bluefin_'s sonar shack was the domain of Senior Chief Dominic LaRusso, a grizzled veteran with a long and colorful service record. LaRusso, in his day, had been a crackerjack sonar operator, with a reputation of being able to squeeze surprising amounts of information out of the old-style systems that predated modern computer-enhanced gear. So he had always been a little bit of a law unto himself, tolerated because of his talents, and even though he was no longer sitting at a sonar console himself, he retained the outspoken, independent manner that had been his trademark for close to thirty years.

LaRusso went on. "Aspect change on _Pittsburgh_. She's coming to a new heading. Zero-zero-zero . . . due north."

"Right," Gordon said. "Chase is making his move. Time for us to make our own." He looked over at his Exec. "Reduce speed to one-third. And take us down below that inversion layer."

"Aye aye, sir. Take her down, Mr. Shelby! Set depth to two hundred twelve feet. Engine ahead one-third."

As the submarine obeyed her human masters' commands, Gordon contemplated his chart once again. He didn't relish the prospect of playing hide-and-seek with a Russian Alfa from the control room of an aging one-time diesel missile sub, even his beloved _Bluefin_. The Alfa wasn't quite up to the standards of the Los Angeles boats, but in some ways her performance was actually reported to be superior. Alfas were faster, and could dive deeper, and that made them submarines a wise captain respected. If Chase didn't draw the Russians away, he was going to have to elude the pursuit on his own, and that wouldn't be easy.

"Two hundred twelve feet, sir," Shelby reported. "Leveling off."

"Sonar, Conn," Gordon said, switching on his intercom mike. "Do you still have *Pittsburgh*?"

"With all that froth she's churning up? I'll say!" LaRusso paused. "Er, yes, sir," he amended. "The return's a lot weaker through the thermocline, but I'm still tracking him."

Gordon set the microphone down. "Deploy the towed array and bring us about. Course zero-zero-zero."

"Sir?" Lieutenant Commander Hogan raised a curious eyebrow. Gordon had gone over the message from Chase with him, and knew the conclusions he'd drawn from it. This was a change to the instructions *Pittsburgh*'s captain had passed to them.

"Just checking the back door," Gordon told him. "I'd like to see if our tail takes the bait."

"Aye aye, sir." Hogan turned away. "Come to course zero-zero-zero, Helm!" He picked up the mike and relayed the orders for the towed array to be deployed. The sonar system aboard *Bluefin* was by no means as sophisticated as what a new sub like *Pittsburgh* carried, but it still mounted a BQR15 low-frequency towed array that could hold its own in most situations.

The sub made her slow, ponderous turn, and as the Dive Officer announced the new heading Gordon spoke again. "All engines stop. Ten degrees up-angle on the planes. Let her rise to one-nine-zero feet, then adjust trim and hold her there." He paused. "Silent running, Mr. Hogan."

"Aye aye, sir," the XO responded.

Once the Exec passed the word, *Bluefin* became eerily quiet. With all but the most essential equipment turned off, and the crew moving carefully and speaking, when they absolutely had to speak, only in whispers, Gordon had the feeling of intruding at a funeral service. The sub drifted, her neutral buoyancy keeping her at a constant depth just above the inversion layer she had used to hide her course change.

Chief LaRusso appeared at the forward hatch of the control room. He padded aft to join Gordon and Hogan. "Contact, Captain," he said quietly. "About a mile aft of *Pittsburgh*, and closing the gap between them. An Alfa, by the look of it, and making some pretty high revs."

"He must be pretty confident Chase can't hear him." Hogan's stage whisper was startling against the silence of the control room.

"More proof, if we needed it, that the Soviets know a lot more about our capabilities than we thought they did," Gordon mused. "I hope that whole goddamned Walker family roasts in hell." He wondered how many of the "incidents" and "accidents" over the years that had claimed lives or cost entire ships might have been caused by leaks from traitors like the Walkers. Then he pushed the thought aside. There were more important matters to consider right now. "Very good, Chief. Back to your post. Commander, take us down to two-two-zero and resume our previous heading. Revs for four knots once we're below the thermocline."

"Aye aye, sir," Hogan said, repeating back the instructions. Gordon straightened up and watched while his Exec and crew got to work once more. They were good people, all of them.

His thoughts strayed to Chase and the *Pittsburgh*. He found himself hoping they were up to the challenge.

Sonar Shack, USS *Pittsburgh*
The North Sea
0322 hours GMT

"You can see it here, sir. And here, and here. He's following us, no doubt about it."

Chase studied the long roll of paper that had recorded the sonar records graphically for the past hour. Small but significant traces left by fleeting contacts showed at each of the points Chief Franco had indicated. They weren't much to go on, but knowing what to look for helped them speak volumes to Chase and his people. Especially Rodriguez, who hovered behind Franco looking interested. He had just been relieved to rest his eyes and ears for a few minutes. Chase didn't want to burn out his star sonar man now.

"Chief, as usual I'm impressed. You and your people continue to amaze."

Franco gave a lopsided smile. "I just intimidate 'em, sir," he said. "It's Rodriguez and these other bums who do the real work."

That made the tall Hispanic petty officer grin. He managed to look proud, embarrassed, and painfully young all at once.

Chase motioned him forward. "Good job, Rodriguez. You're going to feature very prominently in my report when we get home."

"Thank you, sir."

"How's your family doing? I heard on the grapevine that your wife is expecting . . ."

"*Sí* . . . yes, sir." Rodriguez looked a little startled, as if surprised his captain knew anything about him or his family. "I . . . er, I talked to her when we were in Scotland, sir. On the phone."

"Good," Chase said, smiling gently. "I hope everything's okay?"

The sonar man swallowed. "There were . . . some problems," he said slowly. "But the doctors think they have everything under control now."

"That's good. Take my word on this, Rodriguez, your wife and baby couldn't be in better hands. Navy doctors are some of the best in the world, and when it comes to taking care of dependents while someone's overseas, nobody can top them."

Rodriguez nodded. "That's . . . that's what Carlotta said, too, sir. She said she knew everything would turn out all right, because of how good the doctor was with her."

"You married a smart young lady, sailor. Make sure you treat her well." Chase smiled. "I think, once we wrap up this mission and get back to Holy Loch, that I might just be able to cut some orders to let you hop a MATS flight back to the States for a little bit of unscheduled leave. Do you think Carlotta would like it if you could get back to see her in a week or two?"

"Yes, sir!" the petty officer's face lit up. "Yes, thank you!"

Chase clapped him on the shoulder. "Good. Now why don't you go grab a snack in the mess hall? We're going to need that sixth sense of yours again in a while."

"Aye aye, sir," he said. He left the compartment standing taller and striding briskly.

Franco watched him leave. "I wonder if I was really that young once, Skipper. I really do."

"Nonsense, Chief," Chase told him. "I thought everybody knew that chiefs were issued right out of a warehouse in Norfolk, old and cynical from the git-go."

"Wish it worked that way, sir," Franco said with a chuckle. "It'd save a lot of wear and tear, gettin' us all broke in."

Chase laughed. "Well, what say we both get back to earning our pay, Chief? You keep on top of things, and let me know if anybody spots anything worth knowing about."

"Aye aye, sir."

Pittsburgh's commanding officer left the sonar shack and headed aft, back toward the control room, mentally shifting gears as he went. There was a time to play the kindly, compassionate CO, and a time to be a tactician. It was the latter role he'd have to fill in the next few hours if he was going to lure this Soviet boat away and then shake him successfully.

Control Room, USS *Pittsburgh*
The Norwegian Sea
0832 hours GMT

"Over there . . . that looks suitable." Mike Chase gestured toward the monitor screen that was showing a computer-created image of the sea floor ahead of *Pittsburgh*. Using sonar to map out bottom contours and translate the echoes into a map of the terrain around the submarine was one of the benefits of the newer technologies that had been incorporated in American subs over the last few years. It meant that crews were no longer forced to navigate virtually blind when they maneuvered close to the bottom.

Latham leaned forward to examine the contour map. "Yes . . . looks like quite a nice little seamount," he said thoughtfully. "Ought to shield us nicely . . . for a minute or two."

"That's all we need," Chase said. "You know what we need to do."

"Right." The XO gestured to Quimby. "On my first mark, full left rudder," he said. "And dive to two-nine-zero feet. And on my second mark, stop engine. Got it?"

The Dive Officer nodded and repeated the instructions back. Then he moved forward to the helm station and started laying it out to the helmsman and the planesman.

Side by side, Chase and Latham watched the representation of the towering spire of rock that had just missed being a small island creeping closer. *Pittsburgh* would pass close by the seamount. If they could turn quickly enough and place the bulk of the undersea mountain between the American boat and the Alfa, there would be a short period of time when the Soviet sonar would lose contact with them, the sound waves blocked by the terrain of the ocean floor. They wouldn't have much time, but once they had broken contact they could maneuver *Pittsburgh* to a new depth and heading . . . and then go silent. With luck, the Russians would lose her completely.

But their window of opportunity wouldn't be very large. They had to assume that their shadow would be fairly close behind by now, possibly within a few hundred yards. The timing for this maneuver was going to have to be perfect.

Seconds ticked past. Then, at last, Latham straightened up. "Execute . . . mark!"

The helmsman turned his wheel, and the sub began a turn. At the same time the nose tilted downward perceptibly as the planesman guided her deeper. There was a thermocline layer at 238 feet, which Chase was hoping would add to the confusion when the Soviets lost track of *Pittsburgh*.

Latham was watching the contour map again as the computer built up a new view of the terrain ahead of the sub's changing course. An unexpected spine or a second seamount hidden behind the first could ruin their whole day . . . but nothing of the sort materialized.

They must have passed within thirty feet of the rock spire as they turned. "Meet your helm!" Latham snapped, as the sub completed the turn. "Coming up on second mark . . . now!"

The engine noise began to die away as the propellers started to lose speed. The sub leveled out, her hull creaking a little under the external pressure. She continued to move, driven by momentum, but each minute was slowing her further.

"Deploy the towed array," Chase ordered. "And go to silent running."

Now came the hard part . . . waiting. And wondering how successful their ploy had been.

"You have the conn, Rick," Chase said quietly. "I'm going to the sonar shack."

"Aye aye, sir," was the other's soft response.

He made his way forward. All the positions in the sonar shack were manned by intent, vigilant crewmen, including Franco and Rodriguez. Like Chase himself, most of the first-string crewmen had been given a chance at a few short hours of rest during their mad dash north, but were back on duty. They didn't look rested, but they didn't look ready to keel over from fatigue either. Not yet, at least.

As he entered, Franco was standing between Rodriguez and Sonarman Second Class Czernak, his hands resting on the backs of their chairs as he leaned forward to study one of the screens.

"There he is, all right," the CPO was saying.

"What's he up to, Chief?" Chase asked him.

Franco started, taken by surprise. "Er . . . sorry, Captain. Didn't expect you this soon." He straightened up. "We've got a positive contact again. Definitely our same Alfa. He came around the seamount and then started to slow down fast. He must be looking for us now, but so far it's all passive."

"Good." The one thing Chase was concerned about was the possibility of the frustrated Russian sub commander, realizing he had lost his quarry, deciding to switch from simply listening to the sonar hydrophones over to the active pinging of targeting sonar. For the most part, active sonar was something to avoid using unless you were in a combat situation. Not only was it an aggressive stance, suggesting that opening fire was imminent, but it also lit up everything in the area—including your own boat. But if the Russian out there was really serious about locating *Pittsburgh,* he might resort to an active sweep.

If he did, their chances of losing him were low. But so far, it seemed, he was sticking to the regular rules of the game.

"He's slowing some more," Rodriguez reported. "Sounds like . . . yeah, his props have stopped turning. He's drifting, too. If I didn't already have him nailed . . ."

"Looks like he's going to play cat to our mouse,"

Chase said thoughtfully. "Try to keep a fix on him, Chief, but if you can't, just listen for anything interesting."

"Aye aye, sir."

As Chase headed back for the control room, he pictured the situation in his mind. Two subs, each just about the most modern attack boat in its respective nation's arsenal, were drifting silently through the chill waters of the Norwegian Sea. It was a waiting game, now. Whoever tired first would be the loser . . . and it was *Pittsburgh* that had a schedule to keep. All Chase could do was hope that the Russian skipper decided to call it quits so that the American boat would have the chance to slip away and meet up with *Bluefin* off Trondheim.

It was going to be a long, long day.

Saturday, 3 August 1985

Escape Trunk, USS *Bluefin*
Off Trondheim, Kingdom of Norway
1218 hours GMT

"Geez, L-T, why fuck around with this Dive School shit? We all know how to lock out of a sub, fer Chrissakes!"

"Can it, Moultrie," Ted Anderson said gruffly. "We will do this by the book, people. Just because Uncle Sugar sent us a bunch of taxis to ride doesn't mean we skip the basics. We may still have to lock in and out of the sub . . . like if something happens to one of the SDVs, or we find out we can't use them in close to the target because of Soviet patrols. So we practice using the escape trunks, just like we've already been practicing deploying to and from the SDVs, because that way we've got all the bases covered. You read me, Moultrie?"

"Uh . . . yessir." The SEAL, a big, blond man from Alabama whose size was a definite handicap aboard the sub, looked away. Anderson usually rode his people with loose reins, especially when it came to letting them sound off. He was a firm believer in the principle that a little bit of intelligent initiative was far better than an overabundance of blind obedience, but for that very reason the men in his platoon knew when they went too far sounding off.

The platoon's first squad was mustered in the open corridor below *Bluefin*'s forward escape trunk, outfitted in full wet suits and diving gear. Gunn had the second squad forward, in the SDV bay, ready for his own practice runs outside to reacquaint his men with how to operate from the minisubs. They had scheduled this short round of drills and training exercises for a brief period while *Bluefin* lay off the Norwegian coastline, waiting for *Pittsburgh* to rejoin them after playing decoy with the Soviet sub that had been trailing them.

Anderson would have preferred a long and detailed series of training runs, preferably with a mock-up of the target and constant input from satellite recon and humint resources, but that wasn't to be. So he would make do with what was available. SEALs were good at improvising.

"All right, as Chuckles over there has already pointed out, you should all be familiar with the drill here by this time. We've locked in and out of subs often enough that you all should be able to do it in your sleep." He smiled. "Especially you, Burns. You do most everything else asleep."

"Not everything, L-T," Senior Chief Burns replied in a mock-innocent voice. There were laughs from the SEALs. The sub crewman in charge of operating the escape trunk, a BM/2 named Mulligan, grinned as well as he looked on from the control panel at the base of the ladder.

"Must be a clean conscience you've got, then," he said with more than a trace of a lilting Irish brogue. "It must be nice to be able to sleep so well."

"Now, just for those of you who are brain-dead or hungover on that whiskey Callahan smuggled aboard from Glasgow," Anderson said, "I'll go over the drill in nice, easy, one-syllable words you can all understand." He pointed upward at the escape trunk. "I will exit first, and serve as the safety diver for the duration of the exercise. After I'm out, you will all exit the lock in two-man teams. Once you are all outside, we'll take a short swim in toward shore, where you will surface, do a quick recce of the beach there, and then make the swim back. Then you will enter by way of the escape trunk, and we'll have a debriefing back in quarters. Understood?"

"Is it too late to put in for a transfer, L-T?" That was Engineman Second Class Ralph Pond. "Like, to the Jungle Warfare School in Panama?"

"What's the matter, Pond?" Senior Chief Burns demanded. "Too cold for you outside?"

"It's just that I hate what cold water does to me, Chief," Pond said.

"The parts you're talking about won't do you any good anyway, Pond," Burns told him with a malevolent grin. "Not much chance of finding any pussy today." There were laughs all around.

"Right, then," Anderson said affably. "Let's get on with it! Mulligan, if you'll be so kind?"

The Irishman followed Anderson up the ladder to the bottom of the escape trunk. Anderson undogged the hatch and swung it up, climbing into the dark little chamber. He stooped to drop the hatch down again, his last view of the interior of the sub the redheaded, grinning submariner looking up at him from the ladder. Anderson let Mulligan take care of checking the seal on the closed hatch. That was his responsibility.

A light had come on inside the escape trunk, giving a faint but adequate illumination within. Anderson glanced around the escape trunk, making sure there was nothing unusual about the small chamber. Though *Bluefin* was antiquated as far as submarines went, the design of the escape trunk was no different from those used on the very newest boats. It was a cylinder, five feet across and eight feet tall, big enough to hold three or four men if they didn't mind being friendly, with hatches above and below and a ladder running up one side. The upper hatch opened through *Bluefin*'s forward deck, in front of the sail, and when the sub was on the surface it served as one of the regular access points for crewmen moving to and from the deck.

But when *Bluefin* was submerged, the escape trunk was an airlock. It could be used, as now, by divers seeking to leave the boat underwater. Or, in an emergency, crew members could crowd inside and try to swim for the surface.

He checked the positions of all the usual equipment— the battle lantern, the hood for the air bubble where a man could keep his head above water even when the chamber was flooded, the intercom that would allow him to communicate with the interior of the sub. Nodding his satisfaction, he positioned himself inside the bubble and flipped the switch on the intercom. "All ready here, Mulligan."

"Flooding the chamber!" the sailor's voice came back. A moment later there was a throbbing sound of pumps engaging, followed by the swirling rush of water through pipes. At his feet, Anderson saw the water beginning to rise. He slipped his face mask on, set the mouthpiece of his Draeger closed-circuit breathing system in place, and took a few experimental breaths to make sure it was functioning properly. As the water continued to rush in, Anderson double-checked the rest of his gear, the fit of his hood and wet suit, the inflatable vest he wore over his chest, the miscellaneous gear slung from his belt. Every action was familiar, a routine drilled into him as in every other SEAL by numerous training dives beginning in BUD/S training at Coronado and repeated regularly throughout his Navy career.

SEALs were employed on active operations only rarely, in these days of peacetime conditions, but they spent the rest of their time preparing, practicing, and perfecting their craft.

Locking out through an escape trunk was a simple routine, and Anderson knew that the protest from Moultrie had been valid enough in a way. But the lieutenant never liked leaving anything to chance. His men had locked out of plenty of different hatches . . . but never out of *this* one, and he intended for them to familiarize themselves with the quirks of this particular escape trunk on this particular submarine, just in case it became important later. If he had the time and opportunity, Anderson intended to put them through another drill where they'd be locking out four at a time, a considerably more difficult drill in the cramped space. He smiled at the thought, thinking what Moultrie and others would most likely say when he announced it.

Once upon a time Navy divers had exited subs by way of torpedo tubes, rather than escape trunks, a far more dangerous and unpleasant way to get in or out of a submerged boat. Anderson told himself he would have to remember to point that out the next time protests came up. There were so many *worse* things he might inflict on his long-suffering platoon . . .

The water rushing in was around his knees, and chill as it seeped through his wet suit and against his skin. Contrary to popular belief, the rubber and plastic of the wet suit was not intended to keep the diver from getting wet. Rather, it allowed a small quantity of water in, next to the skin, where the rubber insulation and the diver's own body heat combined to warm it up enough to provide real protection against the colder water outside the suit. Anderson thought it was an interesting testament to the Navy's place on the forefront of underwater operations that the original wet suit had been developed by members of the UDT—the predecessors of the SEALs— during the fifties, when they discovered that the rubberized suits originally intended to be worn under a second layer of protective clothing, a "dry suit," actually made

more effective protection by themselves, as well as allowing considerably greater freedom of movement. It
was typical that some iconoclastic Navy diver, protesting
some bureaucratic decision imposed from on high,
should have accidentally created the very basis for diving suits used right down through the years in both military and civilian diving.

The SEAL officer waited patiently as the water continued to rise past his waist. The increasing volume of
water coming in was driving the air out of the escape
trunk and equalizing the pressure with the outside. Anderson's ears popped as he adjusted to the changes. He
was glad they'd be diving in shallow water both today
and on the real op in Russia. One time he had worked
with one of the fancy oxy-helium SCUBA rigs used for
dives at higher pressures, and he hadn't liked it at all.
Of course, trying to maintain anything approaching command authority while sounding like Donald Duck on
acid was a big part of that problem.

Finally, the water had filled the chamber, except for
the small air bubble around his head and shoulders. Anderson removed his mouthpiece for a moment and ac-
tivated the intercom again. "Airlock is full," he said.

"Right," Mulligan replied. "Pressures equalized. You
can lock out any time, Lieutenant. Just don't leave the
doors hanging open, okay?"

Chuckling, Anderson again set the rebreather's
mouthpiece in place, then ducked under the water and
past the air bubble's hood. He guided himself along the
ladder to the top of the chamber with one hand, bracing
his legs against one of the rungs and undogging the
hatch above. It swung up and open easily, and Anderson
carefully swam through the opening and clear of *Bluefin*.

It was strange, the feeling of elation that went with
getting outside the boat. It had nothing to do with claustrophobia—SEALs who showed signs of being "claus-
ties" didn't stay SEALs for long—but everything to do
with the feeling of being free, the master of his own

destiny once more. Useful as the Navy's ships, subs, and aircraft were for getting the SEALs where they had to be in a hurry, these things were not a part of the SEALs' world. A SEAL wanted to control his own destiny, not be carried around like so much cargo. Anderson found it hard to understand the submariners on *Bluefin* who placed so much stock in the technology that made the boat possible. For himself, he far preferred to place his faith in his own abilities and those of his teammates.

Maybe that was why the SEALs at large were still hostile to the SDV program and the men who ran it. Practical though the little minisubs might be, they represented a surrender to the march of technology, another step down a long road that had begun with the "Naked Warrior" of the early UDT days in the Pacific Theater of World War II, where divers scouted beaches wearing swim trunks or less, and carrying no more than a knife, a slate, and a piece of chalk.

Kicking clear of the hatch, Anderson turned in the water and closed it, spinning the wheel to seal it off. Now Mulligan could pump the seawater out of the escape trunk in preparation for the first pair of enlisted men to lock out. With the hatch taken care of, Anderson uncoiled a line dangling from his waist and clipped it to a deck fitting near the hatch, then pushed off the deck and swam upward to fit the other end to a similar clip near the top of the sail. Now even if a man got confused in the murky water, he could use the line to guide himself up to the highest point on the sub, and then on to the surface if need be. Or he could find his way back to the hatch once he located the line.

That job done, Anderson returned to the vicinity of the hatch, waiting.

It took several minutes to cycle through the escape trunk, pumping water out, getting the divers in place, then filling it up again and matching pressure with the outside. Anderson waited patiently, frankly enjoying the sensation of just floating free, until at length the hatch swung open. The first diver out was recognizably Moultrie; none of the other SEALs was as large. Anderson waited until he was out, then took his hand and guided it to the line. Moultrie nodded, flashed a quick thumbs-up, and made his way a few yards higher, where he stopped and held himself in place.

Anderson wasn't sure who the next man out was until he was close enough to see his features through his face mask. It was Carstairs, the cocky little hospital corpsman, who greeted his CO with a sketchy, mocking salute before he moved off to join the hulking Moultrie by the safety line.

They went through the process twice more, with Senior Chief Burns the last man out. Then Anderson joined the men by the line, checked the compass on his wrist, and gave the hand signal to the others to follow him. Seven swimmers moved off, cutting through the chill waters of the Norwegian Sea like aquatic creatures, their rebreathers leaving no trail to mark their passing.

SDV #2
Off Trondheim, Kingdom of Norway
1347 hours GMT

Bernard Gunn slid open the canopy above him as the Swimmer Delivery Vehicle settled onto the sea floor. He waited for "Jinx" Jenkins to push his way out of the minisub before following, propelling himself upward with slow, easy strokes of arms and legs until he was clear of the compartment.

Turning, he looked back at the flattened cylinder. Silverwolf was just coming out of the starboard-side passenger compartment to join Woods. All four SEAL divers were accounted for.

Gunn studied the SDV thoughtfully. The idea for a small submersible that could extend the range and endurance of a combat swimmer was nearly as old as the idea of commando divers; he remembered reading a book about the exploits of the Italian frogmen in World War II who had pioneered the use of simple powered sleds to aid them in attacks on British shipping. Time and time again navies had reverted to the concept, but it wasn't until the SEALs were organized in the sixties that a dedicated SDV program was developed in the American Navy. Ironically, the first SEAL SDV was also an Italian design, the Sea Horse, which carried a two-man crew in a forward compartment and two divers in an aft passenger section. At first there had been no formally organized SDV unit, but by 1969 an SDV platoon had been established by SEAL Team One on the West Coast, and from there the concept had proceeded by leaps and bounds.

The Mark VIII Swimmer Delivery Vehicles that had been assigned to the White Sea mission were the lineal descendants of those early Sea Horses, but they shared little in common with them. They represented the very latest in SDV technology, and had only gone into service fairly recently. Twenty-one feet long, just over four feet across and the same in height, the Mark VIII held a crew of two in side-by-side positions in a forward compartment, and carried four more men in a passenger area astern. There were sliding canopies over each of the crewmen, and one on either side of the rear compartment as well, allowing a fairly swift deployment or embarkation at need. Powered by six rechargeable sixteen-cell silver cadmium batteries driving a five-bladed propeller, the SDV could cruise at depths of two hundred feet at a speed approaching five knots, with a maximum endurance of eight hours' continuous operation. That made the sturdy little workhorses very useful indeed at extending the distance a SEAL unit could strike.

The purpose of the current exercise was to familiarize Gunn's squad with working with the SDVs before they had to face the real thing in the White Sea. Later on they would swap places with Anderson's squad and get in some practice with lock-ins and lock-outs in the sub's escape trunk, and a long-distance swim as well, but for now Gunn was concerned with reacquainting himself and his men with their underwater taxis. After a few minutes of swimming around the SDV, he signaled his men to return to the little vessel and embark once more. They had all trained with SDVs before, at Little Creek in Virginia and off of the USS *Sam Houston* in exercises in the Bahamas, but this refresher course was definitely useful. Most SEALs still thought of SDV work as the exception rather than the rule; though minisubs had been used by SEALs from time to time since the sixties, the idea of a fully integrated SEAL/SDV partnership was still only two years old.

Perhaps that was why there was still friction between the SEALs and the SDV platoons. In a major reorganization of its Special Warfare branch in 1983, the Navy had decreed the end of the old Underwater Demolition Teams and the institution of full-fledged SDV Teams that were supposed to work in direct support of the SEALs. Instead of drawing on SDV assets in special cases, as before, SEALs and SDV platoons were now supposed to work closely together . . . but old habits died hard. SEALs still prided themselves on their toughness and independence, and tended to lump the SDV people in the same category as submariners and others who, so the SEAL credo went, were only there to get the SEALs where they had to be. The SDV men, on the other hand, were drawn from the same pool of BUD/S trainees as the SEALs, and resented the idea that they should be looked down on as mere "taxi drivers" by the same SEALs they had trained beside and faced Hell Week with.

As a result, practice in SDV operations still wasn't all it was supposed to be, and Gunn was glad for the chance to get some training in now. Especially since his nemesis, Vince Harriman, was back in *Bluefin*'s SDV bay supervising matters there. Though the man had been considerably less annoying in the last few days, he still rubbed Gunn the wrong way with his condescending attitude and frequent sly innuendoes about Gunn's competence.

The SEALs returned to their positions inside the SDV with a minimum of fuss, sliding the hatches shut above them. The Mark VIII, like all other SDVs in U.S. service, was a "wet" boat, which meant that the compartments weren't pressurized. Seawater filled the SDV at all times, and breathing gear was needed. However, to extend the use of their Draeger rigs, the SEALs switched from their own rebreathers to an onboard supply of air, removing their mouthpieces and face masks and replacing them with masks connected to the Mark XV UBA system which also supplied the two crewmen forward. The full-face masks of the UBA feed had the added advantage of being hooked up to an onboard intercom system that allowed crew and passengers to talk to one another.

"All secure back there, Mr. Gunn?" The voice of the pilot, Chief Quartermaster's Mate Matt Mikita, was the first thing he heard after settling the mask in place.

He glanced at the others. "As good as we're likely to get, Chief," he replied. "I suppose the operative phrase now is, 'Home, James.' "

"Don't get the idea we're your chauffeurs, Lieutenant," Lieutenant j.g. DuQuense spoke up. He was in the navigator's position, as he would be when the SDVs carried the SEALs on their real operation. "We don't ever book out for proms, and you can forget about trying to find a wet bar back there."

"Hell, the whole damned thing looks like a wet bar to me," Jenkins commented.

The SDV stirred as Mikita trimmed the ballast and powered up the propeller, lifting the minisub off the bottom and driving it in a slow circle until it was lined up on course for the *Bluefin*. Gunn felt a momentary twinge of something between sympathy and envy as he pictured the job Mikita and DuQuense had to deal with. They flew the SDV blind, using nothing but instruments to navigate and maneuver and trusting to the newly introduced Obstacle Avoidance System to warn them if they were about to run into something. He didn't even want to think about what they had done with earlier models of SDV, before the introduction of the OAS.

Gunn decided he was glad to be a SEAL. The work he and his men had to do was simple and straightforward, compared with trying to steer a minisub blind.

Wardroom, USS _Pittsburgh_
The Norwegian Sea
1418 hours GMT

Mike Chase sat at the wardroom table, picking at a belated lunch. He doubted that he was fooling any of his crew into believing that he was actually feeling so nonchalant as to be able to eat, though.

Nearly forty hours had gone by since they had first detected the trailing Soviet Alfa, and it was close to thirty hours since they had maneuvered to lose their pursuer. Since that time, _Pittsburgh_ had been floating, barely drifting in the sluggish Norwegian Sea currents. As hours had stretched out with no sign of their Soviet opposite numbers giving up their own silent vigil, Chase had started to worry that those currents might carry the sub into danger. Choosing between starting engines and possibly alerting their foe, or being dashed against an upthrust pillar of rock, wasn't exactly the best range of options Chase could think of.

The strain was starting to show in the men, too. They were growing tired and on edge, and that was just what it would take to cause someone to make some stupid mistake. Chase could almost imagine someone dropping a stack of plates or a metal wrench on the decks, or hitting the wrong switch and triggering an alarm. Any noise, at this point, might give them away . . . and then they'd have to start the whole game over again.

He didn't want to consider that possibility. As it was they'd be late getting to Trondheim. Would Gordon scrub the mission and head back to Holy Loch if his escort didn't return? Or would he decide to forge ahead on his own, determined to carry out the operation even without *Pittsburgh*'s support? Chase wasn't sure which possibility he dreaded more. Given Frank Gordon's apparent state of mind at Holy Loch, he had a feeling *Bluefin* wasn't likely to turn back, escort or none. But if Gordon did turn back, Chase had little doubt who he'd turn to when the time came to fix the blame for failure. He couldn't help but perceive this as another instance when Chase had let him down.

And he'd be right, though Chase couldn't think of any other way he might have handled the situation. He might have attacked the Alfa . . . an efficient solution, but not exactly the way to sneak into enemy waters.

His one consolation right now was the thought that the Russians on that Alfa couldn't be in any better shape than his crew, and they were probably a lot nearer to breaking. The Soviet submarine service, like the Americans, picked the best and brightest to man their boats, but even so the basic qualities of the two navies were so different that "best" had quite a different meaning to each. American submariners received the very best technical training imaginable, as well as being picked for their stability and competence. In the Soviet navy, even the picked men were the result of a less-than-shining educational system, and discipline tended to be of the rough-and-ready variety that was very good for making slow-witted peasants obey simple orders, but didn't exactly promote intelligent decision making or independent initiative.

So the odds still favored *Pittsburgh* to stay more quiet,

longer. But the odds didn't always tell the whole story.

His head jerked around suddenly as a shadow fell across his half-eaten lunch. Archie Douglas stood there, a solid figure framed neatly in the hatch.

"Captain?" the sailor said softly.

"What is it, Douglas?" Chase replied in the same hushed tones.

"Commander Latham sent me, sir. The Russkie has started his engines and is headed north."

Chase pushed his plate away and stood up. "You're sure of it?" he asked anxiously, then regretted it at once. It was the kind of weakness a commanding officer was never supposed to betray.

Archie Douglas just grinned. "Skipper, I don't know a thing about sonar. But if Bob Franco and Roddy Rodriguez are claiming the Russkies are on the move, then I figure I shouldn't be questioning them."

"How did you draw messenger duty?" Douglas was assigned to a damage control party when the sub was at General Quarters. They had been operating on a modified version of the normal General Quarters watchkeeping arrangements, with a steady rotation of men falling out to eat and rest while the others maintained constant readiness.

"Bad luck, I guess, sir," Douglas said, quiet but infernally cheerful. "I didn't have my hands full of anything when Commander Latham came out of the sonar shack and saw me standing there. So he ordered me to let you know."

Chase nodded. "You know what they say about idle hands," he said with a faint smile. "All right . . . dismissed."

He followed Douglas into the passageway and forward to the control room. The petty officer continued to his damage-control station beyond the control room, but Chase came to a halt at the plotting table beside Latham. The track of their opponent showed plain. The Russians were moving off, all right, and running at a speed that made it clear they didn't care whether they were noticed or not.

"Giving up?" Latham mused. "Or could it be some kind of trick to flush us?"

Chase didn't answer right away. "My gut instinct tells me they're fed up and decided to try greener pastures somewhere else," he said at length. "But I try never to base strategy on my gut . . . too much chance that one of Chef Andre's chili dogs might have thrown it off. We keep on waiting until we're certain he's too far off to spot us. Then we get under way on a course that's directly opposite his, dead slow."

"With a couple of turns thrown in to check the back door," Latham added thoughtfully.

"Now you've got it. Paranoia all the way. I don't see how they could have slipped any other ships into the neighborhood without our hearing their screws, but I want to be careful anyway."

"Right." Latham nodded. Even he looked tired and drawn by the long wait.

"Don't worry, Rick. I think we're finally rid of that stubborn Russian bastard."

USS *Bluefin*
Off Trondheim, Kingdom of Norway
1432 hours GMT

It had been a successful exercise, Anderson reflected as he led his men back toward the dimly perceived shape in the water that was *Bluefin*.

The SEALs had followed his exercise perfectly, using nothing but their compasses to make their way right into a small cove a short way up the coast from the city of Trondheim. There they had spread out to do a standard beach recon job, checking depths and the composition of the bottom at regular intervals right up to the deserted

beach. Then they had turned back, and navigated flaw-
lessly to find their way back to the sub. It was a picture-
perfect run, and Anderson knew a small thrill of pride
at the knowledge that the men of his platoon really were
among the best and brightest the Navy had to offer.

Bluefin loomed closer, hard to see in the murky water,
resting on the bottom. That was one of the characteristics
that made her perfect as the base for commando operations; she had been deliberately designed to be able to
rest for long periods on the ocean floor and still run all
of her onboard machinery. Originally intended to lurk
on the bottom before firing her Regulus nuclear missiles,
the sub—along with her retired sister ship *Grayback*—
had been based on a design quite different from that
used by every other sub in the American navy. Her seawater intake valves were positioned ten feet above her
keel, rather than right along the bottom of the hull, and
this allowed her to make full use of all the onboard systems driven by her water pumps. It gave *Bluefin* a tre-
mendous advantage in difficult situations, since she
could quite literally go to ground on the bottom without
being handicapped over a long period of time.

Anderson could make out the distinctive shape of the
bow, too. One of the bay doors was open, so Gunn's
exercises with the SDVs were no doubt continuing.

With a hand signal, Anderson indicated the deck of
the submarine and the closed escape-trunk hatch there.
Burns gave him a quick thumbs-up and touched Chief
Machinist's Mate Jerry Ehrenberger on the arm. The two
petty officers moved ahead of the rest of the divers, angling toward the hatch. Anderson followed close behind,
once again ready to serve as the safety diver until everyone was back aboard.

The three of them reached their close together, and
Burns spun the wheel to undog the hatch. The escape
trunk had been left flooded after the last of the SEALs
had left, so it was now ready for them to reverse the
procedure and reenter the sub. Ehrenberger pulled him-

self through the opening feet first, using the ladder inside to guide himself down. Senior Chief Burns followed as soon as he was clear, and Anderson closed the hatch behind him and sealed it off. Meantime the rest of the swimmers had arrived to await their own turns.

The throbbing of the pumps expelling water from the chamber was audible to the divers, and it was even easier to sense by touching the hull near the hatchway. After a time the noise stopped, then started again a few minutes later, as the pumps started again to refill the escape trunk for the next pair of SEALs. When he heard the motors cut off again, Anderson opened the hatch and gestured for Pond and Gunner's Mate First Class George Geiger to go through next.

The lock-in process continued smoothly, until at length Anderson was left alone outside the sub. Then, when the trunk had filled up, he opened the hatch for the final time and entered the chamber, hooking his swim fins under one rung of the ladder while he stopped to close and dog the hatch above him. Then he pulled himself down to the bottom of the ladder and found the air bubble. Removing his face mask and rebreather mouthpiece, Anderson thumbed the intercom.

"Ready," he said tersely. After a moment the pumps cut in again, and the water in the cylinder began slowly to recede.

When the last of the water had disappeared, Anderson stooped and opened the hatch on the deck. His SEALs were still clustered below, some already halfway out of their wet suits, others still fully suited but with their hoods drawn back, their rebreathers off, and their swim fins dangling from their hands. A couple of them looked up as the hatch opened.

"Hey, L-T, cool swim," Geiger said. "When can we do it again?"

"A few days from now," Anderson said. He started down the ladder carefully. "In the White Sea."

He was halfway down when something happened—

he was never quite sure what, and none of the other SEALs saw enough to be sure either. Though he was heedful of the bulky SCUBA rig on his back and the awkwardness of his flippers, and careful in how he went down the ladder, somehow he missed his footing and slipped. Even the most thorough training and the most cautious conduct weren't always enough to stop an accident . . . and this was certainly one such case.

Anderson tried to check his fall, but he was tired from the swim and awkwardly placed. He lost his grip and dropped, twisting sideways as he went down, and the only thing that kept him from ending up on the deck in a heap was his left foot catching in one of the rungs. With the leg caught, he dangled upside down, his head only inches above the deck. Had he been one rung lower, he probably would have cracked his head open on the metal plating.

He had clearly heard the leg snapping as it was wrenched painfully in a direction it had never been intended to go. Waves of agony rolled up his leg, and it took all of Anderson's self-discipline to keep from crying out.

Moultrie and Burns were there at once, catching him and working him clear of the ladder to lower him gently to the wet deck below, and a moment later Carstairs was kneeling beside him, examining his leg with lips pursed and a dark frown. The corpsman shook his head slowly and gave Anderson the news he already knew.

"A break, L-T. Nasty one, too."

Anderson nodded grimly and spoke through teeth clenched against the pain. "Tell me something I don't know."

"Better get Dr. Waite up here on the double," someone said. "Looks like we're going to need him."

Forward Deck, USS *Bluefin*
Off Trondheim, Kingdom of Norway
2008 hours GMT

An inflatable raft with an outboard motor was hardly a dignified form of transport for the captain of a U.S. Navy submarine, but Chase wasn't terribly concerned with dignity as he sat in the bow of the tiny boat, watching as BM/3 Drucker steered the awkward craft from *Pittsburgh* across to *Bluefin*. It was strange indeed to have two subs riding on the surface in the pale light of the sub-arctic night, with the auroras flickering over *Pittsburgh*'s soaring fairwater adding an eerie air of unreality to the scene.

The attack sub had reached the rendezvous area less than an hour ago, and to Chase's surprise Gordon had chosen neither to press on nor give up on the return of *Pittsburgh* from her wild-goose duties.

But Gordon had been anxious that Chase come aboard. He hadn't said just what the problem was, but it was clear enough that there was something wrong.

Drucker brought the raft alongside *Bluefin* with something of a flourish, and Chase himself tossed a line up to a crewman waiting on the deck above. Then he hoisted himself up onto the sub's low deck, aided by another crewman. Drawing himself stiffly to attention, Chase quickly saluted the boat's limp, lifeless colors, and then the fairwater where a pair of figures in officers' hats were vaguely visible in the endless twilight.

"This way, sir," one of the sailors said, guiding him toward the forward hatch.

Inside, he was escorted through the control room and aft to the wardroom. Gordon was waiting for him there, sipping coffee and leafing through a manila folder with an expression that hovered somewhere between distaste and concern.

He looked up as Chase entered. "Well, Mike, back at

last, I see," he said, sounding a little sour. "Enjoy your little side trip?"

"Not much," Chase told him. "Our friend in the Alfa was one of those stubborn bears. Wouldn't give up and go away. When he finally got the message that he wasn't invited to the party, he stalked off in disgust. But we still had to take the long way round to get back, because we didn't want to have to tell him no a second time."

Gordon grunted, plainly not interested in Chase's line of banter. "We've got a problem," he said flatly. "While you were gone, the SEAL leader fell down a ladder and broke his damned leg. He's immobilized in a bunk in sick bay now with enough painkillers in him to make an elephant forget."

Frowning, Chase sat down opposite Gordon. "Not good," he said. "Not good at all. Anderson struck me as a level head who could carry off the job. His second?"

"Gunn? He's got some experience. But he's young. And I've heard rumors to the effect that he's not really cut out for the SEALs. A disaster waiting to happen."

"Rumors? What do you think, Frank?"

"I think the kid's jacket looks pretty good." He tapped the folder with one finger. "But I'm concerned about the rumors. Not because they might be true . . . but because if they're floating around, it means he may not have the confidence of his own people. And that I don't like at all."

Chase let out a long breath, thinking. "Are you recommending we abort? I doubt the admiral would be too happy . . ."

"No way, goddamn it!" Gordon burst out. "No way I'm going to let some damn-fool accident derail this op. I just wanted to get your opinions on the record alongside mine. Do *you* think we should abort?"

"Not unless this Gunn kid is a complete screwup. And he struck me as capable enough when we were planning. Thoughtful. I admit he doesn't look much like a SEAL, but it's what he's made of that counts."

"Good." Gordon looked relieved. "I was afraid you might have enough reservations to make *me* rethink things."

"How are you going to handle it?"

"I'm pretty sure most of the rumors stem from the SDV platoon. Our friend Mr. Harriman."

"Ah, the aggressive fellow who likes to blow things up."

"Exactly. I'm going to get everybody concerned together tomorrow and hash it out. But as far as I'm concerned, if Gunn isn't up to the job, I'll find someone who is. One of his chiefs, if need be. But I say we keep going."

"Agreed. Shall we get under way again immediately?"

"Hold on. Let's take a look at what we'll be doing. I don't want to have to decipher anymore of your clever little codes unless I have to."

Chase smiled. "Seems like you did pretty good. But you're probably right. You have the charts handy?"

The two of them bent over the charts for a time, discussing their options and going over new contingency plans they might adopt in case they ran into more trouble. At length Chase leaned back in his seat and rubbed his forehead absently. "I think that covers it. Let's call it a night, Frank. I want to get back and get us moving."

"Thought you'd never ask." Gordon started to stand up, but paused. "Oh, Christ."

"What's the matter, Frank?"

"I just realized. We'll cross the Arctic Circle tomorrow sometime."

"Yeah . . . oh. Right. The ceremony."

"The ceremony," Gordon agreed heavily. "And you know how those bluenoses will feel if they don't get their talent show the night before. Pretty damned late to be organizing the festivities now."

"Well, that's their problem," Chase said firmly. "Tell your COB to do what he can, then let them have their fun."

"Are you a bluenose, Mike?"

"Oh, yeah. Went through the whole routine back in '74. Got my certificate along, too. Nobody's dragging me into their little game." He smiled. "You would have had to go through it all aboard the *Sea Devil*, I guess."

Gordon shook his head. "Before that," he said. "Seventy-five. Aboard the *Ethan Allen*."

"Glad you remembered it. I probably would have sailed right on through and never thought of crossing the circle."

"Rick Latham would have told you. That one doesn't miss a trick."

"Yeah. He's a pretty good XO. Almost as good as the guy he learned from."

Gordon smiled. "Thanks. And you weren't a bad captain, either, in an overbearing, tyrannical sort of way. Come on. Time to get you back to your boat."

Sunday, 3 August 1985

Outside the Enlisted Mess, USS *Pittsburgh*
The Norwegian Sea
0948 hours GMT

Chase could hear the revelry coming from the enlisted mess from a long way down the corridor, and he smiled as he walked briskly toward the sounds of laughter and general hijinks. After the strain of the past few days, it was good to know that morale was running so high.

As Gordon had reminded him the night before, the crews of the two submarines were bound by long tradition to celebrate an auspicious and important event . . . the moment when the boats crossed an invisible but extremely important line, the Arctic Circle.

There were many such traditions in the Navy, going back centuries and embracing many seafaring nations. The most famous was that of "Crossing the Line" at the equator, but the Arctic and Antarctic Circles also involved elaborate ceremonies, as did the international date line. For the most part they were simply excuses for the men to indulge in a little horseplay and relatively harmless hazing, but nonetheless sailors were jealous of their status as shellbacks or bluenoses, and were fiercely

202

proud of the certificates that they were issued to com-
memorate their status.

The ritual had actually started the night before, shortly
after Chase had returned from *Bluefin* and exchanged a
few brief words with Master Chief Torricelli. Within an
hour, Chief Bob Franco, dressed up as the Honorable
Davy Jones, Royal Scribe to His Highness, Neptune,
King of the Deep, was moving through the boat, ascer-
taining who was a certified bluenose who had previously
crossed the Circle. Any who couldn't produce an "official" bluenose certificate was handed a hastily Xeroxed
writ summoning him before the court of Neptune the
next day, to explain why he should be granted permission to pass through the Ocean King's realm, and to be
judged in his royal court. In all, there were seventy-four
bluenoses aboard the sub, leaving fifty-six officers and
men facing the ritual hazing.

There had been a rather impromptu talent contest, too,
which hadn't even gotten started until well after midnight. But life in a sub already held a certain timeless
quality, so nobody was too concerned by the strange
scheduling of it all. The talent show was another long-
standing tradition, held in the enlisted mess with a small
but vocal audience. "Davy Jones" presided over the affair, which in theory was supposed to win him over to
support appeals to his master, King Neptune, to permit
Pittsburgh to make her way safely across the Circle. The
bluenoses got to show off their rather dubious skills in
singing, dancing, and performing in drag for the amuse-
ment of their peers, with the two "winners" receiving
the so-called honor of becoming members of Neptune's
Court for the main ceremony. By long-standing tradition
Torricelli, as Chief of the Boat, would preside as Neptune. Bob Reinhold was unanimously acclaimed as Amphitrite, Neptune's royal consort and Queen of the Sea;
a CPO from Engineering, Tom Coulter, was declared the
Royal Baby. Those who were anxiously awaiting the
ordeal that would make them bluenoses didn't have a

chance to compete in the talent show itself, but a few were allowed to participate in rigorous programs of push-ups and sit-ups to qualify as Royal Guardsmen for Neptune and his Court, a post that offered some relaxation of the ordeals they would face. Archie Douglas, who outperformed all his mates in the push-up category, had appeared particularly happy to be avoiding some, at least, of the hazing. But then, Chase thought, Douglas always seemed to be one step ahead of his shipmates when it came to finding dodges that would keep him out of situations he didn't want to be in.

Now the real ritual was under way. The candidates for initiation were served a cold breakfast and then divided into nine groups of six men each, with bluenoses to watch over them. Aboard a surface ship, the whole ceremony would have been held in the open, in an area large enough for a significant part of the crew to gather around and watch the fun. Aircraft carriers were the best; they had thousands of men undergoing the ceremony at a time, out in the open on their flight decks, where everyone could participate. In the Silent Service modifications to the ritual were necessary to take into account the physical limitations of a cramped submarine, but with typical Navy ingenuity sub crews had developed their own special approach to the day which kept the spirit of the occasion very much alive.

One group of candidates was put through their paces at a time, while the others waited, entertaining their bluenose guardians by bellowing out songs with a naval flavor. As Chase strode down the passageway, he was treated to the conflicting sounds of *What do you do with a drunken sailor?* on one side, and *Now sit right back and you'll hear a tale, a tale of a fateful trip . . .* on the other. It was as incongruous as it was discordant. He was very glad indeed that he had been able to produce his bluenose certificate. Mere rank didn't protect people from the hazing; Chase had heard of battle-group commanders being hauled in front of a CPO playing Neptune on equatorial crossings.

The candidates were moved down the length of the sub's middle deck, starting at the "goat locker"—a sort of miniature wardroom for the sub's petty officers—and ultimately wound up in the enlisted mess hall, which as the largest open space on the boat was deemed the best spot for the main ceremony before Neptune himself. Along this course there were several stops where the candidates were put through demanding or embarrassing tests. At one post the Royal Barber spruced up the candidates with a quick trim to make them more presentable at Court, not always done with royal skill. So far today, Chase had seen two of his men shaved bald and another sporting a rather stubby mohawk. At another station they were quizzed on nautical knowledge and the lore of the sea, with wrong answers being punished by a paddling. At yet another they were given toothbrushes and ordered to scrub a section of the deck. No one was ever actually disqualified by "failing" a test or a challenge, but there were plenty of ways a failing candidate could be chastised. To get from point to point, the candidates proceeded on hands and knees in single file, shepherded along by their guardians.

As Chase approached the mess hall, he saw that a group of candidates was just going in ahead of him, having passed the last of the stations. This was in the crew's small communal shower, where the initiates had been stripped to their skivvies and then placed under an icy spray of water. Without being allowed to dry off, the men were now being herded into the presence of the Court, still wet, shivering, and clad in soaking underwear.

Chase waited at the hatch, watching as the six were hustled into place before the table where Torricelli, Reinhold, and Coulter sat in their simple but creative costumes. Neptune asked questions of their guards, first, assuring himself that they had all undergone the purification rituals necessary to transform them into blue-noses, then interrogated the candidates themselves with demands to know why they felt they deserved the honor of acceptance into his domain north of the Circle. Usually he would be satisfied with their answers and pronounce them bluenoses, but sometimes Torricelli chose to put his new subjects through a few additional ordeals. As Chase watched, he saw Torricelli beckon to Franco, who ordered Rodriguez to don headphones connected to a small cassette recorder. When Franco switched on the tape, Chase could see Rodriguez wince. After a moment "Davy Jones" removed the headphones, and from all the way across the compartment Chase could hear the relentless beat of "Proud Mary" blaring from them. Knowing Rodriguez, that had been the worst torment of all . . .

But then it was over for those six. At a gesture from Neptune they were finally allowed to stand, finally accepted into the Realm of the Arctic Circle as full-fledged bluenoses. Unfortunately, no one aboard had stocked copies of the Bluenose Certificate to issue to the new initiates, since the sub's original patrol hadn't been planned for north of the Arctic Circle. But the omission would be corrected just as soon as they returned from their mission. The Navy actually issued these certificates, along with those for other great milestones in a sailor's career such as Crossing the Line at the equator or sailing over the International Date Line.

Somewhere behind Chase, the next set of victims . . . candidates . . . would be moving along their way.

Rodriguez was accepting the congratulations of his crewmates, who slapped him on the back and offered him a cup of bug juice. The Hispanic sonar man was moving slowly toward the hatch, no doubt hoping to get to his berth and retrieve his clothes. Chase caught his eye and beckoned to him.

The sailor looked nervous as he approached. "Sir?"

"I guess this is a day for congratulations, Rodriguez," Chase said loudly. "It's not every day that a sailor becomes a bluenose . . . or becomes a father!"

Rodriguez gave him a blank look for a long moment.
"Sir?" he repeated.

Holding up the familygram that had come in while
the sub was cruising at periscope depth and checking for
SSIX messages, Chase gave him a broad smile. "I know
it's not polite to read other people's mail, Rodriguez,
but Markowitz let out such a yell when the message
came in that half the control-room crew ran to see what
had happened to him. It's a wonder we didn't go off
course and run into *Bluefin*. And when I saw what all
the commotion was about, I figured I'd deliver it to
you."

Rodriguez took the familygram from Chase and began
to read it silently. Chase, who had already looked it over
in the comm shack, could almost hear the short but
heartfelt message.

> 336. RODRIGUEZ ST/3 8/1: CONGRATULATIONS IT'S A
> GIRL. MOTHER AND DAUGHTER WELL. NO COMPLI-
> CATIONS. NAMED HER MARIA. CARLOTTA STILL AT
> HOSPITAL BUT COMING HOME SOON. TOMAS, AN-
> GELINA LOOKING AFTER YOUR PLACE. ANGELINA
> WILL STAY WITH CARLOTTA. WE ARE ALL SO HAPPY
> FOR YOU. ILY. MAMA.

Forty short words, all that a familygram allowed. Over
the years they had become the lifelines for sailors in the
Silent Service, short but vivid looks into the lives of
loved ones left behind. Births, weddings, engagements,
graduations, all the high points of life back home were
compacted into those messages, together with more
mundane things like report-card grades, home repairs, or
vacation plans. And, always, the soul of the familygram
came across in that final ILY—"I love you." That was
the signal the Navy wanted her sailors to be receiving
when they were away on a long, isolated tour of duty
with precious little contact with the outside world.

Knowing there were still people back home who cared, who thought about them and wished them well, was the best way anyone had found to counteract all the negative factors in a submariner's life.

Chase was glad the message had been a good one. It would probably be taken as a good omen; sailors, even in this high-tech age of nuclear power and advanced computers, were still a superstitious lot, and the birth of a daughter to one of their own as they sailed into hostile waters was sure to give their spirits a needed lift.

Though judging from the roar of laughter coming from a cluster of bluenoses farther up the corridor, escorting the next group of initiates who approached on hands and knees while trying to sing the theme from the Popeye cartoons, morale was already higher than it had any right to be.

Wardroom, USS *Bluefin*
The Norwegian Sea
1315 hours GMT

The wardroom seemed crowded when Gunn arrived, though in fact there were only five officers there ahead of him. He took a seat beside Lieutenant DuQuense, who was looking uncharacteristically sour, particularly when he happened to look toward his CO, Vince Harriman, whose expression was guarded and neutral. *Bluefin* was represented by Captain Gordon, his Exec, and Dr. Waite. It was hard to believe they'd had all the hilarity of *Bluefin*'s Arctic Circle celebrations just a few hours earlier, with DuQuense and Gunn amongst the many crewmen and passengers forced to undergo the hazing at the hands of the sub's small but enthusiastic contingent of bluenose veterans led by King Neptune, Master Chief Preston. Now the atmosphere in the wardroom was anything but happy.

"Sorry I was slow, sir," Gunn said. "I was with Lieutenant Anderson."

Gordon nodded. "Understandable. How did he seem to you?"

"Mad as hell, sir," Gunn told him with an effort at a grin. "A SEAL trains his whole life for the kind of mission we've been handed, and Lieutenant Anderson is pissed that he's going to miss it because he couldn't stay on a goddamned ladder!" Gunn realized what he had said and cleared his throat awkwardly. "Er, his words, sir."

That made Hogan, the XO, smile faintly. The others didn't react. Gordon looked at Waite.

"Just how bad is it?"

Waite nodded. "About as broken as a leg can get, Skipper," he said. "Compound fracture. I'm afraid Mr. Anderson is looking at spending a long time off his feet."

"Which leaves me, or rather us, with a problem, gentlemen," Gordon said quietly. "Can we carry out the mission without the SEAL platoon leader?"

"Yes, sir, we can," Gunn returned promptly. "One man won't make that big a difference in the execution of our mission plan. And we have plenty of time to make adjustments to it on the way to Archangel."

"To put things bluntly, Lieutenant," Hogan said, "it has been suggested that perhaps Lieutenant Anderson's injury leaves your unit . . . short on leadership."

Gunn couldn't help but throw a glance in Harriman's direction. "Whoever made that suggestion, sir, is wrong. Dead wrong. I'm fully briefed on the situation, and there is no reason why Lieutenant Anderson can't assist me in further planning from his bunk in sick bay. I've got some very capable NCOs in the unit as well. I can take over Lieutenant Anderson's duties, with Master Chief Callahan stepping in as my second."

"You're a goddamned junior grade!" Harriman exploded. "And this is a critical mission. You don't have the experience or the seniority to take that platoon up against the Russkies!"

Gordon raised a hand. "Please, Lieutenant, shouting it won't do anybody any good here."

"Sir, I am the second-in-command of the platoon. If Mr. Anderson had been wounded in action, I would have to fill in for him, and he would trust me to do so." Gunn strove to keep his own voice calm and even in deliberate contrast to the excited Harriman. "In fact, this situation is much less trouble because we have plenty of time to make the transition. I don't see a problem here."

Harriman shook his head. "Captain, I'm senior to Mr. Gunn here, and I've had the same BUD/S training he's had. Same class, in fact . . . *and* my overall record was quite a bit better than his. Lieutenant DuQuense can handle the SDV platoon, and I could take charge of the SEALs. I know it's not quite chain of command, but, by God, this mission is too important to entrust to some wet-behind-the-ears junior grade!"

"Yes, sir, it *is* outside the chain of command, that much is certain," Gunn said firmly. "More importantly, Lieutenant Harriman is forgetting the fact that BUD/S training is *all* that he and I have in common. After Basic Underwater Demolition and SEAL school, he was put into the SDV program. He's received a great deal of highly specialized instruction on the care and feeding of those four sea monsters up in the bow bays, and despite our differences of opinion I bow to his superior knowledge of how they work. But I've been through the advanced training that any SEAL has to go through. Ranger School. Airborne training. Jungle Warfare School. All the advanced combat classes the armed forces of the United States have dreamed up over the past thirty years or so. I'll admit that Jungle Warfare training isn't going to help much in northern Russia, but the point is that I am a combat-trained SEAL . . . and Lieutenant Harriman is a superbly prepared SDV specialist. My platoon would not accept him as their commander, and I think the mission would be severely compromised if any attempt was made to put him in that position."

"Suppose we let them decide?" Harriman asked. "Do you really think men like Callahan and Burns would take a chance on some youngster if they didn't have to?"

"No, sir, they will not decide. I don't know how you run your platoon, but Lieutenant Anderson has never considered our outfit to be a democracy, and I'm not about to start now." Gunn met Harriman's challenging stare directly. This had gone beyond the old rivalry. This was the future of Second Platoon they were deciding, and Gunn was damned if he'd risk those men just so Vince Harriman could try to prove that he was a good enough man to be part of the SEALs after all.

"Gentlemen, gentlemen, if you *please*?" Gordon's voice was soft, but it still cut through the wardroom like a whipcrack. "This isn't a debate on your relative qualifications. The only thing I want to know is what is going to be the best way to salvage this mission." He looked at Hogan.

The Exec was studying Harriman. "Sir, I'm inclined to accept Lieutenant Gunn's word on what his platoon can do . . . and how it might react to, uh, unexpected changes. I'll admit that Mr. Gunn is young, and his appearance is, shall we say, not the sort that inspires great confidence." He smiled, while Gunn's ears burned red. "But messing around with the chain of command is never a good idea, sir, in my book. I would expect Mr. Shelby, young as he is, to take command of *Bluefin* if the officers senior to him were incapable of exercising control, and I'd think that his training would allow him to meet the challenge. I don't know SEALs the way I do submariners, but I figure they deserve the same considerations."

Gordon nodded. "That's my thinking as well. Mr. Harriman, you are in command of the SDV platoon. There you will remain. Lieutenant Gunn commands the

SEALs, and you will give him your full cooperation for the duration of this voyage. *He* is now in operational command of the mission. That means that he has the final say on the way your unit is employed. I recognize that you may have problems taking orders from someone who lacks your seniority, quite aside from the personal differences that are so plain between the two of you, but my advice to you is, *get over it*! Because the only other option open to us would be to scrub the op and return to Holy Loch until a replacement officer could be flown out from the States, and as far as I'm concerned that is no option at all. Are you with me on this?"

"Yes, sir," Harriman said, subdued.

"Good. Mr. Gunn, you had better be right about your ability to carry this operation out successfully. Because if I find out I've made a mistake in backing you up, I'm going to be very, very unhappy, and anyone on this boat can tell you that you don't want to be around me at such a time."

"Yessir," Gunn said. "We'll do our part, Captain."

"Good. Then the mission continues as before. Dismissed."

Feeling a little bit of an adrenaline rush after the clash with Harriman, Gunn left with the others. In the corridor outside the wardroom he stepped in front of Harriman before the SDV officer could stalk away.

"Lieutenant Harriman?" Gunn began. "I'll be going over the operational plans with Master Chief Callahan and Senior Chief Burns later this afternoon. We need to start seeing how Lieutenant Anderson's injury might modify the mission profile. I'd like you and Mr. DuQuense to be there too for your input. Will that be convenient for you?" He tried to keep control of a voice that might have cracked or quavered otherwise.

Harriman looked at him with hostile eyes, but his response was crisp and professional. "We'll be ready. Lieutenant." It sounded as if he had to force that last word out.

Gunn nodded. "Thank you," he said, turning away.

It was only after he was alone and on his way back to sick bay that the full realization hit him. He was in command.

Perhaps, he thought, he had been hasty to insist on taking so much responsibility onto his own shoulders.

SEAL Enlisted Berths, USS *Bluefin*
The Norwegian Sea
1512 hours GMT

"Man, did you ever see anything as funny as the look on Silverwolf's face when he thought he was going to have to drink that swill? Priceless! Damn, I wish I'd had a camera with me!"

Silverwolf glared across the table at "Jinx" Jenkins. "Very funny, Jinx," he said in the soft tone he reserved for people he was thinking about pummeling. "And just how is it that you got out of the day's festivities, any-how?"

They were relaxing after the morning's festivities, lounging around their rec room. Most of the SEALs and SDV men—all but Callahan, Jenkins, Lieutenant Harriman, and of course the injured Anderson—had been required to go through the ritual hazing along with about a third of the sub's crew. Submariners operated in the Arctic far more often than most Navy personnel, so the proportion of bluenoses in any given sub crew was considerably higher than it was in other Navy branches. Especially SEALs. Though they trained for all sorts of environments, duty rarely took them above the Arctic Circle, except for the occasional platoon assigned to a NATO training exercise in Norway, or other such odd-ball assignments.

Silverwolf, always a little touchy, had found it hard to take some of the pranks played on him during the course of the "ceremony." But he had forced himself to go through it all. He was a SEAL. Whatever his Team did, he did as well.

Actually, now that it was over he was glad he'd gone through it all. Silly as it had seemed at the time—not to mention humiliating and sometimes downright disgusting—the ceremony had given him a special feeling of kinship not just with his fellow SEALs, but with the submarine crewmen as well. Together they were sailing to the top of the world, and that set them all apart from other people just as surviving Hell Week set BUD/S graduates apart from everyone else in the Navy. It was a distinction he could point to for all his days . . . and maybe, someday, he'd be among the bluenoses when some other ship he sailed on crossed the Arctic Circle, and he'd have the chance to do unto others . . .

For now, he had his Bluenose Certificate, thanks to the pack-rat mentality of Master Chief Preston, who had blanks stored on board even though no one had warned them they were going to the White Sea before they left Norfolk. Decorated with polar bears, reindeer, and other icons of the far north, it proclaimed one John Silverwolf to be a one hundred percent true bluenose, entitled to freedom of travel north of the Arctic Circle, and signed most impressively by Their Royal Highnesses, King Neptune and Queen Amphitrite. A souvenir he looked forward to passing on to his family someday. . . .

Jenkins was grinning at him from across the table, taking a long swig of bug juice before he answered Silverwolf's question. "Hey, I'm a bluenose from way back, kid. I went from BUD/S into UDT-11. First assignment I drew was doing equipment tests on some prototype diving gear in cold-water conditions. Me and six of my buddies were stuck in Alaska for six months. My nose was *really* blue, let me tell you, even before we crossed the Circle."

"So you went from the UDT . . . ?"

"Straight into SEAL Team Five," Jenkins said, nodding. "When the idiots in the five-sided squirrel cage decided they didn't need the UDTs anymore, they just waved their magic wand. Poof! Some of us turned into SEALs, and some into SDV drivers, just like that."

"So what's a West Coast puke doing with our fine outfit, then?" Davis challenged.

"Damned if I know," Jenkins said, shaking his head. "I was happy in Coronado. Sun, sand, California babes in bikinis too small to make a decent handkerchief out of . . . I'm telling you, boys, that was paradise."

"They probably transferred you because they found out about the gypsy curse," Randy Carstairs put in. The corpsman shook his head sadly. "It's such a shame, a fine young lad like yourself, cursed to cause bad luck wherever you go . . ."

Jenkins had earned his nickname after a string of small but unfortunate incidents had started to plague the outfit, starting shortly after his assignment to Anderson's platoon two months earlier. Nobody seriously believed that he had caused any of the problems, but it made for a few good laughs during late-night bull sessions.

"Yeah, look at what happened to the L-T," Danny Woods put in from the far side of the compartment. "He always scoffed when somebody said you were a jinx, and now he's in sick bay with a bad leg."

"I wasn't anywhere around when he fell!" Jenkins protested loudly. "I was forward in the SDV bays with Mr. Gunn."

"So your reach is longer than anyone suspected, huh?" Carstairs said.

"Anybody seen the L-T yet?" Martinez asked.

"Mr. Gunn was with him for a while this afternoon," Master Chief Callahan said. "I guess he's still pretty hopped up on painkillers, so the doctor ain't letting anybody else in to see him yet."

"That was a damned bad piece of luck," Moultrie said. "And I'm serious, not just talking about Jinx here. L-T's all right, you know? A good SEAL."

"Looks like he's gonna have to play armchair quarterback on this op," Senior Chief Sam Burns commented gruffly.

"Think the kid's up to taking over?" That was Briggs, the SDV technician.

"Damned straight he's up to it," Callahan growled. "No thanks to you and your gang. The way I heard it, your fearless leader tried to step in and take over everything."

"So? He has the rank." Briggs sounded defensive.

"But Mr. Gunn's in the chain of command," Burns countered.

"Anyway, Lieutenant Harriman isn't trained to command SEALs," Jenkins put in quietly. "I know. They turned my UDT into a SEAL Team, but we still had a hell of a lot of training to go through to catch up with the real SEALs. I'll take my chances with Mr. Gunn, if it's all the same to you and your buddies from Yellow Cab."

"Fuck off, Jinx," Joor snarled, coming to Briggs's defense.

"That's enough," Callahan said quietly. "Whether any of you believe it or not, we're all supposed to be on the same side here. Or have you forgotten it's the Russkies we're supposed to be playing with, this time out?" Anderson and the other officers had briefed the commandos on the mission soon after the sub had left Holy Loch, and they were now far along with the actual operational planning.

"Look, Callahan, some of us are getting pretty damned sick of having you high-and-mighty SEAL boys ragging on us all the time," Joor said coldly. "Maybe we're all on the same side, but some of us don't like being second-class citizens. So just get the fuck off our backs, will ya?"

"Don't push it," the Master Chief said. "You guys are part of the team. Nobody denies it. You've got an important job to do, same as we do."

"Yeah," Woods said in a stage whisper. " 'Cept they get to do it from inside a floating taxicab . . ."

"Belay that, Woods!" Callahan snapped. "I mean it! Unless you want to swim to the beach without an SDV, and then swim back when you're tired and fcd up and the whole goddamned Russian Navy is out looking for you, *lay off.*"

"Well, thanks, Master Chief," Briggs said. "We appreciate the support."

"And you guys had better start acting your age, too," Callahan went on as if Briggs hadn't spoken. "If you want to be treated like part of our team, then you'd damn well better start *acting* like it. And our first rule is, we look after our own. If all you people are going to do is take digs at Lieutenant Gunn, then you'd better believe we're going to treat you like outsiders. *He's one of us,* fer Chrissakes! Get it through your thick skulls and stop trying to stir up trouble."

"Can't we be loyal to our officer?" Briggs asked quietly. "Or does that only work for you SEALs?"

Callahan shrugged. "Hell, I hope you're loyal to your CO," he said. "Follow his orders, watch his back, and punch out anybody that badmouths him in a bar where you're drinking. But don't you start trying to turn this mission into some kind of competition between Mr. Gunn and Lieutenant Harriman. Your man doesn't have a leg to stand on, Briggs. He may not like it, but Mr. Gunn's in charge of the op. So we all take his orders, including Lieutenant Harriman . . . and including you guys. You can be loyal to your officer without being *disloyal* to anybody else. You get me?"

"Okay, okay, Master Chief," Briggs said. "You've made your point. Get off your soapbox, already."

Callahan gave him a chilly, humorless smile. "Better hope I stay on top of the soapbox, son," he said. "Because up here I can't give you a bloody nose if you keep mouthing off."

Silence reigned for several long seconds. It was Silverwolf who finally broke it. "Hey, Master Chief, you never said how you got to be a bluenose."

"Sonny, I'd tell you about it," Callahan said with another grin. "But it was a secret mission for the suits from Langley, and if I told you, I'd have to kill you. Since we can't afford anymore casualties now while we're still on the way in, I'll have to wait. Maybe I'll tell you after we get done with the op."

"Thanks anyway, Master Chief," Silverwolf said hastily, playing up to Callahan's game. "I guess I'm not really all that curious after all."

"Funny, that's what everybody says when I explain things to them," the veteran said, shaking his head. "I wonder why that is?"

"Can't imagine, Master Chief," Silverwolf said solemnly. He caught a twinkle in the older SEAL's eye.

Control Room, USS *Pittsburgh*
The Norwegian Sea
1645 hours GMT

Chase and Latham were studying the automatic plotting board, which constantly updated the boat's position and course on a scrolling electronically generated chart. As the indicator reached a line on the map, the two officers exchanged glances and grins. "Make a note for the log, XO," Chase said loudly. "At 1645 hours Zulu, *Pittsburgh* crossed the Circle."

There were a couple of loud cheers from elsewhere around the bridge, and not just from the enlisted men. Quimby, the Dive Officer, was beaming broadly, and Stone Jackson was making a thumbs-up gesture.

"I guess old King Neptune decided we were all right, huh?" Jackson commented with a lopsided smile. "That's a relief."

"Man, who'd've thought it?" Quimby said. "A plank

owner and a bluenose, all on the same cruise! All that's left is to turn around and head south so we can cross the Line, too!"

"Sorry, Mr. Quimby," Chase told him. "Not this trip. We have to leave something for you to do next time you're on sea duty. Maybe when you have Mr. Latham's job you can become a shellback."

He gestured to Latham, and they turned back to examine the chart once more. "All right, Rick, I think it's time we got back on a more direct course," Chase said quietly. Since leaving the vicinity of Trondheim, the American subs had been heading more west than north, cutting a wide circle through the Norwegian Sea that kept them moving away from the coast of Norway. Chase and Gordon had decided on the route during the conference the night before. Both were still worried about the Alfa that the *Pittsburgh* had led off, fearing that it might still be lurking in the neighborhood trying to pick up their scent. There was even a chance the Russian captain might have put other boats in the area on the lookout. The last thing the Americans needed was to have more Soviet attention, so they had set their course to look like they were heading toward *Pittsburgh*'s previous patrol sector off Iceland, only edging to the north gradually as they went.

Now they were well clear of the Norwegian coastline, and just across the Arctic Circle, with no sign of company. They'd been running slow with towed arrays deployed and a close watch kept on the sonar readouts, so Chase was confident they'd come this far without being spotted and trailed again.

Latham nodded. "We've lost enough time as it is," he said, sounding uncharacteristically edgy. "It's bad enough knowing we're sailing right into the Bears' backyard, but stretching it out like this is going to make me old and gray before my time, Skipper."

"Sure. And Rodriguez is looking for tickets to a rock concert." Chase smiled briefly, then got serious again.

"Okay, alter course and make for North Cape. Keep the speed down low enough to allow us to use the array and have some chance of hearing what's what out there, but pick up the pace. We want to get in to the White Sea before the Russians have the current sub model in full production and are starting to test something new. I don't think Admiral Goldman would appreciate that kind of a delay, do you?"

Tuesday, 6 August 1985

Control Room, USS *Pittsburgh*
Gateway Station, Off the Mouth of the White Sea
0235 hours GMT

"Stop engine," Chase ordered.

"Stop engine, aye aye," Lieutenant Quimby echoed.

Pittsburgh became still, almost deathly quiet as the single screw stopped spinning and she floated free, submerged under a hundred feet of water just outside the entrance to the channel that led from the Barents Sea past the Kola and Kanin Peninsulas and into the constricted waters of the White Sea.

They were still nearly two hundred miles from their ultimate destination. But here the two American subs would part company for a time. These well-patrolled waters off the northern coast of the Soviet Union were dangerous enough for a single sub to attempt to penetrate. For two to go in simultaneously was an open invitation to disaster, so they had made the decision back at Holy Loch to let *Bluefin* proceed toward Severodvinsk on her own, with *Pittsburgh* holding back and entering the White Sea later for her own cautious look around.

Chase wasn't too happy with the plan, on the whole,

but given the nature of the mission and the location of the target he hadn't been able to come up with any decent alternatives. *Pittsburgh* might have gone in first to scout things out, quieter than *Bluefin* and better able to evade contact if she was discovered. The Soviets were used to the idea of American attack subs probing their defenses here, and if they had discovered a Los Angeles class sub beating at their back door they no doubt would have run her off, but not overreacted. But sending *Pittsburgh* in first risked stirring things up and making it impossible for *Bluefin* to go in to launch the SEALs on their twin missions. Gordon had been insistent that his sub should be the one to go first, on the assumption that she could get her passengers in range to do their jobs even if the Russians realized something was up and increased their coastal patrols, making further entrances into the White Sea chancy.

It made sense, and Chase would probably have argued the same way if he had commanded *Bluefin*. But as it was, the specter of Goldman's order, the one about abandoning *Bluefin* if need be, continued to raise his hackles.

"Anything out there, Rick?"

Latham looked up from the sonar repeater station, where he had been studying information relayed from the sonar shack in real time. "Nothing close, sir. There's a Kresta II heading our way out of the White Sea, close in to the Kola Peninsula and running like a bat out of hell. I doubt she could hear us if you were holding tryouts for a marching band aboard. The Udaloy we spotted earlier is maintaining course and speed. Still looks like a standard patrol sweep, and still well clear of us."

"No subs?"

"Nothing we can see. If Paxton is out here anywhere, he's too quiet to spot." Captain Ronald Paxton commanded the USS *Queenfish*, a Sturgeon class attack sub assigned to Gatekeeper duty. Almost from the beginning of the Cold War, American subs had been kept on duty there, watching the mouth of the White Sea and studying the movements of the Soviet Red Banner Northern Fleet. *Queenfish* had not been contacted as part of Operation Arctic Fox, and if possible was to be kept out of the loop entirely, on direct orders from Dreyfuss and the NSA. The suits didn't like to let one group of assets know what another one was doing, as usual. But Chase knew that Paxton, whom he had served under once, would take an interest if anything untoward started happening, such as a shooting match in Russian waters.

"He might be anywhere from here to Murmansk," Chase said quietly. While Gateway Station was considered to be here, in the strait that led to the White Sea, the sub assigned here had a broad responsibility for watching much more than just this one small but important area. *Queenfish* might be keeping an eye on Soviet fleet exercises in the Barents Sea, or checking on shipping movements around Murmansk, or studying the approaches to the underground submarine base at Polyarny far up the Kola Peninsula. As always, the fleet was overworked and understrength, and even the drive to rebuild the six-hundred-ship Navy under President Reagan's leadership hadn't made much of a dent in that old problem.

"Conn, Sonar," Franco's voice announced from the intercom. "Bluefin's passing us now."

Godspeed, Frank, Chase thought. *Take good care of the old girl. And of yourself.*

Control Room, USS *Bluefin*
Gateway Station
0242 hours GMT

"Make it periscope depth, Mr. Hogan," Frank Gordon said quietly. He gripped the rail by the command station and leaned forward a little to watch the byplay as Hogan passed the order to Lieutenant Shelby, and he relayed the instructions to the planesman and to Master Chief Preston, who was manning the ballast controls.

Bluefin was at General Quarters, with all stations manned and ready for action. Gordon's first string of officers and enlisted men was in place, the people he trusted most after months of service together. He couldn't maintain this level of readiness for long, but for this first phase of penetrating Soviet waters he wanted his best men on the job. Later—if there was a later— there would be a chance to relax their vigilance, once they had passed the treacherous entrance to the White Sea.

The strait between the Kola and Kanin Peninsulas averaged about fifty miles wide, not exactly a dangerously tight passage like the Straits of Gibraltar, the Bosporus, or the Kattegut between Denmark and Norway. The problem was, the passage was close to a hundred and twenty five miles long, and averaged around three hundred feet in depth. A submarine passing in or out of the White Sea was in shallow waters for a *long* time, and that meant she risked detection for far too long. And, once detected, her maneuvering room was limited. Fifty miles from one peninsula to the other might sound like a lot of space, but not when you couldn't get deep enough to hide from enemy sonar searches without risking scraping your hull on the bottom.

Then there was the fact that this strait was close to several major Soviet military bases. It was constantly patrolled by ships ranging from tiny torpedo boats up to cruisers, plus aircraft equipped for ASW operations overflying the area regularly. And there would be subs operating in these waters, too, some stationed here just to watch out for intruding Americans. Gordon could still picture in his mind the tension on Captain Daniel Brady's face when *Sea Devil* had finally started on her way into the White Sea, nine years ago. Brady had waited for a passing freighter heading for Archangel and dropped *Sea Devil* into her baffles so close that Russian sonars just hadn't been able to detect the American sub, a gutsy maneuver that had depended entirely on their staying close enough behind their shield to stay hidden, yet never surge ahead far enough for a collision.

Bluefin didn't have the luxury of waiting for a freighter. She had to get to her target as soon as possible, and that meant tackling the long and dangerous passage on her own. At least they were still confident that the bulk of the Soviet Red Banner Northern Fleet was tied up on maneuvers. The last set of satellite recon photos transmitted through the SSIX satellite link had shown a large number of Russian ships concentrated at the eastern end of the Barents Sea, including the carrier *Kiev* and other large ships. Hopefully the ships they'd left behind would be stretched thin enough to let the Americans slip past even without a convenient shield to hide behind.

"Periscope depth," Shelby reported.

"Periscope depth, Captain," Hogan echoed.

Bluefin was now riding submerged at a depth of sixty feet as she glided quietly through the waters just outside the entrance to the long passage. Gordon couldn't help but feel exposed, but it was necessary. A brief period near the surface was essential, in fact, to everything else they would be trying to do in the next few hours.

"Mr. Hogan, raise the ECM mast, if you please," he ordered.

"Raise ECM mast, aye aye, sir," the Exec responded.

As Hogan passed the orders down the chain of command, Gordon tried not to show the impatience that was rising within him. This intricate dance was all a part of the standard routine of a sub in *Bluefin*'s position, but that didn't make it any easier for Gordon to accept it. They were poised on the very brink of an operation that would make *Bluefin*'s name shine in the annals of the Silent Service, and Gordon begrudged every minute they had to spend on these preliminaries, every second they had to run exposed so close to the surface.

Yet without taking each of those dance steps, *Bluefin* could end up in serious trouble. All of this was routine precisely because it was so critically important to the safety of the sub, her crew, her passengers, and their mission. The Electronic Countermeasures Mast was one of several specialized pieces of equipment mounted on the submarine's fairweather. When raised, it would poke barely five feet above the surface of the water, but it would be able to detect any radar pulses on the surface. The information they gathered would tell Gordon if anyone was using radar from aircraft or distant ships to search these waters, and the type of detection equipment being used—which could often point to the nature of whatever was doing the searching. Since modern radar sweeps could pick up something as small as a periscope at ranges of up to forty nautical miles, it was vitally important that *Bluefin* be aware of what might be scanning the area before they proceeded any farther.

A few minutes passed in silence before Hogan was able to turn back to Gordon with the report from the ECM station. "All clear, sir," he said. "No radar detected."

"Thank you, XO," Gordon replied formally. He turned away from the OOD station and touched the stud that raised the Mark 18 search periscope on the starboard side of the platform. He began a slow, careful visual search of the surface around *Bluefin*'s position, using a low-light setting that made the view clear as day even in the darkness that prevailed above. After he had taken the periscope through a full 360 degrees without noting anything threatening in view, he lowered the scope once again. "Pass the word to the comm shack," he said. "Raise the radio mast. Mr. Lords?"

"Sir?" Lieutenant Dave Lords, *Bluefin*'s Navigation Officer, responded from his post near the chart tables.

"Update our position from the GPS. This will be our last chance to use it for a while, so make sure you've got us fixed *precisely*."

"Aye aye, sir," Lords replied crisply. Gordon thought he sounded a little stiff, as if he resented having the captain put that much emphasis on a job he could very nearly do in his sleep, but Gordon wasn't concerned with the possible hurt feelings of his navigator. What he was concerned with was good navigation, and he aimed to see that was just what they had.

Submarines operating in the ocean depths couldn't count on the old reliable methods of navigation at sea. You couldn't shoot the stars with a sextant, for example, when you stayed submerged for perhaps months at a time. Even modern sophisticated navigation aids weren't available to the sub skipper, as these mostly relied on radio contact with the outside world, and radio—except the slow and cumbersome ELF system—wasn't available underwater either.

So subs were limited to a handful of navigational techniques. One was to match up sonar readings of bottom contours with detailed charts. Sonar was getting so accurate that it was now possible to model the bottom terrain around a sub accurately as she traveled, and by comparing this model to existing charts a good navigator could pinpoint position with surprising accuracy. Unfortunately, that technique required a set of detailed charts to work with, and the White Sea simply wasn't that well-known. Gordon had the nine-year-old charts from *Sea Devil*'s cruise, charts that he had made himself as Navigation Officer under Captain Brady, but they were far from complete. He could use them for a few specific purposes, like locating the deep channel that led in close to Archangel and Severodvinsk, but he wasn't about to place his ship and the mission itself entirely at the mercy of that one set of incomplete charts.

That left SINS, the Submarine Inertial Navigation System. SINS used a computer hooked up to three gyroscopes and three accelerometers to constantly record every motion of the boat in three directions. The computer kept track of all this information to produce a continuously updated report of the submarine's position relative to a specific point of departure. It was a phenomenally accurate system; given an accurate idea of the boat's starting point, SINS could plot a current location precise to within a hundred yards or less.

But errors did creep in over time as a result of tiny inaccuracies that built up gradually as the boat traveled. So before Gordon risked *Bluefin* to the unknowns of the White Sea, he wanted to get an absolutely accurate starting position, zeroing out all those inaccuracies and starting from scratch. To do that, the sub needed to raise a radio antenna above the surface long enough to get in touch with the global positioning system, a network of satellites deployed in orbit which could accurately fix their location.

Hence the trip to periscope depth, one last time before they took the plunge into hostile waters. Back in Holy Loch Chase had argued that they should do it sooner, well clear of the Russian coast, but Gordon wanted to reduce the possibility of any navigational error entering the White Sea to an absolute minimum.

Lieutenant Commander Hogan moved aft to join the Navigation Officer at his station without waiting for orders from Gordon. The XO knew the importance of an accurate fix, too, and while no one doubted Lords's competence or his dedication to his chosen profession, this was one time when it paid to be extra careful.

At last the Exec straightened up from the chart table and moved to join his captain. "Position is fixed and fed into the SINS, Skipper," he said. "Radio mast is down and secure, and we're ready to proceed."

Gordon gave him a thin smile. "Very good, Mr. Hogan. Take us down to two hundred feet, and set course for Severodvinsk. Start us off nice and slow—revs for five knots until we're sure that Kreska isn't going to pay any attention to us."

"Depth two-zero-zero, speed zero-five knots," Hogan repeated dutifully. "Course for Severodvinsk. Aye aye, sir." His voice was level, his face wore the calm, professional mask of a submarine officer doing his duty . . . but there was a gleam in Hogan's eye at the prospect of penetrating enemy waters.

Gordon was sure his own eye held that same gleam. This would be *Bluefin*'s chance to shine. . . .

SEAL Mess Hall, USS *Bluefin*
The White Sea
0618 hours GMT

Gunn sipped at his orange juice absentmindedly, his full attention focused on the blowup of the satellite photo of the shipyard at Severodvinsk that was spread out on the table in front of him. An open notebook lay beside the photo, and Gunn tapped a pencil on the blank page as he studied the facility and went over the plans for the recon operations one more time. He barely registered the approach of someone coming up behind him.

"Mind if I sit, Gunn?" a gruff voice demanded.

He looked up, startled, straight into the steady gaze of Lieutenant Vincent Harriman. The SDV platoon leader had a breakfast tray in his hands and a blank, unreadable expression on his craggy features.

Gunn glanced around the mess hall. There was plenty of free space, even with both platoons spread out enjoying their meals. The possibility of Harriman actually *wanting* to join him left him so bemused that he just shrugged. "Suit yourself, Lieutenant," he said, and turned his attention back to the recon photo.

"Looks like tomorrow's the day," Harriman said as he sat down opposite Gunn.

"If this goddamned boat ever gets us to the target," Gunn responded automatically. It was the same reply he'd made every time one of the SEALs commented on their progress, and it was becoming second nature by now. First they'd had the long trip from the Norwegian Coast to Gateway Station, broken only by the bluenose ceremony on the first day of the trip. Now they were creeping down the long passage into the White Sea, sometimes running as fast as fifteen or twenty knots, other times cutting power entirely to drift for seemingly endless minutes as the sub's crew waited for some passing menace to move past.

Gunn had heard every change in the pitch of the props, every start and stop ordered by the control room, from his berth over the course of a long and sleepless night. An old hand like Master Chief Callahan could sleep anytime, anyplace, on a moment's notice, and wake up ready for anything, but not Bernard Gunn. Not when he was worried about bringing off the recon mission successfully, about the burden of being in command. He'd led the stick of SEALs against the radio station on Grenada, so he already had experience of leading men into a dangerous situation. In a way, experience made things worse for him. Grenada had been a disaster from start to finish, and though he'd carried out his mission, everything had gone sour. He hadn't lost any of his men, but every one of the seven SEALs had been wounded in the fighting, a couple of them seriously. He'd been hit twice himself, and still had the scars on his left arm and across his ribs to prove it.

He knew how many things could go wrong on any op, whether it was a quick sneak-and-peek into a hostile harbor, or a combat mission like Grenada. The old axiom "No battle plan survives contact with the enemy" was the kind of thing that could always get you laughs when you quoted it at a party . . . but it was entirely too true.

And the full weight of bringing his SEAL platoon through *this* mission rested entirely on his shoulders now. It wasn't a feeling he enjoyed.

"You look like you're getting ready to face a firing

squad, not a recon op, Gunn," Harriman commented. "Feeling the pressure?"

"I'll manage," Gunn told him sharply.

The SDV officer held up a beefy hand. "I wasn't trying to make a crack," he said quickly. "Jesus, you're prickly!"

"Maybe I've got a good reason," Gunn said. He took another sip of orange juice and tried to keep his temper in check. "Like having to fight off pushy bastards who want to take my platoon!"

"Yeah . . ." Harriman actually cracked a smile, faint and a bit forced, but a smile nonetheless. "Yeah, maybe I'd be touchy if somebody had done that to me, come to think of it." He devoted a moment to carving up a sausage and taking a bite, then set knife and fork down and fixed Gunn with that same disconcerting look the younger man had noticed before. "Look, Gunn . . . we both know you and I are about as likely to get along as two jarheads fighting over the only piece of tail in a Tijuana whorehouse. I still think I should've had a slot with the SEALs, and God knows you'd've been better at all the technical crap I've had to learn . . ." He trailed off, then cleared his throat. "Anyway, what I'm trying to say is this. I've been doing a lot of thinking the last few days, and I was dead wrong to try to cut you out the way I did."

Gunn raised an eyebrow. "Really? Welcome to the Navy, Lieutenant."

The gibe sent a quick, angry flush across Harriman's face, but he controlled his reaction quickly and even forced another thin smile. "Yeah. If somebody had tried that stunt on me, I'd've kicked his ass from one end of this sardine can to the other, and then flushed him out of a torpedo tube for good measure." He paused. "Gunn, you're the boss, whether I like it or not. And I want you to know that you can count on me and my boys to get your lot in and out of the target. We're pretty good at our jobs, too, you know."

"I never doubted that, Lieutenant," Gunn said quietly. He wasn't sure if Harriman's gesture was genuine, or just empty words to cover his own tail in case there were repercussions from the confrontation after Anderson's injury. The best way to deal with the man was to stay as aloof as possible, and say no more than necessary.

"Thanks," Harriman said. He paused for a long moment. "Look, like I said, you're the boss, and I'm sure you're not in any mood to take advice from me. But whatever you think about me or my way of doing things, I *have* been around a while longer than you, and I'm going to give you some advice whether you're in the mood or not . . . as one officer to another."

"And that is?"

"You're pushing yourself too hard, Gunn. I've been watching you since, well, since you took over the platoon, and it's pretty damned clear you're worrying yourself half to death trying to plan this op." His gesture took in the recon photo on the table between them. "Wrestling with this shit at breakfast . . . tossing and turning in your bunk half the night . . . by the time you and your boys make your swim into the harbor, you're going to be a wreck. And what good will that do your platoon then, huh, kid?"

"There's still a lot of details—"

"And you need to be on top of every one of them," Harriman finished for him. "Because otherwise you might make a mistake, and then people might think old Bad-Ass Harriman was right all along and should've taken command. Right?"

"No!" Gunn said hotly. Then, a moment later, he shook his head. "Maybe. Hell, Lieutenant, you think I don't remember some of those days at BUD/S when it was all I could do to keep from going to ring the bell because I didn't know if I was up to it?" "Ringing the bell" was the way trainees in the Basic Underwater Demolition/SEAL course announced that they'd had enough of the grueling training program. Once a man rang the bell he was out of the program, washed out. "I'm a SEAL and damned proud of it. But it was close. And I've got twelve men relying on me to be a SEAL *and* an officer and get them through this op in one piece. Sure, I've got doubts. I guess you wouldn't, if you were in charge."

Harriman laughed. "And me without my deeds to Florida swampland! Come on, kid, wake up. If you weren't worried you wouldn't be human . . . and then the rest of us would be pretty damned worried instead. You listen to me, just this one time, Gunn. It's okay to be worried. It's okay to have doubts. But it's a disaster waiting to happen if you get yourself so knotted up now that you can't do your job when the time comes. Now I did you a bad turn in the first place by challenging your right to take command. So I'll do you a favor to make up for it. Ease up. I know from the last couple of briefings that you've got damn near everything covered, so quit trying to second-guess yourself. Get some rest, and that way you'll be in better shape to make the hard calls if something does go wrong on the mission." Harriman regarded him for a few moments in silence before finishing. "And if you won't take the advice from me, than get yourself a second opinion, Gunn. Talk to Lieutenant Anderson. I'll bet he'll tell you the same damn thing . . . and I'll bet you believe it when he tells you, too."

"Maybe so . . ." Gunn trailed off, thoughtful. "Why the sudden interest in my well-being, Lieutenant? Wouldn't you look better if I screwed up?"

The other officer drew in a sharp breath, stiffening. "Listen to me, Gunn. I'll only say this once. All I want is to see this op go down right. I thought at first that you were too green to be in charge, and I tried to fix the problem the only way I could think to do it. Now that I've seen I was wrong, the best way I can make sure this mission works the way it should is to make sure you *are* up to the job. You get me?"

"Yeah, I hear you, Lieutenant." Gunn shrugged. He didn't quite believe Harriman, but on reflection he wondered if the SDV officer himself really understood what drove him. Vince Harriman needed to prove himself, to show that he could have been a SEAL, but maybe he wasn't entirely aware of it. And his desire to show his own abilities didn't exclude a genuine dedication to the mission.

The man would never be likable, Gunn told himself. But he was a fellow officer ... and he'd been through Hell Week, just like any SEAL. That was the only thing that really mattered, as far as SEALs were concerned.

"I'll think about what you've said, Lieutenant," Gunn said at length. "And I'll be hoping your advice will be just as good once we're buckled in to those oversize torpedoes of yours and on our way to Severodvinsk."

Control Room, USS *Pittsburgh*
Gateway Station
0827 hours GMT

"Conn, Sonar. Positive ID on target Sierra One. She's *Queenfish*, Skipper. No doubt about it."

Chase fought the urge to give a little sigh of relief, mindful of the image of sub captains as steel-nerved, strong, silent types who never reacted, whether the news was good or bad. But he did relax a strong grip on the railing of the watch officer's station as he straightened up, and he thought he detected just a hint of a smile on Lieutenant Quimby's face as the Dive Officer happened to meet his eyes.

There hadn't been much traffic through the mouth of the White Sea since *Bluefin* had entered the channel, and most of what they had seen so far had been either big, slow-moving merchant ships or a few relatively light patrol boats. The exercises that had drawn away the bulk of the Soviet Red Banner Northern Fleet had certainly reduced traffic in this important thoroughfare. But Chase was still concerned about the possibility of submarines operating in the area. A principal reason for letting *Bluefin* go in first had been the possibility that any lurking Russian boats might have given itself away powering up to pursue her, which would have left Chase to decide what to do about it. But nothing of the sort had materialized . . . until Chief Franco had reported the submerged contact heading their way from the direction of Murmansk.

But it was the American boat they had hoped to encounter here at Gateway Station. Captain Paxton's timing had been perfect, Chase reflected. *Pittsburgh* had to start making her own way into the White Sea soon in order to link up with Gordon's boat in time for *Bluefin* to complete the recon mission and extract herself from the dangerous waters off Severodvinsk.

He picked up the intercom mike. "Sonar, Conn. Keep your ears peeled down there."

"Aye aye, sir," Franco replied.

"Mr. Quimby," Chase went on, replacing the mike. "Get us under way. Course two-nine-six degrees, speed ten knots. Maintain our present depth."

"Ahead at ten knots on course two-nine-six, aye aye, sir," Quimby replied. He looked and sounded a little mystified.

"Something wrong, Lieutenant?" Chase asked.

"Er . . . no, sir," the Dive Officer said. He started to turn away to carry out the orders, but Chase's voice made him check the motion.

"We want to contact *Queenfish* before we enter the White Sea, Mr. Quimby," Chase said levelly. "Now, we could wait for her to join us here, and then scare the pants off of every man aboard by suddenly announcing our presence. And, quite possibly, some junior Weapons Officer with a nervous trigger finger might just punch the panic button and send a couple of torps our way at short range." He smiled. "Or we can meet them halfway, and give their sonar boys plenty of time to spot us and look us up in their files. They won't have *Pittsburgh*'s signature on record, since they started their patrol while we were still finishing sea trials. But they'll recognize us as a Los Angeles boat, and hopefully they'll decide not to shoot."

"H-hopefully, sir?" Quimby looked more confused now.

"Hopefully, I say, Mr. Quimby. After all, some of those Sturgeon class crews are a little jealous of us lucky stiffs who get to ride around in these brand-new luxury models."

A few of the ratings scattered around the control room chuckled at that. There was a healthy rivalry between the crews of older submarines and those aboard the new Los Angeles boats, but anyone who had been forced to put up with some of the compromises *Pittsburgh* and her sister ships had been forced to adopt—like the requirement for a large portion of the crew to hot-bunk instead of having their own private berths—knew that there was nothing luxurious about service aboard the newest generation of attack subs.

Pittsburgh got under way, gathering speed so smoothly that the motion might hardly have been noticed by an outsider. But Chase was attuned to his boat's every vibration. He could feel the beat of the engine, driven by the reactor that lay at the very heart of the attack sub. Some submariners that he knew tried not to think too much about sailing with a nuclear reactor running closer than the length of a football field to anyplace they could be on board. In the early years of the nuclear Navy, misconceptions and mythology had run wild, and it had taken a hardy breed of men to put those fears aside and serve on the new boats. Today there were fewer fears, thanks to the careful schooling given to every man who earned his "dolphins" as a submariner, but it still wasn't easy for some to get past the thoughts of radiation bombarding the crewmen . . . or the awful consequences of a nuclear disaster at sea.

Chase, though, had never shared in those fears. He knew just how much safety had mattered to the men who had designed each successive generation of nuclear submarine, guided by the precepts of the eccentric but brilliant mind of old Hyman Rickover. Unlike the Soviets, who were reputed to skimp on the shielding needed to safeguard crewmen from a reactor's radiation, the shipbuilders at the Electric Boat Division of General Dynamics never lost sight of the human side of the submarine equation. And in three decades of operating nuclear boats at sea, none had yet been lost as a result of a reactor problem.

For Mike Chase, the nuclear submarine wasn't something to fear. It was the ultimate weapon in the Navy's arsenal: fast, stealthy, able to go anywhere and carry out just about any mission. And after years of operating in covert-operations subs under Admiral Goldman, he felt nothing but pride in finally having a nuclear attack boat's deck under his feet.

He roused himself from his reverie to check the sonar repeater. The two American submarines were drawing close together now, and Chase gave Quimby a curt order to stop the boat. As the propeller shut down, *Pittsburgh* drifted free in the cold, still water. Within minutes *Queenfish* had halted as well, less than a hundred yards away.

Chase picked up the intercom microphone. "Communications, Conn," he said. "Patch me into the Gertrude."

"Communications, aye aye."

For a long moment there was silence in the control room as the communications technicians switched their circuits to activate *Pittsburgh*'s Gertrude system. It was one of the most archaic means of communication in use in the Navy, essentially unchanged from the days of the old World War II diesel boats his father had sailed in.

An underwater telephone system, it used simple sound
waves over short distances—longer ranges weren't possible because sound waves didn't carry very far in water.
The Gertrude system wasn't used very often in the
sound-conscious modern submarine fleet, but it was still
the one reliable method for short-range ship-to-ship contact.

Finally, the communications shack announced that
they were ready, and Chase picked up a handset.
"*Queenfish*, *Queenfish*, are you receiving?"

It didn't take long for the other boat to reply. Presumably Captain Paxton had ordered his own Gertrude
rigged as soon as he realized another American sub
wanted to talk to him. "*Receiving five-by-five*," came the
response. "*What ship?*"

"This is USS *Pittsburgh*, *Queenfish*," Chase said.
":SSN Seven-Two-Zero. Mike Chase, commanding."

"Chase? You old barracuda, who did you have dirt on
to get yourself a brand-new attack boat?" Even with the
distortion caused by the combination of water and
the scrambling/descrambling process on each end of the
transmission, Chase recognized Paxton's characteristic
laugh, once described by an admiral as "a cross between
a braying, seagoing donkey and a dolphin on Valium."

"If you're my relief, Chase," Paxton went on, "then
you're a month early. And while I'm not one to look a
gift horse in the mouth, Our Lords and Masters aren't
usually that generous. Care to bring me up to speed?"

Chase proceeded to explain the broad outlines of the
mission, without going into details about what *Bluefin*
and *Pittsburgh* were supposed to bring back from the
White Sea. That was need-to-know information, and
Paxton didn't need specifics. But he did explain that
Bluefin had already gone in, and that *Pittsburgh* was due
to follow shortly . . . and that both boats would be much
more secure if an American sub was standing by at Gateway Station to hold the door open for them, just in case
they needed help with the extraction.

Back in Holy Loch, there had been a major debate on involving *Queenfish* in this way. Chase and Gordon had both argued strongly that a third sub covering the mouth of the long strait into the White Sea would greatly increase the chances of *somebody* getting out with the information they were being sent to secure. Dreyfuss, the NSA suit, had been against involving anyone else as a matter of principle. In his world, you only revealed what you absolutely had to, and to as few people as possible. Surprisingly, Goldman had sided with him, up to a point.

The original proposal had been to alert *Queenfish* to be on station and request her cooperation with the other two subs, but the admiral had been against it because of the threat that their codes might be compromised. Even the most basic rendezvous instructions might have tipped off a Soviet radio watch armed with Navy codes provided by the Walkers that something was going on near the White Sea, and that could have been enough to ruin everything. So the final decision had been to leave *Queenfish* in the dark until and unless *Pittsburgh* or *Bluefin* could contact her.

It was a poor compromise, Chase thought as he explained the situation over the Gertrude. After all, Paxton's commission predated either Chase or Gordon, which made him the senior officer. If he got stuffy about operations being conducted on his turf . . . or if he turned out to be the glory-hunting type who would insist on being at the heart of the action instead of simply providing the support the other two subs required . . . there wasn't much Chase or Gordon could do about it. Not without orders straight from Goldman or some other flag officer spelling things out.

Luckily, Chase's worries were quickly dispelled.

"Understood, Captain," Paxton replied after Chase had finished. "You need us to lie doggo here and keep an eye on the door for you. Sounds a hell of a lot better than scraping my bottom in the White Sea with you guys. A vacation, even."

"Just don't get so busy working on your tans that you don't keep an eye out for us, *Queenfish*," Chase said, chuckling. "It's possible that we're going to be coming out a hell of a lot faster than we're going in, and maybe with some angry dogs snapping at our heels."

"We'll be here, *Pittsburgh*," Paxton said. "Count on it. But you'd better be careful in there. I doubt the brass back at the five-sided squirrel cage would be too happy if you went and scratched the paint on that new toy you're driving."

"Thanks for the warning," Chase said. "I'll try to keep it in mind. Thanks again, Captain. *Pittsburgh* out." He returned the handset to its cradle and turned to look down at Quimby. "Lieutenant, prepare to get us under way again. Five knots to start, and maintain our depth. We'll be increasing speed once we see what the traffic is like."

"Aye aye, sir," Quimby responded. "Course?"

"Huddle with the Navigator, Mr. Quimby. Best course for Severodvinsk."

He straightened up and turned his attention back to the sonar repeater.

Chase thought he knew what Caesar had felt as he ordered the legions across the Rubicon.

Wednesday, 7 August 1985

Control Room, USS *Bluefin*
The White Sea
1225 hours GMT

Frank Gordon leaned over the plotting table and carefully studied the chart spread out there. "I keep expecting the Old Man to chew me out for taking too long," he said abstractedly, hardly realizing he was talking out loud.

"This time out you *are* the Old Man, Captain," Hogan responded from the other side of the table.

"Yeah, but I can still hear Captain Brady's voice in the back of my head. 'For the love of God, Mr. Gordon, haven't you narrowed it down yet? You *do* have us *somewhere* in the White Sea, I hope?' "

"Sounds like a real bastard of a CO, sir," Hogan said sympathetically.

"Regular slave-driver, Mr. Hogan," Gordon told him. "And the best damned skipper you could possibly have if you wanted to learn a thing or two about running a boat. Of course, you're lucky. You get a captain who'll teach you everything and still go easy on you." He smiled at his Exec. "Isn't that right?"

"If you say so, Skipper," Hogan returned blandly. Both men laughed, but their laughter was strained. It had taken better than thirty hours to get this far, hours filled with constant stress. Their voyage across the White Sea had been without serious incident, although frequent sonar contacts had confirmed what everyone on board already knew, that this stretch of ocean was a regular superhighway for the Soviet Red Banner Northern Fleet. They had spotted several surface ships, both warships and merchantmen, plus at least three different submarines during their trip. All of the subs had conformed to known sonar signatures, and apparently none of them had noticed the intruder slipping quietly into their midst. Or so they hoped. Gordon was well aware of the fact that some enemy sub could have picked them up in passing and be following close behind, waiting for a chance to strike without warning.

Probably not, he told himself. The Soviets would be far too sensitive about these home-port waters to play a game of tag. If they thought an American sub was nearby, they would flush it out and send it packing, no doubt with an escalating scale of aggressiveness. Gordon figured they would start by simply making their presence known, and by calling for support from surface ships and coastal patrol boats. They would follow that by going to active sonar pinging, and by having their sub or subs in the neighborhood flood their torpedo tubes as if preparing to fire, a very distinctive sound when heard over sonar that was one of a sub captain's greatest dreads.

If the American intruder hadn't gotten the message by then, the Russians might try more strenuous methods of getting their point across, such as games of undersea chicken or a couple of "practice runs" with torpedoes or depth charges. That was how accidents happened at sea. If an American submarine was damaged deep inside the territorial waters of the Soviet Union . . . well, sorry, comrade, but how could *we* know your spy ship was there? That was the answer they'd get back in Washington, and there would be precious little support for the U.S. position if outraged officials protested the incident.

That was the way the Cold War chess game was played. And in this case the pawns were Navy SEALs, while the two American subs . . . What were they? Bishops? No, Gordon decided with an inward grin. Knights, that was it. The ones with the subtle moves who surfaced unexpectedly in the middle of the board to wreak havoc on a carefully devised plan.

Gordon liked the idea of being a knight. And he wasn't going to allow the Russians to play out this little chess game without handing them a few crooked dogleg moves along the way.

"Right . . . now let's see what we've got here." The old charts from *Sea Devil* had been transferred to transparencies that could be overlaid onto the Mapping Sonar Display on the plotting table, so they could compare the terrain around the boat with the features shown on the old charts. It was a fussy job, made all the harder by the fact that the *Sea Devil* charts covered only a relatively small part of the White Sea. Most of these waters were still mostly unknown as far as Western sailors were concerned, so the trick was to find a match with something they *did* know and proceed from there.

Of course, Gordon thought as he poured over the sonar imagery, all it would take would be one misidentification of a bottom feature, one simple, basic mistake in the whole process. Then, like as not, *Bluefin* would end up plowing straight into shoal water. And that would sink the mission just as fast as any torpedo or antisubmarine missile.

"What about this one, sir?" Hogan asked, tapping a blob on the sonar display that represented a roughly conical bump on the sea floor. It was too small to be called a seamount, but big enough to be a good landmark nonetheless. "This looks an awful lot like something I saw when we were flipping through those charts earlier . . ."

Gordon studied it a moment, nodding vaguely. "Yeah . . . let me think . . ." He pushed one of the *Sea Devil* charts aside, then spread out another one. "This is it, I think," he went on.

Together they positioned the transparency over the sonar display, and Hogan manipulated the controls to shift the view and zoom out until the two fit together almost perfectly. Gordon pointed at a contour line in the middle of the chart, showing gradually deepening water. It, too, lined up with a shading on the sonar display. . . .

"We have a winner," Gordon commented. "Gentlemen, we're no longer flying blind." He studied the chart for a moment, casting back to his days aboard *Sea Devil*. "We've come in about a mile to the south of the underwater channel, I believe," he said. "Mr. Hogan, get us under way again, if you please. Take us on a heading of . . . zero-one-five. Ahead slow, and maintain this depth."

"Course zero-one-five, ahead slow," Hogan repeated. "Maintain depth. Aye aye, sir."

"And don't spare the mapping sonar, either."

Bluefin crept forward, feeling her way. Even with the proper charts spread out to guide them, Gordon couldn't help but feel on edge. Maneuvering in these constricted waters had been a nightmare back when he had been *Sea Devil*'s Navigation Officer, but this time it was worse. This time, there was no Daniel Brady to take the weight of responsibility for the boat and crew on his sturdy shoulders. Now it was Frank Gordon who carried that weight, and the knowledge that the mission, the very safety of *Bluefin* and her people all depended on his judgment brought a sheen of sweat to his brow and an uneasy flutter to his stomach. He had trained for this, and he knew he was up to the ordinary demands of submarine command. But that didn't make things anymore comfortable for Frank Gordon.

But, at last, it was done. The mapping sonar clearly displayed the gentle sloping he recognized as the edge of the channel *Sea Devil* had discovered years before. *Bluefin* had reached her destination.

"Take us down to the bottom, Commander," Frank Gordon ordered formally. "This looks like a nice place to make our nest."

"Aye aye," Hogan said. "Stop engine! Fill the ballast tanks and take us to the bottom!"

Shelby picked up the orders and was passing them on, but Master Chief Preston was already operating the ballast-tank control, flooding the tanks with more seawater to give *Bluefin* negative buoyancy so that she would begin to sink deeper into the chill gray waters that surrounded her.

There was little sensation of motion as the sub slowly descended toward the level stretch of sea bottom their mapping sonar had revealed. This had turned out to be a nearly perfect spot from which to mount the rest of the op. Not only was there a smooth bottom for *Bluefin* to go to ground upon, but it was less than twelve nautical miles from the mouth of the Dvina River, and so perfectly suited as a base for the SDVs. Finally, they were fairly close to the coordinates chosen during their planning sessions back at Holy Loch for a rendezvous with *Pittsburgh* once Chase came up to join them. That wouldn't happen until sometime Thursday at the earliest . . . which gave *Bluefin* time to get settled in and to launch the first SEAL mission.

Abruptly the sub came to a stop, and the motion they hadn't been feeling before was suddenly very noticeable indeed in its absence. *Bluefin* was on the bottom, at rest. She could stay that way for days, provided she could run her snorkels to the surface from time to time in order to run her diesel engines and recharge her batteries.

That would have to come later. Just then Gordon wanted to get settled in and watch the neighborhood closely for any sign of problems.

"We're down, sir," Hogan reported unnecessarily.

"All right, people," Gordon said. "Time to start earning our pay. I want a full passive sonar sweep of the area. If there's a fish out there who's hungry enough to have his stomach growling, I want to know about it. Reduce energy use to a minimum. We'll rig the snorkel and a comm antenna once we're sure we're not getting any unwelcome visitors." He paused. "And pass the word to Mr. Gunn and Mr. Harriman. They can start loading up the SDVs anytime they want, but they don't get to go out and play until I give the word. Okay, let's get to it!"

He smiled as Hogan and the others began to carry out his orders. The mission—the real mission—was under way at last.

SDV #1
The White Sea, Off Severodvinsk
2213 hours GMT

The SDV touched the bottom with a tiny jolt, and Bernard Gunn swallowed a couple of times. This was it . . . the moment of truth.

"We're in position," Harriman's voice crackled in the intercom that was an integral part of the minisub's UBA system. "Try to keep a fix on where we are for the extraction."

Gunn fought back the urge to snap back some angry reply about not needing to be mothered. The SDV officer's warning was perfectly legitimate and by the book. "Thanks," he said, forcing his voice to remain even. "Just stay put for us, okay? It's a long swim home." Twelve miles back to *Bluefin* . . . not impossible for trained Navy divers, but not something he wanted to contemplate, either. "Right. Let's get moving."

He removed the full-face breathing mask of the on-board underwater breathing apparatus, replacing it with his own mask and rebreather mouthpiece. The other three divers in the rear compartment were doing the same. With hand signals, Gunn indicated that two of them should open the hatches overhead.

Swimming out, he took a quick inventory of his gear. It was the minimum necessary for this sort of recon mission: knife; slate; waterproof camera; flashlight; a watch on one wrist and a pressure gauge on the other; compass. If he was better equipped than the classic Naked Warrior of his grandfather's era, he was still traveling light for a SEAL. They all were.

Gunn wondered, as he checked his compass and pointed in the direction they needed to head, whether he had done the right thing as far as the platoon's organization was concerned. The original fourteen-man platoon had been set up by Anderson, with the First Squad under the lieutenant's direct command and Gunn commanding the other. Anderson had assigned Master Chief Callahan to serve as Gunn's senior NCO, to provide the younger officer with the benefit of experience that stretched back to tours in Vietnam. Even though Gunn had been in combat on Grenada, it had been clear that Anderson wanted to be sure his second squad's leadership was up to snuff no matter what.

After Anderson's injury, Gunn had been faced with deciding how to reallocate the leadership duties. He had talked it over with the convalescing lieutenant, and finally decided he should disrupt things as little as possible. Rather than swapping around Callahan and Burns, to give the First Squad the senior man, he had elected to take command of First Squad himself and leave the second under Callahan's watchful eye.

It meant a minimum disruption for the men. But it also meant that Gunn himself had been deprived in a stroke not only of Callahan's reassuring presence, but also of the men he had been training with for months. Each squad had its own unique character, its own way of doing things, and suddenly Gunn was in the company of a group of strangers. It would take some getting used to . . . but they didn't have time for a leisurely program of getting acquainted.

SEALs were professionals. They would do what they had to.

He had decided that First Squad should do the recon operation that night, to give him a chance to work with them on a fairly routine dive once before they had to tackle the more difficult full-scale excursion onshore to break in to the shipyard facility's files. Senior Chief Burns, plus Moultrie and Pond, were the men he'd chosen for the reconnaissance. More than four men would have required a second SDV, and wouldn't have done that much to increase the squad's speed or efficiency. That was something you learned early when you served in the Teams—that "more" and "bigger" didn't necessarily add up to "better" when dealing with unconventional warfare. Had the United States military realized that sooner, the course of the conflict in Vietnam might have gone considerably better.

They used the classic buddy system, splitting into pairs as they swam. Gunn was working with the big Southerner, Moultrie, while Burns was teamed with Pond. With less than a mile to cover to reach their objective, they moved quickly and confidently.

Soon Gunn held up a hand, gesturing for a halt, then pointed toward the surface. The four SEALs headed slowly upward, careful to follow the guidelines for safe decompression. Back on the *Bluefin*, Dr. Waite supervised a large decompression chamber for use after diving emergencies, but none of the men was about to play games with such a dangerous problem as decompression sickness—the bends.

Gunn's head broke water, and he raised his mask cautiously. It was late, but so far north there was still considerable light to see by. Treading water, he slowly began to turn in place, studying his surroundings. The other three SEALs bobbed to the surface as well and followed his lead. Each man was likely to pick up small details the others might miss, making multiple view-points a valuable asset.

To the south, against a backdrop of slowly rising ground, Gunn could see the sprawling grounds of the Severodvinsk shipyard. From his angle, and in this light, it didn't much resemble the satellite images and computer-generated maps he had studied ever since the first briefing at Holy Loch, but he could recognize the outsize shapes of the huge construction halls and the network of piers and docks that crowded the water's edge. It was the right place . . . and *there*, just where it was supposed to be, was the long, low, menacing shape of the newly constructed Russian submarine. The *Akula*.

Nobody knew what the Russians were calling it, beyond the rather bland designation of Project 971 picked up from their human intelligence resources inside the Russian military. *Akula* was the NATO tag, since they had run out of phonetic alphabet words to work with. The name was Russian for "shark," an appropriate handle for a new hunter-killer in the Soviet arsenal. Gunn recalled that Dreyfuss, in one of the briefing sessions, had mentioned that there had been an actual *Akula* in the Russian Navy back in the period around World War I, an early submarine design lost at sea after an accident on a mine-laying mission in the Baltic. Dreyfuss had commented then that everyone hoped the bad luck of the earlier model would rub off on this new boat, but the joke had fallen flat.

Gunn reached out to tap Burns on the arm, then pointed toward their target. The Senior Chief nodded. In silence, all four men fixed their masks and slid under the water.

As they swam toward the docks, the two teams split farther apart. Gunn and Moultrie made for the bow of the sub, while Burns and Pond headed for the boat's stern. Both teams would try to cover the entire boat two or three times over, but by dividing up from the start they made it more likely they could bring back every-

thing they needed even if something unexpected interrupted their work and forced them to break off the
reconnaissance early.

When they reached the dock area and could see the
massive, dark shape of the sub's hull stretching out in
front of them, Gunn once again went to the surface, this
time even more cautiously than before. From less than
twenty feet away, the submarine looked large and threatening, though a part of this was merely the swimmer's
perspective. The new attack boat rode no higher in the
water than any other surfaced sub, and if anything the
fairwater wasn't as tall as most submarine sails Gunn
had seen before, though it was considerably longer than
most. That gave the entire hull a racier look, like the
boat was a thoroughbred where the clunky-looking *Bluefin*, for instance, was a mere draft horse.

Gunn heard voices and froze, then forced himself to
continue treading water slowly and quietly. He didn't
want to give himself away, but neither did he want to
miss out if there was any information exchanged that
might be useful to the SEALs. The voices seemed to be
coming from the landward side of the boat, possibly near
the gangplank, but even though Gunn could hear them
fairly plainly, and spoke Russian, they were hard to understand. It was one thing to speak conversational Russian, quite another to try to piece together snatches of
someone else's exchange from a distance.

He was tempted to try to get closer, but knew that
wouldn't be the wisest move he could make at this junc-
ture.

One clear phrase reached him: ". . . good night for
testing . . ." Then one of the voices called a cheery good
night, and he heard footsteps thudding down a wooden
pier.

Gunn allowed himself to drop under the water again,
and moved closer to the hull.

The surface of the hull was covered by a rubbery material, anechoic tiles designed to absorb rather than re-

flect sound waves to confuse sonar. That was standard for Western sub designs, and had started to appear in some of the more recent Soviet types. Gunn wished there was an easy way to get under that skin to sample the hull metal itself, but there wasn't any practical way for the SEALs to check that. Hopefully they'd find something when they raided the files on shore. The Soviets had recently started using titanium, rather than steel, to build their subs, according to the briefings. This made their hulls stronger and lighter, allowing them to dive to greater depths and get more speed without increasing the size of their reactors or engines.

Moultrie found the torpedo tubes and gestured for Gunn to join him. Together they measured the outer doors to the six tubes carefully. It was hoped that the measurements of the doors would tell what type of torps the Russians were planning to use. Gunn wasn't expert enough to draw any conclusions from what the two SEALs could study, but with luck there would be other experts who could.

They worked their way slowly down the port side of the boat, the seaward side away from the pier, stopping frequently to move up or down along the gracefully curved hull to examine fittings close-up and chalk in notations or sketches on their slates. Moultrie was particularly good at rendering surprisingly detailed sketches where necessary. They also took frequent pictures, but the quality of the water around them wasn't particularly good, and Gunn worried that they might not turn out clear enough to be of use. Archangel and Severodvinsk were both fairly large cities, the shipyard facility was a busy industrial center, and the Dvina River carried factory waste from towns and manufacturing centers far inland. The water around Severodvinsk would have given a Western environmentalist nightmares.

They paused about halfway down the hull and cautiously surfaced again. Gunn and Moultrie both brought their cameras fully into play, taking exposure after exposure of the hull, the deck, and especially the fairwater and the small forest of antennae, periscopes, and other protrusions that rose above it. Again there was little the SEALs could do to identify all these esoteric components, but there were experts back home who could tell at a glance the type and model of a radar or radio antenna, which would help pin down the exact performance range of the boat's electronics suite.

Their photographic work finished for the moment, Gunn and Moultrie dived again and headed farther aft. By the time they reached the stern of the boat, they had a good idea of her size. She was about three hundred fifty feet long, with a beam just shy of forty feet. Even Gunn, who didn't know that much about submarines, could tell that her flattened shape and low sail were designed for speed. He wondered how fast she could go under ideal conditions . . . and how she stacked up against American boats like *Pittsburgh*. While studying the stern assembly he paid special attention to the propeller, one of the items that especially interested the analysts back home. The *Akula* used a single screw, seven-bladed propeller design. During the briefings at Holy Loch Admiral Goldman had told them several times that this could be significant. Apparently older Russian sub designs had frequently used twin screws and propellers with five or six blades, but there were indications that they were shifting their focus to the single propeller with seven blades in their more recent designs. It was much closer to the specs used in American boats, and tended to be much quieter, according to Goldman. And the changeover could well have been fruits of the Walker espionage activities that had forced the Soviets to take a brand-new look at their entire submarine doctrine. They made notations and took photographs, and wondered if this information was something Washington wanted to hear, or something they were dreading.

The two SEALs returned to the surface again to take more photos, this time concentrating on the stern section of the attack sub. The football-shaped housing that rose high out of the water above the stern was, according to their briefings, the preferred design for the storage of Russian towed sonar arrays. American boats like *Pittsburgh* and *Bluefin* stored their towed arrays in a long tube fitted to the port side of the submarine's hull, but the Soviets had opted for this more compact housing instead. Towed arrays, Gunn had learned, had only been added to Soviet submarines comparatively recently, the Victor III being the first class of Russian attack sub to carry them. Again, it was evidence of a comparatively new drive toward increasing the detection capability, as well as the stealthiness, of the newer Russian boats. On the other hand, the upthrust towed-array storage housing looked like it might break up the smooth lines of the hull badly enough to generate more noise. Gunn was no expert in sonar technology, but from what Dreyfuss and Goldman had explained at Holy Loch he understood that even the sounds made by water rushing past the hull of a boat could register on sonar, and the best designs for stealth were those which were smooth and sleek, without awkward projections to cause extra drag and stir up additional noisy currents. Perhaps the fact that the towed-array rig was on the centerline of the boat and aft of the larger fairwater meant that it was already in the wake caused by the sail as it moved through the water; Gordon had brought that up at one point in one of the briefings. Gunn didn't know, and didn't really want to know, all the ins and outs of submarine design. He was a SEAL. His job was to kill people and break things . . . or sometimes just photograph them.

They were working their way forward again along the starboard side when a noise in the water off to Gunn's right made him stop and turn. It was hard to see anything in the murk, but the characteristic growl of machinery was obvious. Backing away from the hull, Gunn nearly bumped into one of the pilings for the boat's pier. Signaling to Moultrie, he carefully surfaced for a quick look around.

Coming up under the dock, he was well screened from any possible observation, which turned out to be a good thing indeed. There were several small work parties visible on the sub's deck, some clustered around lines fore and aft, and one group just finishing the task of dislodging the gangplank that linked the boat to the pier. There was a pair of figures visible at the top of the sail, one scanning the not-quite-dark horizon through binoculars. Their dark uniforms and caps were distinctly different from what the other crew members were wearing, and Gunn supposed they were officers.

The sounds he had heard underwater had to be the engine starting; the *Akula* was getting under way. So the test runs had, indeed, started. The SEALs had been lucky to find the boat in port when they arrived. There was no telling if it would be out on maneuvers for an hour, a day, or a week. Certainly they couldn't count on being able to learn anything more from this sort of recon swim.

Gunn wondered if they had enough of the data Dreyfuss and the NSA analysts needed, or if the raid onshore was still critical to the success of the mission. Lieutenant Anderson had always made it plain that he didn't care for the covert op against the shipyard facility, and Gunn felt much the same. It was one of those Rambo deals.

But it looked like that was all the SEALs had to fall back on. Their target was about to move out of their range, perhaps for good.

Still hidden by the pier and the pilings, Gunn raised his camera and began snapping pictures as the sub crew cast off and the attack boat slowly moved away from the pier. Moultrie was doing the same from a vantage point a little farther up the pier. The *Akula* made a stately sight as she made her way toward the open sea, running on the surface at a slow but steady pace. Gradually the figures on her deck began to disappear below, until only the two officers on the bridge atop the fairwater were visible to Gunn.

And then the submarine was gone, swallowed up in the perpetual twilight.

Gunn gathered his three men in and gestured out to sea. It was time for them to return to the SDV and then *Bluefin*, to make their report and to begin preparations for the next operation, the big one.

At least administrative buildings in shipyard facilities weren't like to suddenly fire up an engine and leave in the middle of a SEAL op. . . .

Bridge, Soviet Submarine *Bars*
The White Sea
2257 hours GMT

Captain Second Rank Viktor Nikoleivich Kalinin took a moment to appreciate the wind in his face as *Bars* made his way north and west into the heart of the White Sea. It was good to be away from land after all the frustrations and delays of the past weeks. The sea trials were already over a week behind schedule, thanks to the bureaucratic incompetence of the idiots at the Severodvinsk yard. Tonight, finally, they could start to find out just what his new boat was capable of.

Tonight, when there were no known American satellites overhead to notice their departure, and when the twilight would help disguise the boat even if there was an unknown orbital eye looking down upon them.

He would have been far more comfortable underwater, in a submariner's natural element. But the schedule of tests was very exact, very demanding, and it called for the first tests on *Bars* to be performed on the surface.

Kalinin's Executive Officer, Captain Third Rank Ivan Ivanovich Usenko, scanned the horizon with his low-light binoculars, muttering darkly into his beard.

"What was that, Ivan Ivanovich?" Kalinin asked quietly.

"What? Oh, sorry, Comrade Captain," Usenko replied. "I did not realize I had spoken aloud."

Smiling, Kalinin shook his head. "You did not, my friend. Not loud enough for me to hear, at least." Usenko had served with Kalinin before, and the two were friends in a stiff, formal way that was always safest to maintain under the watchful eyes of a KGB that didn't like friendships that might outweigh the military man's bonds to the *Rodina*.

"I was just wishing that we could go ahead and take him down. He is not meant to loiter here on the surface like some great clumsy walrus."

"Softly, Ivan Ivanovich. Dmitri Fedorovich might take that as a criticism of the carefully drawn up schedule of tests the Design Bureau has requested us to follow." His words were correct, but his tone was just faintly mocking. Kalinin had no more use for Dmitri Fedorovich Anikanov, the submarine's *zampolit*, than did anyone else on board. It was the lot of Political Officers, who watched the officers and men aboard on behalf of the KGB, to be despised behind their backs but deferred to face-to-face, but Anikanov was a particularly objectionable member of the hateful breed, a thin, withered little man who would have been more at home as a bookkeeper or a bureaucrat than as part of a submarine crew. His fastidious attention to the exact wording of every order was one of the reasons they were running behind on the trials, since he seemed determined to clash with every yard officer they came in contact with in his insistence on supervising everything personally.

No one was going to deviate from the scheduled tests as long as Anikanov was on board.

Usenko shook his head. "My apologies, Comrade Captain. I will not speak so again." But there was a defiant jut to his jaw and an impatient look in his eye.

"Be happy, Ivan Ivanovich," Kalinin advised. "We are

at sea. There are no dockworkers or petty bureaucrats arguing over how long it will take to load sufficient toilet paper for the crew. The skies are clear, and the night air feels crisp without being too cold. These are things we should be celebrating. And in a day or two we shall be ready for the underwater tests. True?"

"True, Comrade Captain," the Executive Officer replied with a grin. "And I just realized that I have something else to celebrate, tonight."

"And that is?"

"I do not have to make a report to our beloved *zampolit* regarding the performance of *Bars* as he left the harbor at Severodvinsk. And this, Comrade Captain, pleases me mightily."

Control Room, USS *Pittsburgh*
The White Sea
2312 hours GMT

"Conn, Sonar."

"Control room," Chase replied into the intercom mike. "What have you got, Chief?"

"Designating contact Sierra One. Range, fifteen nautical miles, closing. Bearing one-six-niner. Speed is twenty knots. Target is on the surface, definitely a vessel of some type."

"Of some type? Come on, Chief, I expect better from you and your boy Rodriguez. What's your acoustical file tell you?"

"It doesn't, Skipper," Franco replied. "That thing's not in any of our files, and Rodriguez doesn't recognize her either."

"Best guess?"

"She's running on the surface, sir, but her engine noise is a little bit like an Alfa. But not as noisy. You

know how the Alfa power plant sounds when they've
got it cranked up."

Chase frowned. A sub running on the surface . . . and
not in their files. That sounded like something they
should be investigating. There might be many subs in
the Soviet Navy that hadn't been tracked and filed before
. . . but whether this was just some ordinary boat that no
one had happened to get on tape before, or their quarry
from Severodvinsk, it behooved him to check it out.

Pittsburgh had allowed *Bluefin* a long head start before following her into the White Sea, but now she was
on course for the agreed-upon rendezvous point. Running at periscope depth, the attack sub had kept an antenna raised to listen in on Soviet radio traffic in the
area, making periodic periscope sweeps to make sure
nothing had gotten past their sonar ears. So far the whole
operation had gone much more smoothly than Chase had
feared. Even the periodic appearance of Red Banner
Northern Fleet ships had not caused any significant problems. As yet, the Soviets seemed blissfully unaware of
the possibility of two American submarines penetrating
the inner sanctum of their main fleet.

"Bring us to a full stop and let her pass, Mr. Quimby.
Then slip us in behind her." Chase rubbed his chin absently. "I want to get a closer look at this guy."

"Aye aye, sir," Quimby said. He began to issue orders
to his crew at the helm.

Chase moved to the raised platform in the center of
the control room. On the starboard side, the Mark 18
Search Scope was already raised, and Chase took up his
stance there. One of the most advanced and versatile
periscope systems ever designed, the Mark 18 had both
standard daylight and low-light viewing capabilities, a
hookup to various onboard video monitors, a still camera, and other features that made it an invaluable window on the surface world.

Rotating the scope slowly, Chase scanned the surrounding waters for a full 360 degrees. They were still

too far away for him to get a look at their quarry, but he knew the other boat was out there . . . and he had a gut instinct that it would be the *Akula* they had been sent to examine.

If it was, they had a golden opportunity to study her at sea. That could turn out to be very valuable indeed, possibly more useful to the NSA and Naval Intelligence back home than anything the SEALs might obtain on their recon missions. Specs, measurements, and photographs were all well and good, but every submariner knew that there was nothing like actually watching another boat's performance to get a real feel for how she handled and what she was capable of.

He reached again for an intercom mike. "Sonar, Conn," he said.

"Sonar, aye aye," Franco replied.

"Start recording everything you pick up from Sierra One, Chief," Chase said. "And I mean everything."

"Already doing it, Captain," the CPO told him. That was one of the advantages of having a highly trained crew. Individual initiative was encouraged everywhere within the U.S. Navy, but it was particularly strong in the Silent Service. These were men who spent most of their off-duty hours studying for the tests that allowed them to advance in their chosen careers; even the newest and greenest men aboard knuckled under to study in order to earn their dolphins, the insignia that showed their status as qualified submariners. They were used to making decisions and working for the good of the boat, and didn't require heavy-handed supervision to get things done.

Chase lowered the periscope. Though coated with radar-absorbing material, or RAM, which reduced the likelihood of having the scope detected when it was raised, Chase didn't intend to leave anything to chance. *Pittsburgh* would lie in wait, silent and still, until the Soviet boat had passed them by.

And then the hunt would begin.

Thursday, 8 August 1985

SDV Bay, USS *Bluefin*
The White Sea, Off Severodvinsk
0024 hours GMT

Water was still streaming from nearly every surface within the SDV bay, and Bernard Gunn shivered as he stripped off the top of his wet suit and felt some of that icy water dripping onto his back. Close by, Senior Chief Burns was pulling his swim fins off of his feet, while Pond and Moultrie were rounding up all of the diving gear and stowing it neatly out of the way.

Harriman and his pilot were talking together in low, urgent tones, something about the performance of the SDV on the return trip. It sounded like a minor problem, nothing to worry about now, so Gunn mentally put it aside until he could tackle whatever it might be on a clear head and a full night's sleep.

"Sir?" a redheaded submariner—Mulligan, Gunn remembered—had appeared in front of him. "Captain's compliments, and would you be laying aft to the wardroom as soon as you can?"

"Doesn't that man ever sleep?" Gunn grumbled.

Mulligan flashed him a grin. "Not so you would notice, sir," he said.

Gunn decided that "as soon as you can" didn't mean that the sub's captain wanted him to appear in the bottom half of a dripping wet suit; the wardroom furnishings weren't really intended for entertaining people fresh from a swim. So he stopped off at his tiny cabin long enough to towel off, change into a dry uniform, and run a comb through his hair. Feeling more or less presentable, he proceeded to the wardroom.

The captain was poring over a report of some kind when he arrived. "Ah, Mr. Gunn. Good. How did it go out there?" He waved the SEAL to a seat across from him.

"Well enough, Captain," Gunn said carefully. "We were able to get a pretty good set of measurements and plenty of photos among the four of us, before . . ."

"Before what?" Gordon asked sharply.

"Before the bloody sub decided to up and sail away on us!"

"They're at sea?"

"Yes, sir," Gunn replied. "Left Severodvinsk at approximately 2230 hours, heading northeast, on the surface. Once we were sure they were gone, we returned to the SDVs and headed back here. There wasn't much we could do once the bird had flown the coop, sir."

"Of course not." Gordon was frowning. "Damn, they must have passed just far enough away that we didn't pick them up. Would have been nice to get some acoustical data on her . . ." He fixed his intense eyes on Gunn. "Your assessment of the information you were able to get tonight. Lieutenant?"

"Sir, I don't know enough about submarines *or* Soviet technology to know how much worthwhile information we've come up with. We have a lot of photographs, basic measurements, some sketches of hull fittings . . . basic survey information. I imagine it will be useful to the folks back home. It's the kind of material Admiral

Goldman seemed interested in. Whether or not it will satisfy Mr. Dreyfuss . . . I couldn't say. He seemed to feel we would learn more from the raid on the administrative building."

"And what's your opinion? Is it still feasible to make the attempt? Or would we be better off wrapping it up and heading for home right now?"

"You've been talking to Lieutenant Anderson, haven't you, sir?" Gunn asked.

Gordon nodded. "He indicated that he's not confident the risks of this land op are justified by the amount of information you are likely to obtain. If you think you've already gathered all the data you're likely to get, then say so now. I'd rather leave here with most of what we need rather than push too hard and end up screwing up the entire mission."

"Sir, if this is about the doubts Lieutenant Harriman raised . . . ?"

"It isn't," Gordon said sharply. "I'm just giving you the chance to go on record. Can the second phase of the mission significantly improve on the information we've already acquired tonight?"

"There's no doubt about that, sir," Gunn said. "If we can find the files Mr. Dreyfuss wants us to find, we can discover a great deal of detailed information on the design and construction of that boat. Is it, in fact, a titanium hull? What are the specifications of the power plant? The electronics, the armament . . . how big is the crew? These are all things we *can* find out . . . but there are no guarantees. There are a lot of risks involved, and a lot of uncertainties."

"I see. So . . . it's really your call to make, Lieutenant. Are you game for another crack at the Reds?"

Gunn shrugged. "Frankly, what I really want a crack at right now is some sack time, Captain. But, come tomorrow night . . . yeah. My men are up for a chance to stretch their legs. This submarine of yours isn't exactly a great place for elbow room."

"All right, Mr. Gunn. Make sure you and your men from the op tonight turn over all the information you collected. I want full reports finished tomorrow afternoon, before you leave the boat again. Understood?"

"Aye aye, sir," Gunn said, standing.

"I'll see you in the morning, Lieutenant. Thank you for your time."

As Gunn left the wardroom and headed for his cabin, he wondered at the Captain's tightly wound demeanor. The man seemed on edge, overeager to make sure the mission moved along smoothly. Of course, Gunn was used to dealing with SEALs, who rarely allowed themselves to deviate from a strict professionalism . . . except when they descended on a bar and cut loose. But it bothered Gunn to see *Bluefin*'s captain putting so much of himself into securing the outcome of the operation.

He shook his head as he entered the cabin. No doubt his own fatigue was making his reactions to Gordon stronger than they should have been.

Tomorrow they would both be fresh. Tomorrow, the SEALs would have the chance to truly test their mettle.

Sonar Shack, USS *Pittsburgh*
The White Sea
0607 hours GMT

"So what do we have, Chief?" Chase asked.

Bob Franco had the look of a seven-year-old on Christmas morning, excited by what he had already uncovered, and eager to find more treasures that still needed to be unwrapped. He had only been in the sonar shack for a short time after grabbing a few brief hours of sleep. Officially, he wasn't supposed to be on duty, but no one, Chase least of all, begrudged him his enthusiasm.

"She's a beauty, all right, Skipper," he said. "You

gotta hand it to the Russkies, they may not have all the high-tech bells and whistles we do, but by God they know a thing or two about building submarines!"

"Impressed, are you?" Chase asked mildly, with a grin.

"Just a little." Franco damped down his enthusiasm visibly and began to report in a more formal tone. "We've been tracking her for better than six hours now, sir, and I think we're getting a pretty good picture of what she's got. From the sound of things, she's working off two reactors, but they don't sound like anything I've heard before. Rodriguez thinks they might not be steam reactors at all."

"What does that mean?"

Franco rubbed his chin. "Well, there've been rumors that the Russians were working with a new reactor type on some of their more recent boats . . ."

That jogged Chase's memory. "Right. I remember seeing an article in the *Proceedings* about it. They were building reactors that used liquid metals in place of water as the primary heat exchange elements. Sodium, wasn't it?"

"Could be," Franco said. "Out of my MOS, Skipper. I was just interested 'cause I wondered what these fancy new reactors might sound like on a hydrophone." He smiled.

"More than enough to keep you busy in the wide world of electronics, Chief," Chase said. "Anything else interesting about the engines or power plants?"

Franco shook his head. "Standard turbines turning the screw. Nothing unusual there."

Chase nodded. Aside from the possibility of the liquid-metal reactors, it sounded like a fairly typical Russian design. American boats tended to go with a single nuclear reactor with massive amounts of safeguards and redundant systems; the Soviet Union more often opted to build two separate reactors so that they had a backup against failure. The single screw was a bit of a departure

from earlier Russian practice, and might have represented an attempt to improve stealthiness. He remembered the encounter with the Victor III the day the first
message from Admiral Goldman had arrived. That sub's
twin screws had been badly balanced, increasing her engine noise and giving her a distinct sonar signature.

"Based on her blade rate," Franco went on, "I'd say
she was capable of making at least thirty knots submerged, maybe thirty-five or forty. Hard to tell without
being sure of her displacement, but I'd say on the whole
she was light for her size, so you can figure she's going
to be a mover."

"Aren't they all," Chase remarked. Soviet submarines
were renowned in the West for their speed and agility,
which American shipbuilders had been hard-pressed to
match. No one was quite sure how the Russians did it,
though there were speculations floating around naval circles lately that suggested they had started using titanium
hulls to produce a lighter but stronger boat. It was one
area where Soviet shipbuilding was just plain better; to
meet Admiral Hyman Rickover's specifications for a fast
attack boat that could keep up with its Soviet counterparts, the Electric Boat Division of General Dynamics
had been forced to make some major compromises in
the construction of the Los Angeles class. By thinning
out the steel hull, they had saved enough weight to allow
the installation of the powerful but massive S6G power
plant, but as a result the LAs were limited in the depths
they could safely dive to. Russian boats didn't seem to
have that problem. They were reportedly able to reach
some very impressive depths when they wanted to.
"What else?"

"Most of the rest of what we've heard is just routine,"
Franco said with a shrug. "Hatches closing, that sort of
thing. There was a clattering just about the time you'd
figure their cook would be starting to get out his pots
and pans for breakfast. About an hour back we heard

what had to be garbage being ejected. Sounded like the same old system. No surprises there."

"Unless they had suddenly developed a way to use their garbage as a new kind of torpedo, I doubt that anybody back home would care that much for improvements in the Trash Disposal Unit anyway, Chief," Chase told him with another smile. "You guys have done a good job. I'm sure Washington will be delighted with your tape collection."

"Thanks, Skipper," Franco said. "We're—"

Sonarman Second Class Carl Czernak interrupted him. "Something weird going on over there, sir!" He manipulated a control, and eerie sounds filled the small compartment. Chase was no expert at interpreting the distorted noises picked up through the sub's hydrophones, but to his untrained ear he thought he could make out machinery noises, irregular clangs of metal against metal, shouting . . . and a long, wavering scream. A moment later the sound of the turning propeller grew ragged and faded out.

"Good God!" he exploded. "What the hell is going on over there?"

At that moment the intercom sounded. "Sonar, Conn," Latham's voice was unruffled, but Chase picked up an underlying note of urgency. "Our friend is drifting. He's shut down his engine and just seems to be wallowing out there."

Captain's Quarters, Soviet Submarine *Bars*
The White Sea
0755 hours GMT

"Why have we stopped, Comrade Captain? This is a most irregular situation!"

Captain Second Rank Kalinin regarded the thin, disapproving features of the boat's *zampolit* with weary eyes. He had been expecting this visit, of course, ever since the accident that had forced them to shut down the power plant and drift while they effected repairs in the engineering spaces. But it didn't make the Political Officer any more welcome in his quarters. Kalinin was tired, irritated, and spoiling for a fight. "The boat has stopped because some shit-for-brains idiot at the Severodvinsk shipyard managed to install a set of faulty pipes in our coolant loop. As a result, the pipe burst two hours ago, spraying superheated sodium into the engineering spaces and putting three of my best engineers into sick bay with severe burns. Until we can replace or repair the pipes, we cannot run the turbines, and therefore cannot turn the propeller. Unless you would like me to have my men rig oars and *row* us somewhere?"

"Spare me the sarcasm," Dmitri Feodorovitch Anikanov told him with a sour, petulant frown. "You are sure this is the fault of someone at the shipyard? Not incompetence on the part of your engineering department . . . or sabotage by imperialist sympathizers?"

Kalinin laughed, not caring about the hostile look he earned from the *zampolit.* "Believe me, Comrade Anikanov, there are plenty of ways for bad pipes to be installed in a boat without requiring the machinations of some capitalist spy." He began ticking points off on his fingers. "First, there are the miserable conditions at the factories these days. The workers are dispirited, and they do not always pay attention to their work . . . when they are well-enough trained to know what they are supposed to be doing anyway. Then there is the lack of competent quality control to reject those items coming out of the factories which are not up to specifications. And there are the contributions of organized crime, who find ways to skim off the best-quality materials for resale on the black market, forcing government procurers to make do with what is left. And finally there is the head of the engineering section of the shipyard, who refused three requests from my Chief Engineer to provide new piping to replace several sections of the coolant loop that he certified as below standard three weeks ago. We were told that all installed pipes had passed the inspections given by the dockyard crew, and that therefore we had no call to ask for replacements. Shall I show you my Chief Engineer's report, Comrade *Zampolit*, together with the reply from the shipyard staff? Or would you rather blame my people for someone else's failure so that you can stage a zealous inquisition and prove your dedication to the party and to the Committee?"

"That kind of talk is not going to look good in your dossier, Comrade Captain," Anikanov said warningly, dodging the issue.

"Screw my dossier," Kalinin said curtly. "Listen to me, Anikanov. And understand me, as well. I have been in command of this boat less than a month, but I know my officers and crewmen. They are good people, dedicated and loyal. I will not have you sniffing around in search of some scapegoat to pin the blame on, when you know as well as I do the abuses that have been going on at the shipyard and elsewhere. We cannot expect to do our jobs well if we are going to have third-rate material fobbed off on us, and our attempts to rectify the problems simply swept under the carpet."

"If there is, in fact, documentation to support your claims . . ." The *zampolit*'s tones were smooth and silky.

"Oh, there is." Kalinin stared him down. The other man blinked and looked away. "Your job may be to monitor the loyalty and correct thought of the personnel assigned to this boat, *tovarisch*, but I would hope in future that you will remember that you are a *part* of this crew and this boat, as well. And as such I would have you working toward the good of *Bars*. He deserves the best from all of us, as he is the best the *Rodina* has to offer." Kalinin relaxed his stiff expression and even forced a tiny smile. "Or at least he will be, when the Chief Engineer finally manages to get the pipes repaired."

"How long do you expect it to take?" Anikanov asked, sounding subdued now.

"It is hard to estimate. We have some spare pipes in stores, of the same high quality as the ones which blew out. And not enough to replace everything that ought to be removed. But the Chief Engineer assures me that he can make sufficient repairs to damaged pipes to allow them to be used again, provided we do not operate at high pressures. So we will be able to begin to limp home in a few hours, hopefully."

"And if the repairs cannot be made?"

"Then we shall have to radio Severodvinsk and request a tow," Kalinin said. "But I do not intend to have *Bars* return home from his first cruise being dragged along behind some tubby harbor tug. He will return to port on his own, if I have to get into the water and *push* to get him in."

Even the humorless *zampolit* smiled slightly at that. "You have little respect for proper authority, Viktor Nikoleivich," he said heavily. "But your dedication is obvious. Very well. Please keep me informed of our schedule as you learn more."

He stood and left the cabin without further words, leaving Kalinin alone with his thoughts.

It galled him to have the first sea trial marred by such a foolish accident. He should have refused even to consider leaving harbor as long as the coolant loop went unattended to, but he had allowed himself to believe that they could keep the pressure in the pipes down long enough to at least get *Bars* through the first day or two of testing. That had been a mistake, and Kalinin did not like to make mistakes.

Fortunately, the Chief Engineer was not amongst the casualties. Five minutes sooner, and the bursting pipes would have sprayed him with the same scalding steam that had nearly killed his assistant and two petty officers. There was still some doubt about Senior Lieutenant Rogov's chances of recovery.

Engineering crews faced more hardships than other Soviet submariners, he thought bitterly. For years now the West had been trying to understand how the *Rodina* could design and build submarines which were so much faster than the boats the NATO allies could send to sea, when all along the explanation had been so simple. Many of the older Soviet nuclear boats had simply had large amounts of reactor shielding stripped out to lighten the vessels and allow them to travel faster. The cost, of course, had been borne by the sub crews, exposed to dangerously high levels of radiation. And the engineers who worked closest to the reactors naturally paid the highest price.

The new generation of Soviet subs had adopted the new titanium hulls to save weight, and restored the shielding their predecessors had done without. But the engineers still suffered most.

When *Bars* returned to the shipyard, Kalinin planned to have a long talk with Rear Admiral Arkov about the problems at Severodvinsk. His men faced dangers enough in the service of the *Rodina*, without being jeopardized by the fools who manned the yard.

Control Room, USS *Pittsburgh*
The White Sea
0811 hours GMT

"Two hours they've been like that. What do you think, Captain?"

Chase studied the video monitor relaying the view from the Mark 18 periscope. The elongated shape of their quarry was framed on the screen, drifting on the surface of the White Sea. She somehow looked less threatening now than she had before, like some great wounded sea beast floating helpless on the ocean currents. "What I think, Rick, is that they've had themselves an accident. You know how things go the first time out in a new boat . . . and this isn't just a new boat we're talking about, but the prototype for a whole new *class* of boats. Lots of things just aching to go wrong."

Latham sniffed disdainfully. *Pittsburgh* had been almost new when they had taken her out of Groton for the first time, but she'd never given them any major problems. Nor did her logs from her sea trials reveal anything like a major breakdown. "Shoddy Russian construction," he said, shaking his head. "If this is their new pride and joy, they can keep it."

"Don't think it, Rick," Chase warned. "That boat might be having a few shakedown problems now, but you've seen what she can do."

They had been following the Russian boat all night, staying discreetly in her wake. Although she had never once attempted to dive, they had learned a lot about her performance from the way she handled on the surface. Chase, for one, was not encouraged by their observations.

The *Akula* was indeed a modern design, not as fast as some older Soviet subs but at least as capable as the original Los Angeles class boats. She was also quiet . . . very quiet. *Pittsburgh*, one of the Flight II LA boats which had incorporated various modifications based on lessons learned from the first twelve boats of her class, was probably even more stealthy than the *Akula* . . . but not by much. The new Russian boat was at least as good at evading detection as the earlier Flight I LAs. And that was grounds for concern.

They still didn't know much about her electronics suite or her ability to detect other boats, but Chase had his worries there, too. That elongated sail carried a whole forest of antennae and periscopes, and there was no telling what sorts of improvements had been incorporated in her sonar systems. Not that Chase was eager to find out what the other was capable of, since there was every chance that a sonar sweep might pick up *Pitts-*

burgh and expose them to the full fury of the Red Banner Northern Fleet.

He stared at the image on the video screen. The American submariners were being presented with an extraordinary opportunity. A brand-new Russian sub was just sitting there in the water, inviting a detailed inspection.

And Chase didn't know if the SEALs had been able to get a look at her or not. If the sub had left the barn at Severodvinsk before Gunn's people could get a look at her, the mission could be at risk.

On the other hand, not knowing how good the Soviet detection systems might be, it was impossible to know whether or not they could get close and really study the other boat. Worse, maneuvering in close enough to get pictures through the Mark 18 scope would be tricky . . . especially if the Soviets were to start their engine and get under way again at the wrong moment.

A sub skipper who made a daring move and brought back detailed pictures of a new Russian boat would be feted and made much of. He might well be promoted to full captain and given an Ohio class boomer to command, or even a slot as a submarine squadron commander.

But if that same sub skipper made a miscalculation, perhaps ended up colliding with the other boat, things wouldn't be pretty. For one thing, a collision with a Soviet sub wasn't the sort of thing that you handled by trading insurance information. There would be serious diplomatic repercussions, especially with the discovery of an American sub deep in the heart of the White Sea. Collisions happened more frequently than either side liked to admit, sometimes resulting in serious damage. There had been a fairly high-profile case within the past couple of years, Chase recalled, where a Soviet Victor III had fouled her props with the towed array streaming aft of an American frigate off the Carolina coast. The Russians had ended up calling in help and were towed to Cuba for repairs.

Somehow Chase doubted that the Soviet Union would allow an American Los Angeles class submarine in its territorial waters to call on other American ships to give it a tow all the way to England or Norway. More likely, the Americans would suffer the fate of the crew of the *Pueblo*, captured and tried as spies by the North Koreans in 1968.

The captain whose "daring and initiative" opened up any of those cans of worms couldn't expect to command a rowboat after that. Frank Gordon's long and struggling career would be a meteoric rise to the top of his profession by comparison.

So Chase had some important decisions to make . . . and he had to make them fast. How long would they have before the Russians started their engine again? Was the information they could hope to gain worth the risks he'd have to run with his boat and crew?

Chase straightened up as the decision took shape in his mind. "Rick, we're going to take a closer look at our crippled friend," he said.

"How close, sir?" Latham asked, one eyebrow raised. For him, it was quite an expressive display.

"Close enough to count rivets with the Mark Eighteen," Chase informed him. "I want you and Quimby to take us in tight. Circle her at, say, ten to twenty yards, dead slow, as many times as you can manage without bumping into her. I'll man the periscope and see how many photos and how much video footage I can get of hull fittings and control surfaces."

"Risky, sir," Latham said quietly. That was his duty. As Exec he was expected to point out the flaws in a captain's harebrained schemes.

"But worth the risk." Chase paused. "Be ready for unspecified maneuvers. If they should get under way again, or if they detect us, we'd better be ready to make tracks."

Latham shrugged. "If they detect us, what can they do? At twenty yards the safeties on their torps will keep them from doing anything." He smiled suddenly. "But I really would hate to go and scratch the paint on our little lady, here."

"Yeah, we'd never get back our deposit," Lieutenant Quimby chimed in from his post near the helm controls.

"That's enough, gentlemen," Chase said sternly. "Work out what you want to do, Rick, before we get into it. Let's look alive!"

They did nothing rash or precipitous. With the staid Latham in charge of maneuvering the sub, everything was carefully laid out ahead of time to avoid any sort of seat-of-the-pants moves; Chase knew that he might easily have given in to the temptation to cut corners or improvise, and this wasn't the situation for that kind of cavalier approach.

So *Pittsburgh* crept in close to her quarry, a cautious bloodhound sniffing its wounded prey. From the periscope station, Chase used the Mark 18 to do a thorough study of the drifting Soviet boat, both above and below the waterline. The video cameras ran throughout, both to relay images to various monitors and to record the entire examination on videotape. And through it all Chase snapped off picture after picture with the still cameras, trying to save as many minor details as possible from different angles and distances.

The American boat slid slowly along the Soviet sub's starboard side, then performed a leisurely turn and came back down the port side, all without apparently alerting the Russians to their presence. Chase didn't know what to make of that. It was true that *Pittsburgh* was under the very strictest conditions of silent running, with all nonessential systems shut down and every man in the crew keeping as quiet as possible. But it seemed incredible that they could pass so close, for so long, without being picked up by the Russian boat's sonar. The *Akula* didn't have her towed array deployed, but surely her passive sonar was listening? Perhaps, Chase told himself, they were shorthanded after the accident, whatever it was, that had forced them to cut their engine. Or perhaps here in the White Sea they weren't at their most vigilant, assuming that no Americans would be crazy enough to test them on their own turf. Or maybe the Soviets simply hadn't made the same strides in detection systems as they plainly had in stealth.

There was no way to be sure, and Chase told himself that he would have to be careful to avoid implying any answers when the time came to write his report. Just because *Pittsburgh* was having a lucky time of it out here was no reason to make assumptions that could lead some other American boat into underestimating her opposition.

With one full circuit of the sub completed, Latham approached Chase with the stiff formality that he often adopted in tight situations. "Orders, Captain? Do we resume our original position?"

Chase shook his head. "A second pass, Mr. Latham," he said. "Just like the first. We'll make sure we didn't miss anything."

This time around, Chase turned the periscope over to Lieutenant Jackson, with orders to concentrate on above-water observations. He sent a runner to summon Chief Franco and Lieutenant Erskine from the sonar and comm shacks, and the three of them huddled around one of the video monitors to study the antennae sprouting like a tangled thicket from the top of the *Akula*'s long, low fairwater.

"I'm pretty sure that's a Snoop Tray radar," Erskine offered, pointing at the screen. "It's hard to see clearly, but the shape looks right." The Communications Officer prided himself on his knowledge of electronics systems of all kinds, especially those used by foreign powers. Chase was willing to grant him the status of expert, within limits. It would be up to the analysts Stateside to go over the recordings and photos to make the final determination.

"Any idea of her sonar type, Chief?" Chase asked

softly. No one was talking loudly, given their proximity to the other sub. A top-notch sonar man like Rodriguez, with the right equipment, could pick out individual voices at this range if the water conditions were just right.

Franco shrugged. "Nothing obvious I could point to and identify, sir," he said. "But the Alfa and the Sierra both use Shark Gill. Unless they've made some radical change, I'd put my money on them carrying the same over there."

He gave an absent nod. That, of course, was the real question. Had there been any radical changes in the Soviet design? Everything they had turned up so far pointed to confirmation of some of the Pentagon's major fears. This boat was designed to overcome many of the flaws in stealth that had plagued her predecessors, that was obvious. She was at least as good as one of the original Los Angeles class boats, though probably still a little less stealthy than *Pittsburgh* and the other Flight II subs. With a titanium hull, the *Akula* could probably go faster and dive deeper than the American boat. Her electronics suite was a matter for outright speculation; the fact that *Pittsburgh* had now completed two full circles around the other vessel without, evidently, attracting any attention at all argued for a problem somewhere, but whether it was hardware, software, or the quality of the crewmen operating the systems was something they would never be able to discover for sure without capturing one of the boats and tearing it apart.

For just an instant the helplessness of the *Akula* was a tangible temptation for Chase. He had a momentary vision of running up the Jolly Roger and trying to take the enemy boat. Smiling, he suppressed the thought immediately.

Instead he turned to Latham. "Rick, we've got about as much as we're likely to find out from hanging around while this guy tries to put Humpty Dumpty back together again. I'd say we'd better get to the rendezvous coordinates before Frank Gordon has some kind of stroke from worrying about us." He paused. "Set course for the rendezvous. Dead slow until we're well behind our friend over there, then revs for ten knots."

"Aye aye, sir!" Latham responded crisply. Was there the tiniest trace of relief in his voice? Latham and Quimby would be able to dine out for years on the story of how they had circled a Russian sub twice without being detected . . . assuming the mission was ever declassified enough to allow any of them to talk about it without being marked as dead men by Dreyfuss and his cronies.

They had managed quite a coup . . . but it would only count when *Pittsburgh* and *Bluefin* completed the rest of their mission and returned to the open sea.

Until then, Chase couldn't allow himself to feel satisfied with anything.

SDV Bay, USS *Bluefin*
The White Sea
1805 hours GMT

"Don't forget, Callahan, timing is everything," Gunn said. "Set off the fireworks too soon, and you can screw up our whole op inside the shipyard. Wait too long, and it won't do anybody any good."

Master Chief Callahan nodded, his expression that of a parent patiently dealing with a child—or a senior NCO putting up with an eager young officer who talked too much. "We lie low until you give us two clicks on the radio, Lieutenant. Then we let 'em know we've been there. Piece of cake."

Gunn smiled. "From your mouth to God's ears," he said. He looked around the cluster of SEALs who had formed a semicircle around him at one end of the SDV bay. Behind them Gunn could see Harriman's people

checking over their minisubs one last time as they prepared for the mission. The minor problem in SDV #1,
which had turned out to be a small fault in one of the
batteries, had been corrected over the course of the afternoon. Everything was ready . . . or so Gunn hoped.
"Okay, any last questions? Problems? If you've got
something you want to get off your chest, now's the
time."

"All I need to know," Martinez said, "is where are
the bad guys, and how soon can I open fire?" He pan-
tomimed aiming a rifle and pulling the trigger. The
young SEAL sounded cocky, eager.

Gunn spared Martinez a glance, then looked at the
other rookie in the platoon, Silverwolf. He was a little
concerned over having both of them in Callahan's squad
for this op. He was sure Anderson had originally set
them up in second squad so that they'd have the benefit
of training with the grizzled veteran Master Chief, but
had the lieutenant intended to keep them both together
when it came time to go into action? The issue had never
come up in his talks with Anderson since the lieutenant's
injury, and Gunn hadn't wanted to upset things by making any major changes in the familiar organization of
things. So now Callahan, with one empty spot in his
squad already thanks to Gunn's taking charge of First
Squad, would have to baby-sit a pair of newbies. Martinez and Silverwolf had been doing well enough in
training, but Gunn well knew that there was a world of
difference between practice and the realities of a genuine
operation.

But even if he wanted to make last-minute changes—
and that was always bad for an outfit's morale—Gunn
didn't think it would be a good idea to take one of the
rookies in with his stick of SEALs. Callahan's unit was
assigned to a diversionary operation, while Gunn and his
men were to tackle the problem of getting into the shipyard and uncovering what secrets they could. The cold,
hard facts were that Callahan's part in things was strictly

secondary . . . and he could better afford to have the newbies with him.

Gunn wasn't terribly fond of having to look at those cold, hard facts. They made him uncomfortable.

Nobody spoke after Martinez, and Gunn nodded the way he had seen Anderson do at the end of a meeting. "Okay, then, check your gear, then mount up. We've got some Russian Bears to annoy."

The SEALs broke up into ones and twos, assembling their gear, smearing faces and hands with waterproof camouflage paint, and donning their wet suits and diving equipment as they continued to talk amongst themselves. After a few minutes, with all of them finished with their individual preparations, Gunn looked across at Lieutenant Harriman, who gave him a slow, deliberate nod.

"All the gear is loaded, Lieutenant," Harriman said. His voice was even, professional. If there was no warmth in it, neither was there any trace of hate or contempt. "You've got a nice mix of demolitions gear on all four vehicles, everything from plastique to limpet mines, and all the trimmings."

"Still wishing you could blow up a few boats in the shipyard, Lieutenant?" Gunn asked mildly, remembering Harriman's suggestion at the first briefing back in Holy Loch.

"Just trying to cover all the bases," Harriman responded, coloring.

"Well, I hope we don't need anything more than the basics, but thanks." Then, turning to Callahan, Gunn said, "All right. Get them aboard, Master Chief. Let's get this show on the road."

"Aye aye, sir," Callahan responded. "Let's go! Let's go! Saddle up!"

The Master Chief's tiny command started climbing aboard the two SDVs at the forward end of the bay, moving quickly, confidently, a study in precision without any wasted motion or effort. Jenkins, Silverwolf, and Davis were soon secure inside SDV #1, and Lieutenant

Harriman and QM/2 O'Dell personally checked the hatches and made a last inspection of the hull before they clambered into position in the bow of the Swimmer Delivery Vehicle. As they did so, Callahan was joining Martinez and Woods inside SDV #3. The old SEAL gave Gunn one long, last look, a level, emotionless gaze the younger man couldn't interpret. Callahan would be carrying an officer's share of the responsibilities for the mission, and while Gunn knew there was no man better qualified in the platoon to take over from Lieutenant Anderson, he still couldn't help but feel a twist of worry deep in his gut.

Then the last hatches were closed, the second SDV crew was strapped in, and a warning siren hooted in the bay. Gunn turned away from the gleaming, flattened tubes resting in their cradles and joined the orderly stream of technicians and other ratings filing aft through the watertight doors. The young, redheaded Mulligan closed the hatch behind him and dogged it shut, and the throb of the water pumps echoed through *Bluefin*'s hull as the bay began to flood.

Callahan's team had farther to go and a job to do before Gunn's men could begin their investigation of the shipyard, so they had to have a head start. But Gunn knew it would soon be time for his own group to mount up and depart.

Soon enough, they would all be walking on Russian soil.

Thursday, 8 August 1985

South Bank, Dvina River
Near Severodvinsk, Russian SFSR
2317 hours GMT

"Arright, keep your heads down and your eyes open."

Silverwolf could hear the edge in Master Chief Callahan's voice. The veteran was flat on his belly, peering through his night-vision gear down the long, gradual slope of a rise in the ground that some might charitably have labeled a hill toward the fenced-in compound where the six Americans had only recently finished a good night's work. The rest of the SEALs were farther back from the crest of the rise, crouching, kneeling, or lying down amidst a tangle of bushes and small trees.

Behind them the gurgle of water was an ever-present siren's song luring them to where the Dvina River flowed to the sea, sluggish and dirty. Unappetizing as those muddy gray-brown waters were, they represented safety and sanctuary to the SEALs. Lieutenant Harriman and two SDVs were waiting, grounded on the bottom of the river close to the bank. When the time came to withdraw, it would be easy to reach the minisubs and then head out to the open sea and the safety of *Bluefin*, nearly fifteen miles away.

Silverwolf checked the action of his AK-47, mostly so he could be *doing* something. He had been through this kind of waiting before, dozens of times, in practice sessions at BUD/S and later on when the platoon had been on maneuvers. But there was something different about being in the middle of hostile territory, alone. The time dragged, and Silverwolf wondered if they would ever get the signal to go from Lieutenant Gunn.

He crept forward to the crest alongside Callahan, who gave him a sharp look but neither spoke nor signaled. Silverwolf looked down at the sprawling electrical plant that had been their target. It was a well-lit beacon in the darkness, alive with lights and movement even after midnight. Oily black smoke roiled from towering stacks, picking up the light from below and providing a fair imitation of a scene from Dante's *Inferno* as the coal-burning generators fed the demand for power for the city of Severodvinsk and the many military and industrial facilities that lay nearby. The filthy smoke would have shocked any Western environmentalist speechless, but according to the briefings the SEALs had gone over this was actually one of the cleaner, nonnuclear generating plants in the Soviet Union.

Still a child of the reservation at heart, Silverwolf was appalled that anyone would put up with such a monstrosity. He found himself smiling. Perhaps the work they had done tonight could be seen as his own gesture toward militant environmentalism, rather than merely an act of sabotage. . . .

Second Squad had penetrated the compound easily, coming ashore from the SDVs and making their way silently to the southern end of the compound. There they had cut their way through the chain-link fence and spread out, moving amongst the massive industrial generators to plant a series of explosive charges in strategic spots. Aside from an uneasiness at being so close to so much raw, crackling power, Silverwolf had gone through the op as smoothly as if it had been just one more drill at Camp Pickett or some other SEAL training facility back in Virginia. By the time Callahan's party had reassembled at the place where they had cut their way in, there were enough explosives laced through those generators to plunge a good portion of Severodvinsk and its environs into darkness.

All they needed now was the word from Gunn.

Second Squad's mission was to provide just enough confusion to cover Lieutenant Gunn and First Squad as they penetrated the shipyard. It was a delicate balance. Stir up too much trouble, and the entire shipyard might end up on high alert. But some distraction was called for, and something that would divert both attention and Soviet troops away from the shipyard for the critical period of Gunn's reconnaissance ashore.

This was strictly a diversionary operation, Silverwolf told himself. But he could still remember an instructor at BUD/S training who had been fond of saying "a diversion can get you just as dead as anything."

He crawled back to join the others, leaving Callahan to his lone vigil.

Shipyard Number 402
Severodvinsk, Russian SFSR
2324 hours GMT

Lieutenant j.g. Bernard Gunn rose out of the water like a phantom in the night and waded ashore slowly, cautiously, taking care to make no sound. Once on dry land he dropped to his knees behind a low retaining wall that overlooked the rugged, rocky shoreline. He removed his face mask and swim fins, then opened the waterproof satchel slung over his shoulder and fished out a set of low-light goggles. With those settled over his eyes, he could scan his surroundings carefully. The half-dark of the summer night was as bright as day to his enhanced vision, and Gunn could detect no sign of movement or activity anywhere around him.

The stretch of ground lay between the shipyard docks they had visited the night before and the huge construction buildings that were the heart and soul of the facility. Gunn noted that the docks were quiet . . . and the *Akula* had not returned.

He made a quick hand signal and produced an H&K MP5SD5 submachine gun from his satchel. Still searching for any signs of life, he crouched behind the wall, waiting.

Six more SEALs climbed onto dry land, two of them manhandling a long waterproof canister that contained equipment and weapons they would be needing ashore. As Moultrie and Geiger set the tube down near Gunn's position, Pond and Burns were already opening it up to retrieve their own weapons and night-vision gear to join Gunn on watch. Then the other SEALs began to shed their diving gear, dropping masks, fins, and rebreathers into the tube and drawing out AK-47 rifles, canvas shoes, and camouflaged fatigues to wear over their wet suits.

Chief Jerry Ehrenberger dropped to a crouch behind the wall beside Gunn, who moved to join the others around the equipment container. He added his own diving gear to the collection there, and pulled on a uniform and shoes that were exactly the same as those the other men had donned. There were no insignias or unit patches, nothing to indicate rank or national origin. Their weaponry was a mix of Soviet and German, their other gear equally diverse in origin. No one could identify them as Americans from their equipment, at least, and should any of them have to leave something behind there would be no indication that it was property of the United States Navy or the SEALs. That was an essential aspect of the mission. No one must know that the Americans had dared send a commando unit onto Soviet soil.

Each man carried poison, too. That was an aspect of SEAL covert ops that was rarely mentioned outside the ranks of the SEALs themselves. Strictly speaking, there was no way an American serviceman could be required to commit suicide rather than face capture, and it would outrage some back home to think that such a policy would ever be considered. But it was a fact of life for men assigned to classified, highly covert operations. In this day and age, no one could hold out against the interrogation techniques available to the KGB and other security organizations. A man who was captured was a man who would talk; the only question was how long it would take to break him. So it was generally accepted among the SEALs that capture was not an option. Poison was one way out. A bullet from a rifle belonging to one of your messmates was another.

When all seven men were outfitted, the canister was resealed. Wielding collapsible shovels, Geiger and Ehrenberger quickly buried the tube under loose dirt and gravel just below the wall, near a gnarled old bush that served as a handy reference point for finding the cache later. Gunn didn't wait for them to finish. With a series of hand signals, he divided the remainder of his men up and then climbed over the wall, his SMG at the ready. Moultrie and Carstairs followed him. Burns and Pond made a second team, crossing the wall about ten yards to Gunn's left and immediately taking up positions behind some bushes while Gunn and his two followers moved in a crouched trot toward the wall of a large building visible several yards away. The remaining two, Geiger and Ehrenberger, would remain hidden behind the retaining wall, keeping the back door open for their squadmates in case of trouble and monitoring the squad's radio so they could keep in touch with Callahan's unit.

Gunn could sense the tension in his men, the intensity of coiled springs wound tight and ready for instant release. This was what SEALs trained for, day in and day out, though many of them did nothing but train and never actually saw a chance of action at all. Personally, Gunn would have been happy to include himself in that category. He had been in combat before, and while it didn't scare him, it was something he wasn't likely to seek out again, either.

All Bernard Gunn wanted was to get in and do the job, then get out . . . without any unfortunate encounters along the way.

Control Room, USS *Bluefin*
The White Sea, Off Severodvinsk
2333 hours GMT

"Ahoy, *Pittsburgh*," Frank Gordon spoke into the handset of the acoustic telephone. "Took your sweet time getting here, didn't you?"

Scrambled and distorted over the Gertrude system, Mike Chase's voice still held a note of triumph. "While you guys have been bottom-feeding in the mud like a bunch of catfish, we've been doing a spot of real work. Tracked and photographed a big metal shark."

Shark . . . in Russian, that was *Akula*, their quarry's NATO code name. That, Gordon thought, accounted for *Pittsburgh*'s long delay in reaching the rendezvous. That lucky bastard Chase must have blundered right into the Soviet prototype sub after it sortied on its late-night sea trials the previous night.

"So you threw a party and didn't invite us, huh?" he replied. "See if I buy the first beer when we get home after that! Good to have you here."

"Good to be here," Chase responded. "Mission status?"

"Phase Two under way," Gordon told him crisply. "Gunn should be ashore by now."

"Excellent." There was a pause. "I'm sending across one of my divers with a copy of all the pertinent data we gathered last night. If you can get together whatever Gunn's people collected . . ."

"Then we'll both be current with everything," Gordon finished for him. "Good idea. That way we just have to divvy up whatever Gunn brings out tonight, and either of us will be able to deliver full reports to the admiral." And if either submarine ran into trouble, the mission could still be completed successfully. "I'll have everything ready for your man when he gets here."

"Thanks, Frank. *Pittsburgh* clear."

He returned the handset to its cradle. The last exchange had been an unpleasant reminder of how much could still go wrong before the mission was over.

And that turned his thoughts back to the SEALs ashore. Both squads should be ashore by now, and in position, but as long as they maintained radio silence there wasn't much more the submariners were likely to learn about what was going on around Severodvinsk. Gordon had deployed a radio antenna to the surface along with the snorkel that was feeding air to the diesel engine and saving his batteries, but so far all they had picked up was routine Soviet radio traffic.

He supposed that was a good thing. Except for a single signal ordering Second Squad to execute their diversionary operation, the SEALs weren't likely to chatter back and forth much . . . not unless a situation developed that was outside the scope of their original plan. In this case, no news was good news.

"Mr. Hogan," he said, stepping down from the OOD position, "prepare to receive a diver from *Pittsburgh* at the forward escape trunk. I'll be in the wardroom if you need me."

But it didn't make the waiting any easier to take.

Shipyard Number 402
Severodvinsk, Russian SFSR
2337 hours GMT

There was just one guard posted outside the administrative building, and no lights showed from within.
Crouching at the corner of an adjacent structure, Gunn
studied the building through his low-light goggles and
nodded approvingly. Everything was pretty much as
they had deduced from satellite photographs and the
mysterious humint resource Dreyfuss relied on. It looked
like an easy job, in and out with little to stand in the
way of the SEALs.

He clicked on the short-range headset radio and spoke
softly into the mike. "Ferret Four, this is Ferret Six. Do
you copy?"

"Copy, Six," Jerry Ehrenberger's reply was prompt
and crisp.

"Lights Out. I say again, Lights Out."

"Understood, Ferret Six. Transmitting code for Lights
Out . . . now."

The wide separation between the two SEAL squads
made coordination difficult. The little headset radio each
SEAL wore with the rest of his combat gear was fine
for tactical communications within the squad, but it
didn't have the range to let the two squads stay in direct
voice contact. On the other hand, the big backpack radio
Ehrenberger and Geiger were guarding was too bulky
for the fast in-and-out operating Gunn and the rest of
First Squad needed to conduct here. So the larger radio
remained at a fixed point, where it could communicate
with a similar unit in Callahan's squad, or even with the
distant *Bluefin* if necessary.

And now, Ehrenberger would be transmitting the two
short clicks they had agreed upon as the signal for Callahan's people to carry out their diversion.

Things, Gunn thought, *should be getting very interesting in just a few more minutes.*

South Bank, Dvina River
Near Severodvinsk, Russian SFSR
2338 hours GMT

"That's us!" Silverwolf said unnecessarily. All the SEALs of Second Squad heard the two quick bursts of static from the radio Martinez had set up against a tree stump in a sheltered hollow ten yards below the crest of the hill, all of them except Callahan himself, who maintained his lone vigil looking down on the electrical plant, away from the others.

Callahan didn't need to hear the signal from First Squad. His headset radio was on, and if he didn't hear Silverwolf's comment, he certainly heard BM/1 Davis make the formal report. "Lights Out," he said. "We have a go for Lights Out."

Leaving Martinez to monitor the radio, the rest of Second Squad moved quickly to join Callahan at the crest. Just as they reached the top of the hill, the grizzled old Master Chief finished extending the antenna on his radio detonator. He thumbed the switch without ever taking his eyes off the target, and without ever changing his expression. Silverwolf envied him that professional detachment . . . and feared it just a little at the same time. Would Johnny Silverwolf ever reach the point where he could simply look on all this as just another job to be done?

Down in the electrical plant, a ripple of fire and thunder tore through the lines of outsize turbines. The explosions didn't quite go off simultaneously, but it was close enough, and as the charges the SEALs had set went off they triggered subsidiary explosions that only added to the chaos. Now there was more smoke pouring upward, and tongues of fire leaping and dancing from shattered machinery.

The man-made lights dimmed as the flames spread, and warning sirens hooted and wailed. Silverwolf spotted a gaggle of workers erupting from buildings on the far side of the complex, most of them half-dressed and in a panic.

Something else exploded among the generators, and a tower carrying high-tension lines crumpled, swayed, and sagged to one side in a shower of sparks.

"Just like the Fourth of July," Woods said with a nasty grin.

"They don't have that around here, Woody," Jinx Jenkins said.

"They do now," Davis said.

"Arright, that's enough," Callahan growled. "We've done what we came here to do. Let's get the fuck out of here before the Russkies decide to come looking for us. Silverwolf, you help Martinez get the radio packed up. Woods, Jenkins, you start for the beach and get our gear ready for us. Davis, you're on back door with me. Got it?"

"Yes sir," Silverwolf said.

"Next time you call me *sir,* Silverwolf, you'll be doing laps around the grinder until you trip over your own long, gray beard!" the Master Chief told him gruffly. "I ain't no fucking officer. Now move it, you squirrels! Move it!"

Shipyard Number 402
Severodvinsk, Russian SFSR
2340 hours GMT

There was a distant, muffled sound, like thunder echoing in far-off hills, and after a moment the lights of the shipyard compound began to flicker and fade. One well-lit area overlooking the docks was suffering a brownout, and as Gunn watched, the guard at the door to the admin building turned to stare at the fading lights.

Gunn gave a hand signal, knowing that Senior Chief Burns was watching from another vantage point close by. Raising his H&K, Gunn waited patiently, Moultrie watching his back while the other SEALs moved quietly into position closer to the target. Even knowing what to look for, Gunn barely saw Burns and Pond coming up on either side of the guard through the shadows that lay heavy across the front of the administrative building. When they struck, it was silent and quick as lightning. The guard slumped from a blow delivered by Pond, while Burns grabbed his weapon and helped ease the body silently to the ground. Carstairs appeared a few seconds later, moving cautiously up to the door with his weapon raised, looking decidedly unlike a hospital corpsman.

Gunn turned and tapped Moultrie on the arm, then pointed toward the admin building. The two of them raced across the open ground to join the other three SEALs.

By the time they got there Burns and Pond had dragged the guard into the shadow of a patch of bushes near the door. Gunn knelt beside the prone body and checked the man. He was unconscious, not dead, and Gunn frowned as he studied the still form. The guard presented them with a problem. Dead, he would be a clue that someone had been in the admin building, and that was something the SEALs didn't want the Russians to know. Left alive, he would tell his superiors he had been attacked . . . same problem. He could be killed and his body carried off, perhaps dumped in the sea, but that would be a difficult job and would increase the risks of discovery.

It was Burns who solved the problem. Searching the body, he discovered a hip flask concealed under the man's belt. Gunn shook out a few drops on his finger and tasted it. The stuff was booze of some kind, probably homemade or brewed by some enterprising soldier or sailor at the shipyard. Grinning, Gunn proceeded to splash the stuff liberally on the unconscious guard's face, and forced a couple of swigs into his mouth. Liquor would explain away a multitude of sins. Even if he remembered being attacked, the guard's story wouldn't be believed; his superiors would probably think he was making things up to cover his drunkenness. Even the blow to his head was easily explained as the result of falling down drunk while on duty. . . .

Burns also found a set of keys attached to the man's belt, which he promptly removed. Those could be useful . . . but they would have to be returned before the SEALs left. Gunn gave his senior NCO a thumbs-up, and the two of them joined the others at the door.

Somewhere, an alarm was wailing mournfully, and the compound's lights were coming back on as backup generators within the shipyard facility itself cut in to take over the load no longer being supplied by the regular power grid. Gunn glanced around, but so far there was no reaction in the immediate vicinity. It would take time for people to realize there was trouble afoot, more time to organize a reaction to it. And hopefully the SEALs would be done long before anyone realized that any part of that trouble was right here in the heart of the sprawling shipyard complex.

Pond had already discovered the alarm box, and a quick check of the keys located one that fit. They deactivated the alarm; then Carstairs took the keys and went to work finding the right one for the door. Gunn set Moultrie up in the position the guard had occupied before; he was a fair match in size and general shape for the unconscious man in the bushes, and in the dark, from a distance, it would look like the man was still on watch. When Carstairs found the key and opened the door, the four remaining SEALs slipped inside and closed it behind them.

The interior was dark, a maze of corridors and offices. Gunn divided them up into two teams again, since only two of them—Carstairs and Gunn himself—read Russian well enough to be able to search out the room and the files they wanted. Gunn took Pond, while Burns and

Carstairs paired off. Splitting up, they began to search the first floor for Room 115.

It seemed to take hours, though Gunn knew that they had been moving from room to room for only about fifteen minutes, when the short-range receiver in his ear came to life. "Ferret Six, this is Ferret Two," Burns said crisply. "We found it."

"Roger, Two," Gunn replied. "On the way."

He and Pond headed back the way they had came, then down the corridor Burns and Carstairs had used when they split up. Moments later they spotted Burns ahead, beckoning them to yet another room . . . one which bore the legend "115" on a plate affixed to the door.

Inside, Carstairs was already at work at a bank of file cabinets that took up all of one end of the room. The hospital corpsman was busy rifling through files, a penlight clamped between his jaws, but he removed it as Gunn joined him. "Whoever's in charge of this mess ought to be sent to Siberia," the corpsman grumbled. "If there's a system to these files, it's beyond my understanding, sir."

"Just keep looking for Project 971," he responded, pulling open another drawer and starting to look. Pond took the light and held it for the two as they searched, while Burns remained by the door keeping watch.

They worked for a while in near-perfect silence, broken only by the soft sounds the file cabinet drawers made as the two SEALs opened and closed them. Gunn quickly discovered that Carstairs had been right in his complaint. The files cabinets were poorly marked, and the files stuffed inside them badly organized. He began to despair of ever finding anything worthwhile when Carstairs pulled a folder out and flourished it eagerly. "Here's something!" he said in a whisper.

Pond turned the light on the cover, and Gunn studied it. The Russian for PROJECT 971 was prominent on the front, written in large, blocky Cyrillic letters. He mo-

tioned for Carstairs and Pond to join him at a table
nearby, where Carstairs opened the folder while Gunn
produced a small camera. Working quickly, they photographed each of the documents in turn, then started
from the front again and made a second set of photos
using the camera Carstairs was carrying. There was no
time to translate as they went, though Gunn couldn't
help but pick up words here and there. These documents
didn't seem to be anything particularly useful; they appeared to be purchase orders for various types of routine
supplies and equipment. But perhaps somewhere there
would be indications of how the *Akula* had been fitted
out, such as parts orders for the sub's electronics suite
or armaments stores.

When they had finished photographing everything in
the file, Carstairs looked up at Gunn. "Do you think
there's more, sir?" he asked.

"Won't know until we've looked," Gunn shot back.
They started back to the long row of file cabinets. There
was still a lot to do, and time was passing. . . .

South Bank, Dvina River
Near Severodvinsk, Russian SFSR
2357 hours GMT

Silverwolf reached the mudflat at the base of the hill
and somehow managed to keep from slipping on the
slick, wet ground. He reached out a hand to steady Martinez, who had to contend with the bulky radio slung
across his back. The young Hispanic SEAL muttered
something that might have been "thank you," but probably wasn't, and Silverwolf flashed him a tight-lipped
grin. He was feeling lighthearted, knowing the mission
had gone off without a hitch. In another few minutes
they'd all be back in their diving gear and in the water,
heading for the two SDVs on the river bottom. And then

. . . back to *Bluefin*, which right now was the closest thing to home Silverwolf could think of.

First time out for the rookie SEAL . . . a slam-dunk success. When they got back to Norfolk he and Martinez wouldn't be the newbies anymore. They'd seen the elephant . . . and lived to tell the tale.

Above them, Davis and Callahan were making their withdrawal with all the care and caution anyone would expect from a pair of canny covert-ops veterans. And down by the water Jenkins and Woods had already uncovered the canister they had hidden when they came ashore. Woods was hunched over the open tube, carefully packing the explosives and other combat supplies from his web gear, while Jenkins crouched nearby with his weapon held ready, scanning the sluggish Dvina and the low island with its crown of low, twisted vegetation half-visible in the twilit sky.

Even as Silverwolf's eyes rested on Jenkins's stocky form, the other SEAL's head jerked around to face downriver. The hair on the back of Silverwolf's neck prickled, as if for just a moment he shared with Jenkins an uncanny sense of *wrongness* that couldn't be explained as anything but a SEAL's intuition for danger.

His eyes strained to probe the half-darkness downriver, but Silverwolf *heard* the threat before he saw it. The irregular throb of an engine that sounded badly in need of a tune-up, growing louder with each passing minute. Already it was far louder than the other sounds that rent the night from the other side of the hill, where the explosions had finally died away but the roar of uncontrolled fires still mingled with shouts, alarms, and the rumble of heavy machinery and fire engines striving to bring order to the chaos of the electrical plant. Those sounds were more a background noise now, while this new disturbance was menacing and immediate.

A shape seemed to solidify out in the gloom, coming into sight around the far end of the marshy island in the midst of the delta. It was long and dark, a humpbacked,

slow-moving form which put Silverwolf in mind of
some legendary sea monster in the few moments it took
his mind to process the information from his eyes into
something recognizable. Then, like a puzzle suddenly
seen at a new angle, all the elements snapped into
place—the long, tapering bow with its flat forward deck,
the built-up deckhouse amidships, the open well deck
astern . . . a boat, looking for all the world like some PT
boat out of an old World War II movie, with clusters of
men on the bow and in the well deck. It was chugging
slowly up the river, well away from the SEALs on the
southern shore. The blazing beam of a searchlight cut
through the gloom, playing along the shoreline, and Silverwolf realized that the men on the forward deck were
grouped around a machine-gun mount.

A patrol boat, making the rounds of the Dvina? Or
drawn here by the commotion at the electrical plant? It
didn't matter much at that point. All that mattered, Silverwolf thought with a sudden catch in his throat and
an irregular thudding in his chest, was that it was out
there . . . and in seconds the men on board were sure to
catch sight of the SEALs.

Jenkins's voice was harsh in Silverwolf's earpiece radio receiver. "Down! Down! Everyone down and
freeze!" Silverwolf cursed silently as he scrambled for
the cover of some stubby bushes. That was the essential
difference training and experience made in a SEAL. Jenkins had reacted while Silverwolf was still coming to
grips with the sudden change in the situation.

The other SEALs were going to ground as best they
could, but there was precious little cover to hide behind.
Jenkins and Woods were flat on their bellies in the thick
mud, both taking advantage of a fallen tree that provided
some concealment. Silverwolf glanced behind him to see
Callahan and Davis crouching behind low scrub.

But Martinez had been caught unprepared by the
warning. Out in the open, well away from anything that
could give him cover, he hesitated . . . and hesitation, as

Silverwolf's SEAL instructors had repeated time and again in training sessions from BUD/S onward, could be fatal in a combat situation.

Martinez had heard all those same commandments, probably knew them by heart as well as any SEAL. But all the training, all the practice, all the lectures and field exercises in the world couldn't tell a man how he would react the first time he faced battle for real.

The searchlight beam swept across the mudflats, missing Jenkins and Woods, blinding Silverwolf for an instant as it flashed across his position without stopping ... and fixed on Alberto Martinez. Too late, the rookie SEAL dropped prone in the mud. His belated reaction had only added to the problem, for keen eyes watching from the deck of the patrol boat were sure to detect the movement.

An incomprehensible shout rose over the uneven splutter of the boat's engine. The searchlight dipped, found Martinez again, and held on him as another shout, harsh and preemptory, rang out in challenge.

And all hell broke loose on the banks of the Dvina River.

The deep-throated hammer of that pintel-mounted heavy machine gun on the patrol boat's forward deck shattered the night. It was only a short burst, and aimed high as a warning shot. Someone on the boat called out a third time, and Silverwolf didn't need to understand Russian to know what that shout meant. *Show yourself, or the next time won't be a warning. . . .*

Martinez was squirming in the mud, trying to break away from the probing searchlight beam and reach a stump a few yards to his left that might offer him some dubious cover. As if he was watching it all in a movie slowed for dramatic effect, Silverwolf saw an officer on the deck of the Russian boat make a curt gesture, and the machine gun swung over and down. It rattled again, sparks strobing bright in the gloom.

Martinez screamed, an inhuman wail of agony. Hugging the mud behind his bush, Silverwolf winced.

Then Jenkins rose to one knee nearby and returned fire with his AK, and in moments the firefight had escalated out of control. Shouts and cries were punctuated by the staccato beat of automatic weapons firing. In an instant, the nighttime stillness had transformed into the chaos of battle.

Other SEALs were joining in the firing. Woods had already stowed his own Kalashnikov, but he yanked it back out of the supply canister, slapped in a fresh magazine, and drew back the bolt. He fired in short, measured bursts, in contrast to the wild, sustained autofire from Jenkins. From the slope behind Silverwolf someone else, Callahan or Davis, joined in.

Silverwolf ignored the urge to jump into the firefight himself, though every nerve was quivering with the need to do *something* to fight back. But in this situation one more rifle wasn't going to make much of a difference, he told himself. And there was something else he *could* do. . . .

He gathered himself in a racer's crouch and burst from the inadequate cover of the brush. The mud seemed to suck at his feet, and it felt as if he was running in slow motion as he sprinted across the open ground to where Martinez lay writhing in the muck. Silverwolf heard a few stray rounds whistle past him, but he reached the injured SEAL without being hit and dropped to one knee beside him. Without pausing to examine him, Silverwolf hoisted his dead weight from the ground in an awkward fireman's carry and staggered the rest of the way to the stump the other SEAL had been trying to reach before.

Lowering Martinez, Silverwolf unslung his AK, but a shout from above interrupted him. "The radio! Silverwolf, the radio!" Callahan paused to fire a few quick bursts from his H&K SMG. "Warn Gunn that we're under fire!"

The boat's searchlight flashed and swung up the hill toward the sound of his voice. More AK fire rattled as

Jenkins and Woods continued to fire, but the Russians on the boat were answering with their own rifles, to back up their heavier machine gun. It was an increasingly uneven contest, and Silverwolf knew the SEALs were outmatched.

He fumbled with the radio on Martinez's back, his mind racing as he worked. How long would it be before more Soviets were drawn to the firefight? It would only be a matter of time before ground troops put in an appearance. Hadn't the whole purpose of the diversion been to draw out their patrols away from the shipyard and into the area around the electrical plant? Ground troops . . . or what if a helicopter or two showed up? The SEALs needed time to get into their gear before they could get into the water and head for the waiting SDVs, and as long as they were pinned down there was no chance of donning that gear or making good their escape. Even if the firefight devolved into a standoff, dawn came early in these latitudes, and with full daylight they would stand even less chance of breaking contact and getting away.

He heard Jenkins fire again, and then a shouted "All right!" as the searchlight went dead. But the machine gun was still hammering away, and Silverwolf heard another scream from the hillside and knew that another of his comrades had been hit.

Finally he had the radio switched on. Silverwolf grabbed the microphone and held it close to his face, "Ferret, this is Mongoose. Ferret, this is Mongoose," he said urgently. "Waterloo. I say again, Waterloo." That code phrase meant the squad was in contact with hostile forces and in trouble. "Squad pinned down and unable to extract. We have casualties." He paused as the Russian machine-gun fire probed his position, bullets pounding deep into the tree trunk that shielded him, sending splinters of wood flying everywhere. "We're taking fire! Repeat, we're taking fire!"

Friday, 9 August 1985

Administrative Building, Shipyard Number 402
Severodvinsk, Russian SFSR
0006 hours GMT

"Ferret Six, this is Ferret Four," the voice whispered in Gunn's ear. "We've got trouble, L-T."

"Go, Four." Gunn replied, straightening up from the file drawer he was searching.

"Message from Mongoose." That was the code name Second Squad was using tonight. "They ran into an unexpected Russian patrol on the Dvina before they could get back underwater. The last transmission I had was, quote, 'we're taking fire,' unquote."

"Damn . . ." Gunn fought the urge to keep on cursing. They still hadn't finished going through the extensive files . . . and they hadn't turned up anything further of interest since that first folder. But with Second Squad in trouble, he had to make some hard choices, and fast. Stirring up trouble around the electrical plant to draw attention away from the shipyard was one thing, but now that it had turned into open combat there was a very real danger that the Russians would tighten their security all around Severodvinsk. That would be even more certain if they discovered that they were fighting American commandos by the banks of the Dvina, and not just homegrown dissidents.

Let them suspect that U.S. Navy SEALs had been deployed from the White Sea, and the entire mission was jeopardized, not just here at the shipyard, but out where *Bluefin* and *Pittsburgh* were waiting to bring them out. If the Russians started thinking in terms of American submarines carrying commandos, they could bar the door and trap the two subs. And the whole mission would be well and truly sunk.

Even if they missed a veritable mother lode of additional information in these files, they didn't have much choice but to abort at once. If they pulled out immediately, First Squad could get back to the subs with what they'd already found. And even if the worst happened with Callahan's men, they might still be far enough ahead of the Russians to win free.

He only hesitated for a moment before coming to a decision. "All right, Four, prepare to extract. Inform Mongoose they're to break contact and pull out as soon as possible. We're on our way now."

"Roger that, Six," Ehrenberger replied. Gunn thought he could hear relief in the man's voice. "Ferret Four, clear."

"Okay, people, time to pack up and move out," Gunn said, closing the file drawer reluctantly. A few more minutes and they might have uncovered more worthwhile documents on Project 971 . . .

Or they might have found nothing at all even if they searched all night.

Gunn swallowed a hint of bile as he thought of Callahan's squad caught in a firefight. There was nothing he could do for them, no way to help pull them out. His responsibility now was to get his squad and the photographs they'd obtained back out to *Bluefin*. He had to regard Callahan and the others as expendable.

Acceptable casualties . . . a phrase he had always regarded as an oxymoron. As far as Gunn was concerned, no casualty was acceptable if there was any way of avoiding losing a man. But he didn't have any options tonight.

If Anderson hadn't been injured, Gunn would have been in command of Second Squad instead of Callahan. Would he have been able to make a difference? Or would his leadership have made things worse, instead of better?

At least he wouldn't be feeling so damned *guilty* . . . .

Burns led the way out of Room 115, and Pond brought up the rear. As they hastened down the dark corridor, a warning siren rent the night.

Wardroom, USS *Bluefin*
The White Sea, Off Severodvinsk
0010 hours GMT

"Captain?"

Gordon looked up from the paperwork on the table in front of him, the stack of reports the diver from *Pittsburgh* had exchanged a few minutes earlier for the material Gunn and Gordon had compiled after the SEALs had made their first swim the previous night. By now Chase was probably starting to pore over those reports, though they weren't nearly as impressive as what the attack sub had managed to amass after her chance encounter with the Soviet prototype.

Hogan was standing in the open door of the tiny wardroom, looking tired and a little less jolly than was the norm for him, but that was easy to understand. This was the second night in a row that the normal watch rotation had been disrupted by SEAL operations. If Lieutenant Commander Hogan looked a little out of sorts, Gordon imagined he himself must look like death warmed over. He'd had precious little sleep over the last thirty-six hours, and it could be just as long again before he had any real chance to catch up on it.

Luckily one of the first things anyone learned in the Silent Service was how to catch a catnap . . . and how to take advantage of almost any opportunity to get some rest, no matter how brief or under what unusual circumstances the chance occurred.

"What is it, Mr. Hogan?" he said, trying to keep the weary edge out of his voice.

"Comm shack just monitored a couple of transmissions from the SEALs. Second Squad has run into trouble on the Dvina. They're under fire, and have taken casualties. Gunn just gave the order to pull out."

"Damn . . . any sign of reaction from the Russkies yet?"

"Just general confusion on the channels we've been monitoring," Hogan told him. "I think things are still developing too fast for them to realize what's going on. No way to know how much longer that'll last, though."

"Yeah." Gordon nodded, hoping the gesture would help to clear his head. It didn't help. "Damn it all, running flat out it'll take at least an hour for Gunn's squad to get back here. Longer for the other bunch even if they can get back to their SDVs. And by then . . . who knows how much the Russkies will have mobilized? I can just see them sending out patrols in time to hear us operating the bow doors during pickup."

"We don't have a lot of choice, Skipper," Hogan said slowly. "Chances are we're far enough out that they'd only blunder into us by accident. . . ."

"Chances are," Gordon shot back savagely, "that there are going to be wounded coming out in some of those SDVs. Damn it, Ed, stick a wounded man in a flooded SDV for an hour and a half and how much worse is he going to be by the time they dock with us out here?" He stood up slowly, gathering his resolution. "I'm not going to sit on my ass out here and leave those SEALs to make it out on their own. We can halve the time until pickup if we meet them halfway!"

"But the mission specs—"

"Damn the mission specs!" Gordon said savagely. "Those men are as much my responsibility as our own crew." He paused, forcing himself to calm down. "Your orders, Mr. Hogan. Reel in the snorkel and the communications antenna and prepare to get under way as soon as possible. I'll join you in the control room shortly."

"Aye aye, sir," Hogan said stiffly. His usual jovial disposition had vanished, and Gordon could read the disapproval in his eyes. But the man was too good an Executive Officer to argue once his CO's mind was made up.

"And set up the Gertrude, Mr. Hogan. I'm going to have to sell this to Chase, too." Gordon turned away. He knew how Mike Chase was likely to react.

Dvina River
Near Severodvinsk, Russian SFSR
0011 hours GMT

"I don't like this, O'Dell," Lieutenant Vincent Harriman growled. "Something's gotten fucked up somewhere."

"Yessir," the SDV pilot, QM/2 O'Dell, replied. Normally an easygoing sort, his voice was taut with worry.

Waiting in SDV #1, grounded on the bottom of the river while the SEALs carried out their mission ashore, had been a strain on both of them. With nothing to do but lie in their flooded control cab, surrounded by chilly water that even their wet suits couldn't completely insulate them from, the minutes weighed heavily on them. According to the original mission profile the SEALs should have been returning as much as half an hour ago, but so far they hadn't put in an appearance.

And then they'd heard the turning screw thrashing the water above them.

Human ears might not be as sophisticated as the sonar gear aboard a submarine like *Bluefin* or *Pittsburgh*, and the SDV's electronics were designed for navigation and collision avoidance rather than long-range detection, but the sound of a boat moving through the water was distinctive. Harriman had heard it often enough before during exercises, and he was sure that was what he was hearing now.

A boat, passing slowly over their position, and the SEALs were late for their extraction. He didn't like that combination at all.

"I'm going outside to have a look around, O'Dell," Harriman said. Before the pilot could answer, he was already checking his SCUBA gear. The SDV crew used the onboard underwater breathing apparatus, just as the SEALs did when they were on board, but like the SEALs the two crewmen had their own swimming gear with them. There was always the chance they might have to abandon their SDV and make their own way to safety.

"Lieutenant . . ." O'Dell sounded nervous.

"What is it?" Harriman demanded gruffly. He didn't plan to let his subordinate talk him out of anything, if that was the man's intention.

"Sir . . . you should take someone with you. Buddy system."

That made Harriman pause a moment. O'Dell had a point. Going out there solo was against every principle of diving, in the Navy or out of it. "Yeah. You're right. But you ain't coming along, O'Dell. You keep an eye on the old girl here. I'll get Joor out of Number Three."

"Yessir," O'Dell said again. "And . . . good luck, Lieutenant."

Harriman switched from the UBA breathing mask to his own mask and mouthpiece, then opened the hatch above him and kicked himself free of the confines of the

Swimmer Delivery Vehicle. He took a moment to orient himself in the chill, dark water, then swam slowly across to the other SDV where it lay on the soft bottom perhaps twenty yards farther up the river. Both rear hatches were still open, and he pulled himself inside of the portside passenger compartment. Donning one of the full-face UBA masks there, he switched on the intercom.

"Joor, I want you to come with me for a look around up topside. You up for that?"

"Uh . . . sure, Lieutenant, if you say so," the SDV's navigator responded. Normally cocky and full of himself, Joor sounded a little less certain than usual now that he was faced with a radical departure from the usual SDV *modus operandi*.

"Then get moving." Harriman took a moment to check one of the lockers along the side of the passenger compartment where the SEALs carried their combat stores. As he had hoped, several of the limpet mines he'd included as part of the mix of demolitions gear were still stowed there. The mines, intended to be attached to the bottom of a steel-hulled boat with a powerful magnetic clamp, weren't the sort of thing Second Squad needed for their sabotage ashore, so they had been left aboard the SDV. Harriman snagged a pair of satchels, put a mine in each one, then exited through the hatch overhead.

If that boat they had heard moving on the surface was interfering with the extraction, Harriman figured a couple of mines would be one way of persuading the Russians to let the SEALs pass.

He handed one of the satchels to Bill Joor as the navigator joined him, and together the two men started for the surface of the river.

Shipyard Number 402
Severodvinsk, Russian SFSR
0013 hours GMT

With distant sirens wailing the alarm, Gunn and the other members of First Squad raced out of the building and into the night. Chuck Moultrie remained at his post in place of the guard, craning his head from side to side as he watched for any sign of trouble. So far, fortunately, there was no indication of a major turnout in response to the sirens anywhere nearby.

But that might not last, Gunn thought. They had to move . . . quickly.

Senior Chief Burns stooped over the still form of the Soviet guard long enough to restore his keys. As he did so, Gunn was already urging Carstairs and Pond to move out. Carstairs had one full set of the all-important photographs in his camera, so if they could just make sure that he escaped back to the waiting SDVs the mission wouldn't be a total loss, whatever happened to the rest of them.

Now Burns straightened up and joined Gunn and Moultrie. "Time to make tracks, L-T?" the Senior Chief asked.

"Like a rabbit in the snow," Gunn told him. "Moultrie, point. Chief, watch behind. Move!"

They moved off along a different route than the one the first two SEALs had taken. It lost them the advantages of covering each other in a leapfrog withdrawal, but it doubled their chances of having one group make it to the shore without getting into trouble. The sound of the sirens rose and fell, making the hair on the back of Gunn's head stand on end. He could almost feel hostile eyes following their every move, could imagine a sniper with a high-powered Dragonov rifle drawing a bead, squeezing the trigger . . .

But no shot came, and no one shouted a challenge. The SEALs made their way around buildings and down wide streets without seeing anyone, and as they came closer to the sea Gunn began to think he might dare to breathe again after all. It seemed that the diversion scheme was working after all . . . the Russians were still concentrating all their attention on the far side of the city, up by the Dvina, and no one had thought to be concerned about security inside the shipyard as yet.

He only wished he knew how the others were faring. They were the men from the platoon he knew best: the crusty Callahan, Jenkins with his bad-luck reputation and hangdog expression . . . the rookies, Silverwolf and Martinez. Davis and Woods, both hard-bitten, competent fighters.

Gunn forced the thoughts from his mind. He had his own group to shepherd to safety. He couldn't do anything to help Second Squad, whatever their situation. And worrying about them could be fatal to the men he *could* look out for.

They spotted the retaining wall and sprinted across the last open space to reach it. As he rolled over it, Gunn saw Ehrenberger by the open equipment canister, handing out diving gear to Carstairs and Pond. Geiger was by the wall, weapon at the ready, his rebreather, mask, and fins already back in place.

They had all made it. So far, so good.

He joined the others. "Carstairs, Pond, Geiger, get moving. Head for the SDVs, fast. If we don't make it five minutes after you get there, head back for *Bluefin*. Doc, you have your camera secure?"

"Right here, L-T," the corpsman said.

"Good. Then get moving!"

"Aye aye, sir," Pond said. "Come on, Doc, let's get wet!"

Gunn and Moultrie took over the watch at the wall while the other three finished gearing up and withdrew to the water. Then Gunn remained in place while Moultrie got his equipment on; the big SEAL in turn took the watch while Gunn hastily donned his diving gear, stuffed his shoes and weapon into the canister, and sealed it tight against the water. He gestured to Moultrie, who discarded his AK and ran down to join Gunn. Together they hefted the weight of the equipment case and started into the water.

Their foray into Russia was done.

Gunn only hoped it would turn out to be worth whatever price the others were paying on the bank of the Dvina. . . .

Control Room, USS *Pittsburgh*
The White Sea, Off Severodvinsk
0018 hours GMT

"My mind is made up, Mike. I'm taking her inshore."

Mindful of the eyes watching him from every corner of Pittsburgh's cramped control room, Chase bit back a curse and spoke into the handset in a flat, even voice. "Even if I order you to stay put, Frank?" he asked.

"Don't give that order, and you won't have to find out, Mike." Gordon's reply, even with the Gertrude's distortions, held a note of appeal. "Those SEALs are in trouble. Every minute we cut down on transit time is another minute my doctor can be working on one of their casualties. And it'll be one less minute the Russkies have to organize a search to find out how the SEALs got there in the first place. It's for the good of the mission, Mike. Can't you see that?"

Chase reined in his temper. He didn't like Gordon's cavalier departure from the established plan, but it was understandable enough. Six SEALs had gotten into trouble ashore, and hadn't been heard from thereafter. Chase himself would probably have taken *Bluefin* inshore in hopes of helping them escape. Just cutting down the transit time from landing area to submarine might be important, especially for the wounded.

But if Chase would have done so commanding *Bluefin*, the Chase who was captain of the *Pittsburgh* and in charge of the overall operation had a different perspective. Getting out of the White Sea was going to be tricky enough. Any extra complications only caused more headaches . . . and risked the moment when Chase might have to face up to Goldman's "the mission comes first" orders.

Frank Gordon didn't want to leave six SEALs behind. But Mike Chase might have to face something far worse—abandoning nearly two hundred men, and *Bluefin*, in order to escape with the information they had gathered so far.

"I should at least be there with you. We're supposed to be covering your ass . . ."

"Negative on that, Mike. Think it through." This was Frank Gordon, Academy roommate and old friend, not Frank Gordon, junior officer, telling his CO what to do. "*Bluefin* has to go in because we're equipped to pick up the SDVs. But if some of the SEALs miss us and head for the original rendezvous, you have to be there so they can abandon the SDVs and let you pick them up. This way we cover all the options." He paused. "Anyway, you have duplicates of everything except whatever Gunn is bringing out. If need be, you can pick up and head for home right now, and deliver everything to the admiral."

"And leave you behind? You think I can abandon you, any more than you can leave those SEALs behind?"

"Those are your orders from Goldman, aren't they, Mike? We both know that either one of our boats is expendable . . . as long as the other one brings home the bacon. Look, it ain't gonna come to that. I'll take us in right up the channel, just like *Sea Devil* back in the old days with Captain Brady. I'll fetch out our lost sheep and then we can all take a nice, leisurely cruise the hell out of the White Sea and back to someplace decent where there's plenty of water under our keels. Okay?"

"Yeah . . . okay, Frank," Chase said slowly, reluctant to commit himself but all too well aware that he didn't have any real options. He could, he supposed, charge Gordon with insubordination and disobedience of lawful orders when they got back home . . . *if* they got back home. But at this point, if *Bluefin* did make it back, Gordon would deserve a hero's welcome, not a court-martial, for what he was trying to do. And there wouldn't be much point in a court martial if *Bluefin*'s inshore run went sour. . . .

"Okay, Frank," he repeated, more firmly this time. "Do what you have to do. But take care of *Bluefin*, damn it. The old girl deserves better than to go down as a monument to Frank Gordon's testosterone count!"

Gordon chuckled, a raw, harsh sound on the Gertrude. "She'll be fine, Mike. Trust me. *Bluefin*, clear."

He lowered the handset. "And take care of yourself, Frank," Chase whispered.

SDV #2
Off Severodvinsk, Russian SFSR
0019 hours GMT

Gunn pulled the passenger hatch closed above him as he entered the SDV, then groped to find the last remaining underwater breathing apparatus face mask. He pulled his diving mask and mouthpiece clear and settled the UBA mask over his head in their place. As he took a deep breath of the SDV's tanked air he glanced at the others in the passenger compartment. Moultrie, Burns, and Ehrenberger were already strapped down and ready to go.

And SDV #4, with Carstairs, Pond, and Geiger on board, had already started back toward *Bluefin* for their pickup.

Mission accomplished for First Squad. But what about Callahan and his men?

"Back to the barn, Lieutenant?" Lieutenant j.g. DuQuense asked over the intercom.

Gunn hesitated for a long moment. A part of him wanted to order DuQuense to head for the Dvina River and Second Squad. He wanted to help those men, to share their danger instead of leaving them hanging in the breeze.

"L-T," Senior Chief Burns said quietly, "you know there's nothing we can do for the others. Not now."

He looked sharply at Burns, wondering how the Senior Chief had read his thoughts so clearly. Then again, all of them were probably feeling the same way just then. It was a point of pride with the SEALs that they took care of each other, and they didn't leave behind their wounded . . . or their dead.

But it would take an SDV traveling at top speed close to an hour to reach the scene of Second Squad's diversionary operation from there, and an hour is an eternity in a firefight. By the time Gunn could be on the scene the battle would be long over, and the SEALs would have either reached their own SDVs and started for home . . . or they would all be dead. And in either case, all Gunn would be doing would be feeding four more men into a stirred-up hornet's nest.

And, anyway, his mission wouldn't be successfully completed until the photographs of the papers they'd gone through were safely delivered to *Bluefin* and *Pittsburgh*. That still had to take priority. Carstairs was on the way out with his copy of the information, of course, but there was still a chance something would happen to SDV #4 on the way out. Gunn couldn't go charging off on some fool's errand until he was *sure* the mission had been carried out, especially when he couldn't hope to help Callahan and the others no matter what he tried to do.

Gunn swallowed. "Back to the barn, Mr. DuQuense," he agreed reluctantly.

No matter how correct the words might have been, they were the hardest he had ever been forced to say.

South Bank, Dvina River
Near Severodvinsk, Russian SFSR
0021 hours GMT

His surroundings had taken on an air of unreality, as if Johnny Silverwolf was only a spectator to the firefight instead of a part of a life-or-death struggle. It seemed as if he saw and heard everything with preternatural precision, yet there was a remoteness to it all that made him feel detached, aloof.

And then Martinez stopped struggling, and in an instant everything changed.

The Hispanic SEAL had been twitching and moaning from the time Silverwolf had first set him down under the cover of the big tree stump. He'd tried to administer first aid to the wounded man, but in the dark, with autofire probing their position over and over again, he hadn't been able to do much for his friend. Silverwolf had managed to bind a couple of bleeding wounds in Martinez's left arm, but there were other wounds, and blood . . . way too much blood. . . .

Martinez gave a final long, drawn-out moan and slumped sideways against Silverwolf's leg. The whites of his eyes gleamed unnaturally bright against the olive skin of his face as they stared fixedly upward, almost as if they were trying to convey some last message of regret or recrimination. Silverwolf looked down at those dead eyes, the spark behind them extinguished now, for long seconds before he could comprehend what had happened. Then, desperately, he tried to find a pulse at Martinez's wrist or throat. But there was none. He was dead. . . .

The rest of the battle receded from Silverwolf's mind as he looked down at the other SEAL. Martinez couldn't die! He'd been the one man lower in the pecking order than Silverwolf himself, the rookie freshly joined from BUD/S and a quick stint at Ranger School . . . the cocky young bastard who made up for his lack of experience with a carefully cultivated SEAL attitude. Friend, swim buddy . . . comrade in arms. Now he was gone.

"Snap out of it, Silverwolf!" a gruff voice ordered. "Give me a hand with the Master Chief!"

It was BM/1 Davis, staggering toward him with Callahan leaning heavily against him. Silverwolf roused himself and sprang up to help them, dragging the Master Chief down into the mud beside the dead body of Alberto Martinez just as the Russian machine gunner fired another burst in their general direction. Answering fire confirmed that Woods and Jenkins were still in the game, but for how much longer? Martinez was dead, and Callahan didn't look good. . . .

"How's the Master Chief?" he asked.

Callahan grunted. Davis shrugged. "He's lost a lot of blood. Wish Carstairs was here to patch him up." He was already cutting away Callahan's sleeves around the ragged bullet wounds in his arm and shoulder. "Damn, Master Chief, your arm looks like ground beef," he muttered as he started to clean the wounds. "Silverwolf, give me a hand here."

The two SEALs worked quickly to bind Callahan's bullet wounds. Through it all the Master Chief seemed groggy and out of touch, and Davis was frowning as he finished with the last bandage. "Shock," he muttered. "And too much blood loss. Damn . . . I don't like this."

"Don't like what?" Silverwolf asked.

"He needs better attention than we can give him here," Davis said. "Back when he was in 'Nam he would have been picked up by a chopper and medevacked straight back to a hospital, but we can't do that. We've got to get him out of here . . ."

"Not much hope of that right now," Silverwolf said glumly. "We're up shit creek without a paddle."

"Paddle? Kid, we don't have a fucking *canoe*!" Davis ejected a spent magazine, snapped a fresh one into the receiver of his muddy Kalashnikov. "Best we can hope for right now is a miracle, Silverwolf."

"Right now I'd even settle for the U.S. Cavalry," he replied. Things were coming back into focus for Johnny Silverwolf. Martinez was gone, yes . . . and the rest of them might soon be following him into oblivion. But in the meantime they were still SEALs, by God, and Silverwolf was determined not to go out without a fight.

Dvina River
Near Severodvinsk, Russian SFSR
0023 hours GMT

Lieutenant Vincent Harriman's head broke the surface of the river, and he was plunged into another world.

The transition from the chill, dark calm of the underwater realm to the chaos on the surface took him by surprise even though he'd been expecting trouble from the moment he realized there was a boat in the neighborhood. What he hadn't been prepared for was the intensity of the clash that had erupted between the boat and the SEALs on shore.

Harriman and Joor were off the bow of the patrol craft, and close to the southern bank where Callahan's men had gone ashore. In the half-light, the vessel loomed large and black, illuminated by running lights and strobing muzzle flashes from a machine gun and various autorifles firing from her bow and well decks. Ashore, things were harder to make out, but intermittent muzzle flashes showed that Callahan's SEALs were returning fire when they could,. Still, the Russians had the advantage in both mobility and firepower. In moments it was clear to Harriman that the SEALs were pinned down, and as long as that boat was able to maintain its position, Callahan and his people weren't going anywhere.

He motioned to Joor to dive, and both men ducked their heads back underwater and headed downward. When they were close to the bottom again Harriman signaled to Joor to join him and detached the slate and chalk that hung from his belt. He wrote quickly on the slate: ATTACH MINE NEAR BOW. 5 MINUTE TIMER DELAY. Holding it up, he pointed up in the direction of the patrol boat, and Joor gave him a quick nod before kicking off from the bottom and swimming toward his target. Harriman followed, but as they approached the boat he changed direction and moved toward the stern of the vessel.

As he drew the limpet mine from its satchel, he was mindful of the thrashing propeller blades only a few feet away. This was going to be a tricky operation, requiring care and no small amount of luck. Harriman grabbed onto a projection on the bottom of the hull, possibly the mounting for a small sonar unit, with his left hand, while he placed the mine against the metal hull with his right. The mine attached with a loud *clang*, and stayed in place when he released it.

He fumbled a little as he set the timer on the mine, cursing inwardly at his clumsiness. If he'd had more chances to practice with explosives, he would have been better equipped for this, but of course as a mere taxi driver for the SEALs he wasn't given those sorts of exercises to keep him sharp. Harriman had to cast his memory back to BUD/S and some of the qualifying tests there to recall details of how to set up the timer. He wondered if Joor was having the same trouble with his mine.

Then he was done, the charge set to detonate in five

minutes. Plenty of time for the two men to get clear. He jackknifed in the water and drove himself deep, feeling the prop wash as the boat slowly passed above him. With hard, broad breaststrokes he swam down, scanning back and forth in search of Joor. But the SDV navigator wasn't in sight, and reluctantly Harriman started up again to search for him.

He spotted Joor, still clinging to the bottom of the boat and wrestling one-handed with the timer. Muttering a curse around his mouthpiece, Harriman swam to join him. With the clock already ticking, there was no time for Joor to keep on trying to set up his mine. He had to get clear before the one at the stern went off. Even outside the immediate blast radius of an underwater explosion, there was always a danger from the pressure waves that radiated outward through the water, which could stun or even kill a man. It was the same principle as dropping dynamite into a lake to bring dozens of dead fish floating to the surface . . . the effects of the blast were greatly magnified in the water.

Impatiently, he attracted Joor's attention and wrote on his slate again. LEAVE IT. SWIM TO SHORE AND HELP SEALS TO SDVS WHEN BOAT GOES UP.

The navigator nodded and started away, swimming rapidly. No doubt he was just realizing that the other mine must already be set and counting down, and Joor didn't look as if he relished the prospect of hanging around to see the results of Harriman's sabotage efforts close-up.

Harriman was about to head for the bottom again, to get the SDVs fired up and ready to move out as soon as the SEALs could reach them. With the firefight, and whatever calls the Russians might have put out reporting their situation or summoning backup, this area wasn't going to be a healthy neighborhood to linger in, and the sooner they got started back to the rendezvous with *Bluefin* the better. But Harriman checked his motion as he noticed that Joor had almost finished the arming sequence on the mine. It was always best to have two explosives in place, in case one failed . . . and this would only take a moment to arm.

He grabbed on to the mine itself and pulled himself closer, made the last few keystrokes needed to set the timer, then shoved himself down and away and started swimming.

The boat, still moving along at a very slow pace, passed over him, a dark shadow more felt than seen. Harriman would have smiled if it hadn't been for the mouthpiece of his rebreather. In another few minutes, the Russian patrol boat would be fiery debris.

And it would be the SDV man, the taxi driver, who would earn the credit for saving the SEALs' collective butt. . . .

South Bank, Dvina River
Near Severodvinsk, Russian SFSR
0027 hours GMT

The standoff continued along the bank of the Dvina.

The American SEALs were still pinned down, unable even to deploy properly under the continued hammering autofire of the pintel-mounted heavy machine gun that commanded the riverbank from the deck of the slow-moving Russian patrol boat. But the Russians, on the other hand, were finding the return fire from shore severe enough to keep them from deploying their Spetznaz naval commandos ashore to flush out the hostiles from their cover.

In the end, the Russians knew, they had all the advantages. They had already broadcast a request for additional support, and any time now patrols would be closing in to seal off all possible escape routes. Then they would have these intruders, whoever they were. Meantime all that was necessary was to keep them in play, hold them pinned on the riverbank while the additional forces came up. But the senior lieutenant commanding the patrol found the situation galling. His Spetznaz were, man for man, a match for any elite forces on the planet, even the vaunted American Green Berets or Navy SEALs. They should have been able to deal with this problem on their own, without relying on back-ups.

So the lieutenant wasn't content to simply let the stalemate stand. He ordered the boat to stand in closer to shore in hopes they could suppress the enemy fire long enough to allow his men to get ashore and fan out.

"Dmitri! Ivan! Grenades!" the officer snapped. He pointed toward shore to the nearer of the two spots they had identified as definite enemy positions, and the two Spetznaz commandos gave him wolfish grins as they reached for the grenades on their web gear. Each man grasped his hand grenade and stepped forward to make a textbook throw. One grenade sailed over the open water in a perfect arc, but landed wide and did nothing more than send a geyser of mud into the air when it burst.

The second grenade never left the hand of the grenadier. A burst of autofire from shore caught Ivan Ivanovich Razin squarely in the chest just as he was about to throw, driving him backward against the well-deck railing. His body hung limp, draped over the stern. The grenade, armed, tumbled into the water directly aft of the patrol boat, sinking out of sight.

It went off underwater a few seconds later, too far down to do any damage to the boat. But the muffled explosion caught Vincent Harriman as he dived for the cover of the SDVs on the bottom, and the sudden wave of pressure knocked the American out cold. Harriman's body, suddenly limp, began to float upward, toward the surface.

And then the countdown was over, and the two limpet mines went off almost as one.

Friday, 9 August 1985

South Bank, Dvina River
Near Severodvinsk, Russian SFSR
0031 hours GMT

Fire and thunder rent the night.

The double explosion tore through the steel hull of the Russian patrol boat as if it were wet tissue paper. A geyser of flame and smoke shot high into the air, tossing men aside like so many rag dolls. Silverwolf, watching in stunned amazement, found his eye drawn to a flashing, spinning object thrown high above the wrecked boat. It was the Russian machine gun, blasted loose from its pintel mount, rotating like some bizarre pinwheel as it fell in slow motion back toward the river.

The aft explosion set off a gas tank, which created a third, distinct blast to complete the destruction. In a matter of moments, all that was left of the enemy craft were a few bits of flotsam and jetsam and a spreading stain of burning fuel on the surface of the river.

"What the hell . . . ?" Silverwolf began, but Davis cut him off.

"Don't look a gift horse in the mouth, kid! This is our chance! Help me with the Master Chief!"

Together, they half carried, half dragged the unconscious Callahan down to the riverbank, where Woods
was once again at the storage container while Jenkins
scanned the water for any sign of survivors, his AK held
at the ready. He had torn strips off his shirt to bandage
a bleeding wound in the fleshy part of his calf, but otherwise he looked none the worse for wear.

Silverwolf and Davis lowered Callahan to the ground
next to the supply canister.

"Do you think he can dive?" Silverwolf asked. "Make
it to the SDVs?"

Woods shrugged. "If he can't, he's a dead man either
way."

"You two get him into his gear," Davis ordered. "I'm
going back for Martinez."

It was hard work getting the wounded man into his
wet suit, but somehow they managed it. By the time they
had Callahan geared up, Davis had brought the body of
Martinez down to the riverbank. It was a SEAL credo:
You didn't leave a teammate behind, dead or alive.

Something stirred in the water close by, and Jenkins
and Davis both had their weapons trained on the spot in
an instant. But the head that broke the water was wearing a wet-suit hood and face mask, and as he scrambled
onto the bank Bill Joor spat out his mouthpiece. "Don't
shoot! Damn it, it's the cavalry!"

Silverwolf looked up from tightening the straps on
Callahan's rebreather gear. "Is that supposed to be a
good thing?" he asked with a grin. Now that the firefight
was over, he was feeling almost giddy.

"Lieutenant Harriman sent me to help get you guys
moving!" Joor said. "He may have blown up the boat,
but you can bet there's more trouble on the way . . ."

"Harriman blew up the boat?" Davis repeated. "Goddamn, now I've heard everything. The taxi drivers are
taking over!"

"You better be damn glad the taxi drivers were there

for you guys today," Joor said. "Otherwise, you'd all be royally screwed."

"Yeah," Woods said, looking a little stunned. "Yeah . . . thanks."

From his position on the bank, Jenkins was staring through a set of night vision glasses at the water near the place where the boat had gone down. "Joor . . . I think you'd better have a look over there." He pointed to where a body was floating on the surface. Even without the night glasses, Silverwolf could see that it was wearing a black wet suit identical to the ones on Joor and Callahan. . . .

"Oh, God . . . not the *lieutenant*!" Joor's voice broke as he said it. He turned and dived back into the water before anyone could stop him, swimming just under the surface with powerful strokes of arms and legs.

Silverwolf looked away. Martinez . . . Callahan . . . now Harriman, all casualties. His baptism of fire was carrying a high cost.

Control Room, USS *Bluefin*
The White Sea, Off Severodvinsk
0034 hours GMT

Gordon stood at the OOD position, willing himself to remain calm and controlled in front of his bridge crew even as his every instinct cried out for him to be doing something, *anything*, to use up the pent-up energy within him. A commanding officer couldn't be seen to fidget or worry, but Gordon was finding it hard to live up to that particular requirement right now. He found himself envying the captains of old-time sailing ships, who could pace their quarterdecks, thinking on their feet or just burning up calories. A submarine didn't have any room for a captain to pace. . . .

He returned his attention to the readouts on the

OOD's panel in front of him. They were maintaining a course straight up the middle of the Dvina channel, their depth steady at 120 feet, their speed a full fifteen knots. That was just about fast enough to qualify as reckless, given the shallow water of the White Sea and the age of the *Sea Devil* charts, but Gordon knew that if he was to make any difference at all to those SEALs out there he had to bring *Bluefin* inshore quickly.

So far, the charts had been completely accurate, and the boat hadn't encountered any unexpected obstacles. He could only hope and pray that would continue to be the case all the way in. Otherwise, *Bluefin* could be in serious trouble.

Studying the readouts, Gordon asked himself if he was doing the right thing. Both Chase and Hogan had tried to talk him out of this dangerous course of action, and from just about every standpoint they had been absolutely right to do so. It wasn't as if *Bluefin* could hope to influence events on shore. By now, the firefight Second Squad had reported was surely over, one way or another. All Gordon could hope to do would be to recover the survivors, if any, a little sooner than they might otherwise have reached safety. Was that worth the risk to boat, crew, and mission?

And what would the brass say, looking at the after-mission reports, even if everything went well and they made it home again? What would *Admiral Goldman* say? Would he decide that he had been right all along about Frank Gordon's character flaws, and sink what remained of his lackluster career?

Right now, Gordon told himself, *none of that matters*. *Bluefin* and *Pittsburgh* had already carried out their mission. Chase could bring home the bacon whatever happened to *Bluefin*. But those SEALs might need all the help he could bring them, and Frank Gordon didn't intend to turn his back on them. Not even if he was offered all the things he'd about given up on—a promotion, a new command, the ideal assignment—as the price for letting those men sink or swim on their own.

It might not have been the Navy way . . . but, by God, it was the right way for Gordon to go. And he was going to see it through to the end, whatever the cost.

South Bank, Dvina River
Near Severodvinsk, Russian SFSR
0037 hours GMT

Silverwolf pulled his face mask into place and took an experimental breath through his mouthpiece. Satisfied that the equipment was all in order, he turned expectantly toward EM/1 Jenkins, who looked awkward wearing a wet suit but leaning heavily on a stick as he hobbled toward the bank.

"Silverwolf," Jenkins said. "Help me with the Master Chief. Woods, you're in charge of the equipment. Right? Let's get moving."

He hadn't said anything about Joor or Davis and their burdens, and didn't have to. They would have their hands full bringing the bodies of the two dead men down to the waiting SDVs. Silverwolf's thoughts shied away from the grisly task, and he focused instead on his own role.

Callahan was conscious, but only barely, and he was weak and disoriented. Shepherding him underwater was going to be a difficult task . . . and one that the SEALs feared would finish the job the Russian bullets had started. No one in Second Squad was a hospital corpsman, but they all had enough basic first-aid experience to know that Callahan had been hit badly. Davis suspected there had been internal bleeding, and certainly the grizzled old Master Chief had lost a lot of blood. The shock of swimming through the chilly waters of the Dvina and the long trip back to the sub might be enough to kill him. But they had no choice but to try.

"Come on, Master Chief," Silverwolf said, hoisting Callahan to his feet in a fireman's carry. "Let's get this show on the road."

Slowly, awkwardly, he guided and supported the wounded man to the water's edge and waded out as far as feet could carry them. Then Silverwolf paused to let Jenkins catch up. With Callahan drifting in and out of awareness as he'd been, he needed to be closely monitored all the way to the SDVs to be sure he was breathing properly. That would be Jenkins's responsibility, while Silverwolf provided most of the muscle to keep the Master Chief moving.

The other SEALs were maneuvering their own burdens into position as Silverwolf waited for Jenkins to fit his mask and mouthpiece into position, discard his stick, and make an unsteady dive into the murky water. Then he eased Callahan down until he was fully immersed and ducked his own head underwater. With Jenkins swimming close alongside and checking the fit of Callahan's SCUBA gear, the three men started downward.

It seemed to take forever to reach the spot where the two SDVs awaited them on the bottom of the river, but at length they saw the two flattened tubes ahead of them, passenger hatches standing invitingly open. Silverwolf angled toward the nearest of the two, towing Callahan. When they reached the SDV, Jenkins helped him get the Master Chief inside. While Silverwolf strapped him into position and substituted the UBA face mask for his SCUBA gear, Jenkins slid into position beside the Master Chief and donned another mask so that he could explain the situation to O'Dell, the SDV pilot.

With Callahan secured, Silverwolf left the SDV again and set off to help the others. Joor and Davis, towing their grisly burdens, were doing all right on their own, but Woods was having problems with the equipment canister, so Silverwolf assisted him in getting it to the other SDV and loading it aboard. By the time they had it fitted into place, the bodies of Martinez and Harriman had been secured in the rear of SDV #1, and O'Dell was already revving up the engine and steering toward the open sea.

Joor took his position in the cockpit of SDV #3, while the three remaining SEALs strapped themselves into the passenger compartment and pulled the hatches shut. They listened to the hum of the engine as the SDV lifted from the bottom and turned seaward, thankful to make good their escape. But Silverwolf couldn't help but think of Martinez and Harriman, the two men who had paid the ultimate price.

Control Room, USS *Bluefin*
The White Sea, Off Severodvinsk
0042 hours GMT

Gordon stepped down from the OOD station and bent over the sonar repeater to study the two targets displayed on the screen. "Looks like we've found a couple of our lost lambs," he said.

His Exec nodded. "On that course, they're headed out of Severodvinsk," he said. "Lieutenant Gunn's team, no doubt about it. As long as the boys in the sonar shack got the ID right. . . ."

"I don't imagine you could mistake the sonar signature of one of those SDVs for too many other things," Gordon commented, smiling.

"How do you want to proceed, Skipper?" Hogan asked.

"Take her to the bottom and wait for them to get here," Gordon said. "They'll have us on their OAS, and they should be able to recognize our profile easily enough." He paused. "The op orders called for Gunn to have duplicate copies of anything his people found in each SDV, right?"

Hogan nodded. "If they found anything," he added dubiously.

"Good. Then we'll send one of them on to *Pittsburgh*. That'll give Chase the rest of the info to add to what we sent over to him earlier. We'll take on the other SDV here and then resume course to meet the other two SDVs." Inwardly, he added, *if they made it out*. "Have Sparks fire up the acoustic telephone, and notify me when they're close enough to talk to."

"Aye aye, sir," Hogan replied formally, turning to pass Gordon's instructions on.

Gordon wished he'd learned how to cultivate a better poker face. He knew he must be showing the relief he felt at meeting up with the first half of the SEALs. Now if they could just recover the others successfully. . . .

SDV #2
The White Sea, Off Severodvinsk
0046 hours GMT

"Are you sure it's *Bluefin*?" Gunn demanded.

"The OAS doesn't lie, Lieutenant," DuQuense replied cheerfully over the intercom. "It's her, all right. Looks like the Old Man got impatient and came to fetch us out himself."

Gunn frowned inside the UBA face mask. He didn't know Frank Gordon that well, but it seemed out of character for the man to change the operational plan so radically. Still, as DuQuense had commented, the OAS identification had been positive. While the sonar systems fitted aboard the Swimmer Delivery Vehicles were by no means as sophisticated as those of full-sized submarines, within certain specialized parameters they were quite reliable. The Obstacle Avoidance Sonar subsystem enabled the SDV to navigate through virtually any sort of hazard it might encounter in the water, and was also designed to identify the SDV's launch vehicle and facilitate rendezvous and docking procedures.

So that was *Bluefin* up ahead, barely three miles out from the Russian coast instead of out at the original rendezvous point ten miles away. It was, Gunn decided, all to the good. They were that much closer to Second Squad, and that would cut down on the time it would take to locate and pick them up. The sooner he knew their fate, the sooner he would be able to breathe easy again.

The SDV continued at full speed, closing the range with the waiting submarine, and Gunn fought to control his impatience as he waited, cut off from the outside world, in the virtually featureless passenger compartment. It was ironic, one detached part of him reflected, that he was feeling so edgy, when just a few minutes before he'd been prepared for another couple of hours of travel time back to the original rendezvous point. But the knowledge that *Bluefin* was close by, and the possibility that they might be able to find out what had happened to Second Squad sooner rather than later, was making him more jittery than a BUD/S trainee going into Hell Week.

Time seemed to stretch out interminably before DuQuense announced over the intercom, "Coming up on *Bluefin* now. Hope they remember to open the garage doors."

At that moment a horrible racket surrounded them all as sound waves buffeted the little SDV. Gunn cringed. "What the hell . . . ?"

"They're using the Gertrude," DuQuense said. "Hang on . . . gotta patch in. Not much call for an acoustic telephone on one of these babies." After a moment he went on, interpreting the sound that continued to wash over the little submersible. "Orders from Captain Gordon, Lieutenant. We're to dock with *Bluefin*. Number Four is to continue to the original rendezvous point. They're to abandon the SDV there and transfer to *Pittsburgh*—

damn, Lieutenant Harriman ain't gonna like it that much!—with their copies of what you got from the shipyard."

Gunn's initial reaction was negative. He would have preferred to get everyone safely aboard *Bluefin* right away and worry about getting copies to the attack sub later, when the immediate crisis was over and Second Squad was accounted for. But then he considered how close inshore they were now, and how much of a risk Gordon must be taking to bring *Bluefin* in this near to both the huge Severodvinsk shipyard *and* the Soviet naval base at Archangel in order to pick up the SEALs. It was only smart to make sure that every scrap of intelligence they had gathered be available on both American submarines. Just in case.

Otherwise, the entire mission could end up being for nothing, if the photos they'd taken of that file folder didn't make it back to Admiral Goldman and the NSA. And Gunn wasn't willing to even consider the idea that this operation might have been pointless. Not when it might have cost some good men's lives over on the Dvina River.

"Acknowledge the orders, Lieutenant," Gunn said.

"Right," DuQuense responded. After a moment he went on. "Number Four's acknowledged as well. She's altering course and increasing speed."

"Godspeed, men," Gunn muttered.

"You can say that again, L-T," Senior Chief Burns added solemnly.

Control Room, USS *Bluefin*
The White Sea, Off Severodvinsk
0051 hours GMT

"SDV Four is on her way, Skipper. Number Two's beginning her approach now. SDV bay is flooded, bow doors preparing to open now."

"Very good," Gordon said, nodding as the Exec summarized the situation. He paused for a moment, before his need to be doing something finally overcame his efforts to appear remote and aloof. "You have the conn, Mr. Hogan. As soon as the SDV bay is secured, get her under way again and resume our previous course and speed. I'm going forward to welcome our conquering heroes."

"Isn't that jumping to conclusions, Skipper?" Hogan asked.

"Hey, these are SEALs. They're always conquering heroes. It's written into their terms of enlistment."

Gordon made his way forward and reached the entrance to the batcave just as the grinding of machinery announced that the outer door was swinging slowly shut. He didn't have long to wait before the huge hatch was sealed and the seawater pumped out. Then the SDV bay crew opened up the hatches, and Gordon followed them in. He felt *Bluefin* stirring from her resting place on the bottom as Hogan obeyed his orders to resume their progress toward the coast.

The SEALs and SDV crewmen were already climbing out of their strange-looking underwater chariots. Gunn was already hastening across the open space toward Gordon, his face drawn with worry. "Captain! My second squad was reported under attack. Is there anything we can do to help them?" He was talking fast, and sounded like he was growing ragged with concern or fatigue.

Gordon held up a hand. "Slow down, son. First things first. Did you carry out the mission?"

The young SEAL officer nodded vaguely. "Yessir," he said. "Don't know how much good the documents we found will do, but we photographed what we found." He shook his head. "That's not what's important now, though, Captain. My men . . ."

"The mission, first," Gordon said sternly. He sympathized with Gunn, indeed he wouldn't have been there to pick him up if he hadn't felt the same way about those other SEALs, but the mission *had* to come before all else. "There was a duplicate copy of everything in the other SDV?"

Gunn nodded again. "Carstairs has it," he said.

"Good. Turn your film over to Chief Matchett in the ship's office, then you and your men report to your berths and get some rest." He smiled. "We'll spare you the debriefing until tomorrow morning."

"And Second Squad?"

"We'll pick them up as soon as possible, Lieutenant. I can't promise you more than that. Now get your men below and get some rest. There's nothing else you can do right now."

The young SEAL officer looked like he wanted to say more, but after a moment he nodded reluctantly and drew himself to attention. "Aye aye, sir," he said.

Gordon watched as he gathered the other three SEALs and led them out of the SDV bay. There were none of the usual high spirits that normally marked the end of a successful mission. All four men were serious, subdued. He remembered what a point of pride it was with these men that they never left a man behind. That was part of what made the SEALs such an elite unit, the camaraderie that bound them together so tightly on duty and off. With half their platoon still unaccounted for after reporting contact with a hostile force, Gunn and his men wouldn't rest easy until they had accounted for Callahan's squad.

Well, Gordon told himself, *neither will I.*

He turned and stalked out of the SDV bay, wrapping his determination around him like a well-worn pea coat.

SEAL Berths, USS *Bluefin*
The White Sea, Off Severodvinsk
0111 hours GMT

"Hey, you know the Master Chief. The Russkie who tangles with him is gonna be one sorry bear!"

Bernard Gunn looked across the table at Moultrie, not bothering to conceal the irritation he felt. The big Southerner just wouldn't stop talking about Callahan and Second Squad, and Gunn didn't need any more reminders right now. But Moultrie didn't notice his look, and Gunn couldn't quite muster the energy to chew him out.

Senior Chief Burns, however, did notice his lieutenant's glance. "Can it, Moultrie," he growled. "Talkin' about it ain't gonna get Second Squad back here any faster."

"Aw, c'mon, Chief, I was just . . ."

"I said stow it, Moultrie! What part of 'stow it' do I have to explain to you?"

Moultrie subsided, and there was a long moment of blessed silence.

Then the intercom broke in on Gunn's bleak thoughts. "Now hear this! Now hear this! Lieutenant Gunn, lay forward to the SDV bay! Lieutenant Gunn to the SDV bay! Two SDVs incoming!"

"They made it!" Moultrie crowed. "What did I tell ya?" He gave Burns a defiant look.

Gunn surged to his feet, ignoring the byplay, and started for the hatch.

"Want us to come, too, L-T?" Ehrenberger asked.

He paused, turned back a moment, and shook his head. "Stay here. Too many bodies'll just confuse things. I'll make sure you guys get filled in as soon as I find out what's going on."

Gordon met him near the batcave, which was still sealed tight as the two SDVs made their approach. As they reached the doors to the SDV bay, the public-address system came on. "Now hear this, now hear this,"

Lieutenant Commander Hogan's voice boomed. "Dr. Waite, lay forward to the SDV bay. Casualties coming in. Dr. Waite, casualties in the SDV Bay."

Gordon strode to the nearest intercom station and lifted a handset from its cradle. "Control, this is the captain," he said crisply.

As Gunn watched, the sub's CO went through a series of emotions—curious, then angry, then plainly disturbed. "Understood," he said at last. "Get us under way as soon as the SDVs are aboard. Back out the way we came in . . . up the trench. Best possible speed." He returned the handset with a quick, irritated slap and turned back to Gunn.

"Sir?" the SEAL ventured.

Before Gordon could speak, the noisy grinding of the bay-door machinery rumbled around them. He talked over the noise, his face a study in determined self-control. "My Exec talked to the pilot of one of the SDVs over the Gertrude," he said. "Two of your men were wounded, one of them seriously. The pilot doesn't know anything beyond that, except he's worried about the condition of the one casualty."

"Who is it? Did he say?" Gunn asked, so worried that he forgot to address his superior properly.

Gordon didn't appear to notice the lapse. "Callahan," he said.

They waited in silence after that, Gunn, at least, plunged into a black pool of depression at the news. Master Chief Callahan had always given the impression he was unstoppable. If he had been so badly wounded, what of the others? What about Martinez and Silverwolf, both newcomers barely qualified to be called true members of the Teams?

At length the SDVs were aboard, the bay doors sealed, and the water pumped out. Gordon and Gunn entered together just as Dr. Waite appeared with a pair of sick-bay attendants close behind. Waite nodded absently toward his CO as the entire group crossed the open space to the cradles that held the dripping SDVs.

One of the forward hatches opened up on the nearest of the new arrivals, and the SDV pilot clambered out slowly. Gunn studied the man, frowning, and stepped forward. "O'Dell? Where's your navigator? Where's Lieutenant Harriman?"

O'Dell gave a kind of half shrug and shook his head slowly. "In the back, Mr. Gunn," he said.

"What? Why?"

"He's dead, sir," O'Dell said flatly. It was as if all the emotion had just drained out of him. The words caught Gunn off guard. Harriman, dead? How could the SDV navigator have been killed?

What in God's name had happened out there?

SDV #3, USS *Bluefin*
The White Sea, Off Severodvinsk
0116 hours GMT

Silverwolf climbed down the side of the SDV to join Woods and Davis, feeling tired and unsteady on his feet. The letdown after being in battle had caught up with him, and he felt more exhausted than he had at any time since the last stages of Hell Week in BUD/S. Then it had been sheer physical exhaustion that had dogged him, after a week of little sleep and constant grueling exercise and activity. Now his fatigue stemmed more from the intensity of the emotions that had hit him once the SEALs had reached their SDVs.

Now they were back aboard *Bluefin*. Strange that it felt like home . . . and stranger still that it represented a genuine feeling of safety even though the sub's position, deep in the territorial waters of the White Sea, was anything but secure.

Lieutenant Gunn was striding forward to meet them, his chubby face betraying concern. As the senior man present, it was Davis who moved forward to meet him.

"It's good to see you back," Gunn said. "We were starting to worry."

"So were we," Davis replied. A shadow crossed his face. "It was rough out there."

Among the SEALs, it was a point of pride to maintain a stoic, uncomplaining façade in the face of real trouble, even if griping and grumbling about day-to-day problems was expected by all. Davis's words, spoken quietly and mildly, were about as despairing as any SEAL was likely to hear.

"Sir?" That was Woods, unable to contain himself. "Any word on the Master Chief?" He glanced toward the other SDV, where the medical people were just getting the rear hatches open.

Gunn spared him an unhappy glance. "Nothing yet. The doc'll let us know." He returned his attention to Davis again. "Where's Martinez?"

"Dead, sir," Davis admitted. "He was caught out in the open when that goddamned Russian patrol boat showed up. They spotted him, and shouted something—I guess it was something like 'halt, who goes there?' or something. When he didn't answer them they opened up . . ."

Silverwolf saw a spasm of emotion cloud the lieutenant's features for a moment as Jenkins spoke. He remembered that Gunn spoke Russian. Maybe he was regretting the fact that he hadn't been there to answer that first hail, and perhaps fool the Russians into thinking they belonged there.

But of course the Russian-speakers had been needed at the shipyard anyway, for the mission to be a success.

Davis continued with his account of the incident, right up through the moment when Harriman's two mines blew up the patrol boat. "If he hadn't planted them and blown that boat, we would never have gotten out alive," Davis concluded. "We were pinned down, and it wasn't until the lieutenant made his move that we were able to get back to the water. A few more minutes and the Rus-skies probably would have brought up more troops and gotten us all. He was a real hero, L-T."

That didn't seem to make it any easier for Gunn. He still looked grim. "Well . . ." He was struggling to find words. "At least most of you made it back in one piece, thank God."

"What now, Mr. Gunn?" Woods asked.

"Now our taxi driver heads for home," he said. "Meanwhile, you guys get out of your gear and lay aft to quarters for a real debriefing. Sit back, and leave the driving to them."

"What about the mission, sir?" Davis said. "Were you able to get anything worthwhile?"

Gunn shrugged. "Who knows? We did what they told us to do. But whether the price you guys paid is justified or not . . . who knows?"

SDV Bay, USS *Bluefin*
The White Sea, Off Severodvinsk
0118 hours GMT

Gordon let Gunn talk with his men on his own; the SEAL officer deserved that much consideration. While the SEALs spoke in low voices together near the bow of SDV #1, Gordon watched as the medical team opened up the rear hatches and started maneuvering a pair of stretchers inside the SDV. Dr. Waite disappeared into the vehicle. After a few minutes the doctor came back out. His expression was glum, and when Gordon caught his eye he gave a minute shake of the head that didn't look at all promising.

His misgivings were fulfilled a few moments later when Waite climbed down to deck level. Gunn broke away from the other SEALs quickly to join them, look-ing expectant. Waite made his report to Gordon, but his words were aimed as much at Gunn as they were at his captain. "It doesn't look good," he said. "Multiple gunshot wounds to the arm and shoulder, and one through his side. None of them life-threatening in and of itself, but he's lost a fair amount of blood and must have gone into shock quickly. On top of all that, he's suffering from hypothermia. His body temperature is dangerously low, and he appears to be in a coma. Completely nonresponsive."

"What can you do for him?" Gunn demanded.

Waite spread his hands. "We can patch up the holes. Get some blood into him. Make him warm and comfortable. After that . . . this is one of those situations where a doctor finds out for sure that he isn't God after all, no matter how often he's thought it. The fact is, tough as he is, Callahan might not make it. And there's no telling when, or if, he'll snap out of the coma and wake up. There's just no telling." Waite turned to face Gordon. "I'll say this much, though, Captain. It's touch-and-go for him as things stand . . . but if he'd spent another hour or two in that SDV heading out to the original rendezvous, it would've killed him. Whatever hopes Callahan has of pulling through, he owes to your deciding to come in and make the pickup inshore."

Gordon shook his head. "It only matters if he really does pull through, Doctor," he said stiffly. "Do your best for him."

"Could you . . . keep me informed, Doctor?" Gunn asked slowly.

"Of course, Lieutenant," Waite said. "But don't expect to hear anything soon."

Wardroom, USS *Pittsburgh*
The White Sea, Off Severodvinsk
0246 hours GMT

"Some people to see you, sir."

Chase looked up as Latham ushered three men into the wardroom. Though each was unique in feature and build, the three shared a look he'd grown familiar with during his days in covert operations—the "killer" look he always associated with U.S. Navy SEALs.

"I take it these gentlemen are our new houseguests, Rick?"

"Yes, sir," Latham said.

He gave a nod. "You three gave us a bit of a surprise," he said to the SEALs. "We're not used to people swimming into the escape lock and calling us over the intercom."

One of them grinned. "Couldn't find the doorbell, sir," he said. "Had to make do with what we could find."

He chuckled. "I suppose so. I'll have to write a memo to COMSUBSPECLANT about the desirability of installing doorbells on all our attack subs. Did you three come out here without seeing *Bluefin*? She was headed your way."

"We passed her, sir," the same SEAL responded. "Captain Gordon passed the word to us to continue here, while he took Lieutenant Gunn's SDV aboard *Bluefin*."

"Ah." Chase leaned back in his chair. "I take it you gents have a copy of whatever you turned up in Severodvinsk."

"Already in the ship's safe, Skipper," Latham put in.

"All right. Good," he said at length. "I imagine you guys have had a long day. Have Mr. Latham scare you up some berths. I'll talk to you again another time."

"Aye aye, sir," the SEAL intoned.

Chase saw Latham's stoic expression over the SEAL's shoulder and had to fight back a grin. *Pittsburgh*'s berthing space was already at a premium, and now three more heretofore privileged crewmen would be hot-bunking so that these extra bodies could be accommodated.

The SEALs filed out of the cabin, squeezing past Latham. The Exec ordered them to wait in the corridor and then entered, closing the door behind him and achieving the closest thing to privacy anyone enjoyed aboard *Pittsburgh*.

"What are you going to do next, sir?" the XO asked quietly. He sounded unusually worried. Was it the possibility that *Pittsburgh* might be in added danger from Gordon's trip inshore? Or was it because he still carried fond memories of the old *Bluefin*?

Chase shrugged. "Carry out our orders, of course," he said. "Set a course for the exit route into the Barents Sea, Rick. Speed . . . dead slow. And order Chief Franco's gang to keep a close eye out for *Bluefin*. I want to know what Gordon's doing right down the line."

"Aye aye, sir," Latham said. He looked relieved.

Chase wished he could share in that relief. But they still had a long way to go, and plenty could still go wrong.

Friday, 9 August 1985

Control Room, USS *Bluefin*
The White Sea
0305 hours GMT

"Looks like we've got some activity around Archangel, Skipper."

Gordon turned to study the sonar repeater. *Bluefin*'s passive sonar sweeps were detecting several targets to the northwest, surface shipping from the looks of them, all concentrated near the harbor at Archangel. They were probably civilian traffic, freighters or tankers outbound from Russia's major northern port, but without detailed study of each of them it was impossible to tell which ones might be warships . . . or what their intentions might be.

He turned his attention to Hogan. "Best we play it safe. Bring us to course three-five-five and reduce speed to five knots. We'll take it slow and easy until we see what our friends over there do."

Hogan frowned. "Sir, we're getting close to the edge of the area the *Sea Devil* charts cover . . ."

"I'm aware of it, Mr. Hogan," Gordon told him. "There's not much we can do about that. Keep a close eye on the mapping sonar and cross your fingers."

"Aye aye, sir. May I also rub a rabbit's foot, just to be sure?"

"Whatever makes you happy, Mr. Hogan. Just remember that it didn't do the rabbit much good."

Sick Bay, USS *Bluefin*
The White Sea
0318 hours GMT

Bernard Gunn studied the silent, unmoving form on the hospital bed, and wondered again how he could have prevented the tragedy that had left Master Chief Callahan hovering between life and death.

And that reminded him of the other two bodies, the two dead men, Martinez and Harriman. Callahan, according to Dr. Waite, at least had a fighting chance. But the other two were dead, irretrievably and permanently dead.

He dropped his gaze to stare down at the deck. As the acting commanding officer of the SEAL platoon, Gunn bore the responsibility for everything that had happened, and he was discovering what a crushing burden it was. He'd had plenty of doubts from the very start about the wisdom of the shipyard-recon operation, but instead of speaking up against it he'd gone along with the idea, helped to plan it in detail. Had the diversionary action on the Dvina really been needed? Gunn doubted it now. They could have reached the admin building without the sabotage at the electrical plant. . . .

More importantly, though, had the raid really accomplished anything worthwhile? From what he'd heard, *Pittsburgh* had scored a major coup and obtained detailed information on the *Akula* at sea, probably a lot more relevant than the single file the SEALs had managed to find and photograph at Severodvinsk. Had the

entire op been wasted? Had he put the men of Second
Squad in harm's way for no reason?

"Hey, Bernie."

Gunn looked up, startled, then realized that the voice
that had interrupted his sour reverie belonged to Lieutenant Anderson. The SEAL platoon leader had seemed
to be asleep when Gunn had slipped in, but now the
injured man was sitting up in his bunk and watching
him through narrowed eyes.

"Sorry, Ted . . . hope I didn't disturb you," Gunn said,
stammering a little.

"Are you kidding? I'm stuck in this sardine can with
my leg in a splint and nothing but four gray bulkheads
to stare at. Being disturbed is the high point of my day."
Anderson shrugged and looked toward Callahan's berth.
"You hear anything more about the Master Chief?"

"Not much," Gunn said heavily. "Doc said it was
touch-and-go. Depends as much on Callahan as on anything else."

"Well, if that's the case, then he's home free," Anderson said, a hint of a smile playing across his drawn
features. "You know how tough he is. I hear those old
Vietnam-issue SEALs used to check out of base hospi-
tals as soon as they could stand upright and struggle into
a uniform."

"Yeah."

Anderson fixed him with an intent stare. "You look
like a condemned man who just heard the governor's
not coming through with the reprieve. Look, Bernie,
Callahan knew the score when he went out there. And
I bet on him to bounce back, if anybody can."

"Martinez and Harriman won't be bouncing back,"
Gunn said flatly. "And they died for *nothing.*"

"Nothing? You carried out the mission, didn't you?"

"So? We got one lousy file folder. *Pittsburgh* probably got ten times as much as we did when they tailed
the *Akula* yesterday. The op was a waste from first to
last, Ted."

Anderson shook his head. "You're looking at it the wrong way, kid. In intelligence work, there's no such thing as a wasted effort if you bring out *any* information, no matter how minor it might seem. The spy game depends on gathering facts, and then more facts to cross-check the first facts, and then a few more just to support what you thought you knew already from the first two sets of facts. *Everything's* relevant. That folder you found might have just what the NSA boys need to nail down something they suspected from another source but couldn't prove. It might have the straight dope on something the boys on *Pittsburgh* thought they saw, but made a mistake identifying, like a sonar installation or a radio antenna. You just can't tell how important it might be."

"But . . ."

"Hold on, I'm not through yet." Anderson shifted uncomfortably in his bunk, wincing a little. "*Pittsburgh* may have pulled off a major coup, but that doesn't mean that what you guys did these last two nights was worthless, Bernie. Another thing you need to remember about intelligence work is that it's always wise to have more than one string to your bow. What if *Pittsburgh* hadn't lucked on to the *Akula* at sea? A few minutes earlier or later and she would've missed the Russkies entirely. Or if either boat had steered just a few degrees differently. Then *all* we'd have is what you guys were able to gather. So don't dismiss it as a waste."

Gunn shrugged. "Yeah. Maybe you're right. But I just can't stop thinking that I screwed everything up. The whole Dvina side of the op . . . it wasn't necessary."

"No way any of us could know that at the time, Bernie," Anderson told him. "Look, if you're going to play Monday-morning quarterback and second-guess everything you did, you're not going to be much use to anybody. We put together our ops based on the information we had and on our best estimate of what we needed to do. I was in it, too, don't forget. We planned the best way we could, and after that . . . well, it was out of our hands. Sometimes you get a run of bad luck, like Callahan running into that patrol boat. So you just count on the fact that you've got good people out there, and you trust them to pull through even when the luck does turn rotten."

"You really believe any of that crap, Ted?" Gunn asked.

Anderson chuckled. "Not really. Frankly, I'm feeling pretty damned lousy about the whole thing myself. But there's not a thing either of us can do about what happened, Bernie. What we have to do is make sure we do our jobs the best way we know how, and try to do them even better the next time out. And beating yourself up over stuff you couldn't control isn't going to do you a damn bit of good. I know . . . because I've been doing it to myself ever since they brought Callahan in."

Control Room, USS *Bluefin*
The White Sea
0414 hours GMT

By rights he should have been asleep in his quarters, but after everything that had happened Gordon wasn't able to even think about sleep. Instead he had come to the control room, to wait and watch as his crew guided *Bluefin* on her course away from Severodvinsk and out of the White Sea. The ships they had spotted around Archangel had gone their separate ways, leaving the way north clear, and Gordon had ordered speed increased to ten knots once they had the ocean to themselves.

Frank Gordon, for one, would be glad to see the last of these waters.

He was letting Shelby, as Officer of the Watch, run the boat from the command station on the periscope platform, while he hovered near the chart tables and tried not to give the impression that he was watching over anyone's shoulders. It was always hard to balance a natural interest in what was going on with the unfortunate effects on morale if the officers and crew began to suspect that their CO either didn't trust their abilities, or was just such a worrier that he couldn't leave well enough alone. Luckily *Bluefin*'s people knew him well enough to recognize this particular variety of restlessness, and they didn't appear to take any of it personally.

It felt good to be in his control room. No matter what the worries or the strains of command, Gordon always felt more connected when he was there. *Bluefin* was his, not just a steel tube filled with weapons and high-tech gadgetry, but an extension of Frank Gordon. He would miss the place, when the old girl was condemned and broken up.

He was yanked from his reverie by a warning call from one of the bridge crew. "Bottom's shelving fast, sir! Shallow water ahead!"

Shelby responded quickly. "Helm! Five degrees up angle on the bubble! Blow ballast tanks—"

But it was too late. At that moment *Bluefin* struck the rising seafloor beneath them, shuddering as she scraped her keel. Gordon had to grip the edge of the chart table to stay upright. Shelby wasn't so lucky. He lost his hold on the rail around the periscope pedestal, and the force of their dragging impact toppled him over one of the rails. He landed hard, and he didn't get up.

The engine was straining, whining, but the sub's forward motion gradually slowed and stopped.

For just a moment, no one in the control room moved or spoke. A stunned silence prevailed. Then Gordon was pacing forward to the watch station, bawling orders that came to him automatically, without his having to think. "Stop engine! Damage control, all decks, report! Somebody get Dr. Waite up here on the double!"

His firm voice seemed to have the right effect on the crew; they began to fall back into their routine with all the competence he had come to expect of them. Gordon paused by Shelby and dropped to his knee beside the Dive Officer. He wasn't conscious, and there was blood seeping from behind a scalp wound where his head had caught on a sharp corner of the platform, but he was breathing regularly.

Standing again, Gordon finished his journey to the OOW post. He surveyed the control room slowly, but except for some displaced charts and other minor gear adrift—and, of course, the wounded man on the deck nearby—there were few signs of trouble.

But Gordon was well aware of the fact that some kinds of trouble came with few outward signs.

Captain's Quarters, USS *Pittsburgh*
The White Sea
0420 hours GMT

"Stopped?" Chase sat up and swung his legs out of his bunk. "What do you mean, stopped?"

Jackson's voice over the intercom sounded apologetic. "Sir, the sonar watch reported some ungodly noises. Then they lost everything . . . including the sound of *Bluefin*'s engine. They think it sounded like she struck something, maybe a really thick muddy bottom. Best guess is that *Bluefin*'s run aground, Skipper."

"Damn," Chase muttered. He hated operating in this shallow, almost landlocked sea. It was worse in some ways than the Persian Gulf. At least there the enemy hadn't been a superpower with enough ships in the neighborhood to crush *Pittsburgh* and toss her aside like a beer can at a Super Bowl party. "All right, Jackson, bring us about. Set course to *Bluefin*'s last-known position. Half speed, and keep the towed sonar array deployed. Keep your eyes and ears peeled for trouble. I'm on my way . . . and please wake Mr. Latham and have him join us. If I can't get a decent night's sleep, then neither will my XO!"

Control Room, USS *Bluefin*
The White Sea
0448 hours GMT

Frank Gordon was angry.

For better than half an hour *Bluefin* had been stranded, and nothing they had attempted so far had helped. The boat was aground, and in these waters it was only a matter of time before some Russian ship stumbled across her, and that would be the end of it.

Or they might stay stuck down here without being discovered, which would be just as bad. The thick, gooey mud they had plowed into was piled up high around *Bluefin*'s hull, high enough to interfere with the intake ports that allowed the boat to run her machinery. Set higher above the keel than was common on most boats, those vents normally gave the boat an edge by allowing her to rest on the bottom for long periods of time. But now they were clogged, so it was only a matter of time before the situation turned ugly.

He had sent a diver out to check around the sub's exterior, and the report hadn't sounded good. They hadn't suffered any serious damage in the grounding, but that thick mud was definitely going to be a problem. Even the propeller shaft was trapped, which meant *Bluefin* couldn't count on powering herself out of the mess she was in.

And now, according to the sonar shack, *Pittsburgh* was about to come alongside the stricken *Bluefin*. That made Gordon more angry than anything else about the situation. He had assumed that Chase was long gone, carrying the information they had acquired with him. Instead *Bluefin* had drawn him back, and both subs were still in harm's way. The mission was supposed to come first, and Gordon had put the mission in jeopardy with this single devastating accident.

"Sir?" Ron King had appeared at the forward end of the control room. "We're getting something on the Gertrude. It's *Pittsburgh* . . . Captain Chase. For you."

Gordon nodded an acknowledgment and picked up the acoustic-phone handset. Chase was taking a risk with this, just as he had done when they'd used the system to contact the SDVs. It was noisy . . . but it was just about the only practical way to conduct short-range communications between two submerged boats.

"This is Gordon," he said flatly.

"Frank, what the hell's happening over there?" Chase's voice was subtly distorted, but recognizable. "My sonar people claim you went off the road and ended up in a ditch."

"Something like that," Gordon agreed. "Got caught by an unexpected bump . . . a muddy one. We're stuck fast. The prop's jammed by the muck, and we've emptied the ballast tanks without even budging a little. We're not going anywhere."

"So what do you want to do about it?"

"We'll keep working at it. Maybe we'll get lucky. Or I might get my divers and the SEALs to clear enough mud away to get the engine running again. Then maybe I can pull her loose."

"That'll take forever, Frank, and you know it. What if the Russians find you before then?"

"Then I set off some warheads and make sure they don't get enough of *Bluefin* to be able to identify us," Gordon told him harshly. They both knew it; that was standard but unspoken policy for covert-ops missions like this one. But Chase wasn't accepting it. "Look, Mike, the mission has to come first. You know it. Get the hell out of here and leave us to do what we can. Or what we have to."

There was silence on the other end of the connection.

Control Room, USS *Pittsburgh*
The White Sea
0453 hours GMT

Chase didn't speak, didn't move, as he contemplated Gordon's words. The man was right, of course. The mission came first. Goldman had ordered him to abandon *Bluefin* to her fate if he had to, and this was exactly the kind of situation the admiral would have had in mind when he framed those orders.

But the two boats weren't in imminent danger as yet. There were no Russian ships close by, no sign that the two American subs had attracted any attention so far. No doubt the clash onshore had heightened security concerns amongst the Soviets, but for all they knew they had been fighting homegrown terrorists or dissidents. There was no sign of an active search as yet . . . which meant that *Pittsburgh* should have time to render some kind of assistance to her stricken consort. But what could they do?

To confirm the situation, he lowered the handset for a moment and sought out Latham. The Exec met his glance and hurried across the control room to join him.

"Still nothing on sonar, Rick?"

"A couple of patrol boats a few miles down the coast," Latham replied. "Nothing else anybody can spot. Not even Rodriguez. And with the towed array out we ought to be able to pick up the sounds of Russian ensigns picking their noses."

Towed array . . . the words struck a chord in Chase.

He raised the handset again. "Listen to me, Frank. There's one way we might be able to get you free, if you're willing to give it a try. Don't do anything stupid . . . and wait for me to get back to you." He hung up the handset and turned back to Latham.

"Pass the word to Johanssen to suit up, Rick," he said. "And see if our SEAL guests will volunteer to help."

"Help, sir?"

"We're going to rig a tow cable, Rick. And we're going to drag *Bluefin* out of there if I have to get out and push." He paused, visualizing how it ought to work in his mind's eye. When he spoke again it was with a fervor that surprised even him. "By God, Rick, I'll not lose Frank Gordon this way!"

Escape Trunk, USS *Bluefin*
The White Sea
0510 hours GMT

Water filled the escape trunk, and Johnny Silverwolf watched as Lieutenant Gunn pulled himself up to the top of the chamber and undogged the outer hatch. Gunn kicked off the ladder and drifted out of the sub, and Silverwolf quickly followed.

He was still a little surprised that he had volunteered for this detail, so soon after the disastrous excursion onto Soviet soil. As Captain Gordon had explained things, the CO of the *Pittsburgh* had proposed a daring way to free the stranded *Bluefin*. The plan was to hook up towlines and use *Pittsburgh* to help pull *Bluefin* free, just as tugs maneuvered submarines in tight quarters within crowded harbors. To make it work, they would need divers to secure the lines, and more divers to do what they could to unclog intake vents and try to ensure the propeller wasn't fouled once the job was under way.

Bluefin, like all subs, carried a handful of divers as part of her crew, not SEALs but specialists trained in underwater repair work. They were the logical people to assign to the technical work of opening blocked intakes and the like. To speed the job up, Gordon wanted a few SEAL volunteers to come forward and help rig the towlines. Before he had even realized what he was doing Silverwolf had stepped forward, along with a few of the others. In the end, Gunn had singled him out as the man he wanted for the job.

Silverwolf wasn't sure if that meant the lieutenant thought he was capable . . . or expendable.

But Gunn had thrown himself into the preparations like a man possessed, and Silverwolf had been hard-pressed to keep up. He could tell that the lieutenant had chosen to participate in the job as a way of distracting himself from the feelings that he was so obviously having trouble coping with in the aftermath of the trouble Second Squad had run into. Callahan's plight, and the deaths of Martinez and Lieutenant Harriman, seemed to have hit him hard.

Perhaps that was what had made Silverwolf volunteer as well, he thought as he joined the lieutenant. The two SEALs moved cautiously forward along the deck of the sub, following the angle upward over the bulging SDV bay. The water here, well away from the murk of the polluted Dvina River, was reasonably clear, but visibility still wasn't particularly good. Nevertheless, Silverwolf thought he could make out an elongated shape in the water off the starboard bow, and he touched Gunn's shoulder and pointed. The other diver followed his outstretched hand and gave a nod.

It was *Pittsburgh*, holding station well clear of the stranded submarine. Silverwolf didn't envy her skipper the job of maneuvering in close on nothing but sonar readings and hunches, but that was exactly what the other sub would have to do in order to get close enough to hook up the towlines and pull *Bluefin* out of the muck.

As they watched, the attack sub nudged in closer. Whoever was handling her had a deft touch; every move was carefully calculated, and within a few minutes the looming presence of the other vessel was something tangible to the divers. *Pittsburgh* lay no more than a hundred feet away, close enough to begin the next stage of the operation.

A pair of divers appeared, swimming toward *Bluefin*

from the direction of the attack boat, dragging something heavy and hard to manage behind them. Gunn motioned for Silverwolf to follow him, and the two moved forward to meet the newcomers. As they drew closer together Silverwolf recognized the markings on one of the divers' gear. It was Carstairs, the SEAL hospital corpsman. Apparently he, too, had been pressed into service to help the makeshift salvage operation. The second diver didn't look familiar. Silverwolf presumed he was one of *Pittsburgh*'s regular diving crew.

They were dragging one of the heavy towlines the subs used in working with harbor tugs. Gunn and Silverwolf took hold and helped to drag the massive cable the rest of the way to *Bluefin*, then started to work securing it to the deck while the other two divers made the return trip to *Pittsburgh* to bring another line over. It had been a long time since Silverwolf had done anything so traditionally nautical as line-handling, but the skills were part of the fundamentals every sailor was expected to learn in basic training, and they came back quickly enough. The size of the cable and the critical importance of securing it properly made things more difficult. Nevertheless, Gunn and Silverwolf had the first cable secured long before the other two divers made their second trip across.

It was slow going, but eventually they had the towlines rigged as well as they could manage. The lead diver from *Pittsburgh* gave Gunn a mock salute, while Carstairs flashed a quick thumbs-up at his SEAL buddies when the final knot was secured and the job was done. Then the two from the attack sub swam for home, and Gunn and Silverwolf started back along the deck, double-checking each line one last time before making their way to the escape trunk and locking in.

The water was still being pumped out when Gunn stripped off his face mask and hood and tapped the controls under the intercom speaker. "Bridge, Forward Escape Trunk," he said. "All lines secured. We're as ready as we'll ever be, Captain." He sounded tired from the arduous work outside, but to Silverwolf's ears there was no longer quite the same air of depression and despair in the lieutenant's voice.

Sometimes the only way to overcome one problem was to be forced to deal with another one.

Control Room, USS *Pittsburgh*
The White Sea
0527 hours GMT

"Sonar, Conn. Status?" Chase spoke quietly into the intercom mike, deliberately striving to keep voice and manner calm and low-key. A commanding officer who projected confidence was, according to all his training, the key to getting the most out of a boat and crew, so Mike Chase was determined to make it appear as if the prospect of towing another boat clear of her muddy resting place was all in a day's work.

He wished he could believe that himself.

"Conn, Sonar," Chief Franco replied. "Still showing one contact, Sierra-One. He's at the extreme edge of sonar range and proceeding on course one-nine-nine. He'll be off our screens in another two or three minutes."

"You have an ID on him?"

"Not definite. He's a small surface vessel, maybe an Osa, but that's more a guess than anything else."

"Keep an eye on him. Report if anything changes."

"Aye aye, skipper."

Chase put down the intercom mike and checked the sonar repeater to his right. The blip that represented the Soviet vessel was faint and at the very edge of the screen, but as Franco had indicated it seemed to be moving away from the two American subs, heading southwest. So far it didn't seem as if the Russians were paying any special attention to their seaward approaches. Presumably they thought the clash on the Dvina had been the work of local malcontents rather than American SEALs. Who, after all, would expect foreign commandos to turn up right in the heart of a sea as thoroughly Russian as this one? It was as unlikely, on the face of it, as Soviet *Spetznaz* commandos attacking a facility somewhere outside of Chicago. . . .

Nonetheless, the Americans couldn't afford to wait there for long. Even if the Russians didn't mount any special effort to search those waters, their routine patrols would still be out, and sooner or later they might stumble across the two submarines. And there was always the chance that the naval exercises would end and major elements of the Red Banner Northern Fleet would return, complicating the chances of escape into the Barents Sea.

They had to act quickly to free *Bluefin*. Chase knew there were risks involved—the risk of being detected when they ran their engines up to full power to try and break the stranded boat free, and the risk that one or both subs would suffer crippling damage during the rescue operation. He was putting everything on the line to save Gordon and the others, and flying directly in the face of Goldman's orders to boot. But Chase would take those risks.

Chase picked up the intercom mike again. "Communication, Conn. Fire up the Gertrude."

He had let Frank Gordon down once, and almost ruined the man's career in the process. This time he would stand by him, whatever the cost.

Control Room, USS *Bluefin*
The White Sea
0529 hours GMT

"We're ready on this end, *Bluefin*."
Gordon took a quick look around the control room,

not quite sure of his state of mind. Chase's plan was a risky one, and Gordon still wondered why he had agreed to try it. If it worked, the two subs would both be free but still deep in Soviet waters. And if it didn't work . . .

Pittsburgh could damage her engine straining to pull *Bluefin* free. Or a wrong move could result in a deadly collision. And above all, there was the chance that the effort would bring the Russians down on top of the two subs, whether they were successful or not.

In any event, Chase was risking his submarine, and the outcome of the entire mission, to help *Bluefin*. And Gordon couldn't help but wonder why.

He knew Mike Chase as a compassionate man, someone who wouldn't willingly leave nearly two hundred men to die if there was a way to save them. But duty often forced choices like that on a commanding officer, and Chase's duty was clear—to get the information they had gathered at such risk back to Admiral Goldman and the NSA. Years of training had prepared Chase, as they had prepared Gordon, to make sacrifices if they were necessary.

So what was making Chase ignore all that now?

Gordon was afraid that he himself was the real reason.

For years the two men had been separated by that wall that had gone up when Gordon married Rebecca and earned the elder Goldman's ire. Chase, caught in the middle between a friend he cherished and a surrogate father who had all but raised him, had been forced to choose between them, and their friendship had gone by the boards. Gordon could still remember the look on his face the time he had used that angry word: "traitor."

It seemed that Gordon wasn't the only one who was still living down events that had happened fifteen years past. Chase, stubborn as always, had said he'd be there for Gordon and *Bluefin*. And in the face of everything that argued against it, he seemed determined to keep his word.

Gordon let out a long, slow breath. There was no turning back now.

"All stations, prepare for . . . unspecified maneuvers," he said slowly. That actually brought a few laughs, from Hogan and Shelby and even the dour veteran Preston. There weren't specific commands in the manual for an operation like this one. "Mr. Shelby, on the mark, blow all ballast tanks, and engage engine at one-quarter speed. Increase if the screw comes free of the mud."

"Aye aye, sir," the Dive Officer responded. The bandage on his forehead made him look like he'd stepped out of a pirate movie, but Dr. Waite had pronounced him fit and allowed him to return to duty.

Gordon lifted the handset to his ear again. "*Pittsburgh*, this is *Bluefin*," he said. "Ready at your discretion, Captain."

"Understood," Chase said over the acoustic phone. "Ready . . . Execute!"

"Mark!" Gordon said loudly.

Gordon leaned against the railing of the OOD station, his hands gripping the railing with white-knuckled intensity. There was little enough he could do to help free his stranded boat, but if sheer willpower could have pulled her loose, his thoughts alone would have already hauled her clear.

He could visualize it all in his mind's eye. In *Pittsburgh*'s control room, the helmsman was signaling the engine room to apply power to the screw, while throwing the rudder over to steer away from *Bluefin*. The attack sub's planes would be angled up for lift, and her Chief of the Boat was no doubt blowing all the ballast tanks to provide even more upward pull.

The towlines would quickly stretch, tighten . . . and *Pittsburgh* would continue to increase her engine power as she tried to pull her stricken companion free.

Did he detect a slight shift under him? Gordon wasn't sure at first, but then *Bluefin* lurched, slid forward through the mud . . . stopped again abruptly. The lines would be under a terrible strain. The slightest weakness, and one would let go . . . which could start a chain reaction as the strain increased on each of the others.

The sub began to move once more, and Gordon found himself gripping the rail of the periscope platform. His lips moved in a silent prayer. It *had* to work.

"Prop's turning!" the helmsman shouted. "We're getting power to the screw!"

"Increase to one-half!" Gordon called, temporarily disrupting the usual chain of command.

He could hear the engine now, straining as it cranked the propeller shaft despite the mud that coated everything. And he could feel *Bluefin* making a valiant effort to lift clear. She was old and battered, but by God she was still game.

"Full speed!" Gordon said. "Gun it! Gun it!"

And they were free!

The change was glorious. In an instant, the sub was no longer in the grip of the soft mud, but once again a part of the ocean itself, surging forward and upward. Hastily Gordon ordered speed reduced. He and Chase had agreed to cut power entirely once the boat was loose—if it came loose—so that they could disengage the towlines and check for damage.

With all ballast blown, the two linked submarines were headed for the surface.

The surface of the White Sea.

Control Room, USS *Pittsburgh*
The White Sea
0545 hours GMT

"Last line's been cast off, sir."

"Very good, Rick," Chase said. "Let's get the boys inside and button up. I'm not happy up here on the surface."

"I'll second that, sir," Latham said. "It's—"

"Conn, Sonar! Contact Sierra-One has altered course and speed." Franco's voice on the intercom sounded haggard.

Sierra One was an Osa patrol boat they had been tracking for quite some time. It had been making a routine-looking patrol sweep parallel to the coast, and had the very edge of ordinary detection range. A sudden change in course and speed did not bode well for the Americans.

"He's heading our way, Conn," Franco amplified a moment later. Heading is three-four-seven degrees, speed thirty knots."

"Radar's confirming that, sir," Jackson added from behind him.

"Conn, Communications. Monitoring an increase in enemy radio traffic. Sounds like they're putting out an APB on us."

"Right," Chase said. He looked into Latham's expressionless eyes. "All preparations to get under way. Get us moving, Rick, and get us the hell back where we belong, underwater!"

"Aye aye, sir."

He picked up the intercom set. "Communications, get me Gordon on *Bluefin*."

After a few moments there was a crackle in the receiver, then Gordon's voice. "Go ahead, *Pittsburgh*."

"Frank, looks like we're about to be the guests of honor at a little party."

"I see the Osa," the other captain replied. "And my Sparks is monitoring the radio. I told you something like this would happen if you hung around and played hero. The noise our screws were making getting this old lady up out of that mud was probably audible back in Holy Loch!"

"No use dwelling on it, Frank. You're loose. Enjoy it while it lasts."

"You have any ideas?"

"Same as off Norway. As far as anybody can tell, all they know is that there's something noisy out here. I want *Bluefin* to make for the exit into the Barents Sea. Silent running, slow but steady. *Pittsburgh* will do a little dash south and west, back toward where we were playing tag with the prototype. We'll make enough racket to draw their attention away from you. Then we'll lose them, turn north, and make our own way out."

"If they mount a full-scale sub hunt, you'll be dead meat, Mike," Gordon said.

"We won't give them time for that, Frank," Chase said, trying to project a confidence he didn't feel. "I figure they'll be sluggish at first. Who's going to be looking for us in the middle of the White Sea? By the time they start to get really worried we'll already be on the way out, and they'll have to cover a lot of square miles of ocean trying to figure out where we're going to pop up next. The important thing is that you get your ass the hell out of here, Frank. And watch out for bumps in the road. The *Pittsburgh* Auto and Sub Club won't be available to give you another tow."

"We'll do it, Mike," Gordon said. He sounded reluctant. "And listen . . . take care of yourself. Don't keep playing the hero if you don't have to."

"I hear you," Chase said. "Godspeed, *Bluefin*."

He replaced the handset and caught Latham's eye. "Let's do it!"

Saturday, 10 August 1985

Control Room, USS *Pittsburgh*
The White Sea
0315 hours GMT

Pittsburgh lay silent and still on the ocean floor, waiting.

The situation reminded Chase of the decoy operation they had undertaken off Norway, but this time the stakes—and the opposition—were considerably greater. Then it had been a single Alfa stalking them, and their only purpose had been to distract the Soviets so that they didn't take too close a look at *Bluefin*. This time around *Pittsburgh* was the only hope *Bluefin* had of pulling enough attention away from the mouth of the White Sea to make the diesel boat's escape a practical proposition. And the opposition they had drawn after them was much more than a single attack sub. A large percentage of the Red Banner Northern Fleet elements left behind in the White Sea during the exercises off Novaya Zemlya must now be concentrated in an intensive hunt for the American attack boat. So far, since cutting their engine and settling in for an extended wait on the seabed, *Pittsburgh*'s sonar sweeps had positively identified ten surface vessels, three hunting submarines, and a number of aircraft doing ASW work, conventional planes dropping sonar buoys in careful search patterns and helicopters passing back and forth using dipping sonar in an effort to get a fix on the intruder who had dared to penetrate their territorial waters.

Being the object of such an all-out search wore heavily on nerves already under strain from the pressure *Pittsburgh*'s crew had been under since first entering the White Sea. It was hard to credit the fact that over the past few days they had run down the long channel from the Barents Sea, dodging the enemy all the way, then investigated the Soviet prototype sub up close in a maneuver that could only be described as daring, only to top that risky operation with the even more hazardous work of freeing *Bluefin* after she was stranded on the underwater mud bank. Now *Pittsburgh* and her crew faced the most grueling situation a submariner could ever run up against, the need for absolute silence and stealth. Every man aboard knew that if they were once spotted by the hunters who cast their nets for them out there beyond the cramped confines of *Pittsburgh*'s hull, the odds of them escaping made the survival of snowballs in hell seem like a reasonable proposition.

But it was a necessary risk. *Pittsburgh* had done exactly what Chase had set out for her to do. All he needed to do now was find a way to extricate them without alerting the hunters.

By now Gordon was almost certainly clear, which meant that Admiral Goldman would get his information no matter what. Chase wondered if Goldman would understand what had compelled him to stand the admiral's orders on their head, to risk *Pittsburgh* in order to have *Bluefin* win free and complete the mission. He wasn't entirely sure he understood it himself, actually. Certainly on any hard-nosed, practical level there was no comparison possible between the two boats. *Pittsburgh* was brand-new, on her first patrol, while *Bluefin* was scheduled for the scrap heap because she was growing old and thoroughly out-of-date. As a fast attack boat, *Pittsburgh* was one of the most versatile subs in the Navy, where *Bluefin*'s major distinction was being the ugliest submarine still afloat. Every ounce of reason and logic dictated that Chase should have followed his original orders and allowed Gordon to destroy *Bluefin* to avoid capture, rather than coming to his rescue and trying to draw off the pursuit.

But logic wasn't everything, Chase told himself as he leaned against the rail of the periscope station and watched Quimby nervously pacing behind the helmsman and planesman at the forward end of the control room. *Pittsburgh* might have turned her steel back on the other sub and sailed away, but if she had, Chase would never have been able to look at himself in the mirror again.

Chase turned to check the sonar repeater. According to the data relayed from the sonar shack, the bulk of the Soviet hunters were extending the search pattern to the south and west, along the direction *Pittsburgh* had been headed before they had found this patch of deep water and a convenient thermocline that they had ducked under before going to silent running. Most of the surface ships were already beyond detection range, with nothing but a Grisha ASW frigate and an Osa missile boat still close enough to show on the sub's passive scans. There was also one diesel submarine—tentatively identified as a Kilo class boat by SR/2 Czernak, who had relieved young Rodriguez so that the sonar wizard could snatch a few hours of sleep. Even the aerial attention in this area had started to die down.

That was encouraging. With luck the Russians would continue to spread out farther and widen their search, leaving this little corner of the White Sea alone long enough for Chase to get his boat clear of the hunters. All *Pittsburgh* needed was an opening, a way to slip past the enemy and shape a course for the open waters of the Barents Sea.

But as things stood it would still be a while before they could try. As long as there were still hunting Soviet vessels close enough to detect the American submarine, he didn't dare try to make a break for safety. These hunters weren't just relying on passive sonar sweeps which could be eluded by keeping noise down and speeds low. The dipping sonars and the dropped sonar buoys were emitting active pings, and those were much more likely to locate their quarry. Even staying put would prove dangerous in the long run. Sooner or later currents would shift the distribution of warm and cool water, or alter the salinity in the area, and the thermocline could vanish in an instant and leave *Pittsburgh* exposed to detection.

It was a dangerous game . . . but it was a game Mike Chase had been training for most of his adult life. And he'd play the hand he had been dealt the best way he knew how.

The one thing that nagged at the back of his mind was the knowledge that he was not just staking his own life on his skill at playing this particular game, but the lives of 135 other human beings who looked to him, as captain, to bring them home safely to wives and families.

That was a responsibility no amount of training could prepare a man to shoulder.

Control Room, USS *Bluefin*
Near the Mouth of the White Sea
0332 hours GMT

"Stop engine," Gordon ordered tersely. "Let her drift with the current."

"Stop engine, aye aye," Lieutenant Shelby echoed.

Bluefin drifted, silent, as every man aboard strained to hear some clue that would reveal their likely fate. It had all come down to one last battle of wits between Gordon and his crew on one side and the Soviet antisubmarine-warfare specialists on the other.

Over the course of nearly a full day they had made their way toward Gateway Station, the mouth of the long channel out of the White Sea. *Pittsburgh* had done her job well, drawing the Soviet pursuit after her into the very heart of the landlocked body of water so that *Bluefin* could sneak north without being noticed. But the Soviet naval officers coordinating the search weren't foolish enough to leave their stable door open while there was still a chance of keeping the horse from bolting. Most of their assets may have been committed to the search for *Pittsburgh*, but regular aerial patrols were monitoring the waters between the two peninsulas that flanked the mouth of the White Sea. There were plenty of capable ASW birds in the Soviet Naval Aviation service, most notably the IL-38 May, Russia's answer to the American Orion patrol aircraft. Fitted with a magnetic anomaly detector that could register the passage of large metallic objects even underwater, plus sonar buoys and other detection gear, the May could spin a very effective web across the mouth of the White Sea. And the IL-38 and other such Soviet aircraft packed their own punch, as well, carrying both ASW torpedoes and good old-fashioned depth charges.

Gordon's only hope of getting through was to choose a time and a place the Russians simply weren't covering effectively. Even with the resources available to them in this bastion of their naval power in the north, they couldn't manage to be everywhere at once, and the active search for *Pittsburgh* had drained off many of their assets. So *Bluefin* had a better-than-even chance of making it through . . . but only if Gordon made all the right moves.

With the sub drifting on the current, they were safe from passive sonar detection, although active pinging from sonar buoys or a pass with the MAD could still pick them up. Luckily the air patrols were laying their sonar buoys in a fairly predictable pattern, and the magnetic anomaly detector was a short-range method of locating a submarine that required a close pass overhead to make a definite contact.

Lieutenant Commander Hogan approached the OOD station. "Just spotted another line of buoys, Skipper," he said. He'd been studying the sonar readings with an eye for spotting the pattern of the buoy deployment. "The new line has a wider dispersal than the last three. I think our boy up there is starting to run low."

"Then this could be the break we've been waiting for," Gordon said quietly.

Hogan nodded. "Provided they don't already have this guy's relief in position," he said.

"It's a gamble," Gordon admitted. "But I think they're stretched pretty thin. I imagine that their air patrols have a lot more ground to cover trying to make up for the fleet elements at Novaya Zemlya, and of course Chase is probably pretty high on their hit parade right about now, too. I think we might just have a few minutes to make a run for it."

"I'm with you. Anything's better than just waiting here until one of them gets lucky and plants a buoy right on top of us . . . or picks us up on MAD, for that matter. We're sitting ducks here."

"Then let's at least try being moving ducks for a while, Mr. Hogan. Bring us on a course that will take us through the widest gap in their last line of buoys. Revs for eight knots to start, but be ready to put the pedal to the metal."

"Aye aye, sir. Eight knots. Course three-five-four should take us through the weakest part of their net." Hogan turned away, raising his voice to pass on the new orders to Lieutenant Shelby and the helm crewmen.

Gordon stood, silent and still, trying to picture the scene from the outside as the sub gathered speed and made her bid for freedom. Ungainly as she looked, *Bluefin* could still give a good account of herself in a situa-

tion like this. She might not be as flashy as a Los
Angeles class, but she was fast and reasonably quiet for
a diesel boat.

All she needed was a little bit of luck. . . .

The harsh wail of an active sonar ping sang through
the transport submarine's hull, and every man aboard
looked up for a moment as if expecting he could somehow see whatever trouble might be dropping down upon
them from above. But minute followed minute, and the
sub continued on her inexorable way northward . . . and
there was no sign of an attack. Another, weaker ping
sounded a few minutes later, but by then *Bluefin* was
already leaving the constricted channel behind. Open
water lay ahead, and deeper, as well. Gordon ordered
the sub to descend as she continued her progress north,
and with each new depth report he felt a little bit safer.

They had left the shallow water of the White Sea behind them. *Bluefin* was free to chart her journey home,
her mission nearly completed.

Control Room, USS *Pittsburgh*
The White Sea
0421 hours GMT

"Aspect change on Sierra Five. He's turning . . . looks
like he's headed south."

Chase glanced over at the sonar repeater as the intercom report from Czernak in the sonar shack ended, noting the change of heading for the slow-moving Kilo
class submarine that had been hanging around long after
the rest of the Soviet hunters had moved on. The Russians weren't fools, and their sailors had plenty of practical experience to draw on since they had first become
a world naval power back in the fifties and sixties. Letting a sub trail the rest of the pack was a sound ASW
tactic. If the Kilo had been just a little less noisy, the

Americans just might have overlooked her, and come out of hiding too soon.

Chase could respect the Russian tactics . . . but he didn't have to like them.

In a few more minutes, they'd have this stretch of sea to themselves, and he could start thinking about getting under way once again. But caution was still whispering in his ear, and Chase couldn't help but play out the likely scenarios in his mind's eye.

Although the activity had died down in the area for the moment, a smart Russian commander would have more backups moving in behind the main search effort, and he would see to it that other elements of his fleet doubled back to recross the same territory they'd already covered from time to time just to make sure that their quarry had not managed exactly what *Pittsburgh* had done, letting the hunt pass by so the sub could make her move for open water. Chase also expected more aerial searches soon, and he had a healthy respect for what helos or ASW airplanes could do to track down and engage a submarine. They might not be lucky enough to take *Pittsburgh* out on their own, but they could tie her up and summon ships and subs back into the area to make the actual kill.

There were too many variables, he told himself glumly. Too many chances for the Soviets to score in this deadly little game. But Chase was all too aware of the fact that the rest of his crew was looking to him to do what he'd done so many times before, to produce the unexpected solution that would end this state of siege and bring *Pittsburgh* to safety.

It was a tall order. One nuclear attack boat pitted against all those Russians . . .

Chase suddenly felt his heart beat a little faster as that one word, *nuclear*, resonated in his mind. He remembered the message he had sent to Gordon before leading the Alfa away on the first wild-goose chase off the Norwegian coast. People saw what they expected to see, what they *wanted* to see, more often than not. That was a truism Chase had frequently exploited over the course of his career as a submariner. It was easy to overlook a sonar contact that appeared to be something harmless or routine.

Just then, every Russian sonar operator in the White Sea was straining his senses in search of a Los Angeles class fast-attack boat. A nuclear-powered American submarine of known capabilities and a recognizable acoustic signature.

But just suppose Chase could present them with something else entirely . . . ?

It was the sort of scheme that might become legend in the Silent Service . . . if it worked. It could equally well go down in history as a primary example of why captains ought not to improvise, but stick to The Book.

Chase remembered the words of Commander Richardson, the veteran submariner who had been one of his instructors long ago. *"You'll find that a lot of people expect you to go by The Book, but they tend to forget that The Book is nothing but a collection of clever ideas thought up by people who couldn't find the answer they were looking for in whatever version of The Book they were brought up on. Unusual situations require unusual solutions . . . always remember that. Don't be shackled by what others have done before."*

This was the kind of unusual situation Richardson had been talking about, Chase thought. So maybe, just maybe, this was a good time to throw away The Book and do a little judicious improvising.

As he reached for the intercom mike, Chase fought the urge to grin. His crew was expecting him to come up with a clever trick. He wondered what they'd make of the scheme he was about to unveil.

Engine Room, USS *Pittsburgh*
The White Sea
0426 hours GMT

"I don't believe it," Engineman Second Class John Bowen said out loud. "I just fuckin' don't believe it!"

Lieutenant Roger Franklin, *Pittsburgh*'s Engineering Officer, shrugged elaborately. "To be honest, Bowen, I don't give a damn what you believe or don't believe. The captain gave us an order. Carry it out."

"Aye aye, sir," Bowen said, but he wasn't quite able to keep from sounding sullen.

But he had every reason to be reluctant, he thought angrily. What the captain had ordered was crazy. It flew in the face of every ounce of Bowen's training and experience. He was surprised that Franklin was accepting it so calmly. Didn't he care what games Captain Chase played with the delicate instruments in his charge?

"Beginning reactor shut-down procedure," Bowen said, his hands moving across his control console reluctantly. He had the reactor watch, manning the one position on the boat which was always crewed, at sea or in port. The idea was to have someone on hand at all times to monitor the performance of the submarine's nuclear reactor, to adjust the position of the control rods to get optimum performance from the power plant at need, or to institute a shutdown in case of an emergency situation.

He had never imagined that he would be called upon to shut down *Pittsburgh*'s reactor when there was no safety hazard threatening the boat ... and especially when the submarine was deep in hostile waters, where they could expect to need to maintain peak performance of all systems in Maneuvering.

But that was exactly what Chase had called on them to do. He had ordered the reactor shut down, and then instructed Franklin to fire up the Fairbanks-Morse auxiliary diesel engine. That was aboard strictly for emer-

gency use, in case of a catastrophic failure that forced
the reactor to go off-line, so the submarine could limp
to safety if she had to. It was never intended to be their
principal means of propulsion.

Using steam superheated by the reactor to turn the
propeller shaft, *Pittsburgh* could sustain a submerged
speed of well over thirty-five knots. The diesel engine
would be lucky to give her half that speed, and the boat's
endurance would be severely limited as well.

And Bowen could think of another disadvantage of
running the diesel engine. It happened that diesel fuel
was a surprisingly effective medium for shielding
against radiation, and the large midship's fuel tank was
the main shielding that protected the crew spaces forward from the reactor's potentially lethal radioactive
output. If Chase chose to run the diesel engines for too
long a period, he would be depleting the fuel supply. If,
later, he chose to go back to using the reactor to power
the boat, he might be putting the entire crew at risk.
Bowen, working closely with the S6G nuclear generator,
had developed a healthy respect for the dangers it posed.
Crew members, and especially the engineering personnel, monitored personal radiation exposure closely and
were hedged in by multiple safeguards to prevent them
from accumulating too large a dose of radiation while
they served their tours aboard. Bowen didn't like the
idea that Chase might be cutting into those safeguards
with this wild plan of his.

Typical, he decided as he actuated the motors that
drove the control rods into the reactor core to separate
the fissionable material and stop the nuclear reaction.
Chase had come to *Pittsburgh* after a career largely spent
in covert-ops boats like *Bluefin*, and he brought a covert-
ops officer's disdain for the safety of his men along with
him. Bowen had suspected something like this might
happen all along. These black-ops types subordinated
everything else to carrying out their missions, and they
didn't care who they hurt, friend or foe, along the way.

Franklin had started up the diesel engine as Bowen was working on the shutdown procedure from his board. He picked up an intercom mike. "Conn, Maneuvering," he said. "Diesel engine is now on-line. The reactor is . . . fully shut down and reading safe."

"Maneuvering, Conn," Chase's voice replied. "Thank you, Mr. Franklin."

"I still don't believe it," Bowen muttered.

"I'd say it's not a bad idea at all," Franklin countered. "In one stroke the captain has changed our entire acoustic signature. Anybody who hears us traveling along under the Fairbanks-Morse will see us as a diesel boat, and the only diesel boats in these parts belong to the Soviets. They'll know that no American diesel subs are deployed to frontline duty. So the tendency will be to assume we're just one more sub of the Red Banner Northern Fleet. That gives us time to duck out of here."

"The safety considerations . . ." Bowen began.

"Nonsense. Shutting down the reactor is a safe procedure. So is restarting it. I suppose if we ran for a week or two we'd deplete the fuel supply enough to cause problems with the radiation shielding, but I imagine the captain will have us back on our regular power within a few hours." Franklin paused. "You've got to hand it to him, Bowen. The man knows how to use his assets. All of them . . . not just the ones everybody thinks about."

Bowen didn't reply. Maybe the Engineering Officer was right, and they weren't running as big a risk as Bowen had thought, but he still didn't like this development, not one bit.

The engine telegraph signaled a request for half speed, and Franklin moved to another panel to transfer power to the propeller and get *Pittsburgh* under way.

The attack boat slowly stirred and rose from her position on the bottom. With her diesel engine filling, and maneuvering with an unaccustomed throbbing, the submarine slowly swung around and gathered speed.

Bowen would probably have been disturbed by Chase's choice of course, as well as by his decision to trade the reactor for the Fairbanks-Morse engine. *Pittsburgh* was headed east-northeast . . . back toward Severodvinsk and Archangel, rather than north toward the Barents Sea and safety.

Wardroom, USS *Bluefin*
The Barents Sea
0851 hours GMT

A knock made Gordon look up from his breakfast, surprised. *Bluefin*'s wardroom was open to all the boat's officers, and any enlisted men who had reason to be there came and went freely, without formalities. "Enter," he said, before taking a sip of coffee. Tired as he was after snatching only a few hours of sleep, the coffee helped him focus a little, but Gordon knew he wasn't going to be able to keep on functioning at the same intense level if he didn't soon get a decent night's sleep.

Lieutenant Gunn entered. "Sorry to disturb your breakfast, sir," he said as he took in Gordon's meal. "I can come back later . . ."

"Don't worry about it, Lieutenant," Gordon told him. "Our watch schedule is so thoroughly fouled up by now that I'm surprised the cook put together breakfast. I could just as well have ended up with pizza and a glass of red bug juice. You wanted to see me about something?"

The young SEAL officer's pudgy face wore an awkward expression. "Er . . . I was just a little surprised, Captain, when I found out we were still on the move. I guess I assumed you'd stick around Gateway Station until we saw whether *Pittsburgh* made it out, too."

Gordon shook his head. "We got clear of the White Sea, and if I had my way we'd throw a party that would make Crossing the Line look like a mortician's convention, Lieutenant. But these are still hostile waters, and we can't tell when the Red Banner Northern Fleet might decide to put in an appearance. Best for us to head for home as fast as we're able. We've still got to deliver the goods to Admiral Goldman before we can really claim the mission's over, after all. We won't accomplish that by hanging around Gateway Station."

"But . . ." Gunn trailed off. "Yes, sir. I understand."

"You're worried about those three men of yours aboard *Pittsburgh*," Gordon said.

"Well . . . yes, sir. I am. After you worked so hard to make sure Second Squad got back aboard safely, it seems kind of strange to us that you're not interested in making sure *Pittsburgh* makes it out." He paused. "If you'll pardon me for speaking freely, sir."

Gordon smiled. "Granted," he said. "Look, Lieutenant, I'm concerned for *Pittsburgh*, too. Her skipper is just about the oldest Navy friend I've got. And I want all of them to get out of there alive. But there's a difference between this situation and what happened the other night. Then I knew that *Bluefin* was the best bet those SEALs of yours had, so I did what I thought had to be done. Worked out pretty good, too. This time around, though, there's nothing *Bluefin* can do to help. All those people aboard *Pittsburgh*, SEALs and bubbleheads alike, are already in the best possible hands. They've got Mike Chase looking after them, and if I was in a tight spot that's the first guy I'd pick to have in my corner. *Pittsburgh* will make it out . . . or she won't. But the odds are in her favor with Chase in command, so I can concentrate on getting this boat home. Understand me?"

Gunn nodded slowly. "Yes, sir. I think I do."

At that moment Dr. Waite came through the door, grinning broadly. "Oh, good," he said. "Didn't know I'd find you here too, Lieutenant."

"What is it, Doctor?" Gordon asked.

"Just thought you'd want to know. Master Chief Callahan is awake, gentlemen. And the first thing he asked for was a beer." His smile broadened. "I think that's a pretty fair indication that he's out of danger."

Control Room, USS *Pittsburgh*
The White Sea, Near Archangel
2305 hours GMT

Chase studied the sonar repeater screen, fighting back the urge to smile in satisfaction. That would have been bad for his image, he told himself ruefully. He knew that most of his bridge crew, even the imperturbable Latham, had been taken aback by his orders to steer back toward Archangel and Severodvinsk, rather than sprinting straight north toward Gateway Station and the freedom of the open waters of the Barents Sea. But now the move had paid off as he had hoped it would, and his reputation for pulling just the right rabbit out of his hat was safe for a little while longer.

Pittsburgh was once again running off of her reactor. He had kept her diesel engine on-line for just a few hours, until she was far enough from the focal point of the Soviet search to be well clear of unwanted attention. Then the engineers had restarted the reactor, and the attack sub had proceeded on her way restored to peak operating efficiency.

Now Archangel lay less than twenty miles to the east. They weren't far from the scene of *Bluefin*'s grounding, running just under periscope depth and hoping there would be no unpleasant surprises in the undersea terrain to catch them as Frank Gordon had been caught the day before.

And their ticket out of the White Sea was barely ten miles ahead.

"This should do us very nicely, gentlemen," Chase

said quietly, gesturing toward the largest blip on the sonar repeater. There were several others on the screen as
well, but nothing close by, and nothing, as far as they
could tell, aware of *Pittsburgh*'s presence. They were
maintaining a slow, cautious speed and minimal noise
emissions, and it seemed unlikely that anyone would notice the attack sub without using an active sonar search.
And who would be looking for her here, back where the
pursuit had started over forty hours ago?

Latham and Quimby both stepped closer to study the
repeater over his shoulders. The Executive Officer, char-
acteristically, said nothing, but Chase caught a tiny nod
and the light of understanding in his solemn eyes.
Quimby, though, looked uncertain. "Sir?"

"That merchant ship, Mr. Quimby, is on a course that
suggests she left Archangel a few hours ago and is heading for the open ocean rather than some other port within
the White Sea." Latham's voice was flat and professo-
rial, that of a teacher delivering an impromptu lesson to
a promising student. That was, after all, part of the job
for senior submariners, to pass on the tricks of the trade
to the up-and-coming new generation of officers and enlisted men who would man these boats in future years.
"She is large and slow, and from all appearances gen-
erates a great deal of noise even under ideal circumstances. And thus she offers us cover."

Now Quimby was nodding slowly. "We get into her
baffles . . . and she masks us while we follow her out."

"We get into her baffles, as close to her as we dare,"
Chase amended. "Close enough to confuse anyone's passive sonar, maybe even to make it hard to pick us out
with active pinging. It's going to be a difficult ride, Mr.
Quimby. See that you and your people stay alert."

"Aye aye, sir," the Dive Officer said.

"All right, Mr. Latham, let's see if we can pull this
one off," Chase continued. "Bring us in behind that
freighter and then see just how close we can come without scratching the paint."

Latham gave another curt nod. "Aye aye, Captain," he said. "Mr. Quimby, increase speed to fifteen knots. Maintain this course and bring us to periscope depth." He glanced at Chase. "I trust you'll let us eyeball the final approach, sir? Or do you prefer that we do it entirely on instruments?"

Chase smiled. "I think we can take the risk of a peek or two through the periscope, Rick," he said. "Just don't make a habit of it."

He stepped back, both literally and figuratively, and allowed Latham to handle the boat through the slow, careful approach to their chosen target. The Russian merchant ship was laboring along at a little less than ten knots, oblivious to the possibility of an American submarine coming up behind her. And under Latham's deft handling, *Pittsburgh* crept in close, until the hammering beat of the freighter's big screws filled the sub's hull, and the turbulence from her wake was strong enough to make the helmsman and planesman mutter curses as they fought to keep the boat on a steady course.

It would be a long and difficult passage, requiring frequent changes of personnel at the helm in order to be sure the men stayed fresh and on top of their jobs. An error in judgment could result in a fatal collision between submarine and surface ship, or lead to a gap opening up between the two that would effectively lose *Pittsburgh* the camouflage she sought. But with all the dangers and difficulties this course of action challenged them with, it still offered the surest way past the defenses the Soviets would certainly have put into place by then to guard the mouth of the White Sea.

Chase suppressed a smile as he considered their prospects. It wasn't exactly the sort of dramatic escape from danger that would have turned up in some war movie about submarines in action, but it was on just such tricks that thousands of encounters at sea had turned over the years. And while it might not have been as flashy an escape as someone like Lieutenant Quimby might have expected or even wished for, Chase was perfectly content with the plan.

For submariners, victory went not to the strong or to the brave, but to the stealthy and the smart.

Control Room, Soviet Submarine *Bars*
The White Sea, Near Archangel
2348 hours GMT

"Surely you will not simply stand by and do nothing, Viktor Nikoleivich!"

Kalinin turned to face his *zampolit*, his features creasing into a frown as he regarded the angry little man. "And just what do you suggest we do?"

They had finally made the repairs needed to get the engines working again, just in time to receive word of the hunt for an intruding submarine in the middle of the White Sea. Kalinin had steered *Bars* back toward Severodvinsk, monitoring the fleet communications with interest but never allowing curiosity to get the better of common sense. After the accident in engineering all he wanted to do was get his boat safely back into port and have a long talk with the bureaucrats responsible for the substandard pipes that had caused the problem. There was no way Kalinin wanted his boat anywhere near the unknown intruder, not when he wasn't combat-ready. In all likelihood, that was an American boat that was causing all the furor, and Kalinin could see no sense in exposing his untried and highly secret command to exposure.

But the intruder, as it turned out, had come to *Bars*.

Sonar had picked up the fast-moving contact, and Kalinin had immediately ordered silent running. His sonar operator had identified the other boat as a Los Angeles class fast-attack boat, but one which matched none of the acoustical signatures of American boats on record.

So it was either a fairly new boat, or one which had never been close enough to Russian vessels to have any acoustic information recorded. At any event, it was certainly American, and certainly dangerous.

And it was over two hundred miles from the area where the searchers believed the quarry was to be found, heading north away from the great port of Archangel, hiding in the baffles of a large, noisy freighter and moving at a slow but steady speed the American commander probably thought low enough to escape passive sonar detection. He would have been right, too, with any older Soviet system, but *Bars* incorporated several new electronics systems, including an enhanced passive sonar suite which was back on-line at last after being crippled by a glitch in the power systems during the first portion of the long and unlucky sea trial.

Bars had spotted the American submarine the rest of the fleet was looking for so doggedly, and now Kalinin faced a major decision.

Anikanov was determined that *Bars* should intervene. Ever since they had first spotted the American he had been pointed in his comments about their passive role, but Kalinin had ignored him throughout. Not even the craziest senior officer or Politburo member would expect a submarine on its first sea trial, and a damaged one at that, to engage an enemy, so Kalinin knew he was reasonably safe from reprisals even if he continued to ignore his *zampolit*'s demands. And Kalinin was all too aware of the number of things that could go wrong if he chose to take action now. The weapons systems were all untested. He had only a handful of torpedoes on board, and most of them were practice weapons with dummy warheads. The repairs in engineering weren't fully reliable, and some of his best engineers were no longer available to him. He had every reason to keep clear of trouble.

The real problem was that he was tempted to see what *Bars* could do despite all that.

But *Bars* was too important to be thrown away before his capabilities were even known. Already they had important practical information about the design of the sub and his sonar systems that would be lost if the fight went against him. Not to mention recordings of the new American boat, which could be important as well.

Tempting as it was to think about taking on the American and proving that *Bars* was his match, Kalinin knew he should not act. Someone like Anikanov, who saw the world entirely in terms of black and white, could never understand such a decision, but Kalinin was made of different stuff. He could see beyond the immediate, and understood that there were times when blind loyalty and courage were simply not the answers to the problems that could face a commander.

Kalinin knew the higher demands of duty.

He looked past Anikanov and caught his Exec's eye. "Captain Third Rank Usenko," he said crisply. "Alter our heading. Come to course one-eight-zero. Increase speed to one-half."

"Course one-eight-zero, half speed," Usenko acknowledged. If he was disappointed, he didn't show it.

"You're turning? Running?" Anikanov flushed with anger. "Fleeing in the face of the enemy?"

"No, Dmitri Feodorovitch, I am doing my duty as I see it. We cannot guarantee success if *Bars* goes up against an American Los Angeles class boat. Not when we are still untested and underarmed. Our duty, as I see it, is to report the American's movements to the fleet so that they can head him off before he escapes from these waters. Otherwise, they might not realize the ruse he is attempting, using that freighter to mask his own noise. We serve a better purpose by making sure this information reaches the proper people, rather than hazarding everything in a gesture which might not achieve anything." He paused and met the little *zampolit*'s eyes with a cold, even stare. "We withdraw. If you wish to challenge my decision, I am sure the admiral will take whatever steps he deems appropriate to . . . punish me."

Anikanov blanched. Everyone knew Kalinin had been handpicked by a senior officer with plenty of political clout, and patronage like that wasn't something to be taken lightly.

Kalinin turned away, gripping the railing in front of him as *Bars* began his slow, stately turn toward Severodvinsk.

Sunday, 11 August 1985

Combat Information Center
Soviet Cruiser *Marshal Timoshenko*
Near the Mouth of the White Sea
2118 hours GMT

Captain First Rank Ilya Ivanovich Khersekov watched the crew of the Kresta II class guided-missile cruiser going about their duties with a calm professionalism that made him proud of the Red Banner Northern Fleet. There were plenty of problems plaguing the *Rodina* these days, from shortages of supplies and raw materials to corruption in high places and low, to the poor quality of education and training of the men taken in to the armed forces. Nonetheless, the Navy had been making progress in recent years in turning the ignorant peasants who entered the service into capable seamen who could do their jobs with a fair degree of competence. If the average Soviet officer or enlisted man still didn't show the same degree of intelligent initiative as his American counterpart, it was nevertheless also true that the men who now staffed the *Rodina*'s fighting ships were better disciplined and far less likely to cause difficulties for their officers by questioning their orders or arguing with their superiors.

Today, it seemed, they would have a chance to see how well the fighting men of Mother Russia performed against their opponents from the West. An American submarine had dared to challenge Soviet sovereignty over the White Sea, and the orders from the highest levels of the military were clear. That submarine must not be allowed to escape unscathed.

His commander was a clever one, Khersekov thought. He had dodged and ducked, drawn off the bulk of the searching Soviet ships on a wild-goose chase into the middle of the White Sea and then somehow slipped past them for a daring return to the waters off of Archangel rather than taking the obvious course and making a direct break for the safety of the Barents Sea. And the ruse of shadowing the freighter *Katun* . . . that had taken a cool head and no small amount of skill to pull off. Had it not been for the report from Captain Second Rank Kalinin, the American commander might well have made it out of the White Sea before anyone realized he was making his bid for freedom.

But fortunately Kalinin *had* made his report, and now the elements of the Red Banner Northern Fleet under Khersekov's command were in position to cut off the submarine's escape.

It was going to be a near-run thing, he thought. Rather than allow the American captain a chance to come up with some new clever scheme, Khersekov had allowed the freighter and the submarine to proceed undisturbed while he mustered his forces to intercept the submarine. That had taken time, more time than Khersekov had wanted to expend, and now the Americans were not far from their goal of slipping into the wide, deep expanses of the Barents Sea. Khersekov knew that if that submarine could win free of the long, narrow straits leading out of the White Sea, his chances of stopping the Americans were slim at best. With open water to maneuver

in and the skill that captain had already shown, Khersekov's small force wouldn't have much hope of tracking the escaping attack sub even with assistance from
aerial ASW assets flying out of nearby airbases. The best
chance to stop the American boat was to trap her in the
channel, and that was where Khersekov had carefully
laid his trap.

And now it was very nearly time to spring it.

He had five surface ships speeding up the channel, the
Marshal Timoshenko the largest and most modern of the
little squadron. They mounted stand-off ASW weaponry
that could launch an attack from up to thirty nautical
miles away, but those weapons did have their limitations. Khersekov would only bring them into action if
he could do so without jeopardizing friendly vessels in
the area.

The real purpose of the surface ships was to act as
beaters, to drive the American submarine into the jaws
of the trap he had set. A pair of Soviet submarines were
the real hunters today. Once the American realized the
danger he was in from the surface ships, the submarines
would cut him off and finish him. No amount of clev-
erness would save the American captain this time. . . .

Khersekov checked his watch. If everything had gone
according to his orders, all the elements were finally in
position. It was time . . . time to show the Americans that
they could not trespass in Soviet waters with impunity.

"Signal the *Katun*," he ordered curtly. "Tell him it is
time to change course."

Control Room, USS *Pittsburgh*
Near the Mouth of the White Sea
2123 hours GMT

"Aspect change! Aspect change! The freighter is turning to port!"

The words from the intercom speaker brought Chase out of a deep reverie. "Mr. Quimby! Watch your helm!"

"Aye aye, sir," the Dive Officer responded promptly. "Do we turn with him, sir?"

Chase shook his head. "Maintain our course north," he said. "We're too close to the gate to start playing games now."

"Maintain course, aye aye."

Pittsburgh had been traveling close to a full day in company with the freighter, and the exit from the White Sea was only a few miles ahead now. Chase didn't know what had prompted the Russian merchantman to suddenly alter course as it had, but that didn't matter now. Not when escape was so near at hand.

"Conn, Sonar. Designating new contacts. Sierra Two through Six. Surface vessels . . . not certain of their classes yet, but they're definitely not merchant ships. All five bearing one-six-three degrees, range two-two miles. Speed is two-eight knots for all of them."

Chase listened as Franco recited the information in a calm, matter-of-fact voice. He wondered how the CPO in the sonar shack could manage to sound so unruffled about the sudden appearance of five Red Banner Northern Fleet warships pursuing the sub. No doubt the Soviets were deploying all their ASW assets in the vicinity to shut the gate before the Americans could make good their escape. Surface vessels, aircraft, and Russian subs would all be closing in, hoping to intercept *Pittsburgh* before she could get away.

He cursed under his breath. Running so close to the Russian freighter had screened *Pittsburgh* from enemy sonar . . . but the noise from their guardian had also played merry hell with their own detection systems. Even Rodriguez, wizard that he was, hadn't been able to pick up anything significant. Now that the freighter was pulling away on her new course, the American boat was getting her first look around her in hours. And Chase wasn't pleased with what they were seeing out there. It was obvious that *Pittsburgh*'s deception hadn't been quite as effective as Chase had hoped it would be.

The attack sub still had a good chance of eluding the Russians baying at her heels, if only they could reach some open water they could disappear in. Right now the bottom was so shallow that they were constantly running the risk of repeating the mishap that had stranded *Bluefin*, and these shallow depths gave the sub no scope for finding a hiding place. There were no thermoclines to use as shields, no chances to pull the kind of clever ruse he had used to duck the Alfa that had followed them off Norway. There was nothing but shallow water and muddy bottom, plus a squadron of pursuing ships back there moving fast enough to easily overtake *Pittsburgh* as long as she tried to keep her speed low enough to stay off of enemy sonar displays.

She could increase her speed and maintain her distance, maybe even open up the range slightly. The old saying maintained that "a stern chase is a long chase," and *Pittsburgh* had the speed to match those ships. But doing so would be like painting a bull's-eye on the fairwater and inviting every Russian officer in the Red Banner Northern Fleet to take his best shot. The ASW armaments of those ships would be able to knock *Pittsburgh* out easily . . . just as soon as they could spot her long enough to get a solid position fix and launch.

So it was run and be bombarded by missiles, or hide and be overtaken by the enemy. Not a pretty choice, by any stretch of the imagination. But it wasn't that far to the open waters of the Barents Sea. If he could just shepherd the boat the rest of the way through the narrows, he could vanish into the depths. Chase had no doubts of his ability to keep *Pittsburgh* out of sight, if only he had a decent-sized body of water to work with.

"Conn, Sonar," the intercom announced in Franco's distinctive voice. "We have an ID on Sierra Five. It's a Kresta class cruiser."

He picked up the intercom mike. "Sonar, Conn. Ac-

knowledged." The Kresta II was a good ship . . . armed
to the teeth. The news only exacerbated his dilemma.

Chase caught Latham's eye. "I want you to start pulling in the towed array, Rick," he began. "Then begin to
increase speed . . ."

"Conn, Sonar!" This time Franco's voice had a sharp,
warning edge to it. "Designating new contact, Sierra
Seven. Submerged . . . bearing zero-zero-five, depth
two-zero-one feet, range ten thousand yards, closing."

"Ten thousand yards," Chase muttered. And the sub
lay ahead of *Pittsburgh*, blocking the way out.

"Looks like he was lying doggo until we came into
view, Skipper," Franco went on. "Speed's only three
knots, but building."

"Belay that last order, Rick," Chase said. "Reduce
speed . . . let's see if we can drop out of sight before that
guy draws a bead on us." He turned before the XO could
even acknowledge the command. "Mr. Jackson, prepare
torpedoes in tubes one, two, and three. And a noisemaker in number four, if you please."

"Aye aye, sir," Jackson responded. "Shall I flood the
tubes?"

At these ranges, the sound of water flooding into torpedo tubes or the outer doors opening could be clearly
picked up on sonar. When a submarine picked up those
distinctive sounds, her crew knew an opponent meant
business. Those preparations would ratchet the confrontation up to an even higher level of tension . . . making
a shooting match that much more likely as nervous Soviet officers contemplated an American submarine
openly flourishing its weaponry.

But that weaponry, ready for action, might make all
the difference.

"Conn, Sonar," Franco interrupted him before he
could respond to Jackson's question. "Sierra Seven is
positively IDed as a Victor III, number two in our files.
That makes her the *Komsomolets Polyarnyskiy*."

At that moment, Chase didn't really care what it was

they faced. All he wanted now was to get past this unexpected guardian and reach the open sea again. The
confined, shallow waters of the White Sea were beginning to make him wish he had never signed on for Goldman's covert recon mission.

"Flood 'em," Chase told the Combat Systems Officer.
"And open the outer doors. Show some teeth, Mr. Jackson, and let them know this is one fox that isn't afraid
to snap at the hounds."

"Aye aye, sir," Jackson repeated. He seemed torn between excitement and nerves.

Chase understood exactly how he felt.

As the Combat Systems Officer began issuing his orders, the intercom broke through yet again. "Conn, Sonar," Franco said. "Torps in the water! Two torpedoes
fired, bearing zero-zero-five, speed fifty knots, range
nine thousand, closing."

In the background Chase could hear a steady chant.
"Torps! Torps! Torps!"

He felt like he should be shivering in fear, but something inside him refused to react to the danger. Instead
he reacted with instincts honed to perfection by years of
training. "Helm! Hard to starboard! Bring us about
ninety degrees . . . that's nine-zero degrees! Increase
speed to one-half. Deploy noisemaker!"

All around the control room the officers and enlisted
men were grim but efficient and determined as they carried out the crisp orders. It was just like a combat drill,
and they responded as they had been trained to react.

But a part of Mike Chase's mind was listening to that
chant over the intercom of "Torps! Torps! Torps!" And
he knew that this time *Pittsburgh* wasn't in any drill.

Turning toward Jackson, Chase snapped out an order.
"Return fire, Lieutenant." Chase was surprised at the
depth and range of emotions that were battling for control inside him at that moment. Worst of them all was
the sheer anger, an unreasoning fury that someone had
dared to shoot at *Pittsburgh* . . . at *his* boat. But he

wasn't about to start letting his emotions override his brain. The last sonar report had showed several surface ships coming up behind *Pittsburgh,* but only the one submerged contact ahead. And those torps had come from that single gatekeeper who was trying to keep the American submarine fenced in. Get past him, and it was clear sailing to the Barents Sea.

Leave him there, and the Russian sub would continue to try to stop *Pittsburgh* from escaping . . . and her captain had already proven that he was willing to risk an incident if he had to.

"Give me a solution, Mr. Jackson," he said.

"Working on it, sir," Jackson replied absently, bending over the targeting computer. In submarine combat, it wasn't enough to just point and pull the trigger. Everything was in motion—the firing submarine, the target vessel, the currents that lay between them—and it took a delicate measurement of all those factors and more to work out where to aim in order to have a reasonable chance of hitting the target. Of course the onboard guidance system and the wire that allowed the sub to steer the torps manually helped, but a good firing solution was the essential first step for getting a hit.

But it took time . . . and every second that passed brought those incoming torpedoes closer. And increased the chances of another launch from the Victor III. With the range closing faster between the two vessels, the odds of outmaneuvering the next set of enemy torps were going down fast.

Finally, Jackson looked up. "Solution," he announced. "Feeding it in now."

"Fire torpedoes one and two," Chase ordered.

"Firing!" Jackson leaned past the enlisted man at the control panel to press the buttons himself. The roar of the torps leaving their tubes echoed loudly through the control room, and Chase could picture the scene in the forward torpedo room in his mind's eye. Burly sailors would be operating the controls that closed the outer tube doors and pumped out the water, then swinging open the inner doors and manhandling two more of the brand new Mark 48 Mod 4 torpedoes into their cradles. Crews competed every day to see who could load their tubes the fastest. Today was a chance for the endless hours of drills to finally be put to use in a real combat situation.

"Torpedoes running," Jackson announced. "Closing on the target. Five thousand yards . . . forty-nine hundred . . ."

Sonar Shack, USS *Pittsburgh*
Near the Mouth of the White Sea
2136 hours GMT

"Torps! Torps! Torps!" Rodriguez chanted. The high-pitched sound of the propellers turning on the two incoming torpedoes was one no submariner ever forgot . . . or wanted to hear again. Racing faster than a sub could maneuver, with a choice of targeting options ranging from onboard computer guidance to "fly-by-wire" direction from the launching vessel, modern torpedoes had little in common with the old-style "fish" popularized in old World War II movies on late-night TV. Today they were versatile and deadly weapons.

And two were streaking through the waters of the White Sea, straight toward *Pittsburgh*.

Rodriguez could feel the submarine beginning to turn, and tried to remember everything he had studied on sub combat. A launch from anything under five thousand yards was almost impossible to evade, so fast-moving were the torps in comparison to their target. When there was time to maneuver, the ideal move was to turn ninety degrees across the incoming weapon's bow. That had always struck Rodriguez as foolish, since it meant presenting the full profile of the sub to the torpedo instead of minimizing the target by turning directly toward or away from it. But it also meant that the sub had a better chance of moving out of the relatively narrow cone of effective sonar guidance that the weapon required to stay locked on target. Whether the torp was on its own or being guided from the firing vessel, even a short loss of sonar contact could result in a clean miss and a long, difficult period as the torp tried to reacquire the target. Spun out properly, and aided by decoys, such maneuvers could drag things out long enough that the torpedo would run out of fuel before it made contact with its target. That was the weapon's chief vulnerability. They just weren't big enough to contain a powerful warhead and a large fuel reserve at the same time.

Beside Rodriguez, Sonarman Second Class Larry Manners was reeling off the distance to the two torpedoes in a flat, steady voice. He seemed completely unaware of the fact that those two deadly little blips on his scope could kill him and every other man aboard *Pittsburgh*. Rodriguez wished he could be as cool about it as Manners.

Pittsburgh was picking up speed, and diving steeply as well, as Captain Chase played out all the cards in his hand. A thermal layer, an outcropping of undersea rock, a peculiar eddy in the current . . . anything might help to break the target lock and cause those torpedoes to miss.

Rodriguez watched as the blips on his scope closed in. It was going to be close, one way or another.

Something else on the screen caught his eye, a new blip that had just appeared as *Pittsburgh* made her turn. Rodriguez opened his mouth to call attention to it, but things were happening so goddamned fast. . . .

The first torpedo passed by, above the diving submarine's hull. For a moment hydrophones weren't necessary to hear the whine of its small but powerful engine. Then it was gone, and Chief Franco was grinning as he leaned between Rodriguez and Manners to study their consoles. "One down!" he said. "One to—"

The second torpedo detonated.

Rodriguez wasn't sure what set it off. Certainly it hadn't struck the hull. If it had, *Pittsburgh* would probably not have survived. More likely, it had plowed into the sea bottom. But whatever it struck, it was close enough to the submarine for the crew to feel the effects of the blast.

The whole hull shuddered, and the force of the blast caused the sub to pitch and yaw. The lights and sonar gear all went dark for a moment.

Then power surged back through the boat . . . and the panel Manners was operating exploded outward in a shower of sparks and whirling debris. Manners took the full force of both the explosion and the power surge, and died instantly. A shard of metal struck Franco across the throat and sent him spinning backward across the compartment, deep red blood welling from the gash across his jugular.

Franco had screened Rodriguez from the flying debris and the sheer force of the explosion, but he didn't get clear of the console fast enough to avoid being jolted by the electrical shock. His whole body went numb at once, and suddenly he realized that he was flying through the air, pushed right out of his seat and across the compartment by the fury of the power surge.

The world was spinning around him for a moment. Then blackness descended. . . .

Torpedo Room, USS *Pittsburgh*
Near the Mouth of the White Sea
2138 hours GMT

Torpedoman Third Class Jerry Connors was sweating profusely as he helped to wrestle one of the Mark 48 torpedoes out of its storage rack and onto the portside loading tray. Even with assistance from two other crewmen—Bergman and Silvano—it was a difficult job, possibly one of the hardest tasks a submariner could perform under combat conditions. The torpedo weighed close to thirty-four hundred pounds, and despite all the mechanical assistance designed into *Pittsburgh*'s torpedo room, it still required brute strength to shift the weapon into position. That had been a deliberate choice on the part of the boat's designers. A completely automated torpedo-loading system could have been installed on board, but automated systems were prone to breaking down when a boat took combat damage, and then the sub would be helpless. Better a system which could keep working as long as there were men with strong backs willing to manhandle their fish into position even under the worst possible conditions.

Connors spared a glance for Tom Edwards, the young petty officer busy "diving the tube" in preparation for loading the torpedo. It was a job he was ideally suited for, calling for someone who was slender and had narrow shoulders so he could wriggle into the opening of the twenty-one-inch tube to check for debris left behind from previous firings, such as loose wire from an old torpedo's guidance system. There wasn't likely to be anything there this time, since Tube Number Four had been used to launch the noisemaker that was trying to divert those incoming torps. But the routine of diving the tube was as ingrained for torpedomen as the need to swab out an old-time muzzle-loader between shots from the deck of a frigate back in the Age of Sail.

Edwards pulled his head and shoulders out of the tube and stepped back from the opening. "Tube is clear!" he announced.

At that moment, the boat rocked violently as the second of the two Russian torpedoes detonated close by. The lights dimmed, and the sub lurched violently to starboard.

And the three sailors lost control of the Mark 48.

It rolled free before any of them could shout a warning, hitting the loading tray hard and then toppling to the deck beyond. Like a wild animal suddenly let loose in the cramped confines of the torpedo room, it ran amok.

Tom Edwards was directly in its deadly path.

The torpedo slammed into his legs, and he screamed as he fell sideways. His head hit the middle bank of storage racks with a dull, squishy thud even as the rolling torpedo crushed both his legs.

"Secure that torp! Goddamn it, secure that torp!" That was Chief Tanner, bellowing in a voice that could be heard over the clangor of the loose torpedo and the babble of his crew.

They dodged past the damaged loading tray in pursuit of the weapon. Connors fought to ignore the wrecked body of Tom Edwards, but he knew it would haunt his dreams for a long time to come. . . .

Sonar Shack, USS *Pittsburgh*
The White Sea
2140 hours GMT

Archie Douglas was the second man from the damage-control party into the sonar shack. PO/1 Randolph was getting the flames that licked at the center console under control with judicious squirts of his fire extinguisher. Archie spotted the sprawled figures on the deck and quickly assessed them. Manners was clearly dead, and so was Franco, with the metal splinter buried in his neck. Douglas looked away as the blood continued to well from the man's slashed throat.

That left Rodriguez. Douglas dropped to his knees beside the young sailor and probed his throat for a pulse. He couldn't find one, and the man wasn't breathing.

Douglas reacted as he had been taught, rolling the body over on its back and making sure the airway was clear. Then he brought his clenched hand down, hard, across the victim's chest. Finally, he used both hands to begin steady pressure across the chest. *One . . . two . . . three . . . four . . . five.* He leaned over Rodriguez and blew into his mouth, trying to force air into his lungs. Then it was back to the chest massage. *One . . . two . . . three . . . four . . . five.*

It wasn't much like it had been in training, a part of him thought with a detachment he wasn't sure he'd ever understand. They'd worked on life-size dummies and on each other when they studied basic first aid in boot camp, but nothing could quite prepare anyone for facing a real-life emergency like this one.

"Come on! Damn it, Rodriguez, don't give up on me!" He administered more air, then resumed his pressure over the heart. "You've got a wife and a brand-new kid waiting for you at home. Breathe, damn it!" *One . . . two . . . three . . .*

All at once Rodriguez was spluttering and shaking wildly . . . but he was alive, and he was drawing breath on his own, and for those things Archie Douglas was happy.

"Let's get him to sick bay!" Douglas said, motioning to two of the damage-control party to help him with the injured man. But Rodriguez clamped his hand around Archie's wrist in a viselike grip.

"Tell . . . the skipper . . ." the sonar operator gasped. "Target . . . target astern . . . submarine . . . another sub in our baffles. . . ."

Then Rodriguez passed out, his breathing shallow and erratic, his gripping hand suddenly relaxed again. Douglas surged to his feet as the other two crewmen joined him and bent to pick up the wounded man from the deck. "Intercom! Where's the goddamned intercom? I have to report to the captain!"

Control Room, USS *Pittsburgh*
Near the Mouth of the White Sea
2143 hours GMT

"Status?" Chase demanded.

"Sonar shack took it hard, sir," Latham reported. "Two dead, one wounded. Two consoles wrecked, the other one's not in very good shape . . ." He paused. "The hydrophones are still working, but the data isn't getting processed."

"Damn it, Rick, we don't stand a chance without sonar. Get it working."

"Aye aye, sir. The damage control party's on it."

"Bring us back to our original heading, Mr. Quimby. Increase speed to full."

"Full speed, course three-four-seven, aye aye," the Dive Officer responded.

"We'll lose the towed array, sir," Latham warned. "At that speed we'll either have to cut it, or it will shear off anyway."

"Then cut it!" Chase said. "Right now what we need is speed . . . unless we want that squadron back there to catch up with us. Anyway, what's the use of the towed array without a working passive sonar system?"

"Conn, Sonar!" the intercom squawked. Chase knew that voice. It was Archie Douglas, who had no right or reason to be making a report from the sonar shack.

He seized the intercom mike. "This is the captain," he said sternly.

"Skipper!" Douglas broke in before he could say more. "Rodriguez was injured when the sonar shack got clobbered, but he told me he picked up another contact. Submarine, astern of us . . . in our baffles!"

"What's the status of the sonar shack now, Douglas?" he rasped. Word of a possible second sub out there shook him to the core, but somehow he managed to remain clearheaded. They had to get the sonar system back on-line if they were going to deal with this new threat.

"Captain, one station is back on line," Douglas responded.

"If Rodriguez is able, have him get on it," Chase said. "I need confirmation of that second submarine, and I need it now!"

"Sorry, sir . . . Rodriguez is on his way to the infirmary." Douglas's voice was bleak. "Czernak's here now."

Chase tried to keep his features schooled at the news. He liked the young Hispanic sonar genius, genuinely liked him. And not just because he was one of the top men in his field, too. Wounded in action . . . and just days after the birth of his daughter, too. . . .

And *Pittsburgh* needed him now. Czernak was capable, but Rodriguez was an artist. Chase remembered telling Latham that no one aboard was irreplaceable, and had to fight back an ironic laugh at the memory. It looked as if they were about to find out whether Rodriguez was irreplaceable or not.

"One thousand yards!" Jackson said, the rising pitch of his voice betraying his excitement as *Pittsburgh*'s two torps closed the range. "Nine hundred . . . eight hundred . . ."

On the sonar repeater, he could see the traces that showed the torpedoes streaking toward their target. Farther aft, one of Jackson's crewmen was hunched over his console like a kid playing Pac-Man, using a joystick control to make minor course corrections over the guidance wire and keep the torp on course.

"Five hundred . . . four hundred . . ."

An erratic and irreverent corner of Chase's brain wished the target was a surface ship, rather than another sub. Although he had only done it in simulations and practice runs against condemned hulks, he had made torpedo runs against surface ships enough times to know that there was a satisfaction to be gained in watching through the periscope as the fish struck home and the enemy ship erupted in debris and flames. Sub-to-sub warfare was conducted entirely by instruments, a cold and calculated affair with no personal touch.

Of course, on the other hand it was a hell of a lot easier to ignore the lives being taken when your "enemy" was a blip on a sonar screen as opposed to a visible ship.

"She's turning, sir," Czernak's voice said on the intercom. "Trying to slip past our fish."

"Not on my watch," Jackson said, his usually gentlemanly Southern tones giving way to something more appropriate to his Civil War general namesake going into battle.

Jackson reached past the crewman to activate the torpedoes' search function. Now a tiny but effective sonar system in each of those two weapons would begin actively pinging in search of their target. And with the range as short as it was, it was highly unlikely the Victor III would evade them for long.

"They've got a solid lock," Jackson reported. "Closing . . . closing . . . Hit! First torp hit him!" There was a momentary pause before Jackson spoke up again. "Second torp hit, too!"

A small cheer went around the control room. "Good shooting, Mr. Jackson," Chase said dryly. His conscience gave him a tiny twinge as he wondered if he had just started World War III by taking on the Russians in a shooting match. But, damn it, they had fired first. And it was his duty to protect *Pittsburgh* and her crew by whatever means came to his hands.

"Conn, Sonar," Czernak said. "The Victor III sounds like she's breaking apart, sir. I think we just got ourselves a clean kill."

"Never mind that now. What about that second sub Rodriguez reported?"

"I'm trying, Captain. This display. . . ."

"If you can't get it on passive, go active, damn it! Give me something to work with!"

"Aye aye, sir." After a moment the distinctive shriek

of an active sonar burst echoed through the sub.

And, on the sonar repeater, an image flickered into being astern of *Pittsburgh*. Rodriguez had been right. There was a second Soviet boat out there.

"Mr. Jackson!" Chase snapped. "Can you get me a shot?"

"Trying for a firing solution now, sir," the Weapons Officer responded. He paused, his head cocked to one side as he monitored a report over his earpiece intercom receiver. "Sir, we've got a problem . . . damage in the torpedo room, and one casualty. Portside rammer's out of action." The rammer was the system that pushed a torpedo from the loading tray into one of the torpedo tubes. Damage to the rammer or to the loading tray meant that two of the boat's four tubes were out of action until repairs could be made. "I've got one torpedo up the spout. After that I can only feed you one fish at a time until they can repair the damage down there."

"I don't care if your people have to hand-deliver the damned things, Lieutenant," Chase snapped, forgetting this one time to maintain the wall of command aloofness he usually cultivated so carefully. "Get a solution and prepare to fire!"

"Aye aye, sir," Jackson responded.

"Conn, Sonar," Czernak's voice rang over the intercom, taut with urgency. "Second Soviet sub is flooding his tubes!" He paused, as if fighting to reestablish a professional demeanor. "Second Soviet sub now designated Sierra Eight. Tentatively IDed as November class SSN." The November was the oldest nuclear sub in the Soviet arsenal, clumsy and noisy by modern standards, but that didn't make it any less dangerous in this situation.

"Hurry with that firing solution, Mr. Jackson," Chase urged.

"Torps! Torps! Torps!" Czernak announced. "Four torps in the water, bearing zero-zero-eight, closing!"

It took a long moment for the sonar operator's words to fully register with Chase. Then he realized what the man had said. He snatched the intercom mike from its cradle. "Sonar, Conn. Repeat bearing! Repeat bearing!"

"Bearing zero-zero-eight!" Czernak said. "They're . . . my God, they're right on top of us!"

Everyone in the control room heard the whine as four high-speed motors drove the torpedoes past *Pittsburgh*. As the sound began to recede, Czernak spoke up again. "Conn, Sonar. New contact, Sierra Nine, bearing zero-zero-eight, submerged. Range is five-five-zero yards, closing. Speed is five knots . . . it's *Queenfish*! I say again, *Queenfish*! Sierra Nine is a friendly!"

A ragged cheer sounded in *Pittsburgh*'s control room.

"Sierra Eight is turning away," Czernak reported a moment later. "He's running . . ." With those four torpedoes on his tail, the Russian skipper would have his hands full. Even if he managed to dodge the barrage from *Queenfish*, he'd be in no position to interfere with the Americans for a while. Which still left the Soviet surface ships and their arsenal of long-range ASW torpedoes . . . if they dared use them while one of their own boats was close enough to accidentally draw fire.

Pittsburgh had a narrow window of opportunity open. It was up to Chase to take advantage of it while he could.

"Flank speed, Mr. Latham," Chase ordered. "Let's show our Russian friends a clean pair of heels!"

"Flank speed, aye aye," the Exec echoed.

Chase descended from the periscope platform and moved aft to the chart tables, where the mapping sonar was steadily depicting the bottom contours around them, still nerve-wrackingly close to the bottom of the submarine. There just wasn't enough room to work.

And when the Russians began to launch their ASW missiles, they wouldn't even have to worry much about preprogramming a depth at which their warheads should explode. *Pittsburgh* wouldn't be able to ride out a bombardment by creeping along the bottom and hoping the warheads were set to go off at lesser depths. Here, there were no lesser depths.

He could feel the submarine straining like a greyhound given its head, speed increasing with each passing minute. But the higher revs from the propellers would be drawing the attention of Soviet sonar operators, who would be reporting the noise to their superiors. . . .

Chase could almost visualize the ASW crews manning their weapons, setting up their own firing solutions, with fingers poised over buttons ready to unleash their birds the moment they were sure of their target and their captains passed the word.

"Sir!" Latham had joined him at the chart table, and he hadn't even noticed. "Captain, take a look ahead. . . ."

The graphical representation of the seafloor on the plotting board was beginning to drop away. There was deeper water ahead . . . and Chase knew that once it began to drop away it did so quickly. They were coming into the Barents Sea at last, and the whole aspect of the ocean floor was changing rapidly as they did.

"Three degrees down-angle on the bubble!" Chase ordered. "Take us down!"

"What depth, sir?" Latham asked, and there was a note of relief behind his words. It was the first time in a long time that he could ask that question in any kind of a meaningful way.

"Just keep diving until I say differently, Rick," Chase said. He paused and grinned. "Or until you start scraping the bottom."

Seconds passed, and still there was no sign of an attack. He supposed the Russians were hoping to get in closer before they started launching, to make sure of a kill. Or perhaps they entertained ideas of hemming the American sub in and forcing a surrender. That would be the biggest coup on the international scene since the day the North Koreans had captured the *Pueblo* back in 1968.

No matter what their reasoning, Chase told himself,

they had made a mistake today. Given enough time, and especially enough water to operate in, a Los Angeles class submarine could win at practically any game of hide-and-seek with her Russian adversaries. It was simply a matter of knowing how to disappear. . . .

"Passing through a thermocline, sir." Latham spoke from the navigation station, where he was bending to look over a crewman's shoulder. "It's now or never."

"You've got that right, Rick," Chase said. "Mr. Quimby, level her out. Reduce speed to one-quarter, and bring us to a heading of . . . zero-four-five degrees."

"Sir, that will take us in closer to the Kanin Peninsula," Quimby protested. "Shouldn't we be getting away from Russian waters?"

Chase smiled at him. "Another lesson, Mr. Quimby. You're a Russian captain, and you've just lost track of an American submarine leaving Russian waters. You want to find her again, so where do you look? Hanging about in the area he's been trying to leave? Or on a course out into the open sea?"

Looking embarrassed, Quimby gave a small nod. "I see what you mean, sir. Sorry."

"Don't be sorry, Mr. Quimby. When you do your stint at the Prospective Commanding Officer's School in a few years, you can stay in your quarters and sleep the day they cover that particular little tactic. Now . . . the course changes, if you please."

"Aye aye, sir! Heading zero-four-five degrees, one-quarter speed, leveling off descent." He turned to the helm station and repeated the instructions to the helmsman and planesman.

As the helmsman transmitted instructions to the engine room by way of the engine telegraph, the sound of the engines altered noticeably. Chase could feel *Pittsburgh* beginning to slow as she turned onto her new heading. Between the thermocline's reflective effects on searching sonars and the reduction of noise to a safe level, *Pittsburgh* would effectively vanish off the screens of the searching Soviet ships. The hunt would go on for some time, of course, with ships, subs, and aircraft all straining their resources to track the elusive attack boat, but the simple fact was that now that she was out in open waters *Pittsburgh* could hide almost indefinitely. It might take time to work her way clear of the searchers and shape a course back for Holy Loch, but they had plenty of time.

The worst was over. Soon they would be on their way home.

EPILOGUE

Thursday, 22 August 1985

Wardroom, USS *Pittsburgh*
Holy Loch, Scotland
0927 hours GMT

"Well, Mike, you did it. Not the way you should have, but you did it."

"Yes, Admiral," Chase said slowly. He and Gordon were sitting side by side at the wardroom table, while Admiral Goldman was opposite them. The diminutive man was looking a little older this morning, a little more tired. Chase didn't know if it came from worrying over the details of Operation Arctic Fox, or if it was just the result of living on the fringes of the Scottish Highlands, where everything was so much more vivid and intense.

Somehow they had pulled it off, Chase and Gordon working together in harness the way they had when they were first starting out as young Navy officers together. Both of them had bent the rules along the way, but somehow they'd pulled it off. Both subs had made it back, bringing out the information they'd been sent to collect. And no one was apt to pay too much attention to bent rules when the mission had been carried out so successfully.

It had been touch-and-go for a while, though. *Bluefin* had enjoyed a day's head start into the Barents Sea and had missed the excitement of *Pittsburgh*'s escape from the Soviets. Chase still didn't care to dwell on just how narrow that escape had really been, and he knew he owed Captain Paxton of *Queenfish* a night on the town the next time both of them were in the same port. Not only had *Queenfish* saved the day with her well-timed salvo of torpedoes, but she had also further confused the Soviet pursuit thereafter. Once *Pittsburgh* had passed by her position, *Queenfish* had taken over the role of wild goose, leading the Russians on a merry chase in the direction of Murmansk while Chase headed farther north.

Eleven days had gone by since then, and the sub crews were settling in comfortably to a new routine there in Scotland—except for Petty Officer Third Class Rodriguez, recovering well from his wounds, who had been flown home on the first available military aircraft heading for the States. He would be with his wife and baby daughter by now. Meanwhile his shipmates had been granted extensive liberty privileges while the men in charge assessed the outcome of the operation at Severodvinsk. Chase wasn't sure if he and Gordon deserved medals, or courts-martial . . . but he knew they had done their best to muddle through. Sometimes that was all you *could* do.

"You did the job, that's what counts," Goldman said, as if picking up Chase's thoughts. He grinned wolfishly. "I can remember a few times when I broke a few rules and got away with it because I brought home the bacon, so how could I judge you any more harshly? Mike, the suits at the NSA flipped when they got those pics and recordings you made of the *Akula* at sea. I think Dreyfuss would like to have your baby. You took a hell of a chance, but you brought back some first-rate material. Better than the SEALs could pick up, frankly, and because you and your people understood submarines you were able to zero in on plenty of important points." He paused. "Because of what you did, and what you achieved out there, Mike, I'm putting you up for the Distinguished Service Cross."

"Admiral . . . ?" Chase was stunned by the announcement. The medal was one of the highest distinctions a naval officer could win, especially in peacetime.

"The drawback is that it will have to be a black award," Goldman went on. "Can't very well go around admitting that our boys were taking potshots at Russian subs, and in Soviet territorial waters at that!"

Chase nodded slowly. The practice of giving out "black" medals, which could not be worn in public but still appeared in a Navy man's service jacket, was a natural adjunct of the Cold War and the many covert operations it had spawned. Chase didn't particularly care about being permitted to pin yet another shiny Crackerjack prize on his uniform . . . but a DSC in his permanent file could do his career a world of good.

That made him glance at Gordon, who sat beside him with a wooden expression. Frank Gordon had come a long way since they had met here at the start of the operation, but it was still plain to see that he resented Chase coming out with the big trophy yet again.

Goldman, surprisingly, looked him straight in the eye and smiled gently. "I'm sorry I couldn't recommend you along with Mike, Frank," he said slowly. That was the first time Chase could remember the admiral ever pronouncing the name of the man who had stolen away his daughter. "*Bluefin* did good work out there, and so did you. But Chase's performance was outstanding."

Frank Gordon managed a reluctant nod. "I owe him a couple, Admiral," he said slowly. He couldn't quite meet Goldman's gaze.

"However, there's something of a consolation prize I'd like to offer you, Frank, if you'll take it," the admiral went on. "I understand your tour on *Bluefin* will be up soon, and you're slated for a spot of shore duty. Is that right?"

"Yes, Admiral," Gordon responded, a little sullen now. Goldman had touched a raw nerve there.

"Well, I need someone who understands submarines and their uses in covert ops to head up a special board that will be drawing up recommendations on the subject for my office. I was going to offer it to Mike, here, but it's pretty clear he likes playing the mainstream attack-boat skipper now. But with your experience, Frank, you'd be perfect . . . and I don't have to tell you, I'm sure, how much of a career booster a special Pentagon assignment can be."

Gordon drew himself up in his seat, clearly surprised. "You're serious, Admiral?" he asked—hardly the most tactful comment to make to a flag officer.

"I'm serious," Goldman told him. "In fact, I can pretty much guarantee that a few years of high-profile Pentagon work would land you your own attack-boat command down the line. If you want it, that is." And again he smiled. It only looked a little bit forced.

"So you'll be gunning for my job again, eh, Frank?" Chase commented wryly.

"Hell, Mike," Gordon told him, "by the time I'm ready to move up you'll be skipper of a boomer. Or my squadron commander."

"God forbid," Chase said. "I'd like to have subordinates who obey orders now and again."

"That was what I told myself, once upon a time," the admiral told him. "It never works out that way. Submarine skippers are too damned independent, and that's all there is to it."

"So did we get anything worthwhile, sir?" Chase demanded. "I mean, worth what we risked? I was afraid we'd get here and find out we'd set off a shooting war."

Goldman shook his head. "Officially, nothing ever happened. An unnamed submarine in the Red Banner Northern Fleet was reported missing after an accident suffered while conducting routine maneuvers. We have five men dead and another who's just holding on, but as far as the outside world is concerned the SEALs were the victims of a training mishap during NATO exercises in Norway, and your casualties, Mike, were the result of a shipboard accident. I expect you to make it quite clear to your men that nothing they've done, or seen, or heard over the last two weeks ever really happened."

"Of course, Admiral," Chase said quietly. He was familiar with the drill by now, and so was Gordon. How well the bubbleheads aboard *Pittsburgh* would react to this typical decree of the covert-ops brass remained to be seen, but he was fairly sure he could count on his crew to do what was right.

"So there it is," Goldman went on. "Neither side admits anything . . . and both sides know we came close to the real thing . . . again. But as usual nobody stepped so far over the line that we couldn't pull back and set things in order."

"They don't suspect we spied on their sub?"

Goldman shrugged. "With the Russians, you never know what they suspect. But they have no proof that we were closer to Severodvinsk than the mouth of the Dvina River. That's what's important. As far as we can tell, Gunn covered his tracks nicely. So the Russians have their new *Akula* to play with—once they work out the bugs—but we know enough about her to know we can still counter her. That boat's pretty damned good . . . about on a level with the Flight I LAs. But we're moving past Flight II already, and we'll have an improved LA in the water in a year or two. And so it goes."

So it went, Chase thought. Another set of intricate steps in the complicated dance that was the Cold War. Perhaps one day it would all come to an end. The Russians would abandon Communism and give up their dreams of empire, and the Americans could stand down and stop playing policeman to a troubled world.

Until that unlikely day dawned, though, it would be the submariners who stayed in the front lines. And Mike

Chase and Frank Gordon would be there, leading the way.

Infirmary, U.S. Submarine Base
Holy Loch, Scotland
1008 hours GMT

Bernard Gunn looked up as the nurse walked into the room. She was a stern-faced, uncompromising type who looked after her charges with a fierce protectiveness, and Gunn had learned there was little use in trying to argue with her when she arrived to perform one of her arcane duties. He started to rise.

To his surprise she held up a hand. "I didn't mean to disturb the two of you, Lieutenant," she told him. "I just wanted to warn you that they'll be coming by in about a half an hour to take him down to catch his ride."

"Half an hour. Thanks."

She left, and Gunn turned his attention back to Master Chief Callahan. The man had seemed like such an elemental force of nature, always in control. Now he lay in his hospital bed, looking old and drawn after his ordeal despite his frequent protests that he was fit enough to share in the liberty the other SEALs were enjoying.

Gunn had visited the Master Chief daily, but after all this time he still couldn't really understand how fate had decided that Callahan should be singled out for such a devastating blow. The man had survived three tours in 'Nam and everything the SEALs could throw at him since. It didn't seem possible, let alone right, that he should have been struck down. The rookie, Silverwolf, had come out of Russia with barely a scratch on him, while veterans and skilled fighters—Callahan, Jenkins, Harriman—hadn't been so fortunate. Jenkins would return to duty, but the doctors didn't think Callahan, tough as he was, would ever be judged fit to return to the Teams.

"I should have been there," he said aloud. Callahan had been asleep since Gunn had arrived at the infirmary today, but Gunn's words weren't really meant for Callahan. "Damn it, I should have been with you guys."

Would that have made a difference? Probably not. From the debriefings of the survivors it was clear that Second Squad had actually gotten off fairly lightly. They could easily have lost one or two more, starting with Jinx Jenkins.

Nobody was calling him that these days. The reminder of their bad luck was too painful to be made into a casual joke to toss around at midnight bull sessions.

"Don't be so hard on yourself, Lieutenant. You couldn't be in two places at once."

Gunn looked up, startled. "Sorry, Master Chief. Didn't mean to wake you."

"Hell, L-T, I've been awake for a while now. I just find they leave you alone if they think you're asleep. Now if that cute nurse from the night shift was on duty, I wouldn't mind being fussed over . . ." Callahan chuckled, then shifted uncomfortably in the bed.

"Maybe I should put you down for malingering, Master Chief," Gunn said with a smile.

"I meant what I said just now, Lieutenant," Callahan continued. "I know you've been blaming yourself for the trouble we got into, but it wasn't your fault. You did what you had to, right down the line. There's no way you could have known we'd get into trouble. It was just damned rotten luck. Never heard of any course that taught you officer types how to avoid that."

"You almost make me believe it," Gunn said. "Almost."

"What's your real problem, Mr. Gunn?" Callahan demanded. "You're not some green rookie coming to terms with losing men in combat. And you know better than to try and second-guess yourself when you were just the victim of bad breaks. So what is it that's eating you?"

Gunn didn't want to force the answer into words. After a long moment, it was Callahan who went on. "It was Harriman, wasn't it?"

Reluctantly Gunn nodded. "I . . . guess so. He said I couldn't cut it, and I was proud of myself for not just rolling over and letting him have his way. But if I had let him take charge of First Squad . . . things might have been different, that's all."

"Harriman couldn't have hacked it in the shipyard, kid. He would have been a bull in a china shop, smashing everything instead of finessing it the way you did. No, you were the best man for the job. Trust me."

Gunn shrugged. "If you say so, Master Chief," he said wearily. "But I still can't get away from the fact that in the end Harriman was the hero. I skulked and slipped away without ever seeing more than a single enemy. He left the SDV and saved your asses with those limpet mines. And he died in the line of duty. That's not the way it's supposed to work, Master Chief. In the movies the bully turns out to be a coward, and the poor downtrodden nobody turns out to be the hero . . ."

"Well, it's time you learned a few more things, Lieutenant," Callahan told him. "First off, there are no heroes here. Haven't you been griping about these Rambo movies? The movie heroes aren't real, and the real heroes will never be in the movies. Fact is, Mr. Harriman was a nasty, unpleasant, arrogant bastard who rubbed people the wrong way just by the way he said 'good morning.' But he went through the same Hell Week you did, literally. And when you've gone through that, it's a guarantee that you won't be found wanting when the time comes to do the right thing. Harriman proved that. So did you, L-T, in a different way. You did what was best for your men, you accomplished your mission, and then, by God, you chewed the ear off of a Navy submarine captain trying to do everything in your power to go in after the rest of us. Don't deny it. Some of the other guys told me about it. In my book, that makes you just as much of a hero as Vince Harriman and every other fool who figured the only way to prove himself worthy of his country was to go out and die messily for it."

"You really believe that, Master Chief?"

Callahan gave him a half grin. "Nah, of course not. You're a j.g. for Christ's sake, which means the only thing more annoying than you is an ensign. We all know that you're really cowardly, shiftless, and generally not worth the effort to swat down. Is that what you'd rather hear, sir? Because I can dish it out all day. So say the word, Mr. Gunn, and I'll let you have it some more!"

Holding up his hands, Gunn surrendered. "Never mind, Master Chief," he said. "I'll go along with what you were saying before . . ."

"Thought you might," the injured man replied with a smile. "Now how about you let me have a few minutes by myself before they start swarming in here to get me packed up for my trip back to the world?"

Gunn took the hint and left Callahan alone. He had a few new things to think about.

Sometimes he wished that life was as simple and straightforward as what they showed in the movies.

Outside the Tourist Information Center
Douglas, Lanarkshire, Scotland
1145 hours GMT

Archie Douglas climbed out of the tiny rental car and closed the door firmly. He looked around the pleasant little town again, smiling. It was good to be back so soon . . . and with an entire three days when no shipboard duties could claim him. There was a lot a man could do in three days in a foreign land, especially with the right person to guide him.

Strange to think that less than two weeks had gone

by since the battle in the White Sea. Rodriguez had
made a full recovery, though scuttlebutt around the boat
claimed that what had really perked him up was the
prospect of getting a MATS flight back to the States so
he could spend some time with his wife and baby. "Ah,
leave, the great power of healing," was the way Reinhold had put it.

Douglas was happy for his shipmate . . . and, to be
honest, he was glad Rodriguez was gone for the time
being. He liked the little sonar technician, but now he
felt a bit awkward around him. Rodriguez was almost
painfully grateful for the way Douglas had saved his life,
and that made Douglas feel uncomfortable.

He put those thoughts from his mind and started walk-
ing toward the front door of the Tourist Center. Archie
Douglas had seen enough of battle for the time being.
What he wanted to rest his eyes on now was a pretty
Scottish girl with a delightful Southron accent and a way
of showing him things around him in a whole new light.

At least until his duty called him back into action once
again. . . .

APPENDIX

Submarine Statistics

USS *Pittsburgh* (Los Angeles Class)
   Displacement: 7038 tons submerged
   Dimensions (feet): 360 x 33 x 32
   Torpedo Tubes: 4 x 533mm
   Speed (knots): 30+
   Complement: 133 (14 officers, 129 enlisted)

USS *Bluefin* (Grayback Class)
   Displacement: 2935 tons submerged
   Dimensions (feet): 334 x 30 x 17
   Speed (knots): 15+
   Complement: 87 (9 officers, 78 enlisted), plus 67
      troops (7 officers, 60 enlisted)

USS *Queenfish* (Sturgeon Class)
   Displacement: 4857 tons submerged
   Dimensions (feet): 292 x 32 x 29
   Torpedo Tubes: 4 x 533mm
   Speed (knots): 30
   Complement: 107

Bars (*Akula* Class)
  Displacement: 8300 tons submerged
  Dimensions (feet): 370 x 42 x 33
  Torpedo Tubes: 4 x 533mm; 4 x 650mm
  Speed (knots): 35
  Complement: ?

Victor III Class
  Displacement: 6000 tons submerged
  Dimensions (feet): 341 x 33 x 23
  Torpedo Tubes: 2 x 533mm; 4 x 650mm
  Speed (knots): 30
  Complement: 85?

November Class
  Displacement: 5300 tons submerged
  Dimensions (feet): 360 x 29 x 25
  Torpedo Tubes: 8 x 533mm; 4 x 406mm
  Speed (knots): 30
  Complement: 80?

Alfa Class
  Displacement: 3700 tons submerged
  Dimensions (feet): 267 x 31 x 23
  Torpedo Tubes: 5 x 533mm
  Speed (knots): 40+
  Complement: 45?

If you liked *The Silent Service*,
don't miss H. Jay Riker's action-packed saga
of the U.S. Navy SEALs

SEALS, The Warrior Breed:
For Extraordinary Heroism

From the early days of the UDT,
through the hell and glory of Vietnam,
to the last days of the Cold War,
nobody takes you there like H. Jay Riker

Coming Fall 2000 from Avon Books

The eighth book in H. Jay Riker's groundbreaking
historical fiction series on the U.S. Navy SEALs
takes the reader back to the early 1960s. It's a
different world, with different rules, and two elite
warriors from an unknown land-and-sea unit have
been sent on a secret mission to a place no
American soldier has ever gone before. This is
before the SEALs were legends, before the North
Vietnamese were officially our enemies. This is
before there could be any official help for two
"military advisors" trapped in a god-forsaken place
no one back home had ever heard of—the Tonkin
Gulf.

Tuesday, 16 November 1982

Vietnam Veteran's Memorial
Washington DC
1345 hours

Steve Tangretti stood still, letting the full impact of the Wall wash over him. He had come expecting to be disappointed by the newly dedicated monument, convinced that it would never live up to those grand memorials of other wars. All the descriptions had made it sound like some feel-good effort by artistic liberals to make one last anti-war statement, one last spit in the collective faces of the men and women who had served in Southeast Asia. Tangretti had wanted a proper monument, something as stirring and patriotic as the Mount Suribachi statue near Arlington Cemetery. But now, seeing the Wall for the first time, he had to admit that he had been wrong.

The long, V-shaped structure of black granite with its row upon row of inscribed names stood silent and somber. Tangretti had never been moved by anything quite as much as he was by this sight, at once a bleak reminder of war's cost and a testament to those who had given their lives fighting for their country. There were more than fifty-eight thousand names etched in that black rock, each name a connection with a real person who had fought in Vietnam and never come home to friends or families.

Perhaps, Tangretti thought, there were some people involved in the construction of the monument who really had intended it as a last great anti-war protest. Certainly it brought home the horrific cost of the War. But the Wall was more than that, whether by design or by accident. It was the recognition each of those individual military men and women deserved, late in coming but powerful in the message it sent. The official dedication had only happened three days earlier, as part of the Veteran's Day weekend celebrations here in Washington. Tangretti had watched the crowds and the speeches on television, but today, at the request of the only son of one of his best wartime friends, he'd come out to see it in person.

He was glad he'd come.

Studying the monument, Steven Tangretti could almost see the jungles of Vietnam reflected in the black granite. A handful of the names on the Wall had a special meaning to Tangretti, though there was nothing special to distinguish them from all the rest in terms of appearance. No ranks or services were identified for any of the names there, so there was no way to pick out the forty-nine men who had been lost from the U.S. Navy SEALs on duty in Vietnam. To find this stretch of the Wall and the one name that had brought Tangretti and his young companion out here today, they'd been forced to check at an information booth which kept files on everyone listed.

That was doubly appropriate, Tangretti thought with an inward smile. It was right for the people commemorated on the wall to all be equals, not divided by rank or service or race or any of the other things that had separated them in life. But it was even more proper that those forty-nine SEALs be anonymous. For years that was exactly what they had strived for, though later on the elite Navy commandos had become famous . . . or perhaps notorious was a better description.

"I found it, sir. Over here!"

Tangretti turned toward the sound of the younger man's voice. Ensign Bernard Gunn was kneeling on the narrow strip of grass beside the Wall, heedless of the damage he was doing to his crisp dress uniform. His look mingled excitement and sadness, and a touch of wistfulness Tangretti had seen in plenty of other young faces over the years.

He started toward the ensign, feeling the weight of every one of his sixty-five years. It was nearly a decade since he had finally accepted the inevitable and retired from the Navy after a career far longer than most, and though he'd been in excellent condition then and had tried to stay fit and active since, civilian life had brought him a full load of aches, pains, and annoying ailments. But Tangretti didn't allow creaky joints to slow him down, nor did he betray any sign of pain in his expression as he joined Gunn.

Wordless, Gunn indicated a spot low down on the Wall. Tangretti leaned forward to study the name etched there in the polished black stone.

ARTHUR J. GUNN.

He looked from the name to the young officer beside him, thinking how different this young man was from his father. Arthur Gunn had been lean, slight, with a wiry build and an impression of coiled strength. His son was a big man, constantly battling a tendency toward flab, with a round face and a placid, laid-back manner. He was slower to speak than his father had been, more quietly deferential, and he had a way of sounding thoughtful when he spoke. "Arty" Gunn's intelligence had been rapier-sharp and quick-spoken, a born leader who could size up any situation and take charge in an instant.

"I wish I'd known him better," young Gunn said quietly. "Seems like he wasn't home much even before . . . well, before that last op."

Tangretti nodded slowly. "I know, kid. Your dad spent a lot of time in 'Nam, I guess. Damn near as much as I did, one way or another. But that doesn't mean he wasn't thinking about you." His own family had seen precious little of Tangretti during the War. The strain had almost cost him his marriage, and he sometimes wondered if he had done right by his son and his stepson by putting in so much time overseas.

Gunn stood up slowly. "I wasn't criticizing, sir. I just . . . think I would have liked to know him better, you know?"

"He would've wanted the same thing, kid. Believe me." Tangretti fell silent, looking down at the name on the Wall and picturing the man it had belonged to.

"Thanks for coming with me today, sir," Gunn said softly. "It means a lot to me. Dad told my mother once that you were the best damn SEAL he ever knew, even if you were an East Coast puke . . . er, sorry, sir."

Tangretti grinned. "Don't apologize for that, kid. That was high praise indeed . . . coming from a West Coast puke like him."

The younger man looked solemn. "I thought you might want to know . . . I got my order last week. BUD/S training."

"BUD/S?" Tangretti looked at the young officer through narrowed eyes. The Navy acronym stood for Basic Underwater Demolition/SEAL school, the high-pressure course where only the toughest made the grade. "You're shooting for SEALs, too?"

"Yes, sir," Gunn said, standing a little taller with a conscious effort. "Yes, sir . . . a SEAL. Like Dad."

"It won't be easy, you know. Even after all this time, Hell Week's still a killer. And I've heard rumors—old contacts inside DOD and all—that there won't be as many berths out of BUD/S come this time next year. There's talk about phasing out the UDTs."

"So there won't be a softer billet if I don't cut it in training?" Gunn said, a hard edge in his voice. "Sir, I know I look soft. A lot of people have underestimated me because of my looks. But if I couldn't make the cut as a SEAL I wouldn't want to go UDT anyway. If I can't be in that top percentage, I'd rather be a black shoe sailor and stay away from Special Warfare altogether. But I *will* make it, sir. Believe me."

Tangretti studied the young officer for long moments before he responded. "You know, I think you will at that, Mr. Gunn. And I've been sizing up potential SEALs for a lot of years, you know. If you've got just half the guts and dedication your Dad had, you'll make one hell of a good SEAL."

Gunn's face, so intense just a moment before, creased in a wide smile. "Thanks, sir. Mom always said you told things straight . . . at least when it came to SEALs."

"Your mother is right. I only lie when I'm talking to captains or above . . . or sometimes to civilians. But never to a SEAL . . . or a potential SEAL." He paused, his eyes resting again on the Wall. "I have a feeling you'll make your dad proud, wherever he's gone to."

The younger man didn't reply. For long moments the two of them—one a former SEAL, the other hoping to become a part of the Teams, regarded the Wall and the name of Arthur Gunn in respectful silence.

And the power of the Wall took Tangretti's memories back to Lieutenant Arthur Gunn and their service together as Navy SEALs, a service that had started before Vietnam had been anything more than a vague name, when Tangretti and his newly-formed SEALs had confidently expected to go into combat against quite a different foe . . .

Don't miss more action under the waves,
where the Cold War really gets hot

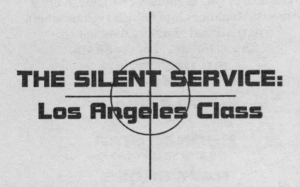

THE SILENT SERVICE:
Los Angeles Class

The next submarine adventure from

H. Jay Riker,

the name to count on in military fiction

Coming in Spring 2001 from Avon Books